Pirate Chains

Second book ~ Against tides

By Syrvat

*"Whether 'tis nobler in the mind to suffer
The slings and arrows of outrageous fortune,
Or to take arms against a sea of troubles,
And, by opposing, end them.
To die – to sleep"*

HAMLET - SHAKESPEAR

Table of contents

Pirate Chains 1
Table of contents 3
Copyright and warnings 5
Author note 6
Prologue 7
Chapter 1 ~ Shadow of doubt 8
Chapter 2 ~ I am a pirate too! 17
Chapter 3 ~ Escape 29
Chapter 4 ~ With bated breath 38
Chapter 5 ~ Word of honor 47
Chapter 6 ~ Pirate Compromise 57
Chapter 7 ~ Dance 64
Chapter 8 ~ Easy mark 75
Chapter 9 ~ Frenzy 83
Chapter 10 ~ Restless hearts 91
Chapter 11 ~ Last resort 99
Chapter 12 ~ My killer 108
Chapter 13 ~ My pet 118
Chapter 14 ~ Blue ribbons 135
Chapter 15 ~ Closer... please? 144
Chapter 16 ~ Oreo 157
Chapter 17 ~ Hit the waves 166
Chapter 18 ~ Dilemmas 174
Chapter 19 ~ The unfilial heir 181
Chapter 20 ~ A pact with the devil's spawn 191
Chapter 21 ~ Cartes sur table 207
Chapter 22 ~ Catching up 219
Chapter 23 ~ Parting ways 227
Chapter 24 ~ Pyry 239
Chapter 25 ~ Ghost from the past 252

Chapter 26 ~ Whips and hopes 261
Chapter 27 ~ His weakness 269
Chapter 28 ~ Please wake up 279
Chapter 29 ~ Illusory smile 285
Chapter 30 ~ The devil's woe 298
Chapter 31 ~ To Ganae 308
Chapter 32 ~ Prayer 318
Chapter 33 ~ While you can 324
Epilogue 335
Author note 336
Also read 337

Copyright and warnings

Copyright © 2018 by Syrvat

All rights reserved. No part of this publication may be reproduced, distributed, or transmitted in any form or by any means, including photocopying, recording, or other electronic or mechanical methods, without the prior written permission of the publisher, except in the case of brief quotations embodied in critical reviews and certain other noncommercial uses permitted by copyright law. For permission requests, write to the publisher at the email address syrvat.novelist@gmail.com.

This story is +18

Expect adult themes and graphic content.
This novel is an adult, gay romance, general fiction. It depicts themes such as piracy, abuse, rape, romance, manxman, gay, travel, sail, adventure, angst, and love.

Author note

Dear reader,

The pirate chain's adventure continues. My babies, Nyx and Agenor face more challenges that will either tear them apart or bring them closer together.

Hope you enjoy our star lovers, as well as more couples rising to meet the tides ;)

Syrvat

Prologue

Nyx and Agenor continue their journey as they reach land. Between his love for Agenor and the pull of Corail, his home island, Nyx faces more difficulties as he tries to cope with the invisible chains of his new life.

[SECOND BOOK. READ 'Pirate Chains ~ Strong tides' FIRST]

... "I'm not going back there Ace... You have no idea-"
The lump in my throat made me lose my voice.
Ace sighed and tried to sound less angry and threatening, "Look, I know you were kept against your will on Martina, so this situation was kind of expected. But there's obviously more to this, right Nyx?"
I opened my mouth to answer him. Explain how his evil Captain was! Just the thought of it hurts so much...... But all I ended up doing was meeting him in the eye once more and repeating,
"I'm not going back to Martina" ...

Chapter 1 ~ Shadow of doubt

∞ *Agenor's POV* ∞

"nnn"

....

"nnnhhh"...

"I... I need to go..."

"Later"

"My God, it's too early for......" He hesitated and I smirked at his half-assed denial. Still too polite. It' adorable, really.

I propped myself on my elbows that were on either side of him. I looked in his eyes daring him to finish his sentence, "Early for what? Say it"

"For... For anything. Whatever, just go back to sleep and let me get to work"

I ignored him and dipped my face in his neck. As usual, I lifted his collar a little and enjoyed sucking on his sweet flesh. Even without the lock, I ordered him to keep the collar on at all times. It just looks amazing on him.

I noticed a red mark that was fading, and I attacked it to bring that beautiful red back to life. I moved to the other side of his neck, working on another mark as he started to moan deliciously.

"Aww! You're biting again! What's your thing with biting??"

"Can't help it", I felt a little guilty to the angry mark that I left. It just looked so exquisite with the contrast between his snowy skin, the black collar, and the redness of the bite. I looked in his sea-blues, trying, but failed to voice an apology.

"You're so delicious Nyx"

He blushed a light shade of pink that lured me to nibble the tip of his left ear. His hands grabbed my sides, and I enjoyed the feeling of his chest as it rose and fell, breathing against mine.

A minute later, I felt soft lips peck my cheek. I couldn't help but smile widely; He's so damn chaste! And I loved his innocence with every bit of my tainted soul.

I knew that if I looked at him, he might get embarrassed and stop, so I kept myself busy with his ear while he slowly kissed my cheek and my neck over and over, then he started licking my jawline.

His tongue felt so fucking hot that I had to reward him; I slid my waist over his, joining our members together and grinding against him through our pants. He moaned under me and I intended to make him do much more than that.

He tried pushing me away, certainly remembering *work*. I hated his conscious sometimes, wished I could turn it off for a few minutes, or an hour... Aye, at least an hour that would be great.

"Baril will be mad, you know?"

I sighed as the mentioned ugly face popped into my head, "Lords Nyx... How could you think of another when you're *here*" I ground on him more making him gasp.

"Nnn... Don't make this harder for me"

"You actually like working with him??" I found that really hard to believe

"He's ok. He tells me many stories. He gets in a bad mood sometimes, but once he relaxes it's 'story time' «I smiled at him. The sexy nobleman in my arms, if you look close enough you could see an adorable childish side of his.

He pouted a little, then said as if he had no choice, "You know your cook better than I do, if he wakes up and doesn't find his galley prepared he might come here"

I slipped my hand in his pants, "The only thing that matters to me Nyx, is when *you* come" He moaned nicely and I didn't give him time to protest; my fingers pressed on him, taking pleasure in teasing his most intimate parts. I moved my hand along his member, squeezing on the head, and descending to the base, feeling him getting harder in my palm and feeling my own manhood growing to claim him...

Knock knock "Nyx! Get the fuck up! I swear to the Fucking Gods if you're slacking again I'm going to get in there!!"

My sweet love stiffened in terror, his member going limb as soon as he heard Baril's obnoxious voice. Then he pushed me aside and stumbled out of bed to grab his shirt, "See! I told you I'll get in trouble!"

I sighed disappointedly and fell on my back, watching his naked back; so fare and flawless, "Remind me who you work for exactly?"

"Baril! And because of you, lately, he got to the galley before me several times"

"That's because you're with a better company"

"Well, I'm not used to being called a slacker." Then he mumbled, "And that company is giving me a bad reputation"

I laughed at that and he rolled his eyes as his fingers ran through his black hair to comb it.

Knock knock knock "**Nyyyx!! I'm fuckin waiting!!** Get the Fuck out or I'm going to drag your ass out myself!"

"Coming! I'm coming!"

I raised an eyebrow at him, "So soon? I thought we'd *come* together?"

He looked at me in disbelief and opened his sweet lips to answer, but his shyness tied his tongue. So he grabbed his pillow and threw it at me before pacing towards the door. He opened it slowly, taking a peek to make sure he was safe. I heard Baril's voice trail away, "I finally get a hard-working one, but they had to twist his habits! Fucking pirates on a fucking bloody ship..."

"Morning Nyxy pixie!"

"Good morning Maren"

The door shut, drowning the cabin in silence.

I liked the silence. A quiet ship, sailing through the waves is the most peaceful place to be. I turned to my side, I should probably go back to sleep as he said.

My hand ran under the black bed sheets, feeling the warm mattress where Nyx was. Fuck that Baril, he's becoming the morning pin in my ass!

I sighed and pulled myself up, deciding to go for an early tour around Martina. Where should I start... the galley maybe?

I walked in on Baril yelling at Nyx. *Who the fuck did he think he was to yell at what's mine??* And I knew Nyx did nothing wrong, it was just the usual Baril ranting and venting his 'charming' mood.

"Oh, Captain! Morning. I see you woke up earlier than usual"

Are you Fucking kidding me?? Whose fault is that! That and the fact that I'm horny AND Fucking hard!!

"Someone woke me up by knocking on my door like a raging bull"

He cleared his throat, then glared at Nyx, who grabbed a broom and escaped into the storage room, it was somewhat funny. I'm glad I came; at least I gave him an escape.

"Well, that's the lazy boy's fault. He used to be the best! He woke up first, worked harder and longer than everyone else! But nah, they had to rub on him. Me Gods, he cleans like a possum!! I'm not letting him become another loss; we have enough of those around here. **Hey!! Get some fucking pickles for your captain to chew on**!!", then he turned to me again, "Want some pickles Captain?"

I glared at him a little. He got the gist and cooled down a notch. Then he started talking and talking, while Nyx ran here and there, from the storage room to the water room and then back to the galley. I enjoyed watching him work. He didn't seem to mind Baril's mood at all. in fact, he was the only one I knew who could stay around Baril all day and not pull a knife on the old man. It's actually the reason why Ace needed to assign different people to help in the galley every time, but now that was easier for everyone since Nyx was magically able to tolerate Baril.

∞ ∞ ∞

Later, we were gathered for lunch. I sat in the large room of the first level of the hull, on one of the benches that surrounded the room. Others sat around on the benches, the floor, or any solid object they could place their asses on. Nyx was occupied, filling the wooden plates, while Yeagar was assigned to help him serve. Baril finished bringing the food he prepared. So he stood there, surveying the distributed portions and glaring at everyone like he wished they'd hurry and die to spare him the effort of feeding them.

It goes without saying that the first one who was served was me. And, of course, the second was Ajax, Yeagar's younger brother. The bulky man thanked his big bro with one sharp nod and started eating immediately.

"Hey!" Nash yelled at them, "How come *he* gets to be served first??"

Yeagar raised an amused eyebrow at him, "Any suggestions, Nash?"

"Aye, plenty! First, after the Captain, you will serve ME. Know your place pirate!"

Yeagar glanced at his brother, both of them trying to hide a devious smile. Then he answered as he went back to grab the plates from Nyx and hand them to others, none for Nash though, "I thought after the Captain, Ace would be next. Don't you think?"

Nash stiffened at that and Ajax went to push the knife further into the wound, "Aye. If you want to be second one day, you should work harder, Nash"

"Huh! That day might come faster than you could imagine" Nash spoke while eyeing Ace who, like always, ate silently.

It's no secret that Nash wanted to be second on Martina. It's probably the most known fact about this crew. But Nash was not Ace. Hell, he wasn't even close to taking his place. He might be in competition with Lou. Aye, Lou would make a fine second in command; he'd even make a good Captain one day if he decides to leave Martina.

But here, I preferred Ace much better than anyone else. He was more than just a crewmember. We go way back and he's best at understanding me and following my orders, there's no doubt about that. IF friendship existed in our world, he'd definitely a very good one. Although pirates can never be real friends, the concept is distorted and relationships are always built based on benefits.

Then again, if there could be love for a pirate, why not friendship? I recently came to the meaning of love; I eyed Nyx who was working silently. *Aye, I came to know what love is. But I can't put it into words; maybe it was the feeling for someone you own, someone you can control and do whatever you want with, but also you'd get the urge to please him and see him smile, you want him to be under your care, nicely protected and in arm's reach every second, he'd challenge you sometimes making life much more interesting but he would never disrespect you.*

I thought about that for another second... *Aye, that's what's called love. But it seems that once there's love, you don't just own, you are also owned; A fact that I've learned the hard way...* My thoughts trailed to a certain night when Nyx got drunk and my ass remembered the hurtful feeling.

I shook my head mentally, when Maren interfered, "Even if we follow that order here, after the Captain, *I* should be the next served. I'm the Captain's trustee. And, take all possible offense from my words, by the way, *I* am higher than all of you! I'm in control of the mast, therefore *I* am more important-"

"Huh! Whatever you say windy, the only thing you're better at is your imagination" Nash interrupted Maren, and before he could answer, we heard a protest, "Meat!! Where's the meat??" I looked at Armpit who spoke the second he was served.

"Everyone's got the same amount. Just stuff your face and shut it!" Baril barked at him and Armpit finally found a tiny piece of dried salted meat, he immediately grimaced and whined, "Me Gods, this thing is thinner than a needle!"

"And it will be this way until we reach land. You pit-holes keep eating and asking for more, and you forget about tomorrow. Be glad we still have some beans" Baril stopped talking when Nyx handed him a plate, served with a smile. He glared at Armpit then started gulping the food in.

Tren hurried to snatch a plate from Yeagar's hand ignoring his snarl. Well, Tren always made sure to eat a random plate; otherwise, if the plate was intended for him he'd accuse Baril of wanting to poison him. And Baril never even tried to deny that.

Armpit peaked on J's plate above his shoulder, "Hey, I'll take those herbs if you don't like them"

"I don't like them, but I'm eating them. I'm not giving you my food!"

Armpit kneeled closer and J shoved him back, "Fuck! THAT'S IT. Don't get close when I'm fucking chewing! Go away!"

"The Fuck, J?"

"That's all you're getting since you went back to smelling like a foul corpse!"

Baril, who finished his food, threw in a comment before exiting, "Aye, if we throw you into the sea it might spit you back on the deck. That's how much you fuckin smell"

Armpit looked unaffected and went back to licking his plate. But J wasn't finished, "Maybe you should learn from Nyx a bit. See? He's always clean, and he smells nice"

Smells nice??

I almost choked at that. *When the fuck did he smell him??*

Nyx completely ignored them; he was used to their ranting by now.

"Sounds good. Hey Nyx, will you clean me?"

Everyone exploded laughing at that, especially when Nyx frowned then tried to cover it. Yeah, worse idea ever. The closest Nyx is getting to Armpit is when he'll throw up on him. But like always, Nyx had to be 'courteous' with his answer, "I... I don't think that's a good idea"

"Why not? I think it's a wonderful idea. That's it, after lunch, you're cleaning me."

Nyx looked like he wanted to cry it made me laugh. And that's when Baril joined us again, bringing Nyx's plate with him, the one that Nyx always hid somewhere in the storage room. And Baril went to serve him his lunch, "Here, go eat. I'll finish feeding the last assholes"

Nyx sat at the end of the bench, and whale, who already finished his lunch, came to sit on the floor beside him with his empty plate in his hand.

"You watch and see fuckers. I'm going to become the cleanest of you all!" Armpit kept dreaming about a new 'clean' life. Even if Nyx tried, I don't think he could do much though. Unless he skinned him. That's the only way you'd get a smell-free Armpit.

"I could give you some pointers. But you should do it yourself. How else will you learn, Mern?"

Nice escape. Armpit looked like he was considering that, before his colorful teeth drew in a wide smile, "Aye, we do that!"

J scoffed and shook his head in surrender, "Me Gods, the only thing that smells stronger than your filth is your stupidity"

Everyone laughed, but Armpit ignored them and went to sneak around the cauldrons pretending he was helping when we all knew he wanted to lick them.

"Hey! Why are you feeding that thing??" Maren pointed at whale and questioned Nyx who shrugged and went to place another spoon of beans on the whale's plate

"Hey! Stop doing that!!"

"It's fine Maren."

"No, it's not! You're being unfair!!"

"Really, Maren? Now you're saying pirates are fair?"

I chuckled at that. Nyx was polite and weak, but not stupid.

"Well... At least you should consider friends first, like ME! If you want to give your food away, I can definitely help you with that"

"I just think it's unfair for Britt to get the same amount as the rest of us. I don't know but, bigger people need more food, don't you think?" then he tilted his head to look at whale, "No offense Britt"

The big thing just nodded. Of course, he wouldn't take offense, the animal was leaching off Nyx!!

Armpit laughed at whale, "Huh, thank Goddess Baril doesn't think the way you do. Or else I'd be left with nothing but one bean!"

We laughed at that, but Maren wasn't finished, "You shouldn't get him used to that though. If one day you decide to eat your whole meal, then he'll eat YOU!"

Nyx rolled his eyes and went back to eating. And without being seen by him, whale grinned and gave both Maren and Armpit the finger.

Armpit put the cauldron that he was carrying away, almost dropping it, "Oh yeah!! Well, **Fuck you whale**!" Then he went to fondle with his pants.

See, normal people, even pirates, flip each other off all the time. It's like a nod or a handshake, nothing to worry about. Armpit, on the other hand, he'd pull out the real thing. He used to drop his pants and send back foul names at whoever tells him to fuck off. It was like that until one day, his prick accidentally touched Yeagar. The pirate went berserk and even his brother Ajax couldn't stop him. I actually had to interfere personally to stop him from chopping Armpit's pecker.

Don't get me wrong, I actually thought the cockroach deserved it. But I didn't want that thing dropped on my deck; it would bring herds of bad spirits to Martina.

Luckily, for Nyx mostly, this time J managed to stop Armpit, and we all got to keep the shit we ate in our stomachs.

My sweet love went back to the galley after that, and I haven't seen him for about three hours.

I was standing by the wheel when a rat came to report to me about a conversation they heard Ace and Nyx talking about. I waited until Ace and I were alone to check about what I heard:

"I heard you spoke to Nyx about the prisoners, Ace"

I felt him tense for a second, and then he went back to his usual calm self, "Aye. He asked me about them"

"I know he asked about them before too"

"Aye Captain. He asked twice before, but today I told him it was better if he never mentioned them and he promised to do so. I also reminded him that he was forbidden from going to the lower hull and he didn't seem tempted at all to defy your order"

Well, reminding him is good. I also prefer him asking questions than going down to verify by himself. What bothers me is the fact that he went to Ace, *why Ace? Why not ME??*

"Captain, since we're on the subject, I wanted to ask if you wanted to treat the prisoners"

"TREAT them??" the idea obviously didn't get my liking at all

"Aye. Earlier, after talking to Nyx, I went to check on them. Well... Chow's jaw wasn't any better, it looked like it healed but in a bad position. It's probably a lost cause for him, maybe if he broke it again but I'm not sure it could get back straight, especially with the scurvy. And........ Ken, on the other hand......"

At the mention of the foul name, I started fuming and my anger was ready to build up. Ace checked me with his eyes before he decided to spell it out

"The second prisoner seems to have an infection. He's having a fever that won't be settled until the rotten flesh on his arm is cleaned. I know he doesn't deserve your kindness, but I think we should either treat him or kill him. We don't need a contagious sickness starting on Martina"

He got my undivided attention with that last part. I took a minute to think about it.

"Alright. First, no one is to go near the prisoners but you personally, Ace. Especially not Nyx. If you need any help take Lou with you. You are to check them again and be sure they don't have an infectious disease. Until you're a hundred percent certain, don't touch them directly, also avoid touching the ground or the walls of the cell. If you have the slightest doubt, we'll throw them both into the sea, is that clear?"

"Aye"

I sighed, then continued, "If they don't have any dangerous disease, then you have my permission to treat them. I spared their lives already, there's no interest in killing them now. Actually, I think what happened to them sent a stronger message to the other assholes. We'll keep feeding them the usual if they can't take it, or if they're too much hassle we'll get rid of them"

"Aye Captain."

He fidgeted a little around me and I knew he had more to say, "What is it Ace"

"Just a small thing... Gods, I hate reporting small things like this. It feels childish"

I looked at him and lifted an amused eyebrow, "Yet too good at it" He always preferred dealing with the tiny things and sparing me a headache. That suited me too, but he felt like reporting this it means that it's still important. So I asked him with a teasing tone, "So, what's this thing that you don't know how to deal with?"

"It's Nyx."

All right, I was more serious now. Ace knows I don't care about a crewmember's feeling or if they slept well or had dreams or not, but when it came to Nyx I had to know every detail. He understood that and I appreciated that.

"Nyx?"

"Other than me, he tried to get others to give him information about our next destination. The when and where. I doubt anyone satisfied his curiosity though, I think they know better than to talk to him about stuff like that. It's still unclear to them if it would anger you or not, so they're avoiding his questions for now."

I sighed and ran a hand in my hair. The food is getting scarce already. Whenever this happens, everyone starts talking about nothing but land this and whore that. *Once again Nyx, once again, you go for others and not me. Did he think I'd get mad if he brought it up? And more importantly, why are you asking Nyx?*

"He's doing it again, being nosy. Maybe he has the right to know. Ugh, I don't know!"

"Agenor, if he's one of us then such information shouldn't be a secret to him. Frankly, I don't see what harm is there in telling him such things"

Harm? So him knowing our destination and the time of us reaching land wrong?? Ace felt my uncertainty and added, "It's only natural for him to ask. Everyone's getting tired of this round and they're all eager to reach land. And my guess is that he's even antsier since he's not used to sailing so much"

Ace was right. But that was not all that's there to consider.

"I don't want him planning an escape, Ace"

"Escape??" Ace blinked as he obviously never considered that option. He looked around the deck for a minute considering what I just said, and then he returned his eyes on me with a small frown, "You think Nyx will try to escape?"

"You don't think he would?"

He shook his head a little and shrugged, "I don't know. But the important thing is what YOU think, Agenor. You know him better"

I nodded, "I do. And as much as I hate to admit it, I'm not sure he has enough here to keep him from wanting to go back home." I couldn't prevent the hint of sadness in my voice and I could see it reached Ace as he too looked straight towards the sea.

"I'll talk to him Ace. Things like this don't remain secret anyway, so I'll tell him myself"

He nodded then went back into the hull after he called for Lou.

Later during the evening, I kicked the door of my cabin open and walked in. I took off my shirt and started burning a cigarette with the help of a lighted lamp beside the small window. As I breathed in the smokes, I expected to relax. But I didn't. My thoughts were inhabited by that small doubt that was slowly tearing through me.

I felt familiar hesitant fingers hold my arm. I turned my gaze to my left and met a curious pair of eyes.

"Hey, everything ok? You look.... worried"

His hand tugged my arm to better check my face. I silently explored his features as I thought about the doubts that refused to leave me at ease. I stood there, debating if I should bring up the subject of our next island. And If I did, should I ask if he wanted to escape or refresh his memory with some threats? What if he never thought about it and starts doing so when I ask him?

I didn't know how much time I remained silent. And despite the concern that invaded his eyes, he offered a calming smile. I felt a nice warmth cloak my heart, a tender feeling that would only visit when he's around.

I turned to face him and wrapped my arms around him. Then I claimed his lips in a breathtaking kiss. When I pulled away, his look was the most luscious; eyes with a deep blue color that only intensified with the hint of excitement.

He smiled at me and that's when I decided. I buried all doubts away, for only a miserable man would dare to wipe such angelic smile.

∞ ∞ ∞

Chapter 2 ~ I am a pirate too!
∞ Nyx's POV ∞

I stood by the side of the deck, my hand holding one of the ropes tugging the sails. I watched as the sun dove behind the horizon, where the sky and the few clouds traveling slowly were painted in a beautiful shade of red. Another hot day tomorrow, I thought.

We sailed south for about a month and twenty-five days, then we turned slightly east. And we sailed in that direction for about three weeks already.

I tried so hard over the days to figure out our exact destination on my own. I had a few ideas, but I still felt frustrated with being uncertain. If we continued in this direction, there were so many possibilities. And judging from the food we had left, I narrowed it down to five possible destinations, and one of them was Ebina.

I really wish it would be Ebina. I've never been there before, but it's a known big island, surrounded by a couple of small ones. Many merchants like to go there to trade or put their hands on rare items. In fact, my uncle is one of them. He used to visit Ebina once a year. I remember him saying that he was thinking about owning a couple of shops there, something about getting the locals to trust him and favor working with him. So if I looked around a bit at the port of Ebina or the market, I'm sure people would recognize his name! The hope gave me a spite of excitement and I kept praying for Ebina to be our next stop.

But I could still be wrong... I have never sailed this far ever before and all my guessing is from what I remember from maps or heard from people who got this far. But if we were sailing to Ebina, we would have gotten there already. We're not exactly following the shortest routes, more like approaching indirectly, like in a circular way. Which is understandable for obvious reasons: Pirates. They don't exactly knock on front doors.

Besides, lately, the Martina crew started fishing from time to time. The sea is not very generous in this area, but they're getting enough to maybe last longer without land. I observe them, hating myself for wishing they would catch nothing. But they do, and every day I try to reevaluate the time left based on the remaining food.

Now, if we were heading to Ebina we should've turned sharper to the East, like, days ago... At this rate, we're missing the island and moving further. And the ones in the following area are not exactly protected islands. People live there and everything but there are no guards to keep the order, so they're what we like to call 'The Shadows'. Full of thieves and....... Damn it... full of pirates. Which makes them a much better fit for Martina than Ebina.

So... If we missed Ebina, I might start praying the food will keep us long enough to reach another guarded area.

I sighed, aware of my own naivety.

"You're praying for land so hard an island will just pop out in the middle of the ocean"

I rolled my eyes to Nash's sarcasm. Of course, I made sure he didn't see that. He doesn't exactly need to be provoked. Even silence is enough fuel to warm him up for a séance of mockery.

"I'm not praying"

"Liar"

"I'm just watching the sunset, Nash"

"Oh, that's very romantic!" said Lou while trying but failing at mimicking a woman's voice, after he leaned his heavy body on my shoulder

Nash snorted, "More like very bullshit"

"Always looking for someone to bully." Yeagar appeared right behind Nash who stepped away instantly. Yeagar smirked at that and his brother Ajax approached from the other side, giving the impression that they were cornering Nash, "Huh! You know him, brother, he likes to play with small fish. What does that make you, Nash?"

"The one who'll fucking slit your throats, that's what it makes me!!"

"Ouch"

..... I zoned out of their ranting. It was always like that with Nash. He'd be either picking on me, or menacing Yeagar and Ajax, who strangely seem to enjoy being insulted by him.

I had no intention of partying tonight. Sailing into the unknown was getting on my nerves. Don't get me wrong, I love sailing; At first, I appreciated just advancing through the waves, never reaching the horizon. But it has been months since I got on Martina and the trip became more stressing by the day. And the truth is... It's not the sailing that frustrates me. It's about my own fate. Where will I end up?......

I wanted to leave for a quieter place. I moved to part from the crazy gathering that started growing, but I felt my right arm being yanked back. I looked back to see Lou's amused stare, "Where are you going?"

None of your damn business.

"Somewhere calm"

"Have you looked around lately? There's nowhere like that on this ship"

I pulled my arm trying in vain to release his grip, "I would like to verify that myself"

"The only quiet place here is the sea. You're not thinking of suiciding again, are you?"

He said that in an amused way and I tried to defend myself, "I never did such a thing!!" Seeing how he was insistent to tease my nerves, I continued in a calm confident voice, "Would you mind releasing me?"

I was glaring at him, but that was just the thing that entertains Lou the most. He leaned closer and said in a low voice, "You want to know where we're heading, right? Want me to tell you?"

My eyes widened for a second to the idea, but I instantly hid my excitement. Lou was one of the most obedient to Agenor and informing ME of our destination had somehow fallen under the cover of defying the Captain. He's just playing with me and for once I'm not falling for it.

"Save it. I already know that"

I tried my best to look calm and composed, and apparently, it worked because his smirk fell and his eyes narrowed, "Oh yeah? Who told you??"

It was my turn to smirk now and I savored the moment. I just loved these rare times when I felt like I won over their teasing.

He studied me for a few seconds, then his eyebrows arched and he dared me, "Or maybe you're just lying"

I opened my mouth to find a smart response to that. Luckily, a thud on the edge of the deck right beside us got Lou startled. He let go of my arm and looked to his left to see Maren who just landed there.

"Whaaaat'ch you're doing?"

Maren released the rope that he just used to swing and he crouched on the edge of the deck with a big smile on his face.

"Maren, please be careful-"

"Fuck! Windy! I've warned you not to Fucking fly above my head again!!"

Maren rolled his eyes and I laughed a little at that. He always managed to avoid everyone's teasing even though he was the youngest AND not very strong compared to pirates like Lou or Nash. Not even Ace could intimidate him, and I so admired that.

I retreated. I didn't really want to spend the evening with the drunken pirates. Lately, they became a bit more aggressive about things. Maybe I'm the only one who noticed, but the eagerness for the land makes them quite impatient and mean.

I walked down the ladder to the hull. I strolled to the water room and drank some water, then I stepped into the hall and looked around. *Agenor is not here, I guess. Which means that he's in the lower hull ordering people around. Or more precisely laying back watching Ace as he ordered people around.* I smiled at the thought. *What a lazy devil.*

I walked back to the deck and into Agenor's cabin. *I'll wait for him here. It's not like I'm allowed down the hull with them. But it's fine. I don't care if I'm not allowed to walk everywhere or know about things like our next land. The important thing is that now I'm living way better than the day I first walked on that deck. I'm much more comfortable with my work and the pirates. Things can't go backward now. Right?*

∞ ∞ ∞

The next day started like any regular day on Martina. After lunch, Maren walked into the galley.

"Tiiiired. Booooored"

"Haven't seen you at lunch today, Maren"

"And so, so **hyngryyy**!! Please tell me there's something left for me?" He tilted his head and I smiled and his hopeful puppy eyes

"Of course. I put it in the storage room for you."

"Ahoy!" He jumped and was in the storage room in a second.

"So... No land yet, huh" I bit my tongue as soon as that came out of my mouth. Damn it, Ace told me I should stop asking such things. I was about to hope Maren didn't hear me when he answered, obviously with a mouth full of food

"Nope, still nothing. I was told we were going to be there like, this morning. I even missed lunch. Fuck, I hoped I'd get to have real meat for lunch, but I guess that won't be happening today"

My heart actually raced at 'this morning'... *We're that close? Maybe, just maybe, my calculations were wrong and we did not miss Ebina after all! What if...*

I turned to find Maren yawning and stretching his arms, "I didn't sleep since yesterday. Me Gods, with that sun, it's starting to give me a headache"

Right, he spent all night watching the sea from up the mast again. Everyone says that he's a brat, that he doesn't do shores well... But he actually takes his work very seriously. I mean, he must have quite the strong will and patience to stay awake, alone, in the dark all night, and that is almost every night for several months! I don't think I could have such perseverance if it was me.

I handed him a cup of water, "Why don't you take some rest"

"Can't, someone needs to look out for other ships. The more we get close to land the more we could bump into someone, you know?"

"Oh... Well, you still need a break. Why not ask Ace to get someone else to take your place?"

"Those fucktards will just start drinking... they're so stupid" I smiled to his sense of responsibility. I always felt that Maren took big proud in *his* crow's nest. He went to drink and my smile fell when he glared at me, "Water, really?? Who the hell serves water?"

"What did you want to have, beer??"

"Well, YEAH!"

"Just drink Maren, it will help with your headache"

"Why, is there an island in the cup?? My headache will only go if we get to land. I'm sick of smelling man butts." His shoulders slumped and he tilted his head back to whine like a child, "I want a woman's butt..."

"You don't have to be rude, just go sleep a little" I pushed him out of the galley and he continued down to the second lowest level of the hull, most probably to find somewhere relatively calm to sleep.

As for me, I had to stay away from the walking pirates; Everyone was cranky and looking for a fight. I climbed the shrouds and took Maren's place. It was truly nice from up here. The Martina definitely looked less scary because everyone walked around the deck without even noticing me looking from above. They were all busy, even Baril. Which is why he left me to clean the galley alone after lunch while he helped prepare things. What things? Everything. Barrels, wooden boxes, weapons... They were moving everything here and there.

I should probably go help, or I might just stay here. In this much calmer level, where it felt relaxing and close to the sky. No wonder Maren loves staying here.

I kept watching the sea, turning every while to watch out for other ship that might spot us from other angles, as Maren said. And I don't know how long it took before it finally happened.

In the distant horizon, a strangely shaped cloud appeared. I gazed at it unbelievingly, until I was certain that I wasn't dreaming: *Land. Land!!*

I jumped out of the crow's nest and almost fell as I forgot that I was still far above the deck. I climbed down the shrouds clumsily and ran into the hull. I was happy. Sincerely happy! I wanted to yell and tell, but it felt unfair to Maren who put so much effort into this. So I climbed down to the second level of the hull, wishing to find him somewhere here because, well, I didn't have the right to go any lower in the ship.

Luckily I found Maren laying on the floor at the side of a room. I called his name, making sure not to wake the couple of others that looked asleep around the room. When he didn't answer I kneeled and called him again. This time he moaned in an irritating way, "Nnn... Go away Ace"

Ace??

We don't have time for this. I leaned closer to his ear and said the one word I knew would wake him up, "Land"

His response was more immediate than I thought. His eyes flew open and he sat up abruptly sending me to fall back on my ass.

"When, what?... Land, did you say land?"

I got up and nodded at him with a smile. He shot to his legs and was already running out of the door in a second. I followed behind watching how he made his way by pushing some pirates away and earning some snarls for that. When I reached the deck, Maren was already up there, looking through his monocular. His smile grew wider and he yelled what sent everyone to halt, "**Laaaaaand!!**"

The cheering, the pirates hurrying to the deck to check by their own eyes, the smiles and sighs, it all made me excited and even happier.

"**Celiaaa**! Your dickhead is back to fuck you, me whore!!" *And that was J, getting all... 'romantic'*

"Finally" Lou said calmly, he looked relieved but not by much. I guess being used to this event makes some pirates immune to the beautiful sight of an approaching island.

I felt a familiar hand settle on my right shoulder. I looked around to find Agenor standing on my left, his hand still holding me close. He looked satisfied but not the least surprised. *Of course, he wasn't, he knew exactly when this moment would come. They all knew.*

He looked at all the excited eyes around us, "Avast ye! Be ready freebooters, we'll be having dinner on land tonight"

The cheers grew stronger and higher. All the troublesome moods were wiped in a second. Some were even whistling and jumping. I wanted to step back to give them more space to stomp around and lean on the edge of the deck to watch the approaching island. I felt Agenor squeezing a little on my shoulder so I turned to look at him. His eyes had a hint of doubt that surprised me. I tried to read him as to why his gaze didn't look happy like when he was talking to his crew, but he looked away from me.

"I guess we'll be skipping our training for today" Ace said to me and I nodded. We've fenced almost every day now, and that was one of the best times of the day.

"Alright," Ace ordered, totally unfazed by all of this, "Heave ho everyone, we got two hours to get all the crap on the deck or you will be missing dinner. Bring everything we need to sell or fill in the deck, only then you can go get your duffels"

Ok. Most of that reached my ears like a foreign language, but seeing how everyone got back to work with more strength summed it up for me.

Agenor led me to the forecastle with him, where he lighted a cigarette and started blowing the smokes free. I was about to go do what Ace ordered us, but I had one last detail to deal with.

"Agenor, where........ are we?"

I finally did it. I asked the forbidden question, and my mind hustled with prayers: *Ebina... It has to be... It IS, yes, it is Ebina...*

He was silent for a moment. One that seemed too long for me. I knew him enough to be sure that he was doing it on purpose, keeping me waiting while he thought about things, or maybe just for the fun of it.

He took a deep breath of fumes then finally answered, "Esme"

And for a second I wished I hadn't asked.

Esme? We have reached Esme already??

Esme. One of the Shadows. The refuge of all outcasts, and the heaven lands for bounty hunters.

I looked at the island that I waited so long to meet, "It can't be... We were supposed to go to Ebina...."

I didn't even know I said that out loud until he smirked at me, "Ebina? Why the hell would we go to Ebina?"

"It's not far from here!"

"True. But Ebina is heavily guarded, especially this time of year. Besides, Esme is as interesting as Ebina, only more suited for our kind"

Noticing my silence, he walked to tower over me. His eyes narrowed as he studied my face, "What is it, was Ebina more to your liking, Nyx?"

YES! A thousand times YES!!

I shook my head vigorously, "No, it's just... Esme is one of the Shadows... it's quite dangerous"

His face softened and I breathed to that, "WE are one of the main reasons why Esme is called like that, so don't worry about such things Nyx. You're part of the Martina now, remember?"

I nodded slowly and watched the island reveal green mountains and forests.

So what if it's one of the Shadows? It's still an island. We'd still be able to rest and walk on a wave-less ground. I don't think my father or my uncle's name would ring a bell around here. But I'm not going to think about such depressing thoughts. I'm going to enjoy stepping on land and........ well, hope not to meet 'new' people.

Despite the slight fear, I still felt happy, and the excitement sneaked back to settle inside me.

"I should go help the others"

"Wait...."

I halted, but before Agenor could continue, the forecastle was invaded. Everyone was following Pin who held a bouquet of straws.

"Captain, shall we?"

Agenor looked a bit irritated at being interrupted, but he nodded anyway, and everyone stepped forward to Pin who snarled at them, "Step back or I'll gut your balls!!"

My eyes widened at the threat, "What's going on?"

Ajax rubbed his hands together in excitement and answered me, "This is it, baby! This is the time we decide who's going to land and who's staying on the ship"

Ace continued explaining, "We need to keep the ship guarded, so we always leave a small team behind. That team will only leave the ship in three days and the next unlucky bunch will take over"

"So? Who wants to pay for the first draw??" Pin looked around him at the hesitant eyes.

"What difference does it make?"

I wanted to swallow my question back when Pin glared at me, "*What difference* you ask?? **It makes all the difference of the world**!!"

J pulled a coin and put it jokingly on Pin's head, who immediately turned his glare at him and caught the coin before it fell, "The first to draw gets all the luck there is!" J said, then he wiggled his big fingers and blew on them, *for.... luck, I guess?*

I wanted to tell him that the odds weren't going to be better just because he's choosing first, but I kept my mouth shut. And I watched like everyone, as he pulled one of the straws.

And as soon as he did everyone busted laughing. I didn't need to ask to know if he was lucky or not, because he dropped on his knees and released a sky breaking dramatic "Nooo...!"

I actually couldn't stop laughing, and everyone took their time to tease him and remind him that he won't be able to 'smell pussy' (their words) for three more days.

Seeing how Agenor and Ace were the only ones laying back, I figured they weren't obliged by this risky game. I, on the other hand, did not stand back like I usually do. I stepped forward, trying to get my chance, just like everyone else. I was in advantage since Pin was close to Agenor and so was I, but I still ended up being pushed back. Well, at least I tried, right?

It was Pin's job to point who will draw next, and everyone needs to witness his share of luck. After the very few more who paid, Pin pushed the bouquet at me, "Your turn punch-boy"

"I... I don't have money"

"I know, but the Captain likes you, so you get to draw before these fuckers for free"

I frankly was surprised by the sudden generosity that was very unknown to Pin. But I didn't waste time, so I pulled a straw before he could change his mind.

I followed the ritual and lifted my luck for everyone to see, "Is... this good?"

Maren was on my side in a second, "Aye, aye! Two words mate: Lola and Trixie"

Some around us nodded, and Nash clarified, "His whore friends"

My eyes widened; Yes, Maren IS trying to set me up with...... women!

"No thanks, I'll pass"

"You can't pass mate! You'll see, those two will do anything," and he lowered his voice seductively, "and I mean ANY. THING. you ask. And since you're *my* friend, I'll get them to do you for a lower cost"

He winked at me and I couldn't even find the words to answer him. He didn't wait for my opinion anyway as he stepped before me and closer to Pin, "Alright! My turn. Nyx brought the Goddess of luck, better do this before she goes back to drinking with some old sailors somewhere"

The bouquet started getting lighter and many kept congratulating me and saying things like, "Heavens are on your side", or "If lucky the first time, then lucky forever"... I knew it was silly, but the impressionable me couldn't help feel more excited about this whole thing.

And the straws were almost finished when my eyes locked on Agenor. I was smiling, but he was far from it. It was almost like he was glaring at me. *Did I do something wrong?*

I decided not to think about that right now and try to be happy with my lucky straw like most of the pirates around me. But the so-called 'Goddess of luck' didn't stick by my side after all.

"You're not going"

The order was calm. Simple. It descended like heavenly fate for everyone to obey.

I wondered who he was talking about until I saw all eyes on me. *Wait, ME??*

"Excuse me?"

"You will be staying on Martina"

I smiled a bit uncomfortably, trying to convince myself that he was joking. But of course, he wasn't. Agenor never joked like that, and the silence that invaded the deck confirmed it.

I opened my hand for him to see my straw, "I picked a long straw. I won my right to-"

"You're not going on Esme"

His eyes looked cold and merciless, making me stop and fail to formulate a protest. That was an order as clear as the day. I was not to defy a direct order.

At the corner of my eyes, I saw someone push the crowd to stand closer to me. I thought someone has stepped in to defend me. In the end, the person just reached for the straw in my hand, "I guess you won't be needing that now"

I yanked my hand protecting the straw, "Get your hands off me!"

The pirate glared at me as if I grew a second head, then he decided against making something out of this, and he retreated after glancing quickly to his Captain.

WHAT THE HELL?? My breathing got heavier and I felt anger filling my head, which didn't really help my confusion at all.

I followed Ace and everyone as they got back to their work. I helped move empty barrels and boxes that we were going to fill with water or food. Everyone was happy, whistling and laughing. I felt the desire to join their laughs, but apparently, I didn't have the right to. And I didn't even know the reason.

And to top it all, the pirates were now avoiding me like the plague, probably scared they'd get stuck with me. No one was talking to me anymore. And as I moved around carrying things to the deck, I never felt more transparent. So ironic, earlier when I was on the mast I appreciated not being seen, but now that I got my wish, it felt horrible and lonely...

I stood in the storage room. It was much emptier than usual with most of the heavy stuff moved out. *Maybe I should just keep myself busy by cleaning here, bury myself in work.* But I didn't want to work. I didn't want to feel the waves right now. I wanted to be with everyone........ *with Agenor.*

"Pssst! Hey, what happened there, mate?"

"You tell me, Maren? You were there! You're always watching everything. Did I do something wrong??"

He looked as confused as I was. My God, I couldn't stoop lower; not only I can't deal with my own shit on my own, I'm actually making a 15-year-old worry about me.

"Look, maybe the Captain heard something or misunderstood something. What I'm sure of is that he likes you, and he also likes to award people who work hard. So don't give up mate, just keep working and he'll see that"

I thought seriously about what he said, and before I knew it, he gave me a quick salute and left.

I swallowed my nervousness and encouraged myself to go back to work with everyone. It was useless to give up so easily and hide, I better do as Maren said and keep working hard.

Which wasn't easy to do. My mind was so distracted and I always worked my best, so now I was overworking myself to exhaustion and all it took was two hours for me to feel powerless.

I saw some pirates take a few things out of the cabin. And like I thought, Agenor was there ordering them. I stepped closer when Agenor walked out while putting on his leather jacket, not even sparing me a glance.

I stepped before him making him halt to stare at me. Coldness crept inside me at the sight of his emotionless eyes. *Why would he look at me like that?*

"Agenor, did I do something wrong? If I did just tell me already, I'm sure it's a misunderstanding-"

"My order is final. You are not going-"

"NO!!" His glare intensified at my sudden outburst, but I'm not the one at fault, am I??

"I have worked hard for this! I followed all the rules and I even won my right to go on land", I showed him the straw, "I did so by the pirate code. I'm part of the crew and I deserve-"

He closed the distance between glaring at me dangerously, and I just noticed how angrier he had gotten in just a few seconds.

"Are you fucking disobeying my direct order, Nyx??"

"N.....no I just..."

I took a step back, but he caught my arm and dragged me to the cabin. Once inside, he whirled me around so I was facing him, and I almost lost my balance if not for his tight grip.

"Now listen to me Nyx. **YOU ARE TO OBEY ME!** If I hear that you did as much as step outside this room, I'll make sure you regret it, is that clear??"

I blinked in confusion to his unjustified anger towards me.

"So what will it be Nyx? Will you obey, or should I get the chain?"

My eyes widened at the threat and I shook my head pleadingly. *My God, not the chain! Not again...*

"Good." He released me by pushing me back. I fell back, and when I managed to look back at him I could swear I saw sadness in his eyes. But I couldn't be sure of it because he immediately grabbed his sword and left after shutting the door behind him with a loud thud.

∞ ∞ ∞

It wasn't long before the commotion disappeared. The crew left the ship except for the few unlucky ones. Time went by very slowly. Agonizingly slowly. So much for 'mate', or 'friend', or 'crewmember'. When it was time for the truth, I am nothing but an outsider. An ex-rich man who owns nothing anymore. I'm not even sure I'm still worth something back home. *What if my uncle took over our business and did better than I?* I felt horrible as I yearned to hope for my family's business to go bad without me. Maybe that would make people forget me less... I'm certain my family misses me. If there were guards searching for me, I'm sure they would have given up already. They think I left willingly, leaving nothing but a letter behind. *Who would look for such a thoughtless person?*

And my cousin Haven, he sure got back from his last trip to find me gone. I wonder what he brought me this time? He always got me presents, at least two. It was a tradition he followed since he started helping his father in business and going to trade trips. Always two presents: a souvenir and a book. I had two shelves full of Haven's books. A couple were in a foreign language, a joke he made to show me that I wasn't the smartest. He seemed to think I was, I never did. He just looked up to me since I am almost a year older than him. Since I'm not there, would he keep the book? Or maybe gift it to someone else...

I love books. I miss books...

I sat on the floor by the wall. The silence around me felt like the worst punishment. As much as I like to believe that I liked privacy, I got used to those pirate's ranting. But I guess I didn't make much impression on them; as soon as 'luck left my side' they were avoiding me, and I was left behind without as much as a small goodbye. What the hell was I expecting? They can't go against their Captain! And why would they defend *me*, it's not like they actually considered me one of theirs...

So after all, I am still the pathetic useless me. Either on the top of the business or the bottom, I still find myself alone in the end.

But this time it was different than before. It didn't feel the same as when my father passed away. This wasn't like the time my mother got married saying that we 'needed a man to stand by the family', as if I wasn't enough... This is different than the time I sent Raya in the decorated carriage to start a new life with her husband... This is far more than when Haven, my best friend, left for the first time to sail with his father, my uncle, and learn about their business. No matter how many times he insisted I'd go with him, and as much as I wanted to, I couldn't just leave my responsibilities behind and sail.

This time was different because loving someone makes you think less about unhappiness. Just being there with the one who fills the void in your heart, it sedates your mind to anything... anything but love. It makes you stronger and gives you a reason to be. I sincerely thought the winds had changed for me. I looked at my right to were the door was, and the scene of Agenor leaving tore through me. Of course, I tried to rationalize this, and the only explanation I came up with was the most hurtful.

He didn't want me on land with him...

The thought of the only person that I truly loved with all my being, casting me away so easily...

My mind started suggesting a thousand reasons: From him wanting to protect me seeing how scared I was from Esme, all to the fact that he was bored of my company. *And guess which one stuck more to my head?*

My heart ached as I realized that since two days ago, he hadn't kissed me not even once. He was always lost in thoughts about something...... Maybe he was just like everyone else, thinking about the women on the island........

The more that single thought replayed in my head, the more I felt stinginess at the back of my eyes.

Women...... such beautiful creatures... Who would have thought that someday I'd feel threatened by them...?

I started shaking as images of Agenor smiling at another woman tore my heart. And as if I could handle more torment, my mind suggested the image of several beautiful ladies I knew back home, in their colorful party gowns, attractive looks, and shining lipsticks. My sick mind showed Agenor, standing charmingly in beautiful clothes, extending his hand to one of them for a dance.

My hands clenched in my hair and I buried my head down between my elbows, trying to just stop my brain from functioning...

No wonder he got bored of me... He said repeatedly how beautiful I was, but maybe that was only because he didn't have real beauty at reach. But now.........

My God, please no! I can't do this... I can't live like this.

∞ ∞ ∞

Chapter 3 ~ Escape
∞ *Agenor's POV* ∞

"Heave ho!!"

H I barked at the stupid pirate and he hustled to row harder. I stood at the front of the boat as it cut through the darkness, with arms folded, and a hellish mood.

I shut my eyes closed and breathed the fresh air of the night trying to calm the fuck down, but it only managed to get me even angrier. Because as soon as I did, I saw those eyes.

I saw *him* falling back, and looking at me with his deep blue eyes, filled with confusion and hurt.

Those eyes... I adored them...

But that was not the kind of confusion that I loved to see in them. *What the FUCK have I done? Why did I have to be such a jerk??* The more I thought about it, the angrier I got. And that's simply because I knew the exact reason behind my behavior; I was fucking scared.

I have never been scared of someone's thoughts before. I rarely cared about other people's opinion; usually, I don't give a damn about what they think. But this time, it was so different. I feared his thoughts so much that I couldn't even find it me to talk to him about it. And as much as I hated to admit it, I knew deep inside me that Nyx still yearned for home. I knew that if he had the chance, he would take it. And I'm fucking mad at him because of that. Maybe I couldn't blame him, seeing how good ties he has with his family and all, but I sure as hell am not going to stand back and let him leave. Shit, I couldn't even stand my own crew without him!

As soon as we stepped on Esme, we made the camp and they started dinner. I couldn't even eat knowing that Nyx was there, alone in the sea. Some even went to buy whores already, and they waited for me to lead the way. But I sent them away. I felt my heart closed for everything; I couldn't even get myself to enjoy the sand on the beach.

So here I am, the almighty Fucking devil, crossing the sea very late at night, looking for the one thing that set a hurricane in my head in the first place: *those eyes...*

I looked behind me and glared at the pirate once more. His arms started moving frantically, and I sighed; any faster and his arms would fall off. I lifted the lamp near my face for the members on Martina to see me and not be alarmed. If they suspected a stranger rowing towards them, those stupid assholes might send an arrow my way.

The boat closed to the ship and a rope was immediately thrown off the deck. I grabbed it and started climbing.

Alright. So......... I Fucked up. That part is clear. Now all I have to do is make it up to him. Well, I doubt he'll be receiving me with open arms; he'll probably start defending himself or send me blaming glares that deliver speeches sharper than daggers; Aye, that's something he's actually good at. All I need to do is explain his mistake for him and he'll be forced to understand.

I stood mid-climb as I realized, *what was his mistake again?* It felt like I punished him for something that was yet to happen. But I was certain it was going to happen!! Is that even logical? Oh, that's so like Nyx, he always gets to my head in strange ways and somehow manages to confuse me. THEN he doesn't even take responsibility and acts as if he knew nothing about it!

I fumed as I jumped on the deck and made my way to my cabin while ignoring the questioning looks of the few idiots around me.

I opened the door allowing the moonlight to sneak more into the room. I looked around the bed and my heart leaped from my chest when I saw the bed sheets lying flat on the bed.

My eyes widened, my breath accelerated and I almost shouted to call the mates to look for my treasure. But luckily, I halted just in time when I felt his gaze on me; I turned to find him sitting by the left wall.

I inhaled deeply to relax a little. The room was drowned in darkness even though he wasn't asleep. I went to lighten a lamp that was by the bed, and then I walked across the room to where he was. I removed my sword and sat on his right, leaving the sword to lay by my side.

He tensed a little but said nothing. He was hugging his knees with his head tilted down. I expected him to yell and start throwing blames, but he just remained as he was, silent, as if he was still alone.

I moved to get closer to him when I noticed something on the floor between us. I lifted it and found it to be a piece of bread.

"Where did this come from?" I asked. It's not like bread was common on pirate ships. We only get to eat it for about two or three days at the beginning of each sail and then it becomes a fantasy until we land.

"Baril sent it" His voice was barely audible, but spoke clearly of his exhaustion.

I smelled the bread noticing it was a little soaked in the middle, "Was there meat inside?"

".... I don't know."

Just as I thought. Baril was kind enough to remember sending some bread and meat for him, but only the bread made it to his hands.

So the horrible moody old man remembered to feed him, while *I* forgot. Fuck... this day just keeps getting better.

Nyx. I treated you that way because of what could have happened if you carried on with what you had in mind. Now if you apologize, I'll forgive you this once. After that, we will both forget it happened. So how about we celebrate and fuck, huh?

My eyes narrowed as I listened to my own thoughts. Thank Gods I didn't voice that. I'm sure somehow he'll manage to make it sound insulting to him.

I looked beside me. He wasn't moving or doing anything; silently gazing at the floor. And when my loud thoughts halted for a moment, I was able to hear small sniffles that he made every few seconds.

Shit. I didn't know I had hurt him that much. Sometimes I forget how sensitive he really is. Why did he have to be so delicate?? I know women that would take a thousand insults and not even twitch!

Then again, this delicate side of his is what makes him so adorable...

I reached my arms around him and pulled him into a hug. I expected him to push me away and I prepared myself for it, but strangely, he didn't. He went still for a second and then buried his head in the crook of my neck. Only then, I realized how sad he actually was...

And when his hands held my arm to keep me from pulling back, I hugged him tighter. I nuzzled his hair and my worries started finding some relief. He fits so well in my arms... How could I not fear to lose him?

I bet he was very tired with all the work during the day and the crying at night. So I remained silent for a while, enjoying having him here in my arms. He didn't look at me at all though, which made me regret even more the way I treated him.

"Nyx, I didn't mean to be that cold to you today. My excuse is both good and... well, unreal for now... Just know that I regret hurting you, I shouldn't have handled things that way... I don't want to lose you... I..... I actually don't know what I would be without you... and that's only because of how much I lo-"

I stopped suddenly when I heard a certain breathing rhythm. I tilted my head to listen closer and my suspicion was true: He was already fast asleep.

I threw my head back and laughed. Aye, I was pulling every nerve inside me to get myself to apologize without sounding like an idiot and he simply skips it all and falls asleep!

I slowly tilted his head back to be able to see him. Even in the dim light of the lamp across the room, I could see the dark circles under his eyes.

I watched his sleeping face and couldn't help smiling at my angel. I kissed his forehead and moved him carefully to a more comfortable position in my arms. Then I closed my eyes and joined his realm.

∞ ∞ ∞

I opened my eyes to find Nyx leaving my arms. I pulled him back and he didn't resist. He sat there for few seconds before rubbing his sleepy eyes and moving away from me once again. I let him stand up and go to the bucket of water under the small window, and then he started his morning cleaning ritual.

"It's maybe around noon already. You're hungry?"

"... Not really"

Of course, that was a lie. He didn't even have dinner last night. Then again, Nyx has a pride that denies him from asking for food or admitting being hungry.

I watched him, a little vexed by the fact that he still wouldn't meet my eyes. Not even when I stood up and walked by him to use the water. But it's alright, I told myself he's still mad but he'll get over it soon. The important thing is that he's safe. He's with me.

"Let's go"

"W-where?"

I didn't like the worry in his tone. *Was he afraid of me now??*

I tried to sound calm as I answered him, "Esme"

He looked surprised, and then his gaze dropped. He fidgeted a little uncomfortable, almost as if he didn't want to visit the island anymore. This is too fucking confusing, but I guess I'm the one to blame for all the awkwardness hovering around him.

I grabbed my sword and motioned him to follow me. I left the cabin and was greeted by J.

"Morning Captain!"

"The boat?"

"Aye, it's ready. Armpit has been waiting for you since you came yesterday"

"Good. I'm going back to the island. Keep your eyes open"

"Aye, aye, Captain!! Euh..."

"What?"

"If you come back... get us some cheese, will you?"

I glared at him making him take a couple of steps back, "w-w-we'll be here Captain! Eyes open and all! You heard the Captain, you shitheads?"

He yelled at his mates and they gave a united "Aye Aye!!"

I rolled my eyes and moved to the edge of the deck. I threw the rope off it, and then I looked back, making sure Nyx was right behind me. I grabbed the rope and quickly climbed down to the boat that was right where I left it the night before.

After I landed on the boat, I watched as Nyx slowly climbed down the rope. I should've carried him down with me; he maybe got used to climbing the shrouds but the ropes are another deal.

Thankfully, he reached the boat safely and we immediately headed towards the shores of Esme.

We reached the land and we got off the boat. We were immediately received by the crew members from the camp that we set right there on the beach.

"Pixie! You made it!!"

The first to greet us was Lou, followed by Ace who had a whore hugging him close. Ace gave me a small nod that told me everything was going fine in my absence.

Nash stepped forward next, tilting his head back like usual and looking down at Nyx, the way he always did whenever he teased him, "Mmm... I wonder what you gave up to get here...."

Hearing no response, I looked behind me. Only to find Nyx standing still, feet soaking in the water as he looked around the island. *He couldn't seem more foreign to all of this even if he tried! Gods, he looks so painfully cute*

I smiled and stepped towards him to talk to him. But a couple of arms around my waist stopped me.

"Captain!!", "Oh my! It's the Captain of Martina!", "What took you so long Captain?", "Nnnh... How come you look more handsome every time you come by", "We missed you Captain", "I'm sure he missed us too, right? Devil sir?"...

∞ Nyx's POV ∞

Hands off.......

Get your hands off him!!

My heart lurched so hard so fast that it physically hurt.

And all I could do was stand there, stupidly speechless, while a herd of half-naked women touched what was mine.

I wanted to push them away. I wanted so much to yell at them all and pull him away from their wandering hands. But in the end, I didn't. I stood there, watching women as they put their hands on Agenor literally the minute we stepped on this damned Shadow island!! They were smiling, laughing, caressing his arms, his chest... One of them was even rubbing her body against his back!! Do these people know anything about decency or how a woman should behave? There was about six of them. They winked and pursed their lips trying to get Agenor's attention. My God, even the one who was once holding Ace has now joined in from far! She was sliding her hand over her body invitingly! And all *he* did was stand there, unaffected, like none of it was happening...... if not for the slight smile on his face.

If he likes such women, why did he bring me here with him? To witness??

"Huh! Look at pixie, you're so red!!"
"Don't let them embarrass you kitten. You'll get used to this"
I'm not embarrassed, you assholes, I'm angry!!
I tried not to glare at Lou and Nash in order not to fuel their sarcasm any further. But their laughs brought more unwelcomed attention to me as the woman once holding Lou left him and walked towards me.

She looked older than me, maybe in her thirties. She wore a long dress showing her long neck and part of her breasts. Her skin wasn't shining and her body was skinny. And despite the lack of jewelry and expensive clothes, she did look a bit beautiful and quite strong.

She circled around me like as if I was a prey, then she leaned to my face and I pulled backward. She tilted her head and smelled me with her eyes closed
"My my, he's a kitten indeed!"
Wha-! Now I'm being called unmanly nicknames by women!!
"Careful there, Trixie, it bites"
'it'??
"I'm not an animal!" I glared at Lou and, of course, that amused him
"Oooh!! It talks too!" The so-called Trixie was still hovering around me, and as if I could feel more uncomfortable, a couple of women joined her, looking at me up and down like they were sizing an object to buy.

Trixie finally put a hand on her hip and pointed her thumb at me while looking at Ace, "Who's this? And don't tell me he's a pirate because he sure doesn't smell like one"

Ace didn't answer her, but Nash took over, "You can be either a whore or a dog, pick one"

"I can be whatever I want" she said confidently as if she hadn't just been insulted, then she added seductively, "And for five coins, I can be whatever *you* want"

"Five?? Windy gets you for three!!"
"So does Ace, because he's the second on Martina. And Maren is a friend"
"We could be friends too; you know?"
"Aye, for five coins"
"Cheap whore"

Trixie simply shrugged and responded with a wide smile. My God, all the crudeness is getting creepy to me. I tried to ignore them and looked at Agenor, who was now talking to Ace. I wanted to go beside him and shoo the women away. But I frankly didn't know if I had the right to.

Suddenly someone grabbed my hand. It was one of the women that were beside me. She smiled at me and pulled me slowly while walking back and away from the crowd, "It's ok, I have something really nice to show you"

I stopped, trying to get my hand back, "Th-thank you, my lady, I don't-"

I was interrupted by her loud laugh, and I knew what got her so amused because I'm so used to this kind of rudeness by now; it was simply because I called her 'lady'

"My Goddess, aren't you funny! Now, if you come with me-"

"NYX!" We both got startled when Agenor suddenly barked my name. I released my hand and went to stand by his side and wait for his orders. Instead, he met me half way and grabbed my arm, "I'll show you where you'll be staying", and he led me the other way on the sand towards a tent.

Before we reached it, Ace called for him, "Captain! Izel is here"

"Oh..."

We both looked behind us and I saw a woman, winking and smiling at Agenor. And I wish I wasn't alive right now to see what happened next...

But I was alive and conscious. And I watched as Agenor motioned at Ace to get closer, then he shoved me to him like a sack of troubles that he needed to deal with, with nothing more than, "Make sure he stays in my tent until I get back"

Once more, with no apparent reason, I'm being treated like a prisoner. I don't get it. Why he got mad and punished me in the first place? Why he left me alone? Why he came back? Why did he change his mind and bring me on Esme? And............... who's this Izel woman that he's leaving me to go meet her...

I couldn't help mu hand that grabbed his jacket, "Where are you going??"

His eyebrows arched as if surprised to the fact that I spoke to him. Then his hand landed on my head to ruffle my hair, and added calmly, "Stay here Nyx, I have some business to take care of and I'll be back as soon as I finish"

He left immediately, and I wanted to be a complete child and tackle him to keep him from going... with a woman...

Ace obeyed and showed me the way. I looked back again to take a better look at that woman but she was already walking away, trying to keep up with Agenor's pace.

"Who's that??"

"Who?"

"That woman... Izel or something"

"They call her 'the whore lord'; she used to be a courtesan. Now she owns several whore-houses here on Esme and the surrounding islands"

So she's... one of those... I had a doubt at first because she looked better dressed but in the end...

"Call me if you need anything"

I nodded at Ace who left immediately. And I just noticed that I was in a tent. I looked around and I recognized some of Agenor's boxes filling half the space inside. So this is his tent. He left me here and went to...

Is this it? Is this how my new life is supposed to be like now? Is this what will happen every time we arrive at land?? I thought we were lovers but...... after all, I'm only a second choice...

And my eyes widened as I came to realize: *So this is why he left me on the ship at first! How could he? How dare he!! I..... I can't... I can't stay here and watch him leave like that again! Who does he take me for??*

Damn it! I felt a burning mix of anger and sadness rising painfully. I felt the tingling in my eyes that announced some tears, but I refused to deliver myself to tears. I'm pathetic, that is certainly established, but I'd be damned if I don't fucking try to keep the last shred of dignity, if I still have any.

I stood there for God knows how long. Thinking so hard that I wasn't able to understand my own thoughts anymore. The only lingering feeling after all of this was the fact that I wanted to disappear. I couldn't think anymore... All I wanted was to make some sense of my life, now my heart feels so crushed that I felt claustrophobic in this tent.

I hurried outside to leave the tent and try to breathe. My mind was very tired and fed up with all of this. I walked toward the sea and felt a small amount of relief when my feet touched the cold water. My senses awakened again and I felt alive for a moment, but I still was in the same situation that I desperately needed to get away from. I looked ahead to the glittering waves... The sea looked so calm and welcoming, and I felt a pull to just walk towards it...

But a simple thought made me turn around and look at the opposite direction: *Home...* I looked around me and found no one in the camp. Few tents scattered around and piles of barrels and boxes. I knew it wouldn't be long before I lost this chance, and almost without thinking, my feet started walking.

In no more than few minutes, I reached the end of the beach and the beginning of the forest. I checked that no one was following me, I gathered my determination and stepped forward. The more I walked, the more I realized how thick this forest was; It had very high trees and a maze of branches, but it still managed to look beautiful with the sunlight sneaking through the leaves.

Many scary and sad thoughts tried to walk their way back to my mind, but I pushed them away and tried to concentrate on finding my way back home. Esme, even if it's one of the Shadows, if there's a whore-house here then this island has enough people for at least one town. And they certainly have small boats to help them travel to surrounding islands. With enough luck, I'll find someone heading to Ebina, and from there I'll do fine...

Yes, this will turn out for the best... Agenor's figure flashed in my memory so vividly that my heart fluttered. I immediately tripped on a branch and sank with hands and knees on the ground.

Turn around. Go back. Don't betray his trust... When he gets back and finds you gone... he'll be angry and sad

Shut up!! I'm not a weak coward and I'm not a replacement for someone else!! I'll prove that! I'll prove that I'm strong and not pitiful! Even if there's no one to prove that to... Well, I'll prove it to myself!! So Fuck him and Fuck you conscious!!

I forced my confusing thoughts back and stood up, then scurried forward. I walked forward and forward, unable to go as fast as I wished. I kept ignoring the voice in my head that pleaded for me to look back, to halt and reconsider, but it was too late. I was too deep in the forest and even if I wanted to, I would most probably not know how to go back. And why would I want to? What would I be going back to? Agenor is busy with......

A lump formed in my throat and sadness started taking over my mind once more. My God, if this keeps up I'm going to because crazy before making it anywhere!

After a while of walking, my body started feeling weak. I was tired and I just remembered that I was barefoot, so I stopped to rest for a minute. My feet hurt and I was hungry, but that was the last of my worries. I looked around me; I avoided ascending a big mountain in order not to get lost, but now I'm not sure if that was the best choice. The voice in my head kept taking every chance to blame me and tell me that I was lost, but I started walking again and kept moving forward.

And just when I was about to lose hope, the sun appeared proud and strong in the sky, announcing that I have gotten out of the forest. I looked around and found the one thing that proved all my doubts about this island: a path. Between the rocks, grass, and shrubs, a path was drawn on the ground, with obvious traces of wheels.

I stood in the middle of the path and looked around, trying to decide on the next direction that I should take.

This is it! One of the ends of this path certainly leads to a town. All I need to do is follow this path and I'll be able to leave all the craziness behind me. *Go home, Nyx... That's it, keep going and you'll get home*

I was encouraging myself and trying my best to stay strong. But strangely, I didn't take any step further. Images of Agenor smiling and smirking at me froze me. And because I stopped, I was once more aware of all the hurt that my heart was suffering.

I don't want to be second... I can't be!!

But I love him... I seriously do

∞ ∞ ∞

Chapter 4 ~ With bated breath
∞ Nyx's POV ∞

I don't want to be second...
But I love him... I really do
I stood outside of the forest, unable to make a decision; my heart pleaded that I ignore everything and just turn around and be with the one it loved, but my mind tugged me to follow the path that I came to find and go back home. It felt so unfair to be forced to make such a choice... In the end, I needed to choose not the life that I wished for, but what thing I'll be able to live without: My love, or my pride.

But my struggle was interrupted by the voice of a man screaming in agony. I turned around in alarm, and a silhouette emerged from the forest. The person was walking back, holding his sword in defense, "Fuck! Who's there?? Show yourself or I promise I'll nail your junk to your forehead!"

"N-Nash!??"

Nash looked back at me as if he forgot that I was there, then he huffed in anger and turned back to face the forest, "Shit... Great! Fucking great..."

And before I could make sense of the situation, Ace stepped out of the forest, his Tashi was unleashed in his right hand, and with the other, he dragged a man by the neck.

The man was on his knees, I've never seen him before, he was wearing filthy rags and he breathed with difficulty. I watched with wide eyes as he tried desperately to release himself from Ace's grip, but with every movement, Ace would squeeze harder, making him whimper in agony.

"Where the FUCK do you come from!?"

Nash yelled at Ace, who answered with a firm but calm tone of voice, "I've been following you."

"Wha-?? Why didn't you say anything, you bastard!!"

"I didn't want to disturb your...", and his eyes locked on me, "... chase"

This means that... Nash was following me? And behind him was Ace??

My whole body tensed and I avoided his eyes. He wasn't the kind to talk much, but his look was almost as ruthless as his Captain's.

"Fucking bastard... You had to fucking take all the fun out of this shit, God damn it" Nash threw his hair behind him, then stomped back and disappeared in the forest, while rambling and throwing insults.

Ace waited for him to leave, then he yanked the man's neck and gave him the glare of death, "I Fucking see you again, and I'll cut your throat without a second thought"

The man nodded frantically and Ace released him. He fell back on the hard ground, his hand holding his side that was bloody and clearly injured from Ace's Tashi. A second man jumped out from behind a tree and helped the first one up. Ace didn't look surprised by him, he just stood still as they both scurried and disappeared from where they came.

Once alone, Ace turned to me and stepped forward; with his sallied sword still in his hand, he kept a steady gaze on me. I've seen that unleashed sword a lot already, I even crossed it countless times during our training. But I have never felt afraid of Ace like I am today.

When he got close to me, my body obeyed me for and unfroze, and I was able to take a step back, "Wh-who were those? Why are you here?? And Nash??"

"Those were robbers. They, as well as many other rogues, live in the mountains and attack people who escape without even taking their sword with them"

I blinked, then looked at my side. *Shit, how could I be this stupid! I escaped without any useful weapon!*

"M....my sword is on Martina"

"We're on Esme to sell weapons! You couldn't steal a shitty dagger to defend yourself with? What if they attacked you??"

I kept silent as I realized that... he was right. I have been so riled up since yesterday, but still, I should've anticipated being attacked by robbers on a Shadow island

".... And Nash?"

"He was tailing you, and I him"

"How did you find me? I mean, no one saw me...." my voice trailed when Ace's eyes narrowed on me, he was trying to look emotionless but I could easily discern his anger.

"We both saw you leave Nyx. You think it would be *that* easy to escape? My Gods, what the hell were you thinking? If you're up to it, then at least be smart about it and plan it properly, damn it! Walking away in the middle of the day without as much as a needle to protect yourself with?"

As he scolded me, the disappointment in his voice couldn't be more obvious. Since I met him, Ace had never hurt me in any way. On the contrary, he was the only one helping me without asking for anything in return whenever I got injured. He even spent hours and hours to train me to be more capable of living among pirates. I owe him and respect him. So when this man scolds me... It hurts

But this is not about Ace. This is about his Captain. Nothing changed. I'm still suffering here while Agenor is away having his best of time with............ I can't go back to *that*. Even if I haven't completely made up my mind to leave, I'm still not going back.

I looked at his unleashed sword and decided not to give in. I knew how dangerous my situation was but I was very tired both physically and mentally, a bit suicidal even. I took a step back and gathered all my courage to look as confident as possible, "I'm not going back with you, Ace"

"Oh, on the contrary, you are going to walk back obediently to the camp and you are not going to make me chase after you." Then he stepped forward threateningly, "I'm very bad at catching my prey alive, Nyx"

A chill of fear made me realize how mad Ace was right now. He values his Captain so much and that's most probably why he's mad at me right now, but what about *me*?

I tried to keep my voice steady but it still shivered a little, "I'm not going back there Ace... You have no idea-"

The lump in my throat made me lose my voice, and I dropped my head when I realized that a stupid tear had already broken free.

Ace sighed and tried to sound less angry and threatening, "Look, I know you were kept against your will on Martina, so this situation was kind of expected. But there's obviously more to this, right Nyx?"

I opened my mouth to answer him. Explain how his evil Captain was cheating on me right this second! Just the thought of it hurts so much...... But all I ended up doing was meeting him in the eye once more and repeating, "I'm not going back to Martina"

He arched his eyebrows in surprise to my determination. He stared at me for a moment, waiting for me to yield, but I stood my ground. In the end, he moved his sword up, then with a swift slash, he forced the blade clean from the blood that dropped on the ground, and he buried his Tashi in its scabbard.

Then he chuckled and I was both surprised and confused to see him smile right now.

"You know who's the one who'll end up in trouble here, right?"

"I know. I'm in the worst situation ever, but that doesn't mean that-"

"Oh, I wasn't talking about you, Nyx. Actually, I am the one who's in deep shit right now. I either let you flee, and Agenor would go all berserk on the crew, he'll hunt you down but you'll most probably be eaten by a bear or a hungry rogue by then, and when Agenor finds out, it will maybe cost us a few lives and limbs before he calms down. OR, I take you back by force and Agenor will most probably skin me alive for putting my hand on you. So you see, your fate is not the only one on the line here."

I listened carefully trying not to fall for his scheme, but even when I knew that he was using guilt to make me back down, it still worked. But will Agenor really get *that* mad if I was gone?

My heart whispered the answer to that without hesitation

"So what is it going to be Nyx?"

I obviously only had to choose between going back on my feet or being dragged, because Ace was never going to let me leave. His Captain ordered him to make sure I stay put and Ace never disobeyed him. I actually don't understand why he let me reach so far. He never talked this much before. It was clear to me that he was only talking this much to avoid using force with me, an effort he was making for the sake of his Captain, not me. This was a courtesy that I better accept or he'll certainly make me regret it.

After much hesitation, my shoulders slumped in defeat and I nodded slowly. He sighed in relief and motioned for me to walk before him.

We went back into the forest and made our way slowly through the trees.

"Why did you let me leave? I mean, if you saw me from the beginning..."

"I was going to stop you right away. Then I saw Nash tailing you. And I wanted to see what he wanted with you so I tailed you both. But I guess he only wanted to see how far you'd be able to go. Too bad those rogues arrived, it was nice to witness your indecisiveness like that"

It's much less amusing when you're the one stuck with a decision to make

"Lords, I can't believe you made me leave a whore mid-fuck, and I already paid her! Now if she had already left the camp, it would your fault, Nyx"

I knew from his tone that he was teasing me, but I still blushed. Having the stoic Ace trying to cheer me up did work a little.

We advanced slowly, mostly because of my bare feet. And the more we got closer to the beach, the more I knew that I was in deep trouble.

We reached the camp and the first one I saw was Nash. He glared at me from the corner of his eye, but immediately went back to throwing insults at the brothers, Yeagar and Ajax, who were obviously insulting and bullying him, something they called teasing.

"Stand in the water" Ace ordered. I did as told, not caring if this was a punishment or whatever. I just wanted to get through the day. But as soon as my feet touched the water and winced in pain

"That's your punishment for being so clever and deciding to take a stroll in the woods with bare feet"

When the sharp pain dulled, I looked at Ace who went back to his emotionless façade. Once again, he's taking care of me... this wasn't a punishment. This was him getting me to disinfect the scratches I got from walking in the forest.

Why was Ace so considerate? I don't need that now... It actually wavers my will to leave.

"Stay a few minutes more, then go rest in your tent. I'll go check if that whore is still around, she owes me another round." He turned around, and just before he left he looked back at me and added, "Oh, and if you plan to cut and run again call for me. I might give you some tips"

Shit, this is so embarrassing. He's practically calling me an idiot!!

I stood there, like he said, moving my dull feet in the stinging water. Why wouldn't Agenor be as forgiving as Ace? Then he'll forget that I just tried to escape. But everyone knew that THAT was not how Agenor reacted to people who disobey him.

My mind was so tired of thinking so I headed to the tent to get some rest. I looked inside and found nothing to sit on or something. Even the boxes didn't seem to be opened yet; Agenor usually makes a little mess every time he changed or went through one of his boxes, leaving his clothes and things thrown over them. It looked as if he didn't even sleep here yesterday, I mean before he came late to the ship.

For a moment there, I felt light-headed. I looked at my feet and the sand started moving in waves... I followed the imaginary tides that swayed me gently. I sat down on the sand, feeling its softness between my fingers.

I love the sand. It's soothing and so clean. I felt like I wanted to go outside, look at the sea and the green trees, but I didn't know if I was allowed to. I was only allowed to stay here. Me, here in his tent while he was....................

The small dizziness disappeared, leaving behind a painful headache. As time passed by, the voices outside got busier than the almost deserted camp I saw when I first got here. I recognized most of the voices, and the ones I didn't recognize were all for women.

"Nyxyyyy!!"

Maren let himself inside the tent. I was about to smile at him, but when I lifted my head, I saw him, standing there with............. A woman under each arm!!

"Maren what are you-"

"Me Gods, I missed you mate!! I even told the girls that I missed you, isn't that right, girls?" One of them nodded and the other one just laughed and buried her head in Maren's neck.

"Maren, are you drunk? It's not evening yet and you're that drunk already"

"Relaaaaaax" he fell on his knees, bringing both women down with him, "We're on land mate, the first few days are always crazyyy!! Crazy, crazy, always crazy...." He went on singing and, of course, the ladies giggled.

"Come on Nyx!! Come join the funnn!"

"I'll pass, thank you"

"No no no, you can't pass, you have to fuck! And you have to do it now because, in a few days, no one will have the money for that, come on"

I felt so embarrassed, sitting there while a woman kissed his face jaw repeatedly. Something touched my knee and I jolted in surprise.

"Ooh, sweet bun, do I scare you?" The woman said, I shook my head quickly trying not to look panicked, and I recognized her from earlier in the day

"Oh, Nyxy! That's Trixie, she already likes you, mate! Nyxy Trixie, Trixie Nyxy... See? You get along already!" He said with a big goofy smile, then drank from a jar that he was holding in his hand.

"Maren, I really don't think you should be drinking that much-"

"Come on man, I promised to take care of you, remember?"

"I'm not the one who needs taking care of right now"

"You know what? I cut us a deal with these two nasties here, believe me, it's going to blow your mind! Listen, how about.... instead of three coins each, we get them both for four!! Isn't that amazing!"

I shifted back a little when Trixie tried to caress my knee again. Her hand fell on the sand and she pouted

"Please tell me you mean something other than what I'm thinking right now"

"How the shit would I know what you think, mate? You're so slow sometimes"

Slow!!

"Here, I'll explain. Two coins per whore, two whores, four coins in all, but wait! It gets better, they agreed that if they get their coins we can both be there, me Goooods, imagine how fun it would be!" Then he started pointing at us one by one, "You, her, and I with her, then you with her, and I with her, **then we fuck them both mate**!!", he suddenly stopped and put a finger in the air to think, then added decisively, "Nope, I'll fuck them both, you watch. You have to fuck, but let's not overwhelm you mate, I mean, the important thing is for you to at least do it once in your life"

My face blushed so hard I thought my ears were going to explode, "I'm not a virgin, you idiot!!"

He stopped to look at me with wide eyes, "Well, of course, you're not, we aaaall know that, mate. I'm glad you finally have the courage to admit it, so we can tease you about your fucking in the open, NO secrets on Martina my friend!"

Is... Is he actually talking about me and Agenor!

I completely lost my tongue to that; now I just wanted him gone, or for the earth to swallow me and get it over with.

Maren laid his hand in front of me, "Come on boy, two coins, just two and I promise I'll get them to fuck your brain out" He wiggled his eyebrows suggestively

"You know I have no money, right?"

"Oh..."

"**What**??" The one that was sleeping on his shoulder woke up screaming, "Are you fucking kidding me, Maren? If I was to open my legs to a broke, I'd rather fuck myself!"

Ouch, I don't know the lady and it feels like she just rejected me. Wait, what the hell am I thinking?

"No no no no!! Calm down sweet puss! Here, drink some, you'll feel better"

He poured into her mouth some of the beer from the jar, then he looked at me, "See? That's why you need to fuck, so you can learn that you should NEVER say that word in front of a whore, she'll spit on you, mate", then he turned back to her, "Look around you, it's the Captain's tent. This little guy here..."

Did he just call ME little??

"Nyxy, here, holds all of Agenor's jewels. And believe me when I say, ALL his jewels, if you know what I mean"

"Ok, that's it!! Get out, Maren!"

"Wha-! You're not going to fuck? I brought you TWO whores man! AND a great deal!! Just try it...."

I ignored his repeated protests as I stood up and pushed him out. One of the women shot me a disgusted glare before she stepped out. The other one, Trixie, wrapped her arms around my waist, "Good thing you sent them away, now I can have you all for myself"

She slipped her finger under my pants and I immediately panicked and pushed her away. She almost fell back

"I-I'm sorry my lady... I-I didn't mean to hurt you"

"Oh, it's fine sweet bun, I'm glad you have it into you to be mean"

She approached me and I stepped back. My God, her insistence was getting me so uncomfortable

"Tsk, tsk, tsk." The tent opened and two other women came in. I suddenly missed my cousin, Haven, he used to take care of all lady related issues.

The first lady was one that I had wished never to see again; Izel, the one who took Agenor away earlier in the day. She walked inside like she owned the place, "I told you a thousand times, Trixie, get the money before the fuck. Get out of my face"

Trixie looked very unpleased, but somehow it seemed like she was used to this. She released me with a pout and left.

Everything with Izel screamed finesse and seduction; from her strong eye-catching lipstick to the way she moved. She eyed the cabin, a frown working its way on her face. She looked displeased with something, she turned to me and said calmly, "Now. I've been told to bring a nice meal to whoever was in the Captain's tent. You don't happen to know a woman that the Captain is keeping here, do you?"

I shook my head, trying not to think about the thousand questions that went off in my mind.

"Mmm, I was almost sure though... Well! Doesn't matter. I was paid to bring this meal to his tent, it doesn't concern us if there was no one here to eat it. Set the food, Cherri"

She motioned for the second woman to come in. This one was young though. She had caramel skin and light brown hair. She wore beautiful clothes and even makeup. If not for the way Izel is talking to her, I would've thought she was her daughter.

"I told you, dear," Izel said to Cherri with a smirk on her face, "you haven't lost your chance yet"

Cherri didn't answer, though. She stepped forward and set a covered basket on the sand, then went to stand behind Izel once again.

Izel went to turn around and leave, but she halted suddenly to ask me, "Who are you?"

I was a bit startled with the sudden attention, but I quickly gathered my focus and answered, "I'm one of the Martina crew"

She seemed more intrigued after I answered. She approached a little, walked her eyes from my toes to my eyes and all the way down again. I shifted uncomfortably, but she didn't seem to care, "A pirate??" The suspicion in her voice couldn't be more obvious.

A pirate... Am I, really? Three days ago I would probably have said yes. Now I'm not sure who I am anymore...

She smirked at me as if she was reading my confused thoughts in my head. She grabbed her dress with the tips of her fingers and curtseyed gracefully, "My name is Izel, a humble courtesan. I own all the whores on Esme, and I provide a few other services. And your name is...?", she held out her hand with her palm facing downward, and presented a polite smile, almost foreign to this entourage. I took her hand lightly and immediately bent to place a kiss on her knuckles, "I'm Nyx Os-"

Shit! What the hell am I doing??

I released her hand an immediately straightened my back, then I tried to continue without looking flustered, "I'm Nyx, I work for Agenor"

But the regaled smirk on her face and her raised eyebrow told me that she caught on my odd behavior. She laughed and tilted her head, "I knew you weren't a pirate. You wreak of courtesy, young man. Interesting...."

Her eyes flashed with interest as she kept eyeing me, stopping a little on my bare feet and releasing a small chuckle. I felt ashamed of my dirty feet and I tried to bury them a little in the sand.

"If you don't need anything I would like to rest if you wouldn't mind"

"Aye, excuse me for keeping you from your chores. So, where's your tent, *pirate*?"

None of your damn business!!

"Why do you ask?"

"Oh, pardon my curiosity, I only wanted to send you a beautiful gift later"

I looked at her questioningly and she explained with a 'matter of fact' tone, "A woman, a whore to be more exact. And it will be on me. Consider it, our way of welcoming you on Esme"

"Thank you for your intentions, but I shall need no such service"

"Oh, really? A pirate refusing a fuck after a long journey in the sea... Interesting indeed...."

I didn't answer this time. It seemed like every time she asked or said something it was to play me, maybe to get some information out of me, maybe to just entertain herself. Right now, I frankly don't give a shit. I'm hungry, tired, and in a shitty situation where I am most probably facing death or worse once Agenor knows what I had done today. So pardon me if I was no ray of sunshine to the woman who pulled him away from me in the first place!!

I didn't utter a word of my thoughts, thank God for that. As much as I'm angry and fucked up, I don't want to deal with the guilt of speaking unmannerly to a woman. Finally, she seemed to get the gist, and she sighed, "Seems like your luck is running out today, Cherri, but we never lose hope now, do we?"

And just when I thought she was heading out, she touched a lock of Cherri's brown curly hair and looked at me in the corner of her eyes, "This is Cherri, beautiful isn't she? I've been raising her for months now, preparing hand training her to meet your Captain..."

My heart fluttered but I tried to keep from showing my feelings. *This young woman was...... trained to be with him??*

"Well, we'll head back now. Please inform your Captain that I delivered what he ordered in time, I leave you to rest now, *pirate* Nyx. And remember, my offer still stands whenever you feel lonely" And she left the tent after motioning for Cherri to follow her.

With the silence that reigned over the tent, the headache settled again. I kneeled by the basket, uncovered it and took in the delicious scent. I went to eat some, I hesitated though. I was very hungry, but who said this was for me? Maybe it was sent for Agenor? And why was that Izel lady here when Agenor hasn't come back yet?

I went against my better judgment and ate a little. The food settling in my stomach made me forget my worries momentarily. When I ate enough, I pushed the basket aside and I crawled on the sand to the only corner that wasn't occupied by any boxes. I laid on the sand; its softness and coldness numbed my senses. And I surrendered to a needed sleep while praying for tomorrow to come and leave in peace.

∞ ∞ ∞

Chapter 5 ~ Word of honor
∞ Agenor's POV ∞

At dawn, I was walking toward the camp. I glanced behind me to the few pirates that I brought along, they were all annoyed. Of course, they were; they would rather drink, eat and fuck whores than being stuck with a Captain in a bad mood.

Yesterday, I was supposed to meet a black market merchant that I did some nice business with several times before. I got to the whorehouse, where we usually meet and discuss, only to find that the old man had died, and a wimp of a servant was there to make the deal, with ME!! I had to sail all the way to Ganae, a neighboring Shadow island, to meet the old man's son and make it clear to him that I don't make deals with servants. In the end, I didn't like the fucker. He was not made for trading and he wanted to get my best weapons for half the price. I gave him a piece of my mind, I seriously wanted to cut his throat for insisting on such a lousy deal, especially for the way he was talking to me as if I *needed* his money. But unfortunately, his mother saved him from between my hands. If I drew a line for killing people, it would be spilling blood with the mother as a witness.

I already know many important people around here. I'll easily manage to get the stuff sold for their proper price. But I'd rather throw everything in the sea with my own hands than make a deal with half-assed merchants.

I walked on the sand, tired and annoyed like hell. This is so expected of the fucking Goddess of fate; treat someone good badly and it will bite you in the ass. And I knew just why my luck in business had turned its back on me today. *This karma bitch works so damn fast.*

I stomped in frustration as that same feeling burnt inside me again: Guilt. I never knew it could be this damn strong. I always did what I wanted, no explanations necessary and no excuses afterward either. And it worked wonderfully so far. Never looking back had made me own one of the strongest pirate crews roaming the seas, along with a name that reached much further than where I actually sailed.

But it seems that things don't exactly work the same way in love. This damn feeling is so beautiful but so fucking complicated! *I mean we were ok, right? We were AMAZING!! But no, he had to sneak around on me and ask others about our destination, while I was almost the only one he didn't confide to!*

It's not my fault, so this fucking karma is unjustified. Ok, maybe just a little bit my fault. I know I've been harsh with him. I could treat any of the pirates that way and they'd still kiss my ring. But, Nyx? Oh no. He has too much pride to swallow such a thing. And he's also too sensitive; I try to be careful with him, but I was bound to fail. He's a nobleman, and you shouldn't expect those to kneel easily.

But he's a gentleman that likes to wipe the floor and serve pirates if it meant that he wouldn't owe them. That's how beautiful his honor is. A strange mix of courage and weakness, dignity and modesty. A sweet combination that observes you behind a set of mesmerizing sea-blue eyes... *Shit, I miss him...*

I accelerated my pace, the light from the few torches that we carried was slowly being replaced by the sunlight.

Aye. I Fucked up. But maybe he'll forget. Oh, that would be great, and it's obviously a childish dream. If only there was a plant that would wipe a few days' worth of memory... Lords, I would pay a fortune for such a plant. I'd give it to Nyx, then have some myself. He'll forget the way I treated him and distrusted him, and I'll get rid of this fucking guilt.

By the time we reached the camp the sun was out on the horizon. I nodded to the pirates that were standing guard and continued to my tent. I saw Ace, laying on the beach, drunk dead with jars surrounding him and a whore asleep beside him. Others were dispersed here and there, most of them asleep, very few still had the strength to drink.

I grabbed a torch and a small bag from one of the pirates that followed me then I dismissed them. I walked inside my tent and my mood softened at the sight of him; laying there on his right side, fast asleep on the cold sand. I cursed under my breath for forgetting to give him sheets to sleep on and cover himself, my head is so fucking in the clouds these days.

I stuck the torch in the sand in the middle of the tent to keep it illuminated and put my sword on the side. I opened one of my boxes and grabbed a sheet. That's my Nyx. No matter what, he would never put his hand on someone else's things. I could keep a pile of gold beside him and he wouldn't touch it. Alright, maybe he'd organize it, but not take any of it. He liked things to be put neatly where they belonged. When we were on Martina, I sometimes threw my clothes on the floor on purpose just to watch him bend over, gather them one by one, and fold them back into my boxes.

I kneeled beside him and covered him with the sheet. Then I removed his hair away from his face to watch him sleep. He was beautiful. Yet a frown seemed to disturb his dreams. I went to kiss his frown away, but before my lips reached him, his eyes flew open. He got startled and went to sit abruptly, and our foreheads met in a painful bump.

He hissed in pain and grabbed his forehead, "Y-you're back!"

"Aye. Go back to sleep. It's still early"

"It's ok." His eyes looked around to avoid mine.

"If you're done sleeping then we'd rather get going"

"Where??"

"I'm taking you somewhere. Oh, and here" I grabbed the bag that I brought with me and pulled a pair of shoes out, "I brought these for you. I ordered for leather ones to be made, but these will do until they're ready"

"y.......you remembered me?"

"Of course I did"

He looked at the shoes in what seemed like a surprise. I grabbed his foot and was about to slip it inside the shoe, but he yanked his foot back nervously, "I-I can do it myself"

He turned a little and started wearing them, but I already caught on the marks on his feet, "You went outside the beach?"

He froze still and I could almost smell his fear. After a moment, he answered, "I..... went for a walk"

For a second I thought my heart had stopped. Thankfully, he immediately added, "Ace was there"

I breathed in and went to fondle with the basket that was set by my boxes, still getting over that mini attack that my heart just felt. I uncovered the basket to find it still filled with food. Bread, fruits, a small kettle filled with nicely cooked meat. Everything was missing a tiny bit. At least he ate, right? Well, I hope he's the one who ate this and not someone else. Then again, if it was that monkey or one of those hooligans they would've finished it all including the basket!

I gathered some of the food in a small bag, grabbed my sword and turned to find him standing up, shifting uncomfortably from one foot to the other. I didn't know if it was caused by nervousness or the shoes. I didn't want to pressure him anyway so I let him be.

Yeah, now you let him be after you beat him two days ago.

I didn't beat him!! I just happened to push him a little. Fuck you, guilt!!

I headed out and he followed. I passed by Ace and told him that I was leaving, I also ordered him to add soberer guards around the camp. He nodded and got up, then went to wash his face with sea water. He looked like he had a strong hangover, and it takes a lot to get Ace to have a hangover. It's either something was bothering him or he really liked the whore and let her fill him with booze. I looked down at the woman that was still asleep on the sand. Aye, definitely the first option.

We left the camp and kept following the length of the beach. The view was beautiful, with no one else in sight. My focus was more on the sound of the feet that followed behind me than the beach and the view. When a small path opened in the thick forest, we left the sand to venture into the woods.

"The last time we passed by Esme was about two years ago. Since then, these forests have grown almost twice the size"

"A-Are you sure of the way? It looks like a maze"

"Don't worry. We're taking a long path, but we're not getting lost any soon"

"Why the longer path?"

"I've been told that during the last six months, a bunch of bandits settled in one of the mountains here. There has always been thieves and criminals around, but it seems like they gathered in some kind of a pack or something."

I stopped to check on him. He was looking around him in worry and didn't even notice me stopping, which made him bump into me. I grabbed his hand preventing him from falling back, and I sincerely appreciated the touch. But he regained his balance quickly and released his hand while averting his eyes.

I sighed, then continued deeper in the woods. About two hours later, we reached the mountain that I aimed for and we started climbing it. It was harder for him to do so, I could tell. So I slowed down the pace a little to avoid tiring him too much.

"What's that noise??" He suddenly stopped to focus on his hearing.

"It's where we're heading. Want to take a break?"

"I'm ok"

"Good."

We climbed higher for about an hour, using my sword from time to time to better clear the path from all the branches and bushes that blocked it.

When we finally came to the destination, we were tired. But the look on Nyx's face was a thousand times worth it.

"It's........ So beautiful..." He said as he gazed at the sight that presented itself before us.

A stream of water walked its way besides our feet, calmly descending the side of the mountain. It reached a cliff and fell freely in a small waterfall.

Nyx walked slowly to the edge and watched the water as it cascaded down for about thirty feet, then joined a small lake. A ball of steam formed where it plunged, adding a beautiful touch to the fair blue lake that was limited by a set of surrounding rocks. And at the further side of it, the overflowing water continued its trip down the mountain slope, where it faced the many trees and bushes, forcing it to divide into a set of tiny streams that pursued their journey in different directions.

I stepped back a little to take in the whole view, and what a breathtaking view it was. My love, standing there, eyes open wide and lips slightly parted, looking around him in complete awe.

"My God... I wish I was a painter... this is so beautiful!"

I smiled and gazed at him, "Aye, it's gorgeous"

He raised his hand and pointed excitingly towards the sea, "Agenor, look! It's Martina!! That's our ship over there!"

A sudden wave of happiness raided on my heart; Was it for the fact that he smiled? That he called my name? Or maybe because he called it 'our' ship?

I didn't register my own moves until I was wrapping my arms around him and bringing his back to press against my chest. With him in my arms, I came to realize how much I actually felt lonely without him. I hugged him tighter, allowing the feeling to fill the void inside me.

It took me a moment to notice that he hadn't pushed me away. Once again, just like when I went back for him on Martina, his hands held onto me. A tiny gesture that pacified a hill of worries in my head.

"I missed you"

HE MISSES ME!!

His whisper was almost lost in the noise of the waterfall, but luckily I was right there to catch it

"I'm the one who's supposed to say that"

He turned around and hugged me back. He kept his head lowered, not wanting to look me in the eye again. It's ok, I'll get him to trust me again. I don't want him to fear me, not to the point that would make seclude his thoughts from me. When confused, he becomes silent and distances himself from those around him. I want to break that limit and be able to hear his worries and complains freely even if they were about me. After all, freedom is what I promised to give him from the start.

Well, as far as freedom could get, which means as long as he's mine, by my side, safe and sound.

He pulled back a moment later and went to gaze at everything, everything but me. As much as I wanted to lock him in my arms, I decided against it and let him breathe.

I kicked my boots away and removed my sword and the new dagger that was strapped around my waist. Next, I took off my shirt and stepped into the river. Then I held an inviting hand to him.

Nyx looked at my hand and hesitated. I worried that he might actually refuse to join me. I smiled and nodded a little to encourage him and to my relief, it seemed to work. I watched with eagerness as he removed his shoes and put them together by some bushes. Then he folded the hem of his pants and walked towards me.

His hand touched mine and I helped him keep his balance as he stepped into the stream and on the small slippery rocks. He shivered at the coldness of the water and I chuckled at that. Once he was in front of me, I gazed at him; he was watching the crystal water as it moved at his feet.

I slid my hands and grabbed either side of his waist. Then I pulled him slowly to close the distance between us. His hands grabbed my arms to steady himself, and we were finally looking straight into each other's eyes.

This is where I apologize to him and all this fucked up situation will go away.

That's what I really thought, but when his eyes watered, I knew he was more confused than he should

"Nyx..."

"What am I Agenor?"

"What?" The waterfall was a bit noisy, but I could hear him well. And his question seemed very weird to me.

"I..... I don't know what or who I am anymore... I feel like I am stuck and I don't know where I belong"

"You belong to ME!"

He shook his head slowly, "I don't know... I don't know what I could do more! Either with my family or here, it's always the same, I am never enough..."

His voice hitched a little with that last word signaling his threatening tears. I know that he was doing his best not only for the sake of keeping his dignity, but also to be noticed and recognized as someone good and worthy. That's why it always relaxed him whenever I complimented him. But right now, where the hell is this coming from??

"Nyx-no, look at me. You are who you are. You are enough without even trying, can't you see that?"

"No, it's not enough!! It never is! Mother needed someone else to lean on in times of distress, and now I try and try but I can't be a pirate. I thought I was doing ok but I was so wrong which is why I was left alone on the ship... And I thought that I was enough, but...... you need someone else to love... I-I'm not blaming you, it's just.... unfair...."

A tear dropped, and of course, with Nyx, once the first one escapes there's a stream ready to spill right afterward.

"You're overthinking this, stop tormenting yourself. Listen, I'm sorry. I really am. I was angry and I just wanted to keep you. It was a stupid misunderstanding and I absolutely didn't mean to push you like that"

"It's ok. I can take it"

Sure you can. Look at how strong you are now!

"But.... there are things I really can't do; I'm not a woman Agenor! I'm a man and I'll always be one!"

Ok, now I'm the one who's confused.

I raised a suspicious eyebrow to that, "You want to become a woman?"

"What? No! Why would you say that? You want me to be one??"

This reeks of a fucking trap

I sneaked a hand to cup him, "I wouldn't trade *this* for the world"

He gasped in surprise, then he immediately blushed in a shade of red that I missed so much and started stuttering. He immediately hardened in my hand and my reaction wasn't less than his. Blood rushed through my veins leaving a sweet tingling on my skin. My left hand held the small of his back to steady him, and my right one caressed him in my palm.

His breathing accelerated and he leaned his head on my shoulder. His moans soon followed in a sweet, low voice that cut through the waterfall's noise.

I meant to go further but he surprised me by pushing my hand away

"N-No... I can't do this... I can't"

He pulled away and I almost whined to the separation. He walked to the edge beside the waterfall and watched the falling water for a moment. Then he turned around with a painful look and pleading eyes, "I don't think I can stay on Esme... I'm better off on Martina"

"You want to go back to the ship??"

"I can't be here and watch you leave *me* to go with a woman!"

I wanted to ask what the fuck he was talking about. He grabbed his hair with his hands and looked aimlessly in the water under his feet while shaking his head repeatedly, "It makes me feel useless and pathetic! No... No, I can't... I want to leave, but I can't leave! I can't be where you're not anymore... and I'm stuck and I can't find an answer, I don't know what I want or what I could give up more!!"

He was obviously confused and very shaken. He took a step back. Luckily I was there to grab him before he fell backward into the lake. I held his face in my hands and his eyes met mine; piercing blue, reaching to the deepest part of my soul, scared and insecure, and once more the blue wavered behind a tiny wave of tears. I like when he cries. As much as I wanted to scold him right now, looking at those eyes, I just couldn't.

"For Gods sakes Nyx, stop working that head of yours" I rested my forehead on his, breathing and allowing him to do the same and relax a little.

When I felt like he would listen and understand me, I pulled away to look him in the eyes with my hands still cupping his face, and said with a determined confident voice, "Now listen to me carefully. I. AM. AGENOR, Captain of Martina. I do as I like and no one dares dictate my actions. No one, Nyx." I saw the hurt deepen in his eyes, so I softened my voice a little before I continued, "That being said, I haven't slept with anyone since I stepped on land"

His eyes widened in disbelief, "I don't know who the fuck told you such thing, I'm going to find them and skin them alive. I'm not saying that I wouldn't if I wanted to as I said, I don't take orders from anyone. But I haven't even considered that, Nyx. The only one I seriously want to be with and want to own and fuck is *you*"

"You...... you didn't?? But they were all over you the second you reached the beach! And..... Izel?"

"What about her?"

"You... left with her..."

I sighed, both relieved that he's starting to talk and get back to his normal self, and annoyed that he's pushing me to explain myself

"Her whorehouse is where I meet with merchants and make deals. This time it was a total time loss, though"

"So you weren't with her??"

"Sure, she was there. She takes care of the food and serves booze"

"So you weren't alone, right?"

The optimism and hope in his eyes were exquisite. My Gods, was *this* what was bothering him?? He's probably innocent but that mind of his loses reins every time it takes over!

I held still, letting him get more eager for an answer. He lost patience quickly though, "Tell me... Please, I need to know"

I chuckled and moved to hold his waist and hug him close. He was obviously jealous and as troublesome as it was, it was a full ego boost for me.

I lifted him a little and set him on a rock at the edge. As expected, he got scared and looked behind him and down the waterfall. His hands held my shoulders in fear of falling back. With one hand around his waist, I secured him, and with the other around his neck, I made him look at me. Right now, I was sure that he was going to stop any rogue thoughts in his mind and listen to only me, "Your jealousy is so damn sweet, Nyx" He flushed red again and I continued before he could protest, "It didn't even occur to me to hold someone other than you. That is how much I love you and want you... When you were away, I was angry and annoyed, and all I wanted was to go back and touch you... Make sure that you were safe, with me and no one else"

The happiness glistered in his eyes and a beautiful smile tugged his flushed cheeks slowly. I took my time to watch his cheerful face and erase every shred of guilt inside me.

"See, you were making a fuss about nothing"

He nodded, "Yes, I was wrong... I'm sorry, I really am"

He's the one apologizing?? My Gods, one COULD wipe a few days' worth of memory!

He seemed to think a little. A few moments later, he leaned in for an innocent kiss that sent a raging fever down my spine. *How could a tongue-less kiss carry so much effect?*

By the time his honeyed lips left mine, I was more than ready to fuck him. But my perverted thoughts were interrupted by a sweet voice saying something that made me hold my breath:

"I love you Agenor. I love you more than I could imagine, and I will never part from you for as long as I live. I can't live away from you... I promise you, from today on, I will never try to escape. I will work harder to become the man that you'll be proud of, I'll do my best to be enough." and he sealed his promise with another kiss.

His words played in my mind over and over again. My heart never felt more vulnerable, its beat became strong and warm. And as I felt his tongue invade my mouth, I was a goner. I fell in love with him right that moment all over again. He had taught me the true meaning of love, and now I discover that you can still fall in love once more with the same person even when the first love is still blooming... *Does that make sense?* And once more I was in a sweet state of confusion that only Nyx could lead me to.

I stood there feeling the weak lamb take control over my heart and mind, AND tongue. I pulled back in a painful separation, "Nyx, you really mean it? You don't want to go home?"

The confident nod that he gave me wiped my last shreds of uncertainty.

"I do want to be home. But I think my home has changed. I belong where you are. Agenor, I give you my word of honor"

And I swear up and down to protect you and love you for as long as I drew a breath...

I attacked his mouth and sucked on his lips hard. I was sincerely happy. Happy to know that I was no longer keeping him from what he yearned for. I was certain that he still loved and cared for his family. But now he had enough to keep him by my side VOLUNTARILY!

I released him to let him breathe, and I watched as he panted in my arms, "You are enough Nyx. You are more than enough to me. I know I'm making you into a pirate, which you're doing great by the way, but even without making any effort, you already are the most courageous person I know. I love you so much"

I turned him carefully, making sure to keep him from slipping into the transparent lake in front of us, "Look around you, Nyx. This is a piece of the world that you're in now. This beautiful nature is all ours and more. And that...", I grabbed his right hand in mine and raised it to point to the sea, where the Martina stood proudly in a vast pool of tiny glistering waves, "That, my love, is *our* ship. That is *our* home"

He nodded slowly and looked at me with a smile. He wasn't nervous or scared anymore. He was calm and I even dare say that he was happy. I gazed at him for a long moment and only came to realize it when rosiness took over his cheeks. But I didn't back down, I smirked at his shyness that I loved the most; it was one of the best signs of his innocence and his unique personality.

"Nyx, do you trust me?"

"I do. I trust you"

I caught the hem of his shirt and undressed him slowly, then threw the shirt away and it landed beside his shoes. He leaned back to avoid slipping and I held him close to me; a hand around his waist, and a hand on his forehead, "Look ahead and don't close your eyes"

"Euh... ok, but why- AAAAAh!!"

I took a little jump forward and we ended up flying in the air together, only to dive along with the waterfall into the small crystal lake.

∞ ∞ ∞

Chapter 6 ~ Pirate Compromise
∞ Nyx's POV ∞

I swam my way out and coughed the water that I had inhaled. I turned wiped my hair off my face
"You crazy crazy pirate!"
I yelled at Agenor who was circling around my feet like a shark. I yelled again hoping he'd hear me from under the water. But it looks like making me suddenly jump off a cliff was not enough, he actually caught my feet and pulled me into the lake again. I tried to swim up once more but he held my waist and brought me in front of him, and when I saw him, I forgot my need to breathe.

Under the crystal water, his aura looked heavier and stronger. With his silver hair forming a halo around him, his victorious smirk, and his gray eyes that looked straight into mine, Agenor looked out of this world. His smirk widened when I had stopped struggling, and he pushed his lips on mine. I couldn't close my eyes though, I kept them open to take in every detail and every move his muscles made.

We slowly floated to the surface and I broke our kiss to breathe. Few seconds were all I got as he captured my lips in his again. I obeyed. I surrendered without hesitation. My mind was so relaxed after all the thinking, the fear, and the confusion that I had felt in the past few days. He told me that he hadn't slept with anyone else. Agenor wasn't the kind to lie, simply because he didn't need to, and I believed him completely. I loved him.... a sedating feeling that once not blurred by confusion, it takes complete control over one's soul, and I gladly let it.

I couldn't remove my eyes away from his. I reached to move a strand of his hair from his face and ran my fingers along it.

"I love you, Agenor"

The once cocky smirk became a sweet smile. He reached his hands around my neck. He held the collar and felt it moving a little.

"What are you doing?"

He didn't answer though, just gave me a reassuring smile. Soon I felt a cold breeze against my neck and saw his hand pull back taking the collar away with it. I held my own naked neck in surprise.

"We're here alone Nyx. No one to be afraid of, no one to bother us"

I watched as he swam to the edge of the small lake, he removed my necklace and freed it from his long hair. Then he attached it to the collar and set them both on a smooth grey rock, away from the water.

I caressed my neck enjoying the feeling of freedom, and I looked up in the sky. I closed my eyes and felt the hot rays of the sun combined nicely with the cool clear water. I felt blessed. And I silently thanked God for easing my pain and clearing my confusion.

My quiet prayer was interrupted when strong arms wrapped around my torso. I laid my head back and rested on his broad shoulder. He held me close and I relaxed, allowing my legs to float on the soft water. I smiled as we swam around, one arm dragging me with him, and the other one moved in the water. If there were heaven on earth, this would be it.

"I knew you'll like this place", he murmured before he dipped his lips in my neck. He kissed and sucked on my flesh. I shivered, my neck somehow felt sensitive after being covered by the collar for months. I tried to pull my neck away, but of course, the bastard laughed and bit me.

"Awe!!"

I tried to free myself, and as soon as he let me go, I turned around and took revenge by splashing water to his face again and again. He laughed harder with my determination to beat him with water. And when I didn't stop, he looked at me playfully, and I knew he was up to no good. He lunged towards me but luckily I was able to dodge and swim away, which was a bad idea, and I should've known how much he loved a chase.

We kept swimming around, chasing each other around the small lake. He caught me countless times and it didn't take much for him to do so; one pounce was mostly enough for him to reach me. I giggled as he dove and tickled my feet. I tried to do the same: I dove and chased after him under the glistering clear water. He was obviously faster, but I got to him soon enough because he had to turn to avoid the rocks at the edge of the lake. I grabbed his foot and went to tickle him, but he swam towards me and gave me a peck on the nose. I smiled at him, forgetting how precious the air that I held was, and most of it escaped with the smile, so I immediately swam to the surface to breathe in.

Agenor joined me, and on his way up, his hands held my hips, and he ascended while leaving small kisses on my chest. A sparkle traveled my spine and I could feel my skin burning with eagerness where he kissed.

I cupped his face gently, "Who knew, you could start a fire underwater"

The smirk that I got as a reaction warmed my heart. I leaned in and our lips joined for a luscious kiss, followed by a hungry bite to my lower lip.

"You seriously have a problem with the biting thing. I mean, what are you, a wolf!?"

"Hahah! Actually... I've been told that I was a tiger"

He swam towards me, and when he closed the distance between us, he lifted my chin and approached his head until our lips brushed together, "A silver tiger, was it?"

I couldn't hold the smile that broke free, nor the blush that invaded my face when I remembered the night that I had called him that. He chuckled and leaned in to lick my ear, then added, "I missed touching you so much". His hands went around me and cupped my backside.

"A... Agenor...."

"Nnnnh"

His hands squeezed harder and I felt the blood rush faster in my veins. I tried to breathe and cool down, but when our hard ones touched, I pushed him away.

"We can't do this-"

"What? Why??"

"Because we're outside, obviously"

"So?"

"I'm not doing indecent things on a mountain full of bad people!"

He chuckled and wore a teasing smile, "*bad people*??"

"Yes, the thieves and cruel people that you spoke of earlier!"

"The one you should worry about is right *here*" He pushed his groin on mine and I gasped at the sweet friction despite the fabric of our pants getting in the way. He took advantage of my surprise to rub against me. The arousal started climbing to my head and my breath accelerated. I opened my eyes to find him lustfully gazing at me.

"I... I can't go further here.... we... we shouldn't do indecent things in the open..."

Hearing my words, he halted then looked away and sighed. He looked annoyed and I didn't know if that was because he was too excited to stop, or if he was fed up with me. I........ am an uptight person, my cousin Haven always said that. He also said I should 'loosen' up. I couldn't, or more correctly, didn't know how to be easygoing. And now, Agenor must be thinking the same thing. Maybe, if he was with someone else...... they certainly wouldn't refuse him a thing... *There you go Nyx, yet another thing I can't do.*

"Hey"

I raised my eyes to find him looking at me with an arched eyebrow, "Don't."

I looked at him questioningly until he tapped his finger lightly on my forehead and added, "Don't let that brain of yours lead you to a frown. I forbid that"

Syrvat

I looked away uncomfortably. I felt embarrassed that he could read my thoughts so easily. He's right. Of course, he is, he's Agenor. The smart charming man that I love. I rubbed on my forehead a little and nodded, "Sorry"

He chuckled and leaned in to whisper in my ear, "There's something you need to learn as a pirate, it's called *Compromise*". With that, he pulled back and gave me a foxy smile, before he swam away.

A part of me wanted to panic and keep him from turning his back at me. But I trusted his smile and remained still, watching his body slide elegantly under the surface, his legs paddling a little then stopping when he was by the waterfall. He rose, facing the cascading water, and somehow, time seemed to go slower; I felt hypnotized as I walked my eyes across his wide shoulders, gazing at his muscles that tensed and relaxed under his skin. He ran a hand to push his silky hair back, making few socked silver strands hug his upper arm. And the glistering water slid freely on his shoulders, making its way to dive back into the lake. He was enchanting. And the more I observed, the more I realized how much he fit perfectly in the raw beauty that surrounded us.

He turned slightly to the right and his arm stretched towards me. I looked at his confident piercing eyes, then at his hand that he held open for me. My arms and legs moved on their own, guiding me to join him. As soon as I did, he received me with a warm smile. He pulled me closer then lifted his left arm under the waterfall. The cascading water that met his arm split, inviting us in like open drapes. He put his free hand on my back and guided me further. I swam forward, crossing behind the waterfall, and I lifted my head to watch it flow right above my head.

Agenor followed behind me, causing the water drapes to close and trap us both in the small space between it, and a smooth wall formed by a pile of dark gray rocks.

I span around in my spot slowly, eyes wide open despite the small droplets that often escaped the waterfall and dove towards us. I looked in awe at the trees, the sky, and the sun, as they revealed themselves differently behind a wall of a small glistering blur.

Agenor hugged me from behind and pulled me closer to him, "So? You like it here?"

"I..... never thought one could look from behind a waterfall... It's so amazing"

"Aye, it is"

"How did you find this place?"

He chuckled and leaned closer to my ear, "*We* found it, Nyx. This is *our* safe place. What do you think, is it *private* enough?"

He didn't wait for an answer though. He found his way to my neck and started sucking and tickling the sensitive skin with his tongue. His right hand slid up my left side and his middle finger rubbed against my nipple. I flinched forward and he hugged me stronger with his arms, one around my waist and the other around my chest, pulling me and making me straighten my back once more. His fingers started working on my nipples, pinching and squeezing, then rubbing with enough pressure to numb the pain. His head moved to the other side of my neck, determined to leave marks all over it. My hand held his head, and the other reached down to caress his thigh. I could feel his hands and his mouth grope and suck me harder by the second, making me feel hotter despite the cool water that surrounded us.

I tilted my head and was able to place a kiss on his forehead. Feeling my eagerness, his eyes rose to mine and the lust in them made my groin ache. His hand pinched my nipple hard and I moaned in pleasure. But that didn't keep my lips from pursuing his as soon as the surge of pleasure was bearable. Our mouths touched and a tingle of playfulness danced in his eyes, making him pull back to send me a cocky smile. I didn't care though, I wanted to kiss the bastard so bad. My hand reached back to cup his neck and coerce him into meeting my stray lips. He kept gazing at them, allowing his lips to brush and lick them slightly, only to pull back a second later... touching and parting... purposely tormenting me and creating an enticing trance...

Impatient with his games, I padded my legs in the water to rise a few inches more and finally get what I wanted to claim. Our mouths sealed and our tongues didn't ask permission to meet and dance. I gladly took control, kissing and nipping on his lips. I enjoyed his docility for a moment until his kiss became wilder and his mouth started to claim every bit of mine. We fought for control, both smiling and enjoying our excitement. I bit and sucked his lower lip making him release a groan. My smile grew wider and I gave him a victorious look without leaving his lip to rest.

My triumph was interrupted though when his left hand groped between my legs through the pants. I was already hard to begin with, and when his palm caressed my member possessively, I flinched to the fire that rode my spine. He chuckled and nipped my ear then said, "What's wrong Nyx? You look like you *need* something, maybe I can help?"

Since when were you this polite??

"S.... stop..."

"You sure?" He rubbed me harder and I held his arm, unable to push him away and risk losing the arousing feeling of his large hand rubbing against my arousal.

I was breathing heavily and moaning, "A... Agenor...."

His palm gave my groin a strong squeeze then it slipped further inside. His thigh parted my legs, and his middle finger rubbed between my ass cheeks until he found my entry. His middle finger pushed harder against the fabric making my member twitch with pleasure. I squirmed and moaned louder, but Agenor hugged me tighter to keep me still and his finger forced its way into me, pushing the fabric inside my ass. His finger moved inside me looking to dive deeper and making me unable to keep control any longer. My orgasm tore through me as my back arched and I released my loads.

∞ *Agenor's POV* ∞

I was hugging him tightly against me, feeling his every move as his body pulsed to release his milk. I pulled my happy finger out and eased my grip on him to allow him to breathe. He looked back at me with blue eyes, hooded with love and pleasure. I guess the poor wolf forgot where he was for a second there because he stopped swimming and sank a little. He immediately panicked. Thank the Gods I was right there to catch him and pull him back up.

I laughed a little at his innocence and helped him reach the wall of rocks to lean on, "There, cute, you're fine Nyx, just breathe"

"...s... sorry... I... forgot about the lake..." He blushed shyly while breathing heavily. He sure looked exhausted. He was grabbing one of the rocks and keeping himself from sinking once more. I was supposed to let him rest now. My cock, on the other hand, had other plans.

I reined myself the best I could, but my groin went rogue on me. It stuck behind his and started grinding on him. I lifted my hand and put it on his, we were both leaning on the rocks together now. My other hand couldn't wait any longer and it was already untying my pants and releasing my eager length.

"Agenor...."

I felt guilty for not giving him the rest that he needed, but his weakness was even more arousing and I couldn't wait a second more, "Nyx, I want you... I want to fuck you so badly"

My left hand reached around his waist and tugged on his pants until they were untied. Then I yanked them down to free his soft ass.

"Agenor, I... I want you too... I want you inside me" His sweet voice carried those unexpected wished to my ears, making me thicken even more. I held my impatient shaft and pushed it inside him roughly.

"Ah!!.... Oh, God... Agenor...."

I pushed hard once again, then a third time before my cock was buried inside him to the hilt.

"Finally...." I said passed clenched teeth, and it felt like the thought was shared by my cock because it refused to move from the heavenly warmness that hugged it tightly. I leaned in and nuzzled his left cheek, "I Fucking missed you so much, Nyx"

He panted a little and a painful moan slipped past his lips, "I missed you too"

"You're so fucking tight"

"Y-You're the one who's bigger! It hurts..."

I chuckled and the vibration seemed to make him moan even more, "Never keep me waiting to hold you, or it might feel more painful" I gave him a thrust to prove

Pirate Chains ~ Against tides

my point. Which did work because he moaned louder, but he also clenched his ass and squeezed me more inside him.

I groaned in pleasure and grabbed his waist with my right arm. I started moving inside him quickly, unable to play gently anymore. I parted his legs wider and had to push his pants further down to open him properly for me. With my left arm holding the rock and keeping us breathing above the water, I laid back a little to be able to invade him deeper.

I reached to hold his shaft in my palm and I stroke him. Squeezing around his swollen head, then sliding down to his hilt at the same time that my own hilt banged his hole. Our groans joined and rose against the noise of the waterfall that shielded us from the outside world. And my cock was so thick I could feel it oozing inside him.

"Agenor... I'm going... I can't-ugh"

I squeezed a bit more on him and stopped rubbing him. I was further my own limit but I couldn't skip a chance to tease my love, "Ask for it Nyx, I'll grant you what you ask"

He looked back and reached to cup my face, his eyes drowned in arousal and sweet despair, "Please..." I leaned in to kiss him and he eagerly kissed me back, "Agenor... please let me come"

I couldn't deny a pretty please from such a beautiful lover. I picked up the pace, and he threw his head back on my shoulder. I thrust in him harder and slammed my waist against his soft ass. Not more than a minute later, I exploded inside him in several shots, he came hard and his ass squeezed tighter on my shaft, milking every bit of my cum.

I pulled out of him. He turned and put his hands around my neck. I hugged him around the waist and gazed at him. His eyes full of satisfaction and love, and his body relying on mine to carry him, giving me the control that kept me content, "You are so beautiful"

My lovely angel

∞ ∞ ∞

Chapter 7 ~ Dance

∞ *Agenor's POV* ∞

"Ready?"
"Aye"
He threw our stuff one thing after the other from above the cliff. I only bothered to catch my sword and the bag of food. Our shoes and shirts just fell in the bushes.

"Careful when you climb down!"
"Ok, ok"

I should have climbed the damn cliff myself, but he insisted on helping. He's acting tough, yet I can see his obvious hesitation while he's standing at the edge and looking down.

"It's alright, I'll come get you! Just stay where you are, Nyx"

He frowned to the idea and I went to climb the rocks anyway. He looked like he was thinking for a second, then his eyes lit up, "Wait! Just a second!"

I halted and was about to ask him to stay put, the cliff above the waterfall was not very high, but if he slipped he could get injured. Then again, *would he be my cute angel if he obeyed and just did as told?* Instead, my eyes opened wide and my heart skipped a beat when the daring baby wolf jumped off the waterfall, butt first into the lake.

I ran to the edge of the lake and waited until he resurfaced, "Did you see that! I jumped! It was amazing!!"

His eyes were shining with excitement. I laughed and applauded to encourage him, "That was really brave of you"

"You damn right it's brave! I can do it on my own, so next time I'd appreciate if you refrained from pushing me"

"Heheh, I can't apologize for that, it was very entertaining"

He slid his hand on the surface of the water to splash me, but it was too weak to reach that far. I laughed a little, but my attention was caught by something much more interesting. I blinked, then looked once more to make sure, and I was barely able to hold my laugh.

Once he regained control over his breathing, he swam towards me. I stood up straight and crossed my arms, waiting for him to get close enough. He went to climb on the rock to get out of the lake when I stopped him, "Are you sure you got everything?"

He thought for a couple of seconds, and then nodded, "The necklace! You still got it, right?"

"I got the necklace. But you're certain that you didn't leave anything behind?"

"I'm sure" He started crawling up on the rock as he continued, "I looked around before I jumped"

"Nyx"

"Yes?"

I looked down pointing to his legs. He gave me a questioning look, then tilted his head and checked himself: He was top-down naked.

"OH MY GOD!" The embarrassment that took suddenly invaded his face was indescribable. I squatted and the laugh I was holding in busted free, while he dropped back into the water and tried to hide behind the rocks

"W........ Where are my pants!!" His face was getting more crimson by the second, "Please don't laugh"

"Sorry" I apologized but I was still laughing. He just looked so damn adorable, pouting, naked in the water, hiding from... no one actually other than me, and I already knew him; *inside out,* I might add.

"Here, I'll find it for you"

"I don't know what happened!"

I jumped into the water; my goal was now to stop tormenting him and make him comfortable. I couldn't keep from looking back at him again, though, engraving the whole picture deep in my memories. My voice was calm, though, trying not to sound amused, "It must have gotten loose when you dove into the water. I'll look for it, please do as I say and stay put this time"

I raised an accusing eyebrow and he pouted. I laughed lightly, and right before I dove I heard his sweet voice, "Be careful!"

I'm not walking the plank! I'm just taking a tour underwater in a tiny lake. Of course, I kept that to myself and just swam deeper. There wasn't any difficulty, really, the water was crystal clear. It took less than a couple of minutes to find his pants that followed the flow and traveled to settle between a set of rocks at the bottom.

I grabbed the pants and thought about staying here a little more. I was weighing the pros and cons of teasing and worrying him when I remembered the way he looked; childishly pouting and hiding. I laughed, losing most of my air, so I turned and swam in his direction.

The remaining of the afternoon wasn't less blessed. I used my sword to clear a place for us to sit by the lake. We talked and laughed, I made sure to tease the butt-naked incident out of him, which cost me a kiss and some flirting to keep his mood away from pouting. We were both hungry and we ate everything I had brought with me. I made sure to stuff him well because I knew that he didn't eat well in the past few days. I was built for hunger and tough times, but Nyx was much frailer; let him skip two meals and he'd start showing signs of fatigue.

He laid his head on my thigh and I let him surrender to an hour of sleep. It goes without saying that I remained awake with my sword by my side and my senses aware of my surroundings; I was almost sure that no one was around, but the beauty of nature shouldn't make us forget where we really were. I looked down, watching him draw slow and peaceful breaths. I knew he was going to like this place, but he enjoyed it more than I had expected. And I could even swear that in the last couple of hours, he forgot that he was on Esme.

He woke up later and insisted on taking another dip in the water before we left. I didn't want him to catch a cold, so after some negotiations, he agreed to let his pants dry on the hot rocks under the sun, while we enjoyed another quick tour behind the waterfall.

∞ ∞ ∞

When we reached the camp, the sun was dipping into the horizon. The beach was busy; some mates were lying here and there, drinking or playing games, others were gathering some wood to start a fire. Ace walked by us. He greeted me with a nod, "Captain"

"Ace, everything ok for the day?"

"Aye Captain"

He pushed a sword in Nyx's hands. Nyx looked at his sword in surprise, it was the Jian that he left on Martina. Strangely, he just responded with a weak, "Thank you..." and Ace didn't even reply. He just gave me another nod and walked away. My God, I swear he's getting less talkative every passing day.

"Boy!! I heard you made it to land in one piece! Where the hell have you been all day?? -Oh, hey Captain"

Alright, I'm fine with Baril acting all 'Nyx works for me' from time to time, but his questioning every time Nyx wasn't in the galley was pissing me off. I didn't spare him a look, just a small 'Hey' and that was generous already

"We went to look around. Esme is really beautiful! I guess it's not as bad as I expected"

"Hah! Of course it's beautiful, have you seen the whores? Expensive, but they ride to please"

"Euh... yes, I saw them. Here, let me help you with that" Nyx paced towards Baril and took the wood off Baril's hands

"Put that by the pile next to those fuckers over there, we're going to party hard tonight"

Nyx smiled at him and went towards a herd of pirates to do as told. He was tired from all the walking, yet he's still helping with work! I should just command him to sit his ass down and rest. Then again, sometimes I should let him do what he wants. I looked back and saw him biting his lip to prevent a laugh while Ajax and Yeagar pointed at Nash and teased him. Lou stretched his leg to trip him, but he easily avoided it and smiled victoriously at the bully, then went to organize the wood into a pile like nothing happened.

He's happy, he's safe. That's all that mattered.

I turned and went to join the herd of idiots. Sometime later, we were all sitting around the fire, drinking and eating. Ace was already half drunk, still bothered by something. If I knew him well, it had to be something he almost screwed up; something that went wrong but he managed to fix. Now, all he needed was to tell me. And to think that after all the years we spent together, he still doesn't know that the best way is to step forward and just spill the truth. If he's too eager to torment himself, let him.

A pair of blue eyes drew me out of my thinking when Nyx handed me a stick with some nicely grilled meat. I nodded my thanks to him and bit into the food, while he sat beside me, nipping slowly into a hot sweet potato.

In the distance, we could see torches closing slowly towards us. From the way the silhouettes swayed, I recognized the whores coming to earn some coins. Of course, the commotion started around us as soon as they figured who was heading their way.

"Captain Agenor"

Izel bowed her head at me politely and the flock behind her did the same. I always applauded the way she kept her hyenas in line.

"Izel" I took another bite into my meal and continued, "To what do we owe this late visit?"

"My girls wanted to please your crew" as soon as she said that, her 'girls' scattered among the wolves who received them with open arms and groping hands. The bulgy guards that she had with her put some covered boxes on the side and joined us around the fire; she always chose fighters with enough muscle that would make bandits think twice before thinking of laying a finger on her. Unless they paid first, of course.

Izel walked closer, that new child following right behind her. She ignored the lustful looks and vulgar words that the men sent her, and her eyes traveled to watch her whores being caught and fondled.

She sat beside me and I ignored her colorful dress that fell on my right thigh, "I expected you would visit us to spend the evening" when I didn't answer her, she continued, "I even prepared the girls for your men, and a nice room for you, Captain"

"Thank you Izel, that will be unnecessary. As you see, these hooligans can enjoy themselves anywhere"

"Of course" She sounded disappointed. Which is understandable; these people make a living out of providing whores and rooms to fuck. And they do their best to fill those rooms.

"When you didn't show up, Cherri here insisted on bringing you a present. Cherri, come serve the Captain"

She ordered the new girl and she obeyed. She walked to my left holding something in her hands, and I felt Nyx shift uncomfortably. The girl bowed her head a little, "My name is Cherri, I've been waiting to meet you, Captain"

No matter how much she sweetened her voice it was obviously the result of Izel's training. I've seen so many whores to know the difference between a woman who wants to be a whore, and a woman who was forced to be one. She was a bit odd though; she was obviously much younger than the other whores, she was well dressed and looked quite clean, unlike most of the whores who wore old skirts and ragged dresses.

I nodded at the girl, she definitely looked new at this, "If anyone bothers you, feel free to kick their ass, Cherri. And.... stay away from Britt, he tends to crush the newbies.... literally"

Britt, who was sitting a few feet away with his hand inside a whore's skirt and the other holding some food, he looked at Cherri and smiled deviously. Izel laughed in her unique way, loud and composed, while Cherri smiled at me in a seductive way. I glanced beside me at Nyx; he was looking away, gazing at the sea. Cherri approached more and looked at him, but when he didn't move away, she sat in front of him, almost blocking his view of the fire.

She put a hand on my left knee, "Agenor, I brought you some expensive wine. I've saved it just for you, *my Captain*"

I chuckled. *my Captain*, Nyx rarely called me that, usually when he wanted to ask for something. And when he says it, it was so fucking sexy.

She uncovered a round jar, then poured some of the red liquid in a small cup, "Here, hope you find my present delicious"

I took the cup and smelled the alcohol.

"She's very well mannered, don't you think, Captain?"

I didn't get what the fox wanted. Usually she claps her hands, the whores gather around, and I just chose one or two for the night.

"You know I hate games, Izel"

She brushed her fingers along my arm, "On the contrary, Captain, I know that you love playing games"

"Not when it feels like I'm the one being played"

She withdrew her hand dramatically, "Oh, I would never dare. Especially not with the most famous and handsome pirate"

I glanced her way and she winked. I went to taste the wine, she continued, "Cherri is simply a special gift I've been preparing for you for months now. She's well trained, but not touched by many-"

"I thought you kept whores, Izel. I didn't know you raised courtesans"

That must have stung because she went silent for a moment. Izel used to be a courtesan, a whore only for the highly born. She seduced a rich Lord, who spoiled her and made her his favorite. As soon as he fell ill, his wife tormented her for months, until one day, she escaped, murdered the Lord and his wife, stole whatever she could carry, and ran to Esme. From that day on, she was no longer a courtesan, just a cheap whore for anyone to buy.

Izel cleaned her throat and continued, despite the hinge of anger in her voice, "She's clean, beautiful, and very obedient. My only wish is to serve you and keep you content. I've noticed that you almost never sleep with the same whore twice, so I handpicked the one that would be to your liking. I also trained her in the ways of pleasuring men. I'm sure she'll please you until you wouldn't stop *coming*.... Captain."

The girl's hand slipped on my thigh again with a sexy inviting smile. She was a tempting little devil, and a few months earlier, I wouldn't have thought twice before grabbing her hair, yanking her down, and making her suck me. Izel wanted me to test her and I wouldn't refrain from doing so.

But today, the devil had changed. As I looked at her inviting smile, the only think I could think of was how beautiful that shade of rouge would look on Nyx's lips.

I laughed at the idea, and the idiots around me echoed my amusement. I felt a hand tugging my shirt from behind. I knew exactly who that hesitant hand belonged to.

I peeked to see Nyx still looking away, this time he wasn't just embarrassed from the way the mates behaved with the whores, he was too tense, almost shaking. His eyes turned to meet mine and I could swear if I made the wrong move right now those eyes would shed tears.

As much as I liked to torment him, I believed he has been through enough lately. I pushed the cup his way. He didn't move, just looked at me with pleading eyes. *Still unable to trust me?*

I lifted the cup and nudged his cheek with it, "Try this. I'm sure you miss such fancy liquor"

"No, thank you. I'm not drinking tonight"

He looked away and tried not to show his anxiousness. But I was too familiar with the way his lower lip pushed into a cute little pout. I put the cup on his mouth and raised it, making him drink it all before he could protest.

Once the cup was empty, I pulled it back and raised an eyebrow at him. He blinked a few times, "It's.... Actually pretty good"

I laughed lightly and that seemed to brighten his mood.

"You're having another one" I said as I shook the cup to the new whore and she hurried to pour more liquid. Izel remained silent. She shared a very quick look with Cherri and I knew that she already figured what was going on. I have no idea why she went through the trouble of keeping a 'hand-picked' whore for me. And with her plans falling apart, she could be resentful. One should never trust a whore, especially not a shrewd bitch like Izel. So I made a note to myself to keep her away from Nyx.

The liquor was very good though. We enjoyed it very much, and I refused to share it with the thirsty wolves that wanted a sip. We were going through the second jar already. Nyx grabbed yet another cup from my hand and emptied it down his throat. His cheeks were colored with a shade of pink, he wiped his mouth with the back of his hand, and that is when I knew that he was tipsy.

We were eating and laughing when that whore, she's called Trixie I think, she came and dropped on her knees beside Nyx. Then she put her head on his lap and closed her eyes while humming. Nyx looked baffled. I reached and pushed her head back enough for it to fall off his lap. The bitch whined, but didn't wake up.

"Nyxy!! Having a party without me?? Not cool mate!"

"Hi Maren"

He was half naked, his pants untied and his hair more rebellious than ever. He was leaning on another bitch, but someone else grabbed and pulled away. Maren almost lost his balance and caught himself at the last second.

"What happened to you?? You look like a mess"

"Aye, these two little kitties here drove me so hard..." The boy grabbed his pants in pain and everyone laughed

"Your dick's going to fall off, monkey" Lou teased him. For once Maren looked too tired and hungover to answer with a smart comeback, so he settled for just, "Fuck off cunt face" He stepped behind the crowd and fell back on the sand.

"Maren, are you ok?" When he didn't bother to answer, Nyx meant to go check on him. I grabbed his forearm and sat him back, "Just let him rest. He's used to this". He didn't look too convinced, so I kept him busy and handed him another drink.

"So, you're the favorite that everyone is talking about?" Nyx lifted his eyes to the whore that stood before us, her hands on her hips. "You're so cute, just like this bitch Trixie said." She put her foot on Trixie's leg. The drunk-dead bitch didn't even notice "And... I hear you were a good lay"

I almost choke. I wiped the wine that I spilled on my chin and glared at Nyx; *A good lay? How the FUCK could anyone know that!!??*

"How about a private sail down to the Celia heaven..." Her finger traveled down her cleavage while she opened her raised leg slowly. Her short dress moving and revealing more and more of her inner thigh right before his face.

Now was the *'How dare you'* or *'How rude of you'* part of the evening. We all waited for the speech to come, but when a moment of silence passed, I turned to see him staring ahead, frozen like a statue. *Wha-!! Just when I wanted him to act like the gentlemen that he is, he is actually looking at her thighs!*

"I.......I......." he stuttered like a child, and of course she laughed and leaned closer to him, "What is it sweet bun?"

I Fucking do nothing and he's all jealous. Now he's almost having his face between a bitch's legs?? Fucking Lords, if they laid a hand on him they'd eat him alive!

I kept my features cold and, as much as possible, unaffected. Only my hand moved on its own and spilled my cup of wine on Trixie's face. The whore woke up suddenly with a gasp and the standing bitch lost her balance and fell back on her ass.

Everyone laughed hard. Good for her. Whores always act this way. I knew it, I was used to it, and I was asking Nyx to get used to it. He was not though. He was used to the fancy educated ladies. And from what I understood from his stories, the most the ladies gave up publicly was a brush on the arm or a seductive wink. Esme definitely ran on a different scale.

Nyx woke up from his daze as soon as the whore fell, "Oh God! I'm sorry!! Are you ok?"

Is he apologizing to a whore? Why would he do that?? He went to help her get up. She smiled at him and didn't let go of him, "Mmm want me to forgive you sweetie? You have to dance with me"

She pulled his hands as she forced him to move around and dance with her. I thought about grabbing Nyx and pushing the whore to the fire, then again, this was actually not a bad idea. The new whore filled my empty cup. I swallowed the burning liquid in one go and watched.

He was smiling awkwardly, trying in vain to pull away. A couple of minutes later, the whore that was sitting in Nash's lap, stood up and started dancing for him. Izel motioned to the new whore with a sharp nod and like the girl pushed Trixie away, then moved to sit by my side, where Nyx was. Good, now I could watch without her hair standing in the way. I felt Izel motioning another order to her and she skillfully slipped her arms around me; one hand around my waist and under my shirt, the other one traveling up my thigh.

Usually, as a pirate I was almost never not in the mood. Our harsh life in the sea fed our thirst to women even more than landlubbers. And even if I was sated, I would just ignore the action and enjoy the feminine attention. But in this case, it was obvious by now that if Nyx turned around and saw her, he'd be not just mad at me, but he'd feel depressed, he'd feel less than enough.

I sighed, pushing the devil in my head that thought it was nice to see Nyx tormented by the fear of losing my love. I wiggled my empty cup in her face without looking at her. She froze for a second, and without looking, I knew she was looking at Izel, maybe waiting for her orders like a trained dog. I intentionally let my annoyance show and snatched the jar that she set on the sand beside her.

Before she could find a new strategy, Lou crouched in front of her. He nodded at me, "Captain"

I nodded back and he looked down at the girl, "Mind if I borrow this little peach here?"

I smiled at my subordinate, "Enjoy"

Lou smirked and stood up, pulling the girl up with him. Izel moved and caught her hand, "What do you think you're doing?"

Lou looked down at her with an amused eyebrow and said with a matter-of-factly tone, "She's a whore. What do you think I'm going to do with her??"

"She's not selling tonight. "

Lou yanked the whore releasing her from Izel, "She's a whore. And I'm paying."

Izel glared at him for a long moment. She was the Whore Lord on Esme. She could walk over half my crew and they wouldn't complain. The other half, on the other hand, she couldn't command or act like she was doing a favor in providing them with whores. Those were stronger than what she or her bulgy guards could handle. And the difference between Martina and other crews, is that we had more strong pirates such as Ace, Nash, Yeagar and his asshole of a brother... and Lou was one of the best on my ship. She disrespects one of them and she'd risk her whore house to be burned and her whores fucked for free. That's why Izel slowly retreated back to her place, reluctantly dropping the fight with her eyes glaring daggers at him. And Lou loves nothing more than harassing someone.

He smirked at her once more before pulling the whore and walking away: Let's go peach"

"It's Cherri!!"

"I think that was popped already"

He pulled her out of the circle and away in the dark, smirking at the cheering of his mates that were envying him for what they called a 'tight whore'. I laughed lightly and poured more wine into me, enough to make me forget the stiff angry bitch sitting by my side.

I lowered the jar and found the area around the fire to be busier. Several dancers joined the fun, dancing and circling around the fire. The wolves watched them with hungry eyes, staring at their hips and bodies, swaying and moving like snakes. Some danced solo, others whirled around each other, while flashing their asses and bosoms to their audience.

My eyes settled on two of them that were coercing a certain someone to dance. One standing behind him, pulling his hands up in the air, while Celia moved her arms in waves in front of him, sometimes swaying down then up again, others kicking her heels on the sand and clapping her hands in the air. I watched intensely, somehow having him trapped between dancers looked extremely erotic. With the wine obviously slowing him down, the sweet angel surrendered to the enchanting trance, he followed the hands that took turns in pulling and circling him. At some point, he started to follow their moves more easily, his feet chasing the rhythm as he moved around the flickering fire, with a spellbinding smile tugging his lips.

When one of the dancers pulled a pirate into the game, and soon more and more joined the fun. As the circle grew busier, my eyes traveled to keep track of the one I adored. He disappeared for a minute and I frowned. A minute passed and my heart pinched. I was about to step in and get him when he emerged from the crowd, pushing the pirates away and making his way out of their messy moves. He looked around, and when our eyes met, his smile came back to life. He walked towards me, stumbling a little, barely keeping his balance from the drinking and moving around. As soon as he was by my side, he sat down and laid his head on my lap.

I froze for a moment; he never showed affection in public before. I chuckled when he snuggled even more on my thigh, with his eyes close and his lips slightly parted, the drunken angel was already passed out.

I ignored the chuckles and remarks of those who didn't have their hands stuck up a whore' skirt. I put my arm on him and resumed drinking, while the tips of my fingers secretly played with his hair.

∞ Nyx's POV ∞

I woke up when Agenor calmly called my name. I rubbed my eyes and sat down, "Nnnh... Why am I asleep on the beach?"

"Funny story"

I didn't remember. Lately, whenever that happened, it meant that I got drunk and did something wrong.

"Hey, you should go to my tent. I'm going to the town; I need to take care of some business. Want to tag along?"

I tried to think about that, but my head had this huge headache.

"I want to........ but I don't..."

He chuckled and I felt his hand ruffling my hair. It felt nice...

"Go rest in my tent, Nyx. I'll be back around noon, ok?"

I nodded and pulled myself up. God I felt like a real mess.

Agenor left and I made it to his tent. I found a bed sheet and lay it on the sand in a corner, then I immediately joined it and went back to sleep.

When I woke up again, I turned around and was about to stand when I saw that girl, Cherri.

"I'm in lots of trouble because of you, did you know that??"

I hesitated at that, mostly because I figured what she meant. My mind wanted to respond the way I was raised to, bow slightly and apologize even if I wasn't in the wrong. But I refrained from it.

"You know, Izel saved my life..."

Our eyes met but she looked away, then continued, "I was kidnapped from my village... Pirates. They took me away after they killed my father. They forced me to become a slave.... cleaning and cooking for them. At night, they wouldn't even allow my body to rest. After that Izel bought me and since then I felt like I still had hope..."

She sighed, then looked at me, "You pirates are really ruthless. Your kind kept me against my will, abused me... raped me!"

She went silent for a moment, with her eyes piercing accusations into mine.

She was like me, I thought. Kept against her will.... raped....

I felt guilty. I didn't do those hideous deeds, but I am a pirate. *I....... am one of those who did that to her....* "I'm...... sorry..."

She stood up abruptly, "Whatever, I don't expect the likes of you to understand. Today I heard that some rich boy was also kidnapped from a guarded island. I think the merchant mentioned....... Mila, was it? Anyway, the boy's mother was so sad that she had fallen sick. I guess even rich people suffer from pirates... It made me remember my mother......."

My heart kicked so hard I could hear it echoing in my ears. My breath accelerated as my mind tried to work what I just heard....... Mila... someone rich... from Mila!!

My body moved on its own. I scurried to stand in front of Cherri, my hands grabbing both of hers, "Where did you hear that from? Merchant?? You said it was a merchant??"

"Why are you asking?"

"I..... I need to know... Please, my lady, just tell me!"

"Yes. A merchant that works on Mila. He was just here."

"What? Here??"

"Aye, he left about twenty minutes ago. He's sailing to Ebina, and from there back to Mila"

Mila! Someone is here from Mila!! And mother, oh God, please don't let her get harmed....

My heart squeezed tightly in my chest, and I realized I had to move fast

"T....... Take me to him!"

∞ ∞ ∞

Chapter 8 ~ Easy mark
∞ Nyx's POV ∞

I panicked.

At last I had news about home, yet it was not good news at all.

Cherri mentioned Mila because that was where most of the merchants did their business. Corail, *my home*, it's a small island, very close to Mila. And how many high-born men could've been taken by pirates in the past few months from there!!

Wait.... how did they know that I was still with pirates? Agenor sent two letters that I wrote and signed, explaining how I was fine, and that I had sailed to take some time off or something.

But this can't be just a coincidence! A man from Mila....... and he has a mother....

She said the mother was very sick. How sick is she?? Is it physical? Is she, like, worried? Sad? or ailing to the point that she couldn't leave her bed??

I remembered all the times mother had skipped her meals in order to guilt us into heading by her wishes. She's not evil or anything, she's actually a very good person, and an even better mother. She's just... a bit stubborn sometimes, but it was all for the sake of her family.

My heart pinched and tightened in my chest; If somehow she knew that I was kept by pirates.... God, that would easily make her fall ill!! What.... what if he refused her meds? or worse, what if she refused to eat!

Oh God! Raya!! She's due in what? A month?? Or has she already given birth?? How could I forget when my own sister is due to have a baby!! I was so occupied with the damn work that I neglected my own sister! my only one!

My breath accelerated while my mind sewed ugly scenarios in my head. There were a thousand ways how things could go south on Corail, yet I wasn't there to take responsibility. I wasn't there for my own family... And even worse, *I* was the cause of most of those scenarios...

I lifted my eyes to meet Cherri's. She was looking at me in surprise, then her expression changed into one of disgust, "Let go of me!" She yanked her hands back, I hadn't even noticed that I was holding them.

"That's what you pirates do! Just because you carry swords and pricks you think you can take anything you want!!"

What? This is definitely not the time for this!

She went to walk around and past me, but I stood in her way again and lifted my hands open in front of her to try and calm her, "I'm sorry! I apologize. I won't touch you, I promise! But, please, right now I need to meet that merchant"

"What?"

"Would you please ask him to come here, I truly need to talk to him, this is really urgent!"

She scoffed and put her hand on her waist, raising an eyebrow at me in disbelief, "*You need*? You think just because you need to talk to him you think he'll jump into a pirate camp?? He has a small business to run, and he's heading to the port to sail to Ebina right away. Why would he risk being robbed by pirates for someone like you? AND Why the Fuck would I give a shit about what *you* need?? You really are something, I come here telling you that you got me in trouble with Izel and you still have the nerve to ask for a favor?"

Yeah, he would never want to meet pirates, so I need to go meet him! I need to get Cherri to help me here. Because of me, Izel failed to push her to Agenor. What do these people want? That I step back and help her untie his pants??

I breathed in and out, but it didn't help with the worry that weighted on my heart. After a moment, my mind seemed to work again; *I'm a pirate now, Agenor wants me to act like it and that's what I'm going to do.*

Then it hit me; Pirates make deals.

"Listen, you help me this once and I promise to help you with Izel"

"Huh, what you're going to do? Fuck me and throw me a few coins??"

"No! I don't mean it like that. I don't know how but-"

"Forget it"

"Please wait.... I-I'll talk to Agenor! I'll ask him to help you. Please just don't move! I'll be right back"

"Hey! Where the hell are you going??"

"One second!!"

I ran out of the tent, looking around and searching. But I couldn't find the silver hair. There were few pirates lying on the sand or gathered to drink and play games, and the camp was a lot emptier without the weapons and boxes that were piled there. I spotted Lou, sitting near Amos on a small barrel, both drinking.

"Lou!" I called and ran towards him

"The princess is up; I see"

I ignored his tasteless teasing, "Have you seen Agenor?"

"Not here"

"Where is he??"

"He went to town. Took everything to sell. I doubt he'll be back with any of that shit. He looked eager to finish his deals and get it over with"

"Ace?"

"Your Godfather went with the Captain. Your monkey buddy is still sleeping, I think."

Amos was glaring in my direction, but I had no time to lose on his way to vengeance shit. I looked around, who could I trust here? Who would help me without going for the merchant's belongings, nor waiting for the Captain to get back??

"Almost everyone is out. There are only those drinking bastards over there and a couple of sober guards", a smirk gained its rightful place on his face like usual, "You're stuck with me, pixie"

This was hopeless... I can't rely on Lou, there's no guarantee he'd want to help me in the first place. And even if he did, he'd certainly ask for something in return and I had absolutely nothing that was mine! Even my dagger is Agenor's!!

I looked around once more, then went back to Agenor's tent before Cherri got even more annoyed and decided she'd leave.

Amos yelled behind me, "You don't want to drink with us?"

"I'm going to sleep"

Once inside the tent, I took a decision without actually thinking about it, "Take me to him"

"I'm through with your stupid games, little pirate"

"No! You have to let me talk to that merchant, I only want to ask him something and I promise not to hurt him. In return, I'll ask Agenor to help you, and I'm sure he can"

"And why would the Captain listen to *you*?"

"He'll help you, I promise! Even if I can't he'll find a way"

She seemed to be thinking about that for a second

"Please, Cherri"

She sighed, "Fine. I'll take you to the merchant. If we leave right away, we might be able to catch him. I know a shortcut, follow me. And you better fulfill your end of the deal"

"Wait! I.... I can't just leave like that"

"Why not?"

"Because.... Doesn't matter. I'll sneak out"

She frowned and stared at me, and for a moment I thought I saw something new in her eyes; sympathy. Then her eyes settled on my leather collar. I didn't want to be rude, but I couldn't waste any second more

"Cherri.... will you help me here? You can leave the camp and I'll sneak out and join you"

"And how do you intend to do that exactly?? It's not like the camp is empty, and excuse me but, you don't look very sharp in this kind of thing, or in anything at all actually"

I was about to tell her that I'll find a way and that she should just leave and wait for me, but she continued, "I'll distract your shithead mates. You sneak out then. Just run towards the forest and when you can no longer be seen, walk east. You'll find me there, something tells me I'll be leaving after you yet getting there before you"

In her twisted insulting way, she was trying to help me. I nodded, then hurried and put my shoes on. I was panicking and in a hurry, but at least I still remember Ace's scolding. So I made sure I had Agenor's dagger around my waist and I grabbed my sword. When I turned to leave, Cherri had already left the tent. I sneaked out after I made sure no one was looking my way. Now the hardest part was leaving the camp and reaching the forest without being spotted.

I watched behind another tent, as Cherri walked towards the pirates. She circled them and stood on the other side, making them all look the other way. I noticed that her dress was pulled down, revealing her naked shoulder. I felt so dishonored, having to rely on a woman's help and pushing her to reveal her body to help me. This was against everything father had taught me, but I managed to those thoughts aside because I had no time for a winy conscious right now.

When everyone was looking at Cherri, some were even trying to touch her, I walked away towards the trees. I kept looking at the pirates, though, making sure they were looking elsewhere. When one of them stood up, I halted and crouched. I remained still until Cherri walked away from the herd then suddenly she fell on the sand. I hesitated, my first thought was to help her, but she glanced my way in a certain way that told me she did that on purpose.

Suddenly I saw Amos's eyes on me. He saw me!! Oh God, he's going to ruin this and I'll never get to know what happened to my mother!!

I panicked even more, but Amos averted his eyes and went back to drinking. I was frozen for two seconds, trying to understand what had just happened, but my mind urged me to continue and close the small distance remaining to the forest.

∞ ∞ ∞

It has been around half an hour since we started wandering in the forest. My hand holding the pommel of my Jian tightly, I kept looking around us in fear of meeting any thieves. The distance that we crossed wasn't praiseworthy though, Cherri was walking very slowly. I tried getting her to walk faster, but she wouldn't. I even suggested that the forest was dangerous for her and that she should show me the direction and give me the merchant's name, but she threatened to turn around and break our deal. And when I tried again, she told me to shut it. Literally! She looked me in the eyes and said "Just shut the fuck up"!! She's so rude and I frankly didn't know how to deal with her to make her walk any faster.

She was also a bit weird; she tried to lead me through some bushed and when she found it hard to continue that way she just took another and didn't deviate to return to the first direction that we were heading to!! I'm probably not used to finding my way in the woods, but I can easily detect when our direction changes

"Cherri, please, if we're lost just tell me"

"Ugh. I told you we're not fucking lost!!"

"But we're getting farther from the direction-"

"Just walk pirate!!"

Another fifteen minutes passed. The woman is following some crazy path, it's not even the easiest to go through! She's either doing this on purpose or she has the worst sense of direction I ever witnessed!

I decided I couldn't let her waste more time than she already had. I walked past her and stood in her way, "Look, we can't keep going like this! I get it, the forest is dense and it's difficult to navigate in it. But I can help us get faster to wherever we want! Just tell me which is the correct direction, is it east? Or tell me something like, the port, is it close to where the sun rises on Esme?"

She wasn't looking at me. She wasn't even listening! She wore a frown as she scanned the trees around us over and over again. I thought maybe she was trying to recognize where we were, so I let her be for a moment.

Suddenly I heard some bushes moving behind me. I whirled around and saw a skinny man with colored teeth smiling wickedly and approaching us. I pulled my sword out, two more men stepped out from behind a tree, and in a few seconds, we were surrounded.

Cherri went to walk away, but I held her arm and brought her back behind me, "Don't worry my lady, just stay close and I'll protect you" I tried to reassure her but I was in need of some of that myself! My mind was already torn with thoughts and worries about my family, and now this? I was in deep trouble...

One of the rogues attacked me. He had a long old knife. He tried to stab me, but I avoided him. Our swords clashed and I moved mine in a way that forced his knife to leave his grasp. He retreated only for two others to attack.

If not for Ace's training, I wouldn't have had a chance. This was a real fight, and I didn't hesitate to aim at them in order to protect myself and the woman that was in this situation because of me. I made sure to keep her right behind me and to slash at anyone who tried to get close to us.

More people appeared and I started losing hope of defeating them all. Hell, I couldn't even push them back and at least give a chance to Cherri to save herself! I decided that I it was better for us to back out, the forest is thick and it would maybe allow us to gain some distance. *God.... I don't have time for this!*

I reached behind me and grabbed Cherri's arm once more, "Cherri, we need to retreat, we can't stay here or they'll get us--AH!!"

I was suddenly pushed forward. I tried to hold my balance, but I tripped on a small rock and fell face first on the ground.

"God!! Where the fuck were you?? I've been walking him around like an idiot for hours, damn it!"

"Hey, don't bitch, bitch. We were watching you. And it was like what, half an hour or something?"

"Yeah, well, the deal was not to watch you twit!"

A foot stepped on my hand that held the sword. I reached for my dagger and slashed towards the leg. I hit it and its owner hissed and cursed, freeing my right arm. I scurried to regain my feet and took a protecting stance.

"Shit, you idiot!!" Cherri yelled at the filthy man and he spat on the ground then glared at me. They started closing the distance, I glanced repeatedly at Cherri, who was standing away from me, crossing her arms with an angry frown.

I was panting and I forced my mind to give me an explanation to all that was happening now, "Ch..... Cherri! What the hell's going on??"

"Shut up!! You fucking deserve this!! You think we don't know about you?? You had a perfect life!! You were high-born AND rich!! Doted by your family like a fucking prince, yet you still need to take things from people like ME!! You're so fucking selfish and you're so fucking stupid!"

She glared at me and I could feel the hatred radiating off her in heavy waves, then she threw her hand in the air and looked at the other men, "Fuck! I fulfilled my end of the bargain! I leave the rest to you, and your boss better carry out his part of the plan properly. The last thing we need is a fucking failure" She said before she turned around and started walking away.

I couldn't help the confusion that hit me; what the hell's happening? Is she with the rogues?? Her words sounded clearer than a confession, yet my mind somehow refused to believe; why would she do that? what about the merchant?? and the news from Mila!?

I didn't notice that I had lost my concentration until my sword was attacked by another, and it was thrown away.

'If you can't do hand-to-hand bouts, then you better hold on to your sword more than your own life' Ace had once said to me. And now I lost my sword and had nothing but a dagger to protect myself with.

I raised the silver dagger in their faces threateningly, and I stood between the smirks and the colorful teeth. I knew it was a matter of seconds before they charged at me. I tried to work my head into finding a way out, anything... But I was stuck. And my mind was so confused, it refused to work, not even to save my life.

Cherri suddenly started yelling then screaming. One of them was holding her and trying to keep her from leaving

"Let go of me you dirty shit!! This wasn't the deal!"

"It is now, whore"

"Hey! Get your hands off of her!"

I tried to run towards her, but before I could hit the guy that held her, a punch threw me back on my ass. Then it was followed by a foot crushing my hand. I reluctantly let go of the dagger and the man took it away from me. Then someone drove a punch right in my stomach, another one in my face, and that was all it took to defeat me. They pulled my arms and my hands were tied behind my back tightly with a rough rope, then both Cherri and I were carried away, deeper into the mountain.

I didn't know how long it took for us to reach their hiding. The rogues took us into a large dark cave inside a mountain, and we were thrown into a large hole, few feet deeper than the rest of the cave. I moved my eyes around trying to find any way out; the hole was surrounded by the cave's wall from one end and a set of iron bars on the other. It looked like a large cell, with many shackles attached to the walls. My heart started pacing faster at the sight of all the restrains... This didn't look like any normal cell... And a shiver took over me when the word *slave* crossed my mind.

Cherri's yells, insults, and screams didn't spare her from being thrown into the cell with me until someone came and decided he wanted to have his way with her. The ugly man yanked her, leading her outside the cell. Cherri kept asking for their leader but they laughed at her. I ignored the couple of other men that were beside me, holding torches and watching the scene with creepy smiles. I couldn't use my hands as they were still tied behind my back, so I plunged headfirst into the ugly bastard's ribs, causing both of us to fall on the hard ground. Cherri escaped to the other side of the cell and crouched in fear.

The man roared and grabbed my hair, "You fucking pirate!! You think because we have a buyer that we wouldn't hurt you!?" He yelled while punching me several times in my stomach. I couldn't utter a word anymore. I only coughed and drew the best breaths I could, and even curling didn't keep his punches from causing damage.

I was in a lot of pain when the other men managed to calm their friend. My mouth tasted weird from the blood and my ribs hurt. I was so damn weak, unable to save my own ass or even save a woman in need. My feet dragged as the two men pulled me back and replaced the ropes with the shackles that were attached to the wall.

I sat there, trapped and drown in shame as Cherri's screams for help filled the cave and faded slowly. Then I was left alone... Despite the scorching sun outside, its rays didn't reach this far in the cave. The breathing was heavier with the weighting darkness, with nothing but my anger towards myself to keep me away from unconsciousness.

I am a failure. She said I deserved this, maybe I did.

I failed my father and didn't protect my mother and keep her safe... Now she's probably sick because of this unfilial son...

I failed my Captain and didn't think twice before disobeying him... I'm so damn stupid!!

I failed my lover... he trusted me and I betrayed him...

He said there's a buyer! I don't want to become a slave! I might never see him anymore!!

Agenor.... please......

∞ ∞ ∞

Chapter 9 ~ Frenzy
∞ Agenor's POV ∞

"**Where the fuck is he??**"

I twisted my hands in his shirt and yanked him closer, my eyes glaring daggers at him

"I have no damn idea!! He was asleep! In your tent! Since.... like, two or three hours ago! He never left!"

"You were in charge! I let you in charge and it was YOUR RESPONSIBILITY to prevent this from happening!"

Lou stared at me in fear and confusion. I knew the fucking bastard for years now, and he never lied to me. I pushed him back releasing his shirt. He almost fell but caught his balance. I looked around, scanning the camp, the eyes of my crewmembers... anything that could show a hint of a mistake or treason.

My mind couldn't think anymore, all I could hear was something inside me panicking and repeating *'no no no... this can't happen...'* like some fucking idiot in denial. I had to stop that annoying fucking voice in my head that was blocking my thoughts and driving me insane! So, I did the first thing that cleared in my head; I punched the closest bastard around me that I could reach. I didn't even register who the fuck it was, just a pathetic unconscious asshole with a busted bloody nose.

I came back from town moments ago. I was so fucking excited, I had sold all my weapons easier than I expected and actually had the times to buy several things. When I went to my tent, it was empty. I actually never thought of it at first, but when I walked around the camp and inside every other fucking tent, blood drained from my face as I realized that he was actually missing.

I hadn't even suspected this might happen!! Not after everything that happened yesterday. But, now that it's already a reality, I couldn't help the bad feeling that invaded me. It was as if he was in danger. I need to figure this out immediately!! This is a fucking Shadow island!! If he could face all kinds of trouble at every corner!!

He's young, handsome, and doesn't give a dangerous vibe... if he crosses a rogue or a black market merchant they'll fucking have him on lunch!!

"YOU!" I pointed at Yeagar, "You go get me that whore Izel, I need her kneeling before me in less than thirty fucking minutes!"

"Aye Captain"

Then I turned to Armpit "Go check for him on the ship and get back fast"

"He couldn't have reached the ship-"

"You'll Fucking hold your tongue or I swear to the Gods I'll rip it out of your throat!!" Lou took half a step back and went completely silent. I had never threatened him before this day. But until now, he had never screwed either:" And you better pray we find him well or you'll be the first I'll be coming after" He stiffened even more and took a fucking vow of silence.

The rest of the crew avoided being too close from me. Seeing how I treated Lou was an omen for them. They kept their distance while remaining cautious with their words and attentive to my orders.

Maren didn't utter a single word. He searched the entire camp several times already. He usually escaped me whenever I was angry, but now he was standing beside me. He was holding his monocular and kept watching Martina. As soon as Armpit arrived, Maren handed me the eye. I could see them hurrying into my cabin then into the hull. A few minutes later Armpit climbed off the ship, and J waved his arms in big moves, motioning a negative answer.

I sent Ace with few others to check the surrounding beach and forest, in case he had just wandered there somehow. My crew was running here and there.... yet no sign of him. *There was no fucking sign of him!! Nyx wouldn't escape...... NO HE WOULDN'T! He made a promise and for once his honesty is playing to his favor!*

Then what...? Lost?? He couldn't have left the camp in the first place!

What if... someone took him!

My heart raced faster. There was more chance of him being taken by someone than him leaving or taking a walk. And on Esme, if you're an unprotected target then you're fucked!

"Captain-"

"**What!**"

Despite my obvious rage, Ace took a step closer, then he spoke at a lower voice, "Agenor, I checked your tent and.... the Jian is missing."

"His sword??"

"Aye. If Nyx was kidnapped, he couldn't have taken his sword along. And if he had the time to grab it, then he certainly had the time to yell or ask or help."

I listened to him, trying hard to get my head wrapped around this. I tried my best to keep a stoic face. He continued, "I spoke to some of the those who were here. They said the sober ones didn't leave or drink, even Lou remained on camp all time.

They also confirmed that Nyx came out before noon and went back to sleep after he asked for you"

"Me?"

"Aye, they say he was running around looking for you"

What the fuck does that mean?? Did he look for me because he needed me or was he waiting for this chance to leave...? And when he does it, he wanders alone on a Shadow island!??

I took a moment to breathe through my boiling thoughts, and I decided.

I don't fucking care if he left on his own or if he was forced. I don't care if he wants back or if he wants me to give him the chance to flee. HE IS MINE, and I'm Fucking getting him back!

"NASH"

"Aye Captain!"

"You wait here for Yeagar and Izel. As soon as they reach the camp, get that bitch to talk! I want you to make her spit what she knows or spit her guts. And if any of her guards bother you, kill them on the spot"

"Aye!"

"Captain, we should go look for the boy" Baril said and he was right. There was no use of wasting a minute longer on the beach. At least if we move right now we should be able to catch him if he was to sail on a boat, voluntarily or not.

"Baril, you stay here with Nash and send a word if anything happens." I needed to move with speed and despite Baril's obvious anxiousness over Nyx, his limping leg wasn't very helpful.

I turned to the rest of my crew, "We're going to turn this island upside down before sunset! If you meet a rogue, try getting him to talk! Otherwise, keep your eyes and ears open! Fail "

I sent two teams, one to the port and the other to the town. I took Ace, Maren, Britt, and Lou with me to search the forest and the mountain.

We separated and I started walking deeper into the mountain, my blood burning and my mind raging. *I have to get him back. I don't give a damn what anyone wants, not even him! All I need is to get him back.*

And I didn't know what was better to hope for: him being caught, or him leaving on his own...

∞ ∞ ∞

Hours had already passed. It was closing to sunset and I still haven't found him. My rage became a constant state for me but seeing how the sun was signaling the rapid time, I was more worried that angry. I was almost feeling bad for those I brought with me too, I wasn't quite the easy Captain to work for when I'm in such state of mind. Even Maren hadn't uttered a single word.

Britt was holding a pathetic rogue for the hundredth time today, shaking and pushing his face into the dirt to force him to confess something... Anything!! And no matter what horrible sickly deeds he blurted out, nothing had any connection with who we were looking for.

This time, I didn't let Britt release him. I threatened his life if he didn't lead me to their main hideout and he agreed. I was surprised to know that they actually had several holes around this thick forest where they hide, but one of them was the main one. I had to check there before the sunsets, even if it meant being surrounded by most of these bandits.

The way there wasn't easy. I had no doubt the bastard wasn't leading us through the best path but I didn't kill him yet. Britt kept beating him every time I felt like the little trash wanted to cross us, and it was enough to make him lead us faster each time. Once we were close enough, we could see several people sitting close to a large opening in the mountain, with some men getting in and out of the cave, and a couple of them standing like they were on guard duty. It looked like a good place for a hideout, and these fucking rogues look more organized than what I expected.

The piece of shit that led us here begged us to spare his life and release him, saying that he did as told and that his leader would take his life if he knew about him revealing the hideout. He was of no use to us anymore, and I didn't care if he blurted anything to anyone. Not with what I was about to do.

I ordered Britt and Maren to step back and carefully watch their surroundings, while the rest of us went to find out if Nyx was inside that cave.

Maren went to argue but I shut him up with a silent glare. We separated after I passed my sword to Maren, Ace and Lou then did the same. We couldn't just step in and ask questions, these shits would never answer anything unless beaten. And I had no Fucking time to lose on them.

Then we revealed ourselves, pretending as if we were lost in the woods like brainless idiots. The rogues were nicely startled, they surrounded us immediately and started poking their rusting weapons and spears into our direction. After a few minutes, the band believed that they were stronger than us and that they 'captured us'. So they led us with the tips of their spears into the cave.

It was quite large. Soon the sunlight faded slowly and the torches that the rogues carried helped enlighten the place. I looked behind us, there were at least a dozen bandits escorting us, most of them held spears. Shit... seeing the number of thieves inside and outside the cave, it will be hard to just walk out the same way we came in.

They kept nudging us to go further for a few minutes more before we reached the end of the cave. And the large cage surrounded by iron bars that we arrived at confirmed my suspicions; these rogues are into the slave business.

As soon as one of the torches was close enough, my heart stopped, and I froze. There was Nyx. I found him! **I Fucking Found Him!!**

I kept my own feelings at bay. I could hear a sigh coming from Ace's direction, what happened wasn't his fault since he was with me all day, but he knew how tormented I was.

The fucking stupid head that we brought along almost revealed that we knew Nyx. As soon as he saw him, Lou gasped and yelled, "Fucking Gods he's-!!"

He was interrupted when he tripped forward by my foot that was suddenly there. I was funny how he fell forward seeing the number of times that he tried to trip Nyx. And suddenly I was ready to actually laugh.

When he heard the commotion, he raised his head suddenly. I couldn't tell if h was asleep or in deep thought. From the way he looked, he was obviously exhausted. My eyes focused on the bruises on his face.... he got himself beaten up.

The thought of someone putting a hand on him made my mouth taste like acid. The cage's door opened and we were led inside. As soon as our eye met, Nyx's eyes widened and his face lit up with an unbelieving smile. He went to speak, and it took everything in me to look away from him.

I could feel his disappointment weighing on my heart, but I silenced the fucking bastard that knew nothing but pounding harder and harder in my chest. I kept my cold eyes as I stared at the shackles that were distributed all around the cage. And the way Nyx was sitting with his hands behind his back, he was obviously chained.

I chuckled bitterly under my breath; *The irony, he left MY chains for this?*

The wave of relief that I felt the second I saw him has now settled. And all the questions about how we came to this situation in the first place wanted to rush out.

We were pushed towards different directions. I walked on my own to the one ahead of us. Lou and Ace were already bound each on either side of the cage. I chose my own spot and someone kicked the back of my knees forcing me to kneel. I was still looking towards the wall when someone cautiously grabbed my hand in front of me and locked them with a pair of shackles. I shook them; breaking out of these would be kind of a trouble.

I turned and sat, leaning back on the wall. The rogues were grinning victoriously from side to side like they accomplished a miracle:

"Fuck! We're lucky like shit today!!"

"Aye! The boss will be proud!"

"Aye! Hey, I saw them first!! I get to tell the boss!"

"You saw shit! You screamed first, that's for sure"

"Fuck you! I'll be the one who tells him! .... euh, where is the boss, by the way?"

"He went to get someone with money"

Their grin grew wider. One of them kicked Nyx's leg as a show of dominance, he yelped a little in surprise and pulled his legs to his chest. I barely held myself from lunging towards the smirking bastard. He seemed to feel the weight of my glare and as soon as our eyes met, he cleared his throat and walked away.

They released shittier comments before they walked out of the cage and locked it. It took a few minutes more of them watching us and sticking their spears through the iron bars in an attempt to scare us. Then they retreated outside the cave, leaving us behind in the dim cell.

∞ ∞ ∞

I closed my eyes and enjoyed the silence for a moment. I breathe repeatedly, allowing my mind to relax; we've been running around the island for hours. I desperately tried not to imagine what could've happened to him… I know we had our ups and downs since I got him, but this was the first time he actually wasn't under my care. And I HATED IT! I refused the idea with every bit of my heart and soul! Now I knew that I preferred arguing with him a thousand fucking times than having him out of my grasp for a second.

Despite my anger, I couldn't keep my eyes from glancing his way. His head was tilted down and he looked miserable. A part of me wanted to ease his obvious distress; tell him that I was here and that I will protect him no matter what. Yet the other part wanted to smother him for leaving me and betraying my trust.

Heavy moments of silence passed before I heard his weak voice, "Sorry…"

I didn't answer him. I just kept looking forward, holding a cold stare at the iron bars. I felt Ace and Lou's attention on both of us, but I ignored them all.

Time passed. It felt like hours for me, but in reality, it could've been a dozen or two minutes.

"…. I'm sorry… I sincerely am…"

Good. He should be. And even if he wasn't, at such a situation he could only voice an apology, no matter what void it would be. It's like someone you trust stabbed you in the back, and when he gets caught, he apologizes, what other choice does he have?

When I didn't budge, I could see him at the corner of my eyes looking at me. Then he moved to approach me, slowly on his knees. I could tell from the way he shifted that he was in pain. Fuck they must've punched him in the stomach or something! They're **fucking rogues**! He's lucky they didn't roast him alive!!

He couldn't close the distance between us, though. One foot remained between us when the chain attached to the shackles found its limit. As soon as it pulled him back, a small whimper left him. He looked back as if that would make the chain have pity on him and stretch longer.

He sat on his heels, with his hands pulled behind him, and he tilted his head forward in an attempt to meet my gaze, "Agenor…. please talk to me…" His voice was raspy and sad. My chest tightened and I felt my heart leaning towards him, but I couldn't. I was in pain too. Just when I trusted him he goes and pulls this on me!

"…. Agenor I didn't betray you, I swear!"

"Bloody Fuck, boy! I was held responsible for your fuckup; did you know that?"

Nyx's gaze dropped and I glared at Lou. I FUCKING OWNED HIM!! I am the only one allowed to order him around AND I was the only one with the right to scold him!!

Lou cussed under his breath and kept quiet. Then Ace took over, unlike Lou, he was able to control his tone, "Nyx, what happened?"

Nyx looked up at Ace like a child trying to defend himself, "I had my sword with me! I took my sword to protect myself and I was able to hold them back! But they were too many... I fought them, but then they grabbed Cherri and when I tried to save her-"

"Cherri??" I glared at him. *What the fuck was he doing with that whore??*

"That bitch left the camp already! I saw her! Everyone saw her!!"

If Lou saw her leave, then...?

I was fed up with this. I stared coldly at Nyx, "Just what the fuck happened, Nyx?"

"I... I didn't escape! I was coming back, I swear! I just sneaked out to go meet a merchant-"

"Oh, so now you're doing business on Esme??"

"Shut your trap!" I barked at Lou, and both he and Nyx flinched in fear. I turned my glare back at Nyx waiting for him to continue

"I..... I heard... I mean... That merchant, he has news from Corail!!"

My heart fell at the mention of that name; *Corail....* his island... the only thing I still can't compete against; *his home...*

"Huh! Bullshit!"

"SHUT UP!!" We both said in unison, and instead of cowering, Lou raised a teasing eyebrow at us.

Nyx didn't bother with him more he turned back to look me straight in the eyes, and despite the slowly fading light, I could see the worry on his face.

"Agenor," he continued in a calmer voice, "I didn't escape, please trust me!"

"You promised, Nyx! I believed you!"

"And I kept my promise!! I just had to leave for like, half an hour... hour tops! Just don't think that I betrayed you! I would never... please, Agenor..."

I didn't know how to respond to that. Somehow, in the very poor light I could feel his pleading gaze fixed on me, and even without clear sight, I could imagine the look in his eyes, that blue radiance that I came to be obsessed with. I sighed, I couldn't see how he could escape yet still not betray my trust. And I decided that I was yet to understand what happened before answering him.

"Age-"

Nyx went to speak again when we heard voices approaching in the cave. The light started flooding the cave as shapes of men danced on the walls.

"I still don't know why the fuck you bring me all the way here at such late hour. What the fuck's so important that is couldn't wait till morning!!"

"As I said, I had a boy for you-"

"You spoke only when I was already on this shit of a mountain!!"

"Ah, I told you for the hundredth fucking time, it's a good trade! You've been looking for one-"

"Watch your tongue with me you shriveled cock! Just because you gathered a bunch of trash and named yourself king of the fools you think we're equal!! Even your business is shit! All the people you provide are either sick or ugly!"

"Well, this one's neither! I've been told that he's quite the handsome-"

The shadows stopped and one of them approached the other threateningly, "*You've been told*?? You don't even know for sure!!??"

"Hey! Don't piss on me! The deal was for me to ship him off as fast as possible! Just take a look at the damn creature then decide."

"Boss!", a third voice spoke, "We caught more! They're strong! I caught them! I saw them first and caught them!!"

"What? Holy shit!"

They resumed walking, and a few steps later we could see a herd of rogues, one of them taking the lead in stride, who I assumed was their boss, and right behind him a fairly young man, nicely dressed, with clean, expensive clothes and a cloak that hid most of his face. He was followed by a few sturdy men in armors. Seeing their attire, and the rogue that spoke earlier about a 'man with money', it was obvious who the man in a cloak was.

"Oh, God..." Nyx tensed. His eyes were open and he gazed in fear at the approaching men. He must have understood by now that the cloaked man was a slave merchant.

I looked at him and whispered in a commanding tone, "Sit back and don't breathe a word–Hey! look at me... **Not a fucking word**!"

He swallowed. Then he sat leaning his back on the wall and lowering his eyes.

Now let's see if he could obey such a simple order!

I watched the iron door squeak open. I just hoped Nyx would refrain from talking back at any of these bastards or attempting to teach them some manners!!

∞ ∞ ∞

Chapter 10 ~ Restless hearts

∞ Agenor's POV ∞

The one they kept calling 'boss' walked inside the cell. I hesitated to reveal who I was to him and maybe try to cut a deal, but that could go either way. He could remove these shackles or he could hand us to the guards of Ebina and collect the bounty on both Ace's head and mine. In that case, dead or alive, I'd be taken away from Nyx and he wouldn't find a way out of here.

A rogue followed inside, holding a torch to better illuminate the cage. The boss walked his eyes on the four of us, "Holy shit, where did you get all these??"

"I told you, boss! I caught them!"

The boss arched his eyebrows in a disbelieving way, "Fuck, they must've been dead drunk or something...", then he turned to the cloaked man, who was watching from behind the bars with his guards by his sides, "See, Zaire, told ya I had nice merchandise for ya!"

The man entered the cage slowly, making sure to keep his distance from us, "It's Lord Zaire for you, you stupid sack of sheep shit!" His face was still shadowed under his cloak, but his voice spoke of his young age and shitty attitude.

The boss looked away and rolled his eyes, making sure the merchant's guards didn't see him. Then the so-called Zaire tsked and walked further inside, with his nose held high like he owned the place, and he approached Ace carefully, "Actually, you are right for the first time ever".

"Got some best quality with these two, ey? Ya should be more generous if ya want to hav'em!" The boss said while motioning at Ace and me.

"Hey! What the fuck??" Lou protested, and I mentally rolled my eyes. *So now he wants to be sold as a slave?? I swear he was out of his fucking mind since I scolded him! He never acted like this, not even when he's hammered!*

I didn't even bother to glare at him. If Lou wants to convince a slave-merchant that he's worthy of being a slave, let him.

Zaire turned to Lou, "You would be sold easily, or I might keep you as a guard. We'll see... You, on the other hand...", then he turned back to Ace, who kept an expressionless face, "You look like the perfect gift for my sister's birthday"

"Euuh... That sis of yours, does she look good?"

For that, Lou received a punch on the face coming from the boss. He groaned and shook his head, and I almost thanked the boss. Nyx watched the hit with scared open eyes, then he remembered my words and pinned his look to the ground.

Zaire pretended as if he didn't hear Lou and kept sizing Ace. A minute later, he walked slowly towards me. He did the same up-and-down look that blessed Ace with earlier. Then he chuckled, "You know, my lovely older sister just broke her last toy. Since then, she's been having too much free time; sticking her fucking nose in my fucking business. And when she's bored, she cripples a slave or two, making them totally worthless. And ugly!! I guess that snake-bitch's luck is back, two gifts on the same day..."

The boss interfered, "You can keep one and sell one!"

"Yeah, I could... Do they fight?"

"Euuh... Yes! Yes, they do!" The boss tried to fake confidence, but Zaire immediately saw through it, "You don't know, do you? Forget it" then his eyes moved to my bound hands, "This one's obviously a sword fighter. Mmmm... I could train them for show fights"

"Aye, they'll look good in an arena"

"They might, yeah." He remained silent for a few seconds then turned to the boss, "Shit, I feel almost bad for them if that slut took them. There have been the occasional broken boys, but sometimes, I actually couldn't find the fucking slave! It's like she swallowed them, or something!"

"Charming woman"

"Right? She's my blood and all but fuck, the only thing wider than her mouth is her vagina!" And he turned to me again, "That frozen cunt is the reason for all my troubles... These might bring me more profit if they could keep her off my back. I'm sure if I wrap them nicely, they'll keep her busy for quite some time"

"Great!! Fucking lucky day!! So, let's do this! We talk money. I say we round up the price, ey? Fifty coins each! Two hundred for all, and that's friends' price"

"Are you fucking me??" Zaire scoffed, "I'll give you fifty for these two, and fifteen for that dick-mouth over there. And don't dream of more! Otherwise, you can drag them to the port tomorrow if you want to test your luck. Just know that I'll be there with all my guards this time, and I'll get them for much less"

The boss looked unsatisfied, "Oooh, come on! I've got a whole fucking mountain to feed! And you know how the business goes limp in winter-"

"I sincerely don't fucking care. You should all choke on your own cocks, if you ask me"

The boss grimaced in annoyance, then breathed a displeased, "Fine"

Then what he added immediately after that, got me to flinch for the first time today, "What about *him*?"

Nyx stiffened when he felt the weight of all the eyes on him. So far, the conversation was brushing past him, and I wished that by some miracle they'd forget about him. But, as always, a fucking miracle was too much to ask for!

Zaire glanced his way quickly, "He's small. He might die in the hull before I could even sell him!" He sighed, then added, "I'll give you five coins for him"

"Five?? No fucking way!! That one's actually what I wanted to sell you in the first place! I owe twenty to the man who gave him to me!"

'man'? Did he just say that a man gave Nyx to him??

"Look fucking closer!! He's just dirty because my idiot cockless shits dragged him in the mountains and ruffed him a little. That one's not like the usual pieces I sell you, he's a highly born nobleman! I won't hand him for less than thirty!"

"A nobleman??" Zaire sounded skeptical. He threw the hood off his head, revealing a pair of green eyes, and a short brown hair. He kneeled with one leg on the floor and walked his eyes on Nyx from his toes to his head that was lowered. Feeling Zaire get closer to him, Nyx tensed even more; his knees pressed hard on each other, he closed his eyes and kept his mouth shut.

"He.... does look quite odd, this one. Where did you get him?"

"Why the fuck you care! Once you buy him, he's all yours. His past wouldn't matter"

Zaire sighed again, "You don't fucking know, do you?"

"I told you, this was a quick trade. So? You going to take him or not??"

"Hey! Where do you come from?"

Zaire waited a few seconds but received nothing but silence.

Zaire pulled his sword. My heart picked up so quickly and I almost charged at him. The boss already took a step back. And I barely stopped myself when I noticed that he hadn't unleashed his sword. He held the fancy looking scabbard and pinned the pommel under Nyx's chin. He forced him to tilt his head back, making his head hit the wall, "I. ASKED YOU. A QUESTION."

Keep. Your fucking hands. Away from him!!

My breath got heavier, and my hands rolled into balls and pressed so hard that my knuckles started turning white. I wanted to shove that sword somewhere unpleasant, but I was still bound by the shackles, and any move could make things worse, right now.

Nyx didn't answer him, but his eyes were open now. Looking straight into Zaire's and, of course, he was glaring daggers at him. Somehow, that seemed to amuse Zaire, because a smug look spread on his face, "Holy fuck, he actually looks like a high-born! Has the same vibe too"

"See? Told ya!!"

He chuckled, "He's probably around the same age as me. And those eyes are so...... Your stupid men bruised his face, you goat shit!"

"Those will fade in a couple of days. Then you could mark him yourself"

Zaire smiled at that and tilted his head to the side. His eyes trailed to Nyx's collar, and he kept looking back and forth between his glare and his collar. Finally, he spoke, "Mmmm... I might actually keep this one for myself. Not a free man, though"

"Wha-?? He's not owned!"

"Well, he's collared"

"Fuck! Let me see"

The boss pushed the rogue that was holding the torch and walked closer. He looked at the collar, then stood and shook his head, "Nah, it's a piece of leather. Just remove the fucking thing, brand him with your seal, and he'll be all yours".

"Yeah, but, that's most likely a pirate collar. Which means...." Zaire looked at me from the corner of his eyes and I knew that he figured it out. He laughed lightly, "I see. You, clever rogue, got a handful of wolves from the same pack"

"Huh??" The boss didn't seem to get it, but Zaire didn't bother with him. His eyes narrowed at me a little, and he remained silent for a moment, then he said to me, "Have we met before.... *pirate?*"

I couldn't even hold a smirk. *This boy was a bit clever. In a few seconds, he figured that we knew each other, that we were pirates, and that I was the one who owned Nyx.*

His smug attitude faded for a moment and he seemed uncomfortable with my smile. He kept staring at me as if searching for my identity in his own memory. The boss looked impatient to finish the deal; he pushed his filthy elephant foot and kicked Nyx on his leg, "Hey! Talk to your Lord! Tell him your name!!"

A tick formed on Nyx's jaw and his frown revealed his anger at being treated that way. Zaire lifted a hand, motioning to the boss to stand back, then he said in an amused tone while gazing at Nyx, "It's ok. I don't need to know his name. And yes, I'll buy him. But I'm keeping this one for myself. He'll be MY pet, from now on. You like your new name.... *pet?*"

Nyx tried to move his head away from the sword's pommel, but Zaire pushed it harder, "I expect a sweet attitude from you, pet. Believe me, you wouldn't want to try my punishments right away. Behave and I promise to make you meow for me in pleasure like a cat in heat. Come on, let me hear your voice, pet, call me *Master*"

"I'M NOT AN ANIMAL, YOU JERK!!"

For a moment, everyone went still, looking at Nyx as if he grew a second head. I sighed, *it was actually too much to ask for, he had to talk back!*

"Attitude, huh? I like that" Zaire stood up with a devious smile and excitement in his eyes, "I love wild cats" he held his hand to the filthy rogue that was standing behind the boss, and he handed him the torch. Then he brought the torch closer to Nyx while talking, "Because I enjoy training a wildcat"

Nyx pushed himself back harder into the wall, trying to stay away from the torch. He was scared, seeing the fire so close to him got him shaking and breathing fast.

"Leave him alone!!" I glared at Zaire, but the bastard only spared me a smirk and went back to focusing on Nyx.

"Now, let's try this again. Say '*Pleaaaase forgive me Master*', and you might spare that pretty skin of yours a painful scar"

Nyx kept looking at the approaching flames. He refused to yield and I knew that his fucking dignity was getting him in trouble yet again. And when he felt the dangerous heat too close, he whimpered in fear.

As soon as I heard him, I lost reason. I lunged at Zaire and snarled at him. He backed out immediately and almost fell back.

I leaned forward in front of Nyx to shield any retaliation from these animals, then I glared at Zaire, unable to keep the coldness in my eyes, nor the threatening tone at bay, "**I told you to fucking leave him alone!!**"

Zaire froze for a moment with his eyes open wide while he stood behind his guards that appeared immediately in front of him. And I couldn't tell if he was scared or just startled. The boss pulled out his sword out and started towards me, "Who the fuck you think you are, slave??"

I prepared myself to receive a stab. Hell, I welcomed it! It was a nice chance to get to steal a sword in this shit hole. But Zaire called the boss back and adjusted his cloak, then pulled up the hood, "Don't touch them. They're mine to discipline as I please"

The boss stood back reluctantly, while still glaring at me as if that would make me shake in my boots.

"Fuck, fine. Then give me my damn money and let's get this over with."

"What about the whore?"

Both men looked at the skinny rogue, "What whore?"

"We've got a whore too! She's so fucking beautiful"

"Where the hell did you get a whore from?"

"She brought the boy to us, and we just *invited* her to stay"

"When the shit were you planning to tell me about that??"

"S..... sorry boss, you came straight to the cave and-"

"Where is she?"

"She's playing with the mates!"

"You fucking bastards, fucking a whore all by yourselves! Not even waiting for your boss!!" Then the boss pushed the miserable thief not so nicely outside the cage, "Let's go you cockless ass!"

"A-Aye boss!"

Syrvat

"Zaire- I mean, Lord Zaire, you might want to take a look. Maybe I'll be selling you five souls today"

Zaire didn't answer. He gave me one last glare under the shade of the hood before he turned on his heels and left.

Their voices walked further away and the insults that the boss kept throwing at his imp faded along with the light of the torches.

∞ ∞ ∞

I inhaled deeply. *Fuck, that could've gone really bad.*

I looked back at Nyx, trying in vain to distinguish his features in the darkness. And even without seeing him, I could hear his quivering breaths; he was still frightened.

I lowered my voice, trying not to scare him even more, "Nyx, you're ok?"

He could only answer after a moment of trying to calm himself, but it didn't work much, "I....... I'm.... fine..."

I sat on my ass and leaned my head back on the wall. I sighed deeply, thinking about how I could really appreciate a cigarette right now.

We sat in silence. Thankfully Lou and Ace refrained from releasing any remarks or trying to lecture Nyx, he obviously couldn't take any of that right now. Maybe the way I had just lost control there with Zaire for a moment... *Fuck, that torch was too damn close... It actually felt like he was going to scar him!*

"A... Agenor..."

The hesitant weak call for my name claimed my attention. I looked at his direction, imagining the painful scared look tainting his eyes

"I..... I don't know what's going to happen.... but I need you to know that I didn't betray your trust." He went silent for a moment, then continued, "It was all for my mother...."

His mother??

"A merchant from Mila said that she was........ sick..."

"What??"

"My mother is sick, Agenor! It's my fault and it's my responsibility to take care of her, but... I... I betrayed her... And now you think that I betrayed you-" His voice heightened and his breath got more frantic.

"Nyx, how the hell could someone know about your mother? And how did they even know you to give you the news!??"

"I-I don't know! Maybe a coincidence, I don't know! I wanted to tell you, but you weren't at the camp, and-and I was going after the merchant to ask him before he sailed away but we were caught! Then Cherri pushed me, and then they caught her... I don't get it!! Now the merchant has left Esme, and Cherri is kidnapped, then.... *you*"

I listened with my teeth squeezing against each other so hard they felt ready to shatter. I listened as he told me the story of him being conned without even realizing it! And of course, it always had to be about his fucking home! Whenever he hears about them, he loses reason!! Now he's endangering himself, chasing after a lie and about to be branded!!

I wanted to shake him so badly, yell at him and make him open his eyes to the fucking truth!

And that's when I heard his small light sobs in the dark. He was sniffling and breathing frantically. He thought he was the reason for all this shit that we're in, and it wasn't quite false.

But it wasn't his fault only. I should have thought ahead and prevented such things from harming him!! I only asked Lou to watch for Izel, thinking she might try and pull some trick on Nyx if she came to the camp in my absence. But I didn't suspect the new whore to go to such extent. Still, she couldn't have done it alone, either Izel is involved or not, someone must've given them the exact thing that would make Nyx go into a frenzy. And I am almost certain of who the fucking bastard was!

sniffle sniffle

My heart ached, and I wished I could just discard his stupidity and forgive him, I mean listen to him! He sounds so confused.... and so damn cute!

"Uughh, for shit's sake, not the crying!"

"Shut it, Lou"

"Come on Captain, the pixie's crying! Just tell him the truth, we're not becoming slaves, not today anyway"

"If you don't shut it, I might sell you myself!"

What the hell?? Isn't he supposed to hate Nyx for this shit we're in? I swear to the Gods I'm going to beat the fuck out of Lou when this is over!

sniffle "I'm sorry Lou, Ace... I'm truly sorry about all of this"

"Yeah, whatever" Lou didn't sound happy with the apology, he probably prefers annoying and teasing him rather than accepting a decent apology. Ace, on the other hand, took it in stride, his voice as calm and normal as always, "It's ok Nyx. It will be ok"

Why is HE telling him that we'll be fine?? Of course, I'm not going to let us get 'enslaved' just like that! But Nyx probably needs to feel like shit a little. That way he'll maybe, JUST MAYBE, think with his head from now on and not blindly follow his heart.

I sighed again and used my hands to caress my temples. Aye, this is definitely not entirely his fault. I knew exactly how attached he was to his family yet I did nothing to shield him from such cons. Now look where we are; chained to a wall in a cave slave cell and about to be transferred to a slave ship. It was MY responsibility to protect him from this world that I forced him to accept.

I leaned my head his way and rest it on his shoulder. I meant to calm him, but somehow that made him shiver even more. It was hard not to be mad and him, but it was harder to be so. I moved closer until our shoulders connected. I wanted to calm him; it would be dangerous if he was still panicking when Zaire comes back.

".... Agenor....", he whispered, "I can't believe I got you into this mess... When they brought me here, I wanted to see you so much! If only for one time! But I failed you..."

I tilted my head and kissed him. I meant to aim for his lips, but I caught his cheek instead. He turned my way, "I promised to protect you Agenor...."

I whispered back, "No Nyx, *I* promised to protect *you*, and I will"

I kissed him again. Our mouths met and his eagerness to kiss me back warmed my heart.

A day. Less than a day I've been separated from him, and I'm already going crazy: I'm mad at him because he acted stupidly, without thinking or even doubting for a second the sincerity of others. I'm furious at myself that he got beaten by some pathetic rogues like a lone wolf. I ache because he's suffering as he thinks that he caused his mother to be sick somehow. And I miss him, less than a day yet I feel so hungry for him...

I kissed him harder, claiming his tongue with mine. And the more he yielded, the sweeter he became.

Aye, I love him. He's a respectful highborn, both smart and stupid, both noble and pirate. And I'd fucking give my life just to keep him safe.

I released his lips, allowing him to breathe, "We'll talk about what happened later. I need you not to think about any of that right now. Just stay calm, and believe in me. You'll be safe, Nyx, we all will, ok?"

He released a small sob, then whispered, "Just for coming so far and looking for me... I could never repay that kindness" I laughed. That reminded me of the first day he spent in my cabin when I told him that I saved him from drowning, he said that he was going to 'repay my kindness'. At that moment, I knew that his charms surpassed his looks... I knew he was something different and precious.

"Oh! The Captain is laughing!! That's a good sign!"

"Shut up Lou"

"Aye, aye Captain!"

I nuzzled his hair, and after I let him breathe and sniffle a bit more, I took more advantage of the darkness, and I kissed him again.

∞ ∞ ∞

Chapter 11 ~ Last resort
∞ Nyx's POV ∞

I didn't want this moment to end. I didn't want to go back to reality.

Even though we were surrounded by darkness, I was aware that we weren't alone. I tried to control myself and make no sounds with my mouth and keep any moan from finding its way out. But I didn't want to let go. I wanted to keep kissing him for always. I wanted to open my eyes and find us on the beach or even in the cabin on the ship... Anywhere but here...

Anywhere but the dark slave cage with the shackles and the ugly people that wanted to take us away.

I wanted to forget about my mistake when I perused that merchant alone and got us all imprisoned in a mountain cave.

I wanted to forget about my own mother that was probably very sick because of me, her unfilial child

A moment later, Agenor released my lips. His forehead rested against mine and we remained silent while we caught our breaths.

"Feel better?"

I nodded, then I remembered how dark it was in here, so I answered, "Yes, I'm ok"

"Did they beat you badly"

"Nothing I couldn't take"

He went silent for a moment. I knew he was angry. I could feel it radiating from him in waves. He was maybe still angry with me, maybe angry with the rogues?

I sighed; angry with all of us, is more like it.

"Agenor, what are we going to do?"

He shifted a little, then answered, "Improvise"

"What? How??"

"When they release these shackles, we'll find a way out of this mess. Until then, do not speak. Try not to draw attention to yourself, we don't want them to consider you a target."

I remained still, my shoulder resting on Agenor's. He spoke to me like I was the weak troublesome one. It hurt because I knew it was the truth.

Time passed heavily. We waited in the dark, with nothing but far voices and Lou's few remarks to break the silence. With our shoulder touching, I felt much calmer. But as soon as the voices started approaching again, I could no more ignore the situation that I put us in and pretend like everything was fine. Agenor pulled away, and I was nervous once more.

∞ ∞ ∞

"Five silvers"

"Wha-?? Did you see her?? She's young! And beautiful!"

"She's a whore AND she was fucked by the likes of you! Five silvers are too fucking much. I'm already giving you a fortune today. I'm definitely certain this is the most you ever made or will make out of a single deal! So stop giving me a fucking headache! If you argue more I'll make it three for that whore. Fuck, she's not even conscious!!"

The boss chuckles, "Euuh... me men like to play rough"

"That's the most disgusting thing I heard this week, and I work in selling fuck-toys to old men!"

The boss glared at him but didn't answer. They reached the cage and that skinny rogue opened the iron door. They flooded inside, the boss's and Zaire's guards. Too many to handle... I tried counting them without being noticed, there was probably a dozen of them!

'Improvise' he said... Oh God, please save us...

I stole a peek at my mates; Agenor wore a cold stare that could freeze hell. His back sitting up straight and his shoulders not sloped in defeat nor tense, I wondered how he could master such a confident attitude when he didn't even have a proper plan! At that thought I mentally slapped myself, this was MY fault! I should be the one working a plan to get us out, not shrinking in fear and blaming others!

But I was out of it. I couldn't even think properly! It's not just my first time being held in a slave cage, it's actually the first time I saw a slave merchant!! They don't actually roam the streets in the guarded islands.

I glanced at Ace. Following the example of his Captain, he laid back, looking relaxed and calm. I almost believed that, but when I saw his eyes, I knew he was focused on keeping track of everyone around him. I got used to that fake-uninterested look appearing whenever he suspected someone would try to bother or training and intervene in our sparing, and by someone, I mostly mean Nash. I never solicited that kind of look, though; he could always beat me without faking boredom.

I was drawn out of my thoughts when several spears aimed at each one of us. I looked at the rusty points, which I shouldn't have because my breath immediately accelerated. I've never seen a spear this close! Corail is not exactly made for hunting, and rarely would someone walk by carrying one. So those I've seen were mostly displayed for sale. I never felt the need to examine or hold any of them.

I also read about them, in a book that explained the different kinds of weapons and how a warrior should choose the one that goes with his personality and stuff like that. The spear in that book looked long and gave quite the 'warrior' aura to the fighter. The ones I'm looking at in this cave were ugly, old, and rusty, but I found them to be much scarier than a normal blade.

I swallowed. And my fear must've been obvious because the three men that held spears to my head and neck were smirking. On my left, Lou kept snarling and insulting the rogues and Zaire's guards. Somehow, the commotion he was making pulled all attention to him, drawing more spears to be pointed at him, and less pointed at me.

The boss was talking back at Lou, exchanging nasty insults. Zaire, on the other hand, walked towards us. He stood to my left. I felt his gaze weighing on me. I didn't know if he was looking down at me or Agenor but didn't lift my eyes to see. I kept my looking straightforward, trying my best to keep my shoulders from shivering, while Agenor took on the task of glaring at him.

Zaire crouched beside me, and his hand reached to hold a lock of my hair. I moved to release it from his fingers, but as soon as I did, his hand caught a full grip of my hair and pulled.

Agenor lunged towards him, "I told you to leave him the Fuck. **Alone**!!"

My eyes widened in panic when the spears touched his neck and chest threateningly. The ones aiming at me were now menacing him! Zaire pulled on my hair hard, making me slide closer to him and away from Agenor. I groaned in pain but that didn't keep Zaire from gripping my hair even harder and forcing me to tilt my head back. I looked at him. His eyes were linked with Agenor's glares and he was smirking.

I glanced at the corner of my eyes to Agenor, "Stop.... please, don't!" I pleaded for him to yield but he didn't. He kept pulling at the shackles and trying to charge at Zaire. I don't even know if he heard me! He was so drawn into his glaring contest with Zaire that he didn't even try to push the spears away! Unlike me, his hands were tied in front of him so he could at least try to defend himself!

Seeing how Agenor's threatening glares didn't soften, Zaire's smirk slid wider, his hand reached for one of the spears, with one finger, he pulled the spear slowly until the point reached my throat.

I didn't even dare to gulp. My breathing heightened and I didn't know what to feel anymore! I was both relieved that Agenor had one less spear aimed at him and I was panicked that it was aimed at me!

Words boiled on my tongue; I wanted to tell them how shameless and coward they were to threaten us with our hands tied!! *This was so damn unfair...*

I kept my mouth shut though because I remembered what Agenor told me. I felt the spear thrust harder and my collar painfully pushing on my neck. And I realized that the collar was the only thing keeping the spear from tearing my throat. Once more I was indebted to the damned collar.

Agenor retreated and sat back. I couldn't look at him, but I didn't try to; was he scared? Angry? Sad? Defeated?? It felt like if I saw any of that right now I would break.

Zaire laughed under his breath. He moved closer and his face was only inches away from mine. I fought the urge to glare at him, just kept my eyes looking forward. He leaned in and said with an amused demanding tone, "Now that I hold both your weaknesses, I'll take my time disciplining you both. And if you obey, little one, I might let you see your friend for a minute." He tilted his head to the side, "I can't wait to brand you... I won't just take pleasure in punishing you, we will also have lots of fun together... And I'll reward you when you behave. Now, I bet you'll do as told and be a good boy? Won't you, *pet?*"

I'm not a damn animal! I wanted to yell at him again, but I didn't. Agenor asked me not to speak or provoke any of them and I really wanted to obey him, better late than never, right?

Nevertheless, the silence didn't seem like the best answer right now. Zaire nodded at one of the guards who immediately drew his spear back from Agenor and taking an attacking stance, preparing to shove the sharp thing in his chest. I immediately nodded vigorously, "Yes! Yes! Please, sir, don't hurt any of them!"

His hand released my hair and his fingers started caressing the numbness that spread on my scalp, "Good. Very good". He was gentle now, but it didn't feel any better. His touch felt so demeaning and I wanted to kick him with my legs or hit his head with mine. Of course, even I knew that I had to come up with a better idea than those.

Zaire reached his hand back at the boss, "Keys", he said. The boss shifted uncomfortably, and when Zaire glared at him for the delay, he sighed, "Zai-"

"Lord!"

"**Lord. Zaire.** I think you're forgetting that we get paid before delivering the goods"

"Have you lost your mind? Or don't you have one to begin with!! You think I'd walk into your shit mountain with that sum of money on me? I only brought a few silvers, never thought you'd actually sell me something decent for a change"

"Then we got a problem! How am I getting my money?"

"You, idiot, will come with me to the port. I'll give you your money there"

"Oh yeah, you don't trust **us** with the money, why should I trust that you wouldn't make me a slave?"

Zaire grimaced, "I'll pretend I didn't hear that"

The boss reluctantly gave him the key, and Zaire turned towards me while grumbling, "Fuck, I don't know what's more disgusting, your idiocy or your fucked up ugly face"

I tried to remain as still as possible as he fondled with the shackles. My hands were free, and I brought them painfully in front of me. I caressed my wrists and kept looking at them. I didn't want to raise my eyes because I felt Zaire's on me.

"What do we say....?"

I couldn't help the frown that refused to dispel

"Come on pet. **I don't. Like. To wait**"

"Th.... thank you..."

"Thank youuuuu??"

This is damn torture! I sighed, "Thank you, sir"

"No. Look at me: Master. From now on, I'm your Master"

I couldn't. I just couldn't say it! Especially not with Agenor behind me!!

I just wanted to cower and go back to sitting beside Agenor. Maybe go back to when the cave was dark when I could pretend as if we were alone.

Zaire fumed. I was making him angry. I shouldn't be doing that!!

Fuck!

"Thank you............. M... Master"

He patted on my head as if I was a cat, "Good

"Come on, pet. Up we go" He grabbed my left arm and pulled me up as he stood. I immediately flinched and held my ribs; they hurt so much I couldn't stand straight, and I went to sit down again if not for Zaire's hold. He removed my hands away and lifted my shirt.

"He's bruised everywhere you fucking dick head!!"

"I told you", the boss said with a fed up tone, "me men like to play rough"

"Fucking moron. I should be kicking your hairy ass for this"

"Why do you care so much anyway??"

"He's mine now! I'm the one to bruise him! I don't like to treat injuries that I didn't cause!"

"Whatever..."

I took the chance to look back at Agenor. He couldn't move much because of the spears, and that pained my heart. *I drove him into this! This is all my fault!!*

Somehow, he read my thoughts. A forced small smile tugged his lips and he nodded slightly to reassure me. And even though I couldn't see any way out for us, his tiny smile was so relieving, like a beautiful light in the darkness of this cave.

"I'm heading out. Get those two"

"Yes Master", the guards answered.

"Let's go" He pulled my arm, forcing me to walk despite the pain in my stomach. We stepped out of the cage, and every time I wanted to look back at Agenor, he'd yank me roughly, making me barely keeping my balance.

∞ ∞ ∞

"Pet, on the way to your new home, I'd like to hear your story. Mmmm, highborn... pirate... slave... sounds really interesting"

I ignored him. I focused on looking back and not breaking eye contact with Agenor...

We headed to the exit of the cave. We took a turn and I was no longer able to see the cage behind me. Zaire held my left arm and dragged me beside him. One guard walked by my right, clearing the path with a torch in his hand, and the second guard walked behind us.

Zaire was walking steadily fast. His stride confident, he was giving orders to his guards to prepare the horses and the restraints once we reach the exit. I tried to slow him down by pretending that I couldn't walk properly. Pretending wasn't actually difficult to do; I was in a good deal of pain in my ribs and my sides from all the punching and the kicking earlier, so I just used that and exaggerated a little. Zaire didn't suspect a thing, he was totally ignoring me and talking to his guards.

Once outside the cave, I knew there would be more rogues. Despite the late hour, I doubted all of them would be asleep with people coming and going in their mountain. I had to do something before we stepped out of here; From all those who were caught in this cave, I was the only one walking without restraints! Maybe it was because they could sense my weakness compared to the others, but it doesn't matter right now! Think of something...... anything!!

I remembered the last 'reassuring' smile that Agenor gave me before we left the cave and my heart pinched. I have to act or we will truly become slaves! The life of the ones that I care about the most was about to get ruined! ALL BECAUSE OF THE STUPID ME!!

My mind that refused to work since I met Cherri, ticked again. I didn't ponder or calculate anything though, I had absolutely no second to lose. So I acted almost without thinking.

With my left elbow I pushed Zaire to the side, then yanked my arm hard, he didn't move much, but the surprise was enough to make him release my arm. The guard beside me immediately turned to defend his keeper. I ignored everything and just ducked a little and reached for the closest object: the torch.

I moved the torch quickly from side to side while turning around, forcing both Zaire and the guard that was beside me to retreat. A spear immediately attempted to stab me; it was the second guard. I sidestepped quickly to avoid the spear and hurried to walk back and step away from them. When I looked up, Zaire was glaring at me with his eyes wide open, and the guards were fuming, both angry and scared of their Master.

They went to charge at me, but Zaire lifted his hand to stop them. Then he reached forward with his hand open upwards, "Come here, pet, it's ok, don't be scared" his voice was calm and, unlike the look in his eyes, gentle.

Why is he talking to me like I was a scared cat? What the fuck he thinks I am??

He took half a step forward and I retreated a couple back. Then his voice became threatening, "You don't want to do this, pet. Do you know what happens when you disobey your Master?"

He waited, but I didn't answer. Fuck him! He's so rude! And he's talking in a weird fashion! Like I'm a stupid child or an animal or something! He sounded scary in a lunatic way

"Fine. I'll give my guards the order, and once I do, they'll catch you immediately. If you don't surrender on your own, RIGHT NOW, and be a good pet, I will make sure your branding is so long and painful it would give you nightmares for months"

I frowned a little at the idea and he caught up on my fear. He removed his hood back, then started walking very slowly towards me while speaking, and I walked backward, "Have you ever seen a slave being branded, pet?"

My breath accelerated and I swallowed... I never saw such a thing, but I could certainly imagine the horror.

"Branding is crucial for slaves. Once marked, you are owned by your Master, just like a dog or some cattle. It's a very important ceremony; First, we heat the branding iron. The slave is held still while he watches the iron turn vivid red like fire. The Master holds the scorching iron and melts the slave's flesh. The pet screams, cries... he can smell his own burned flesh... he pleads for mercy and makes a thousand vows just to get it over with. But, only I, the Master, could make the pain stop. And once the branding iron removed, the pet would have a beautiful scar in a bleeding pattern, right above his heart. Of course, I could use some potions to ease the pain, after all, I'm not a monster, right? But that only applies for OBEDIENT pets. The rebellious ones, on the other hand, they get branded over and over again until either there is no more flesh to melt, they die of the excruciating pain, or... they surrender"

I was frozen. I hadn't even realized how close he was right now, nor the fact that I was leaning back on the wall of the cave, staring at his psychotic look.

"I... I..."

"you... you... what? Who do you want to be, pet? My nice new toy with beautiful eyes, or the dead tortured corpse?"

I was shaking. It felt like the flames of the torch were being drowned by his merciless look. That look that didn't give a damn about what I felt or what I wanted. He wanted me to choose – No, he demanded my answer! What the hell am I supposed to say?? No matter what I said, I was admitting being a slave!!

The weakness in my heart caught up with me at a bad moment. I wanted to whine... I wanted to complain like a child and tell him that I didn't want to become a slave! I didn't want to see that flesh melting branding iron! I didn't want a symbol carved on my heart!!

I......... I wanted to cry and ask Agenor for help...

"A... Agenor..." I whispered because that was all I could manage

"What? SPEEK UP, pet!"

He yelled at me, and the way he did that was so demeaning. So I used the little courage I had to raise my voice and pretend to be strong enough to actually make a threat:

"You touch me and you'll be walking the plank on Martina!"

His eyes narrowed, as he didn't expect such an answer. Then he sneered, "Martina? Really?? That pirate crew? Now, why would they give a shit about an ex-highborn near-future-slave?"

I scoffed. I'll never know where I got the courage not to cry right now, all I knew is that I tried to mimic Agenor's cocky attitude. So I channeled that familiar arrogant aura of his and smirked, "I am a pirate, a Martina pirate. And if you dare to lay one finger on me, you'll be slaughtered before the next sunrise by my Captain... Agenor"

He was frowning already, "You know Agenor? The pirate devil??"

"Aye. And *he* knows *you*"

He thought about that for a couple of seconds, then his eyes widened. He looked behind him to where the cage was, then he looked back at me, "That.... That was Agenor!??"

I didn't know if revealing that was good or not, but hell with it. There was no going back now, so I smirked wider and nodded.

His eyes widened even more, if possible. He ran his tattooed hand through his hair and mumbled, "Shit... Fuck!! I knew I saw him somewhere!! How could I forget that face?"

"So you've seen him before?"

"Only in one of those 'wanted' papers-wait, is that his second in there?"

I didn't need to answer, he already figured it out and cursed under his breath.

"So what will you do, *Master*? Surrender... or die...?"

I expected him to answer immediately. For all the effort and the acting I did, I thought I deserved a quick ending to all this mess. Unfortunately, Zaire didn't answer right away. He kept thinking, and I realized he was weighing his chances between being killed if he enslaves us, or being killed if he releases us.

That was when an excruciating scream resonated in the cave. The guards turned around in alarm and looked at Zaire, waiting for orders

"What the Fuck?? YOU! Go check what the bloody hell is happening in the cage!"

The appointed guard ran back inside while the screams continued one after the other, and a smaller commotion seemed to start outside, on the other end of the cave.

"You will come with me-" Zaire said to me while turning around and reaching to grab me, but he was interrupted when I kicked the back of his left knee with my foot. He lost his balance and I pushed him to fall by hitting him with the torch on his back.

As soon as he fell, he tried to get up again and went to curse me, but his cloak caught on fire from the torch. Zaire cussed and panicked. He pulled hard on the burning cloak to tear it away from his body.

His guard ran to his rescue and grabbed the cloak and yanked it hard. I turned to use that second of distraction and flee, but I couldn't just... leave!!

I was trying to decide what to do when I saw Zaire's sword on his side. I grabbed the handle and unleashed it, then I immediately stepped back. The guard was stomping with his foot on the torn cloak to put out the fire, but when they heard the sound of the sword leaving its scabbard, they both froze and looked back at me.

Zaire stood up and pushed the remaining fabric of his cloak angrily behind his back, "Give me. My Fucking sword back!"

When I didn't answer and just took another step back, Zaire motioned for his guard to attack me and added a simple, "I want him breathing"

The obedient guard strode my way while grabbing his spear with both hands. As soon as I was close enough for the spear to claim my head, he thrust his weapon. I dodged it and tried to attack the guard, but my sword couldn't reach him. So I attacked his spear instead. The damn thing was made of iron! It kept clashing with my sword, and despite my fast moves, my swings were not strong enough to disarm the trained guard. But I didn't yield. I kept kicking his spear away from me while making sure not to get close to Zaire who looked ready to pounce on me on the first chance.

Fed up already, the guard cursed and started using both ends of his spear to attack me. His moves became quicker and more aggressive now, he was actually trying to kill me. And Zaire said nothing to call back his enraged dog.

The thrusts hastened and if not for Ace's training, I wouldn't be moving this quickly and dodging all the blows. The guard aimed his spear at my heart and thrust assertively. In a split of a second, I span quickly to avoid the sharp point and stepped alongside the spear's length, closing the distance between the guard and me, I lifted my sword to my side......

and I stabbed.

∞ ∞ ∞

Chapter 12 ~ My killer
∞ Nyx's POV ∞

Time seemed to go completely still.

The only thing I could hear was a pained groan and my own heavy breathing...

The only thing I could feel was the blade of my sword that I couldn't swing anymore, surrounded by tearing flesh

The only thing I could see was the blooded smudge as it grew wider around the blade...

My heart slowed down dangerously, I felt every beat kicking in my chest like it wanted to leave it. My eyes stared at the end of my sword that started shaking, and they refused to lift and see the agonized face.

'Don't drop your sword'.... 'Never let go of your weapon'.... 'If you're unarmed then the game is over'... Ace's voice resonated in my head, and my shaking hand refused to unclench and release the weapon.

The timeless moment felt like an eternity. It came short when Zaire stepped out from behind his guard and pulled his shoulder back. The body slid out of the sword and the guard fell on his back, with his hands clenched on his bleeding side.

I came back to my senses when my eyes met the guard's.... *he was suffering.... he was dying... I killed him!!*

I jumped over the torch that was laying on the ground and dropped on my knees beside the guard. Zaire got startled and took a couple of steps back to protect himself. With the sword still glued to my hand, I tried to use my free hand and my fist to stop the bleeding, "Y-You... You were supposed to dodge that!! You should've stepped slightly to the side! Why didn't you dodge that!!"

The guard didn't utter a word; he was busy trying to breathe through the pain. On the corner of my eye, I saw Zaire take a step towards us. I looked at him immediately, "Help him!! He's going to die! Do something!!"

Zaire didn't move though; he didn't even attack me. He just tilted his head to the side and stared at me, like he was watching a weird scene develop before his eyes.

Another scream tore through the cave from the inside out. I looked back and saw the light getting closer and silhouettes dancing around. The torch didn't seem to be still so I couldn't tell anything from the moving shadows.

"A-Agenoooor!" I called, my voice husky and shaking with fear. I hoped my shout would reach him despite the noises and the screams... No answer came back from the deeper end of the cage...

I expected Zaire to escape, but he grabbed my arm and yanked me, "We're leaving, NOW!!"

His grip was so strong; I couldn't pull my arm free. His other hand went to grab the sword, but I refused to be unarmed again, "Get away from me!!"

I slashed the sword his way, forcing him to release me, and we both fell on our backs. I scurried to get back on my feet. I was shaking like a leaf in a storm, but I didn't let go of my sword nor escaped. I walked closer to Zaire; the bastard wasn't leaving without me and I wasn't going to become a slave!

I slashed the sword on my side to release the tension in my arm, then I joined both hands to hold it steadily. I swiftly laid the blade on Zaire's shoulder, threatening to slit his throat. His eyes trailed up slowly until they met mine; his glare was cold and enraged. And only when he lifted his chin higher, I saw the cut that traced the length of his right cheek.

His face was cut, but he didn't even try to stop the blood that oozed out.

I felt even more scared than before. The fact that this man didn't care about his own bleeding injury was frightening to me... But I had no time for drama.

"You got lucky so far"

I pressed the blade harder on his neck in an attempt to shut him, but he didn't even flinch, "You know I can't leave without you, right?"

"What! Why??"

"You, lucky pet, are the only card that might protect me from the devil. So unless you slit my throat right now, I'm going to take you back with me and trade you for my safety if needed." Then he mumbled with irritation, "This whole thing was a fucking mistake"

Right now I didn't care about his reasons. I glanced at the dying guard, then I nudged Zaire a little with the sword, "Help him!"

He didn't budge, so I pressed my sword a little harder on his neck, the blade was very sharp, it immediately started drawing blood out. He winced and I urged him again, "Put your hands on his injury! Now!!"

"Why the fuck am I going to do such thing? He was a slave!"

"He IS a man! A person! And he's dying!!"

"Because of you, if I recall well"

"Just put your damn hands on his inj-"
"............ Nyx?"

∞ Agenor's POV ∞

As I walked further, I could hear his voice among the screams and the noises. I headed towards the exit of the cave, and then I raised my hand for my men to stop and I halted at the scene that appeared before my eyes.

There he was, standing unharmed, holding a foreign sword to a slave-merchant's neck, while he knelt before him.

I watched in awe... a strange feeling filling my heart at the sight of his sword that drooled crimson fluid, and the severely wounded guard that lay on the ground.

Did...... did he.........?

"Help him!", he said sternly, "He's your servant!"

His whole body was shaking, but somehow that didn't belittle the beauty of his stance.

"Nyx?"

As soon as my voice reached him, he looked back and his face lit up with relief.

"A....... Agenor...."

I couldn't deny an admiring smile.

"I-I was coming to get you! How did you escape??"

HE *was coming to free* ME*?? That was so fucking adorable*

My smile grew wider and I started walking towards him

"H-help me Agenor! The guard.... the guard he...he-"

Both our attentions were caught when we heard a cracking noise.

We looked at Zaire, his hands were on the guard, but not the way Nyx ordered him to; he had one hand on the slave's shoulder and the other gripping hard on his face. He broke the slave's neck.

His hands retreated and he wiped them on his clothes, then added, "There. Fucking problem solved"

Nyx's mouth dropped and his eyes widened in terror. I didn't need to ask to understand what just happened, one look at Nyx and everything was clear to me.

Zaire smirked at Nyx who couldn't utter a single word. I strode towards them, and when Zaire saw me coming, he tried to scurry back and escape. I could see the fear in his eyes; that special kind of fear that only danced in the eyes of those who heard about the devil.

I grabbed his bloodied throat and lifted him in the air.

"Captain!! Captain Agenor, is it?? I-I-I didn't know! I didn't know who you were and-**He**! He brought me here! That fat ass mountain goat!!" He was motioning at the boss, who was withered in Lou's grip, "You Fucking sneaky shit!! You tried to sell me Martina pirates!!"

"I didn't know you fucking Lord!! I didn't-" Lou brought his head to meet the boss's, forcing him to shut the fuck up. Zaire went to cuss some more and I tightened my grip around his neck preventing him from talking.

Ace walked to Nyx, "You fought well! I'm proud of you, Nyx"

*Wha-! **I'm proud of him!!** Why the FUCK would he be proud of my Nyx??*

At that instant, Maren ran inside holding a torch, "Nyxy!! You're alive!"

"You're alone?" I asked him

"Britt is outside, Captain, torturing a bunch of rogues by sitting on them. They were too easy to beat! Too many though, they're like... a nest of disgusting cockroaches. First, we thought you were going to spend the night here, but then we heard the screaming, so we figured we'd clear the exit for you"

"Good" I threw Zaire roughly against the wall. He groaned and fell on the ground, "Take care of that", I ordered Ace, and he went to grab Zaire and drag him outside.

"Lou, put that shit behind the bars with the others. I have no use for him"

"Aye, Aye Captain!"

"Captain!! I didn't know! I swear by the Goddess of the forests and the mines!!"

Lou shook the boss to shut him up while dragging him back to the iron cage and mumbling, "There's no such fucking Goddess, you stinky goblin"

I approached Nyx and pulled him into a hug, both feeling him safely return to me, and keeping him from gazing at the corpse any longer.

He killed... He killed a fucking trained slave!!

I tightened my arms around him, that image of him holding the bloodied sword to Zaire's neck kept flashing repeatedly in my memory, sending a tingling wave in my body. He looked amazingly hot! My cock pulsed just from thinking about it!!

I nuzzled in his hair moving down slowly to whisper in his ears, "You are so brave, my love. You're so fucking brave!"

"I..... the guard, he attacked me! I swear he...."

"You did what you had to do. You protected yourself, and you brought Zaire down to his knees! You're so strong and brave, Nyx... You are the bravest pirate I know"

I ruffled with his hair while still holding him tight. And I genuinely smiled wider when his free hand hugged me back. He was still shivering, but it's alright. He will have plenty of time to relax and embrace his new life.

I sighed in satisfaction; *He had never felt farther from Corail and closer to me than he does right this second.*

I started walking him out. He tried to look back at his work of art, though. I shouldn't let him. I was aware of the fragility of his heart, and a good lover would protect the one he loves.

But I wasn't 'good', was I? Despite the pain that I knew he was feeling, I eased my grip and allowed him to look at the dead slave. He stared at it for a moment, as if waiting for the corpse to come back to life. Then, his unbelieving and fearful eyes focused on the small pool of blood.

Then I put my arm around his shoulders and we headed outside. He didn't resist, just followed my lead, and I was certain he didn't notice that his hand still held his crimson sword tightly.

∞ ∞ ∞

We stepped out of the damned cave, only to find bodies scattered and piled up all over the place. They didn't look dead, though; with the light of the torches, I didn't see any deep wounds or scattered heads.

"Is this what you meant by *clearing our way out*?"

I teased Maren, who grinned brashly, "Aye! I kicked most of their asses, Britt just helped with one or two"

Britt smirked but didn't say a thing. If I knew my crew well, this was definitely mostly Britt's work. He likes to knock out his enemies then pile them up.

I nodded at Britt and he nodded back. Then he moved his huge body towards us and pushed a sword and dagger to Nyx.

"My sword! Thank you Britt"

The big fellow smiled and walked away. I grabbed the Jian and threw it at one of my men, "You won't be needing that. You have a new sword now"

Nyx looked confused for a second, then he peered at the sword in his hand like it was the devil himself. He shook his head thoroughly, "This is not mine"

"Yeah! Because it's mine!" Zaire yelled and I just noticed that Ace had his hands bound behind his back and a rope around his neck and into Ace's hand. They were standing beside a nicely decorated horse. I guess that also used to be Zaire's.

"Shut him the fuck up, Ace, I don't need a slave merchant's blood on my name"

If I'm known as the pirate that kills slave merchants, that could make fewer people ready to make deals with me. I didn't need that. Being feared is nice and all, but I didn't want to be seen as the enemy of the black market merchants.

Ace tugged on the rope roughly making Zaire wince and glare at him.

I looked at Zaire's sword; it was actually a very nice one. A little longer than the Jian and much fancier. I also assumed it had much more experience than the plain Jian, "That sword suits you more Nyx, it's a sword you earned"

Nyx looked down at his sword again and I could almost hear him blaming the sharp blade.

We couldn't stay here long though, I strode to the horse and climbed up on it. Ace handed me the rope that was attached to Zaire's neck and I took it. I gave the horse a nudge and approached Nyx.

As soon as his eyes lifted from the sword he looked around like he remembered something... Or someone, "Where's Cherri??"

"Passed out over there!" Maren pointed at the trees

Nyx started walking away when I moved the horse to block his way, "Where do you think you're going?"

"The girl! We can't leave her here, they'll hurt her again!"

"She's a mischievous fucking whore and she got what she deserved!"

"You don't understand"

"I don't fucking give a damn, Nyx!"

"But they... They did bad things to her"

"She came to the mountain on her own and made a deal with rogues! She chose to be here-"

"Nothing justifies rape, Agenor!!"

....

....

Fuck, that stung.

I couldn't look away from Nyx's determined eyes. The horse started shifting as if it could feel my anxiousness. When I looked away, Britt was staring at me with a pair of amused arched eyebrows. The fucking blowfish, he's smarter than he looks.

I sighed. Maybe bringing her along wasn't a bad idea, I'll get to make her talk later. So I nodded at Britt, who smirked before he disappeared for a moment, only to come back with the unconscious body of that whore laid on his shoulder.

I didn't wait any longer, I had a feeling Nyx would run to the slut to see if she was fine. And I preferred killing her than letting Nyx touch her or ever come near that bitch again.

I nudged the horse and moved beside him. I leaned down, grabbed him around the chest, then lifted him and sat him in front of me. He hissed in pain and I wanted to punch myself for hurting him more than he already is.

∞ ∞ ∞

We climbed down the mountain, making our way through the darkness.

I could feel Nyx's nervousness; with one arm tugging at the horse's reins and the other holding Nyx tight, I could feel the rhythm of his breathing grow hastier. And I knew, that head of his was working again. Was he thinking about how he screwed up? Maybe it was about how much he loved me?......... Aye, I'd like him to think about that. But it would probably be about the slave guard that he killed, I'm certain I'm still going to hear about that sooner or later.

After a while, I guess he couldn't swallow whatever thought that was tormenting him. He turned his head to talk to me, his gaze hesitant to meet mine, "Agenor"

"Yes?"

"Eumm... Are we going to the port?"

"The port??" *Ok, this one I hadn't expected*

"The merchant...." He looked back at Britt, or more precisely at that whore, then he continued hesitantly, "I know I caused so much trouble today, but I really need to go to the port!"

I sighed. It's not that he's that stupid, he just refuses to believe the truth, and that bugs me even more

"There's no merchant from Corail, Nyx. That bitch simply lied to you"

"I know she did, but... what if she didn't lie about the whole thing? What if there was a merchant and he actually heard some news about my family?"

I didn't answer. Nothing I'll say will make him understand right now. He was still so confused and drowned in all of this to see the truth. He was in my arms, he was safe, that all that really mattered, and everything else can wait for later.

I sighed heavily and just continued down the slope for almost a couple of hours more. During that time, Maren and Lou kept talking and teasing each other, Ace rarely intervened, and Zaire kept whining like a little brat.

Nyx remained silent for the rest of the ride. He was very tired and still wary of everything that happened. He laid back on my chest and I nuzzled his hair from time to time, just to remind him that I was there, I will always be there for him.

As soon as we made it to our beach, I found almost everyone there. Some were still looking around the island, but most of my crew was back already. Everyone kept talking to Nyx, saying how worried they were. Of course, most of those were just mocking him, but some meant it, like Baril who kept talking to him like a lost son or something. Others started their daily portion of teasing, like Nash and Ajax, and continued even with the fact that Nyx didn't answer any of them.

I found Izel in a complete mess. She was obviously crying, which was very unlike her. Locks of her once very long hair were scattered beside her, and some of her clothes were torn. Nash and Yeagar obviously did their job well trying to get her to talk. She threw herself at my feet as soon as I landed begging for mercy, and she went and did the same for Nyx! Which was actually a smart move.

Nash believed she genuinely didn't know a thing about what happened, she only threatened to send Cherri back to her father. Apparently, Cherri's father sold her to Izel to cover his debts, so Izel menaced to toss her back to her father and ask for her money if she didn't sleep with me and make me pay her generously and 'shower her with gifts'.

Nyx kneeled and grabbed Izel's shoulders. He helped her stand and she gave him a pleading smile. Nyx didn't return it though, he looked at his hands that were still soiled with the slave's blood, then walked away. I sighed, then followed him after I gave a few orders for them to guard the camp well and make sure to keep an eye on the brat Zaire, who still whined about the scar that Nyx gave him.

"Nyx, wait! Where are you going??"

Syrvat

We were walking on the beach, a couple of minutes away from the camp. He halted as soon as he heard me, "I'm not going anywhere. I'm not I swear, I just......."

I stood beside him trying to decipher the look in his eyes. With the full moon and clear sky, I could see the mix of sadness and confusion that hovered around him like evil spirits.

"Agenor... Today I fucked up so badly! I'm so stupid!! I betrayed your trust... I put you in serious danger... I made my mom sick... and I...", he was facing the sea and looking at his hands in obvious denial, "I..... I killed a man! I took a human's life!!"

"No, treasure, you protected yourself!"

"But I didn't mean to kill him!! He kept attacking me and I was dodging all his hits, but when I stabbed him he was supposed to dodge that! He should've just... moved away as he should have!"

"That was a real fight, Nyx. You were able to avoid his spear because you trained hard almost every day. But he's not Ace, he was weaker and you beat him. You finished him before he could finish *you*"

I still saw doubt in his eyes so I continued, "I didn't get to you in time Nyx, and I'm sorry for that. But if you didn't take that fight seriously, he could've killed you! Do you want that to happen?"

He shook his head cutely like a little child discovering death for the first time. I held his hands in mine and he tried to pull them back while mumbling, "th-the blood!"

I chuckled and held his hands assertively, "I'd give up anything to see you safe, Nyx. If it's the life of someone else, so be it, I don't fucking care about any of them, I only care about you"

He took a brief moment to think then his eyes lifted to meet mine, "You weren't late"

"What?"

"You said you didn't get to me in time, that's not true. I could only win because Zaire sent the second guard away when we heard the screams from inside the cave"

That was a tiny bit of information that actually filled my heart, "Well, I want to hear details about how you managed to get your new sword. You know how much I love to watch your spectacles, and this will be the first one with you sober, I think"

He smiled, then added, "Actually... I stole the torch first, and Zaire's cloak caught fire so I was able to take the sword"

My eyes widened at that, "You... You set his clothes on fire??!"

He nodded and I looked into his deep eyes; the doubt and fatigue still swarmed, but there was a kindle of excitement that wanted to impress me, and fuck did it work

I leaned in and met his lips with mine. I kissed him wildly, unable to slow down. I kept pushing to kiss him more and ended up laying on top of him, with the tides dangerously close, reaching to soak us. I sucked his lips and nipped on his tongue.

Once he was panting, I allowed him to breathe, but remained on top of him, covering his body with mine.

I pulled back and propped myself on my elbows to take in his beautiful eyes that I could never get enough of. He looked at me appreciatively and said, "Thank you for coming to get me. I don't know what could've happened if..."

I nodded slightly, "Don't worry, I will always hunt you down, Nyx"

He chuckled and the sound drove me above the clouds. I gazed at him, a thought popping in my mind, "Your mother, she's not sick, Nyx"

"...... I know. I know it was a lie, it's just......."

"How about you send her another letter, will that make you feel better?"

His eyes widened with hope and appreciation, "Really!! I can do that??" I nodded and he continued, "Can I tell her to send me one too??"

I shook my head slowly, "Even if she did, you won't be here to receive it. We don't exactly sail on a schedule"

He nodded, "It's ok, I understand, just being able to tell her that I'm fine is really enough! But... How will she get the letter?"

"I'll look around town, I'll certainly find someone heading there, or somewhere close to Mila. I'll just pay him enough money to make sure he'd actually deliver the letter"

He lifted his head and met my lips again. His eyes twinkled and I knew from his voice that he was holding back his tears, "Thank you! Thank you so much, really!! I know I caused trouble today, but I'll be more careful I swear! I won't let you down ever again"

His honest words always had a huge weight on my heart. Even when he screws up, his sincerity strips me from every shred of anger. I brushed his hair with my fingers and contemplated his smiling lips.

It seemed like his worries will never stop in this endless night unless I found a way to occupy him. A moment later, he looked up at me with a frown, "Agenor, am I a killer now?"

I gaped at him for a second, then I laughed aloud. *I wasted more souls than I could remember and even I didn't call myself that!*

"No, love, you're not a killer. You can't be a killer with only two victims"

"One! Just one!!"

I smirked at him, "I was hit from first sight... *I am your first kill*"

The way his shoulder shrunk slightly, I could tell he was blushing. His shyness always had its adorable way with him. I ran my fingers through his, bringing his hands above his head, then I dipped my head in his neck, fighting the collar for his sweet flesh. The more I tasted him, the more I lusted for his body. I kissed my way down his chest and attacked his nipples. One by one, I nipped and sucked on them until he was a withering mess under my control. My eagerness traveled my body and always ended up in the same place; thickening my cock that ground on him and pushed him to harden. I moved one hand down and held him through his pants. He moaned as I caressed his full length, painfully and teasingly slowly with only the tips of my fingers. I bit hard on his bud and he shuddered underneath me, moaning loud while releasing his sweet milk in his pants.

He was panting heavily when he tried to pull his hands back from where I held them above his head. I strengthened my hold and leaned in to whisper in his ear:

"Tsk tsk tsk, I still haven't punished you for what you did today, Nyx. And I intend to take it nice and slow"

∞ ∞ ∞

Chapter 13 ~ My pet
∞ Ace's POV ∞

I pulled him to the side, "You don't have to entertain him, Maren"

"Leave me alone, Ace. It's not like I have Trixie to play with"

He yanked his arm from my hold and paced back to the circle of wolves around the fire.

I sighed.

The night didn't last long. It was already late when we reached the camp, and there were no whores to fuck. So aside from the sober guards, everyone drank their hearts out.

Even the damn prisoner! Somehow, with his hands tied behind his back, he managed to pull Maren into a drinking game. But, the way I see it, Maren just ended up serving the scum beer and cracking jokes to amuse him. They're all having fun together as if they forgot who Zaire was and what he almost did. Or maybe the fact that he's a slave merchant is what makes the mates interested in him.

"Good boy, Maren... You're a goood boy"

There it goes. Zaire is fucking drunk and even imprisoned he managed to score a servant.

And why the Fuck is Maren acting so happy with Zaire's praising??

I stood up and walked away. If I stayed any longer, I might punch Zaire myself! The Captain said to let things rest for the night and that he'll deal with everything tomorrow.

Aye, he wanted to stay by Nyx's side, even after I told him that Amos had disappeared from the camp.

I did send a couple to track him though, but the actual hunt will start in a few hours. He could hide under a mountain or sail far in the seas, Agenor will still find him. And the longer it takes, the more revengeful the devil will be.

I walked around the camp. It was a sleepless night anyway, might as well check on the ones on guard duty. But as I walked by and spoke to them, my eyes kept drifting back at the fire by the beach, at the middle of the camp; many were drinking and singing with their ugly voices, Maren was jumping around teasing his mates, and... *Fuck, he's laughing with Zaire again.*

It's not an unexpected behavior, actually. Maren is a very friendly person and he doesn't quite pick who to be friends with. Either he sees good in everyone he meets, or he doesn't give a shit, or he might simply be that stupid.

He's as mischievous as pirates come, but he's nice to be around. He likes to laugh, tease, make bets and trick people into his 'favor deals'... He genuinely likes whores, sometimes it feels like he likes them not just for the sex. He doesn't look down on them like most of us do, which always gains him many favors, going from a kiss on the cheek to a free fuck.

He's what... 15, I think? A brat, that's what he is. A monkey brat. The only kid that doesn't weep when he sees my sword, even when it's bloodies from taking a walk into once living people.

He's a brat who likes to talk back at me. Sometimes I swear it feels as if he's pushing to provoke me. But, I don't get easily provoked. He knows that, yet he never stops trying. Hell, even Lou never protests if I order him or give him chores! That monkey thinks he's somehow better than the crew when it comes to doing menial chores.

I watched as he squatted in front of Zaire and kept talking. He was probably telling a silly story since at one point, everyone by the fire, Zaire included, busted laughing.

I sighed again, heavily this time.

I can't remember when I started observing him, I mean, more than I did to every crewmember.

Actually... that's a lie. I know exactly when I started noticing his every move.

Shit, I really need to get drunk. Somehow, no matter what liquor I gulped, it doesn't feel like I'm doing it right in this endless night.

Despite the unjustified frustration, the sun always ends uprising.

I walked on the beach until I reached my Captain. Nyx was sitting beside him while he pretended to sleep.

"Morning" Nyx whispered before going back to watching the sea. I responded with the same, swallowing a comment about the dark bags under his eyes. He didn't sleep, it seemed. Either my dear monstrous Captain kept him awake all night, or he couldn't forget about his first kill.

"Someone's coming!"

Armpit stepped to my side while looking at the end of the long beach. I looked closer for a few seconds until I could see the moving silhouettes that were still quite far for now.

"Men," Armpit continued, "lots of men, and a horse!"

The smelly bastard had an eye sharper than a hawk. If I was ever forced to say something good about this stinky creature, it will be his strong sight. He stared more at the horizon, with his eyes that seemed like they wanted to pop out and escape his skinny face.

Nyx stood up and tried to see clearer. He had to wait a couple of minutes for it. That was also when the ones on guard duty noticed them and alerted the rest of the pirates, the awakened ones, anyway. One after the other, they joined us with their weapons in hand.

"Agenor, wake up" Nyx called for the Captain, "Get up! I know you're awake!!"

I chuckled when Nyx nudged him with his foot and the Captain only groaned. He turned to lie on his back this time, eyes still closed, ignoring all of us.

"Oh me Gods! A woman! A Fucking beautiful woman!! I'm not drunk, am I??"

The mates started to get agitated. Just mention a cunt and they'll howl to the moon.

Nyx stepped closer to Armpit and spoke in a low voice, still not grasping the fact that privacy was a legend in our life, "Euuum... Mern, can you see what their weapons are?" Then he lowered his voice even more, he should've known by now that the lower the voice, the more we'd tilt our heads to eavesdrop, "... Please tell me they're not iron spears...."

"Don't know about iron, but they're all spears alright! The ones on the sides have swords but in the middle they all carry spears"

Lou frowned, "Sides and middle? How many are they??"

"About two dozen"

Nash turned to Armpit with a smirk, "How many is there in a dozen, Armpit?"

"Euuuh... Too many! A dozen means too many"

"Heh! You don't even know how to count, you gross imp!"

Yeagar jumped on the chance to tease, "Oh let the imp be, Nash, you don't need to prove you're an asshole. We all know you can read, write, and count. We just don't know if you can do it correctly-"

"I'll prove it when I count the balls that will drop when I slice your dick!"

Yeagar grinned and his brother, Ajax, sighed and handed him a coin, "Fuck... Fiiiiine, you got him pissed, you win. The next opening will be mine"

Nash cussed and charged at them just when Lou pushed him back to prevent any ball cutting in this bloody hysterical morning. Nash's insults started pouring and the black brother's laughed. I ignored them when Maren whistled, "Feeeew, so many visitors. Good! I'm not drunk yet!"

When I looked back, he was holding Zaire's arm, who stood as one of us despite his hands that were still tied behind him.

"Why the Fuck are you moving the prisoner around?"

"Chill Ace, he just tagged along"

There. He's doing it again; talking to me but looking away! I'm not the only one who changed. Actually, I only changed because of that fucking behavior.

Zaire smirked at me, "Hey relax, I'm not going anywhere. Don't take your frustration on the cute pet"

Cute???

Pet????

I glared at him, and his smirk grew wider before he turned his sight to watch the approaching parade.

The noises grew louder, cheering for either Nash or the annoying brothers. Some were alarmed by the approaching guards, others excited to meet the woman that rode the black horse proudly.

"Oh, God... This can't be... They're slaves!! Those people wear the same outfit as Zaire's guards!!"

I looked closer to see that Nyx was right.

"A... Agenor...." He tried to wake him again, but Agenor had developed this new hobby where he liked to torment Nyx.

Some started accusing Zaire and asking him questions. The asshole ignored all of them. He actually didn't answer any of them until Maren asked him nonchalantly, "Are those folks yours, mate?"

Zaire smiled at him and answered calmly, "Yes. Sadly, those are my.... *folks*"

When they came quite close, we could all clearly see them: They were about thirty like Armpit said. The bigger ones held long big knives; their heads completely shaved, and every stomp sent the sand escaping the other way. A single horse strode in the middle, and on either side of it, few men walked less threateningly. Unlike the guards, these ones wore their hair long, and... Well, almost nothing else really; small pieces of clothes barely hung to their hips to hide their junk, and their skins glistered under the sun. Those were obviously sex slaves. Some of them carried about five small fancy looking boxes,

Behind the hose, another shadow walked very heavily. He was obviously the one setting the slow pace. I looked closer, he was covered with a cloth from head to toe, but you could see the unbelievingly heavy shackles that he dragged painfully in the sand. He was probably a new slave of hers or something.

All the slaves wore the same kind of collar and the same snake shape tattoo on their chests. They advanced slowly, very slowly, while surrounding the beautiful black horse. I raised my sight and a pair of mischievous green eyes decorated the illuminating face of the woman that elegantly rode the horse. Her shining blond hair fell on her right shoulder, above a very revealing white dress.

Zaire sighed soundly, "Watch out for your cocks everyone. The bottomless cunt is here"

When she was about twenty feet away, she raised her hand elegantly and all the slaves halted. She nudged the closest with her foot and he pulled the horse slowly forward. They stepped closer, and she took her time to walk her eyes on each one of us, eyes that were obviously used to sizing and picking men. Strangely, she never even paused on her brother. You could tell they were.... a close family.

Now, I watched the charade silently, but it was all developing with the cheers and the rudeness of the mates, who's tongues hanged out of their traps like parched wild animals.

After a long moment of observation, the woman's eyes set on Lou, "I guess you're the proud Captain of Martina?"

Nash scoffed, and for once I agreed with the tall infant. Lou smirked and pointed back towards the laying body on the beach. She looked at Agenor and hummed sexily, "Mmmhh... Even better...."

That one sentence set off about five howls among the starving mates.

"Looks like I came quite early. As soon as I heard, I ran to meet you, Captain Agenor. I didn't want to risk you sailing without.... *introducing you*..."

She said the last part suggestively while her waist ground slightly on the horse. Zaire was right, she was a total slut. A very beautiful one, though.

She waited a little, only an answer never came from Agenor, only the foul suggestions of the herd of animals that she was facing.

"May I speak with you in private, Captain? I have a very... *tempting offer*"

Again, despite her suggestive tone, Agenor didn't budge. And as much as I liked to stick around and watch, we had a rogue wolf to hunt, so I needed to help wrap this up.

"I guess that's a no for a private meeting," I said calmly, "why don't you explain the reason for this visit and get it over with?"

"Ace, am I right?"

I nodded and she smiled, "The second on Martina...", she walked her eyes on me from head to toe, then she added with her head tilted to the side, "I can prove to you that you don't always *come* second"

I hid a smirk while the whistles went crazy. Armpit couldn't take it anymore, he walked a couple of feet towards the horse and fell dramatically on his knees with his hands open and facing upwards, "Me Goddess! I've been waiting to meet you! Please have mercy on this poor soul, and Fuck me brains out!!"

She simply grinned and raised an eyebrow, then looked away completely ignoring the idiot goblin. Then she looked at me, "I am Enya, a slave merchant. And I am here to make a deal with your Captain, also...... get to know him better, I hope"

"Trying to cut a deal to free your brother?"

"Mmmm... It depends on how you see it. But before we waste time talking about meaningless things-"

"*Meaningless*??" Zaire scoffed, but his loving sister completely ignored him and continued, "I'd like to offer your Captain a peace offering"

"Peace offering? I didn't know we were at war. Not until you showed here with your guards anyway"

"Oh, these? Please don't misjudge my friendly visit, Ace. These are here to protect, not attack. You wouldn't imagine the number of men who want to put their hands on me, and these slaves are here to prevent them from doing so. The ugly ones, anyway"

"Fuck, I should've had a sister" Ajax cussed, and Yeagar nodded, "Aye," then he looked at Zaire in pure jealousy and shook his head, "Lucky bastard"

Enya smiled seductively. She winked at Ajax who grinned mischievously and licked his lips. Zaire only rolled his eyes. I was surprised he didn't lash out at his sister's dismissive attitude.

"You're saying you're not here for your brother?"

"My idiot sibling caused you trouble and made it look like we were enemies. I am here to remedy to that unfortunate accident." She sighed, obviously trying to earn sympathy, she didn't need to, she already had all the votes around, "I advised him not to do business with that old mountain goat, he delivered nothing but ugly slaves who were either sick or lacking a fucking limb. But he ignored my words and climbed a mountain full of rogues in the middle of the night anyway. He got what he deserved if you ask me"

"Fuck you!" Zaire yelled, and Enya smirked, "I'm planning to, little brother"

This was taking too much time. Agenor didn't seem interested in making deals with a slave merchant. He strangely never liked them. We weren't very different, we all ran aside from the laws, but slavery was something he wanted to stay away from.

I'm almost certain he still hasn't decided what to do with Zaire, but I believe that should wait after the hunting party.

"I'm afraid your trip will be cut short, Enya. I guess my Captain is just not interested"

She looked at Agenor in confusion; I guess she wasn't used to being ignored. That was understandable, I mean, who would?? She was a gorgeous slut, powerful, and... well, obviously open for a fuck. I bet even Agenor wouldn't have ignored her if they met a few months back.

"At least allow me to show you my gift"

She looked back and motioned for a couple of guards to step forward. He slaves approached slowly, dragging the chained covered man along with them. The man was obviously barely walking, he was hunched forward and each step looked like his last.

"I ran into someone who you might be interested in"

She reached her hand and uncovered the silhouette revealing a heavily chained pirate

"Amos!??"

We gasped and immediately unleashed our swords. There he was, beaten and bound with shackles, the traitor looked around him with nothing but hatred in his eyes. As soon as he saw us, he glared at us deeply, and when his eyes met Nyx, he started snarling at him like a wild animal.

"You fucking highborn!! You're an abomination! I should've killed you!! You want to be a pirate? You want to be a fucking Martina pirate?? Come! I'll give you a fight! I'll rip your throat and kill you with my bare hands!"

Startled, Nyx took a step back and watched with petrified eyes.

"You dare to talk, you disloyal rat! You betrayed your Captain!!" Lou took a step further and many did the same. Our anger was more than justified; Amos made a deal with the rogues and deceived a crewmember, and even though some might argue that Nyx isn't actually one of us, he still is the Captain's property, his most precious one obviously.

But no matter the anger we might be feeling, even Lou who was about to be punished for letting Nyx leave camp, there was one person who was the angriest and the most revengeful among us.

The devil was awake in a second. Agenor stood up, he glared at the helpless prey with eyes that could freeze hell. He stepped behind Nyx, and slowly reached and pulled out the dagger that rested under Nyx's shirt. Then he walked past him and towards the traitor.

Amos shook his head and groaned pleadingly. Looking back and forth between Agenor and Nyx, begging for mercy from the first and blaming the other, he thrashed around trying to escape the heavy shackles and managed to push the slave guards back. I immediately took their place and forced the unlucky bastard to stand still. I kicked his leg forcing him to fall on his knees and wait for his fate.

Agenor halted in front of Amos. He tilted his head to observe the fear that thrived in his eyes. Then, very slowly, he pushed the dagger into his heart, while observing his soul leaving his body.

The corpse fell with a loud thump on the sand. Pirates and slaves, everyone remained silent, as we contemplated the fate of those who betray the devil.

Agenor stepped back, but before he walked away, he kneeled down and put his hand on Amos's chest, soiling it with his blood. Then he turned around and approached Nyx. He put the dagger back in its scabbard around Nyx's waist, then raised his palm that dripped crimson fluid. He stared at Nyx's frightened eyes for a moment, then said jokingly with a calm voice, "So.... *am I a killer now?*"

I guess only Nyx understood that joke because a sad smile escaped him. He lifted his own hand and joined Agenor's, "I guess we both are", he said, trying to sound confident but his shaking voice failed him. Agenor chuckled, his free hand held Nyx's head from the back, bringing him to a small hug. We watched in silence as he caressed his hair gently.

"I appreciate the gift, Enya", Agenor said as he turned around to face the slave merchant who was still a bit nervous, "but if it's your brother you claim, I'm afraid you'll need to offer more"

Enya gathered her focus back, forcing her eyes to leave Nyx. Then she immediately called upon her killer smile, "I want to do business with you, Agenor"

"I'm afraid we sold all our weapons"

"Unlike my idiot brother, it is not weaponry that I seek. It's fancy jewelry."

"Jewelry?"

"Golden necklaces, expensive items... I'd like to expand my business and I have some very rich clients on a few guarded islands."

"I see... Well, you saved my crew a hunt, the least we can do is welcome you"

Enya's smile widened and she sounded surprised as she asked, "So we have a deal?"

"I do have expensive items that I think you might like. If you can pay for them, then we have a deal."

She smirked and motioned to one of her slaves with one finger, "Money is not a problem here, Captain", she said as the slave opened one of the small boxes and all our eyes widened at the sight of gold, "I heard you are loyal to those who never deceive you. The real gain for me here is our alliance"

I scoffed. *Alliance?* Her true aim is probably to spread the word that she does business with the devil. Many tried to lure Agenor into slavery but he stayed away from it. Now she gets to be the only slave merchant that makes deals with the Martina crew. Smart move, actually, rely a little on Agenor's fame to thrive her own business. But there was still one unsolved matter here.

"I guess the next thing you'll ask them to kill me?" Zaire said, too calm for someone who's actually facing death, or worse, torture.

Enya sighed and faked a pout, a cute one I might add, "I would love nothing more than to stop caring about you, little brother. You've been a pain in my ass since you woke me up from my deep sleep the day you were born. And to top it all, now you're taking control over all our slaves!! But, this weak sensitive heart of mine refuses to deliver you to death. SO," she turned to Agenor, "May I propose you show mercy to my idiot brother here and give him a chance to redeem himself?"

Agenor smirked, he always liked devious women, they amused him, "What do you have in mind?"

"Mmmm, I hate to admit it but if you kill him that might bother me. Yet if you simply set him free that will bother me for sure. Let's say... he sails with you for a while. He'll work to compensate for the trouble he caused both of us-"

"Are you **Fuckin** kidding me!!"

Zaire exploded at last, but his sister ignored him completely, "He fights well! You could test hi if you want. Just take him as a crewmember. He'll get to grow and become a man under your command. We set a specific time, a year maybe, and we meet for more business" She ended her argument with a wink, causing a wave of stupid grins to break among the crew.

She was actually putting her brother aside for a whole year in order to take over the business! I suddenly feel for the brat.

"Whoaaah, your sis is so smart! And hot!!"

Maren said admiringly and Zaire only scoffed and cursed under his breath.

Agenor looked at Zaire who actually took a step back at the weighting attention, then he nodded, "We might work something out"

"Wha-!!"

"Great!! Now, I was hoping to officially seal the deal with you, Captain"

Agenor chuckled at the suggestion. He reached and put his arm around Nyx's shoulder then pulled him to stand beside him, "It's too early to do business Enya, you're welcome to stay around as long as your guards behave. If my crew feels any threat, they'll slit all their throats in a second, yours and your brother's included." He paused watching the threat settle in Enya's eyes, then he continued, "Let's eat! I'm fucking starving. Oh, Ace, go bring some of the fancy things I have in my cabin, Enya here might want to take a look"

"Aye Captain. I'll also change the team on the ship, we didn't get to do that on time yesterday"

"Fuck, I forgot about them. J must be crying by now"

The pirates laughed. A couple of them carried the body away. They'll find a tree with a nice view to hang him on for a couple of days.

Enya sighed heavily while looking at Nyx, "I guess I won't be invited to your tent, Captain?"

Agenor smirked and looked at Nyx, who blushed a little. Enya finally surrendered, "Well then, permission to have fun with your crew, Captain?"

"Permission granted. Although that will be on your own risk, Enya"

She whipped her hair behind her seductively and turned her horse a little to face us:

"Well, who wants to fuck?"

And the howls broke again.

∞ ∞ ∞

As soon as the boat reached the shores, J jumped out and buried his face in the sand. After a dramatic display, he stood up and ran out of the camp towards the pleasure house, while yelling, "Celia! Your dickhead is back, me sweet cunt!!"

Agenor laughed and didn't even bother stopping him. He was busy feeding Nyx and trying to keep him smiling.

I took a tour around the camp, I put Agenor's boxes in his tent and found out that Enya already settled in another one. She had her slaves stand guard around the tent while she fucked whoever she pleased inside.

I walked closer and saw the black brothers standing in front of her tent, waiting. They didn't have their weapons on them, so I guessed that was the rule if they wanted to get to fuck the slut. They were grinning and Ajax rubbed his hands together mischievously. They were certainly preparing for something. At one point, they nodded at each other and both walked inside the tent. You could hear yells breaking free as soon as they did and I recognized who's voice it was: Nash. I laughed, the brothers managed to bother him even during his fuck time.

I looked around making sure everything was in order: the team guarding the ship was changed, we set more mates on sober duty because of all the visitors we have, we had enough food for the day, the hunting was canceled and the devil is sated. Enya paid for her slave's food and it didn't seem like any of them would be looking for trouble, as long as they could hear their mistress's satisfied high moans.

Only two playful wolves were missing. I asked where the hell Zaire was and one of the mates pointed at the forest, he said Zaire and Maren went to play a game or something.

I cussed and walked into the forest. I swear to the Gods if Zaire manages to escape I'll kick that monkey's ass myself before Agenor gets his turn!!

It didn't take long to find them, though. Zaire still had his hands tied behind his back, and he was leaning against a tree.

"Let me get this straight. You don't intend to escape at all?"

"For the hundredth time, NO. I'm not going to escape! We're going to be mates soon, right? Just take the fucking ties off, it's so damn uncomfortable"

"Mmmm... I don't get it. You should be fleeing with your tail between your legs by now. Do you even have any idea what kind of deal your sis got for you??"

"That fucking cunt, can you believe her??!! Sending me to live with fucking smelly pirates!!"

"Aye, they fucking smell a lot... But, aren't you scared? We're a pretty scary crew, ya know?"

Zaire smirked, "Who hasn't heard of the Martina and their cruelty. But no, I'm not scared. I'm probably not a pirate but I spent my whole life in black markets, and believe me, despite what you might think, slave merchants are way scarier that pirates"

"So you agree to the deal?"

"Do I have a choice? I'm afraid if I say no, your Captain might kill me. If by some miracle, he doesn't, then it's worse, my sister will! I'd rather wipe fuckin horse shit than give her the satisfaction! And have you seen what your Captain did to those who escape? That was pretty awesome. Kind of cool, actually. Clean kill, slow, cold, kind of boring but traditional... I miss those..."

"Great!! So you agree!! You'll see, mate, we'll be having lots of fun! We drink all we want, we party all night, and we raid a lot! And the stronger you are, the better share of the goods you'll get!"

Zaire sighed, "I don't really care about shares for now. I have a feeling stepping on your ship will be as boring as hell, but it will at least spare my head. I hate to admit it, but lately, I've been pissing the shit queen Enya a lot. She needs some time to forget that..."

"Aye, but you will need money, mate. For bets, favors, more food, better weapons... Always keep a couple of coins in your pocket, they might save your life"

Zaire chuckled and smiled at Maren, "You're wise for your age, kiddo"

Maren put his hands behind his head and grinned happily to the comment.

"You're cute... I usually pick cheerful boys like you to keep for my own pleasure"

"Aye, I'm handsome alright"

"You know...... the thing that's bothering me the most in this deal is the fact that you pirates never allow women onboard. BUT, if you and I could manage a deal, the trip might actually be bearable"

What the FUCK??

Maren arched an eyebrow, "Oh yeah? What kind of deal?"

"I want you. I will keep you as my personal pet."

"Your pet?? Heh, I'm not a slave, Zaire. I have one and only Captain I answer to!"

"And I won't keep you from obeying your Captain. But you can also obey me. You will serve for my pleasure and I'll take care of you: feed you, cloth you, protect you... If you're a good boy, I'll reward you. I might not be in a very advantageous situation right now, but you'll be surprised at how fast I can turn things to my favor. And if you disobey, I'll punish you. You should try it, you might actually beg for a punishment"

I waited for a smart-ass comeback, but it never came. Maren looked like he's actually intrigued by the idea. Zaire immediately caught on that and continued, "With an adorable pet like you, I might end up pampering you all the time." He moved away from the tree and closer to Maren, "Tell me, pet. Have you ever pleased other men?"

Maren nodded nonchalantly.

"How many?"
"Many"
"Fucks??"
"Blows"
Zaire smirked and continued with his questioning, "Did you enjoy it?"
"Only once"
My heartbeat picked up.
"You enjoyed it only once? Were all the others that ugly?"
"No. but I only offered once"
"I see. So you never enjoyed those you were forced to suck"
Maren shrugged like it was no big deal, which made my chest ache. I've never heard any specific details on Maren's past life, and I never pried. I usually don't give a Fuck about people other than Agenor, but somehow a tug in my heart claimed otherwise.
"How about you give it a try? As much as it sounds tempting, I'm not going to force you. Not now anyway. This is a deal, pet. Suck me, if we both like it, I'll keep you like mine"
Maren didn't answer. I tried to understand the look in his eyes but I couldn't; he was not happy nor mad, but he was considering the outrageous offer.
After a moment of silence, Zaire straightened his back and smirked, "On your knees, pet", he ordered with a commanding voice. And to my greatest shock, Maren's knees bent and he went to fall on the ground before him.

∞ ∞ ∞

"What are you doing here?"
"Ace??"
Maren stepped back and Zaire rolled his eyes and cursed under his breath. I grabbed his arm and pulled him out of the forest. I whistled for a couple of mates who came running and ordered them to keep him inside the camp under their watch.
"Not so fast, monkey. I need to talk to you"
I walked back into the forest, Maren dragging his feet behind me, nagging about me being bossy, how he didn't do anything wrong, and that he kept the prisoner safe.
When we reached a bit further, I turned around, grabbed his shirt and pushed him against a tree
"What the Fuck's wrong with you, Ace??"
"What the Fuck's wrong with *you*! Do you have any idea what deal you were going to make??"
His eyes widened and I could actually discern a hint of embarrassment, which was a first for Maren, "You heard that?"

"Aye. I heard. And I want to know what the FUCK you were thinking?"

"I....... That was just...... It's none of your business, Ace!"

"Are you fucking kidding me?? You were about to kneel for that jerk!! He's a **fucking** slave merchant, Maren! He's used to fucking and torturing people all day! You want to get yourself into that??"

His eyes blinked and he remained silent as he thought about what I said.

"And that's not all. If Agenor knows, he might kick you out for following someone else! And if other pirates heard, they might turn your life to hell!! Have you seen what happened to Nyx??"

I glared at him, and his brown eyes didn't leave mine. A moment later he mumbled, "I haven't thought about it that way..."

"Of course you haven't!"

He didn't retaliate for my scolding and just kept looking at me. I could see thoughts swarming in his head, but I couldn't catch his feelings.

I breathed trying to calm the fuck down. I was getting angry unusually fast. I didn't know what the fuck had gotten into me.

I toned my voice down, I wanted to pull away but I couldn't. So I surrendered to the question that kept pestering me, "Why did you tell someone like Zaire about your past?"

He looked surprised for a second, then he answered, "Because he asked"

It was as simple as that. With this monkey, everything seemed so simple.

"He did ask but he doesn't care, Maren"

This time he broke our eye contact and looked down while mumbling, "He looked like he might care"

"So what, you want to be his pet??"

"I..... I want to be... something... you know, like Nyx"

Nyx??

*So all he wanted was to be loved? But why did you go look for that with **Zaire**!!*

And I actually knew the answer to that: *Because he asked.*

I sighed, trying to remain calm, "You're not like Nyx, Maren"

The sudden sadness that invaded his eyes was too obvious to hide. He escaped my eyes again, "I know. You will never look at me the way you look at him..."

"What's that supposed to mean??"

"I see how you stare at him! I know you like him!"

I grabbed his curly hair and tilted his head back to force him to meet my gaze, "Are you fucking joking, right now!??"

He simply shrugged, "I won't say a thing, Ace. I know Agenor might be pissed like hell if he heard anything about it. I might be the youngest among you, but I don't stab my mates in the back"

"I do not like Nyx. Aye, he's different. Probably interesting. But I do not like him! I help him because he's important to Agenor"

He nodded. I waited for a protest but it never came. So I eased my grip on his hair. For once Maren didn't seem like he wanted to win a conversation. And that somehow made me feel bad.

"Is this about what happened last time??"

His eyes widened at the memory of the incident that we both never spoke of. And for the second time, the disappointment in his eyes was too obvious to conceal.

He shook his head slowly, "No, don't worry. I won't bother you anymore. It..... it was my fault. I should've known you wouldn't like it-"

"Who said I didn't like it?"

"That part was obvious, Ace. You practically ran away. I thought I might've had a chance but... I never thought you'd hate it that much"

I sighed. *Was that what he thought during the last couple weeks??*

"Maren. I was half-drunk. All I remember was my cock in your mouth and your head moving up and down my shaft. And the next thing I know, I'm coming all over your face. When you opened your eyes, you... you looked so lost! I even doubted that I forced you into that somehow"

"No! You didn't force me! I'm not a kid anymore, I can't be forced! I offered, because I wanted to"

I watched his eyes gain that familiar twinkle in them. His lips tugged into a hesitant smile as he asked, "If you didn't hate it... Did you enjoy it?"

"I did. So imagine my surprise the next day when you refuse to get down from your almighty tower, not even to eat!"

"I thought you hated me..."

A light smile took over my glaring, "Why would I hate you, Maren"

"Really? Good. Because I like you! I like you, Ace! And if you don't hate me, then I'll try to get you to like me! I'm pretty likable, you know? I'm charming and smart and funny and handsome! I'm very important!! I'm the Captain's right hand!"

Technically that's me, but ok.

I couldn't help the laugh that ran free, making his eyes glister with more joy, "I'm probably not very strong, but I'm very fast! I'm good with raids! And-"

"Are selling yourself to me, Maren?"

"Aye! Please buy me!!"

I chuckled at his delightful enthusiasm.

"So you're looking for a lover?"

"Aye... but it has to be you"

"Why me?"

"Because...... because you're brave and cool... you're boring sometimes but you still look handsome even when you annoy people with stupid chores"

I raised an eyebrow at that, trying to hide my amusement, and trying to keep his words from making my heart thump stronger than it already was.

I gazed at his big hopeful brown eyes, looking for fear or hesitation. And the only conclusion I came up with: This brat was more daring than I ever thought.

After a moment of gazing at each other, he moved away from the tree, then fell slowly on his knees, "I want to be your pet"

"What? Do you even know what that means??"

"It means that you'll care about me! You'll notice me! You'll let me touch you and you'll touch me, and I really want that!", he put his hands on my thighs, "please..."

A thousand 'no's ran around in my head, but a single 'yes' beat them all.

I ran my fingers in his curls and observed his eyes. He remained calm. He wasn't talking back or planning schemes. He wasn't joking and making bets. He actually meant that!

Are you kidding me? Maren, on his knees, silent and calm! He looked strangely very adorable... with his hopeful eyes that looked up at me pleadingly, with that hint of fear of being rejected.

"I have rules" I said sternly, and he immediately nodded, "I can do them!"

"First rule. I don't know how long this will be, but it will be secret for now. I don't want you to risk being in danger because of this"

"Secret. Done!"

"Second rule. You will be honest with me at all times. If there's something that bothers you or that you don't like, you will tell me without hesitation. Even if it was about breaking this, do you understand"

"Aye!"

His hands squeezed a little on my thighs sending a strong wave of pleasure to my groin. All the possible other rules flew off the deck for now, and I bit down on my lip to keep myself from showing any emotions.

I can't believe what the fuck was happening. And I was agreeing on this!! I should be in the camp right now, with all the slaves walking around. Instead, I couldn't pull myself away from this sight; Having Maren kneeling before me somehow felt very empowering. Looking deeper into his eager eyes, I could feel his need to get my acceptance. And that made him look even more beautiful.

"Tell me, what do you want to do?"

"I want to taste you again! And..."

"And?"

"I... I want you to tell me if you like it"

Fuck, last time I felt horrible for making him do that. I was fucking drunk, and as soon as I came, I walked away. I obviously should've said something...

I ran my thumb over his lower lip, his tongue hurried out to lick it. He sucked my thumb and the simple action made my cock harden.

I pulled my finger away, and he responded with an adorable pout.

"Untie my pants, Maren"

His eyes widened in surprise for a second, then he nodded and went to do as told. His hands hustled to tug the ties, and I noticed that he was shivering a little. I didn't know if it was out of excitement or fear of rejection, all I knew was that a clumsy Maren was very cute to watch.

As soon as the pants were undone, he pushed them down to my knees, and his eyes stared hungrily at my length.

"Put your hands behind your back and hold them together"

He looked confused for a moment. I raised a dissatisfied eyebrow and he immediately did as told. Silently, I might add.

Good. Very Fucking good.

"Use only your mouth"

As soon as I said that, his attention was brought back to my member. The first thing he did was unbelievingly arousing; he walked his nose slowly up and down my cock while breathing in my sent. And the way he kept doing it proved that he actually liked it. With an action as simple as that, my cock was already throbbing in eagerness to fuck his face.

I tried my best to keep myself in control and not urge him. Then his lips joined in, distributing small kisses all around my junk, sending butterflies in my groin.

His teeth bit slightly on the sensitive flesh beside my cock making me throw my head back and groan in heat. Fuck, he hasn't even sucked me yet and I'm leaking already!

I breathed to calm myself. When I looked down, a pair of brown devil eyes were staring at me. And when he noticed my breath that started coming out in puffs, his tongue ran along my cock from the hilt to the head, then his mouth immediately closed around me.

"Fuck... Maren..."

He sucked me in and out of his warm mouth, with his tongue playfully teasing the swollen head from time to time. The sounds that his mouth made felt incredibly erotic... My hands held his hair tightly, and soon I was moving my hips and fucking his mouth deeper and deeper. His moans grew louder and surpassed mine, while his ass wiggled cutely.

I pushed his head out, allowing him to breathe before I put my cock in his mouth again and reaching the back of his throat.

The more he needed to breathe, the more his mouth tightened around me. And I enjoyed keeping him there for a few seconds before releasing his head and letting him pant. After depriving him of air a little, I assumed he might rethink his position. Instead, his hands that he released a moment ago were gathered again behind his back, and he smiled while his chest heaved.

I smiled back at him and held his head again. He opened his mouth and leaned in to take my shaft in, this time he managed to actually take it all the Fuck inside, I couldn't wait any longer. My hips pounded his face while gaining in speed, I groaned deeply as I shoved all my cock in him over and over, until I released my loads in his mouth with in several strong thrusts.

I pulled back while I heaved, and looked down at Maren. He swallowed and my milk oozed out of his mouth, but his tongue ran to catch even more. I gazed at him, sincerely wondering how he could look that beautiful... He smiled gently and leaned in to kiss my cock. And I could swear my limp member was ready to go again.

"Time to go, Maren"

He smiled and nodded obediently. It was still unbelievable how the Fuck could he be so docile!!

He grabbed my pants and pulled them up, then he tied them nicely. When he stood up I was surprised at the wet smudge on his pants

"Did you come, Maren?"

His cheeks reddened for the first time as he answered, "...... twice"

I chuckled and leaned in taking his lips in mine. He froze for a couple of seconds then his hands hurried to hug me tight, almost desperately.

Fucking adorable monkey

∞ ∞ ∞

Chapter 14 ~ Blue ribbons

∞ *Agenor's POV* ∞

I took his hand and pulled him up with me as I stood, "I have something to show you"

"Show me?"

"Aye"

"What is it?"

I stepped over some mates who were drinking and eating around us. These mates were the ones refused by Enya or who had already fucked her.

I looked behind me quickly and I chuckled. It was amusing to watch the way Nyx walked around them, throwing apologies and hurrying to join my side.

"It's in my tent. Let's go"

He stumbled behind me when someone grabbed his foot, "Why the hurry Nyx? Ya ain't drunk yet!"

"No thank you. I've had enough"

"Ya need ta drink boy! I hear ya made quite the mess while we were stuck in the sea"

I groaned and turned around. *Can't these fuckers just leave him alone! I'm happy he's not facing danger being among them now, but I hate it when they're acting fucking friendly.*

And of course the others just have to join in, "Me Gods, if I were there, you wouldn't have stepped one foot outside the camp, storm-boy"

"Aye! I would've caught you! And I would've taught you a lesson on how to be a good pira-"

I stepped my foot on the pirate's back, forcing him to lean forward. He immediately let go of Nyx's foot and grinned back at me, then he handed me a jar with a colorful smile. I rolled my eyes and jerked my head for Nyx to follow me, which he did gladly.

"**Nyyyyx**!! Come help me carry this shit!!"

"Coming!"

"Hey! Where are you going??"

"Just a minute, please!" he said while running to help bail.

That fucking old man treats him like his own servant! It's so damn frustrating. I just need them to like him juuuust enough to not harm or bully him! Any more than that and it's too much. I mean he's fucking MINE! So just stop......... noticing him! Look at how beautiful he is... leaning down, being all cute and helpful, smiling to that ugly Orc while carrying a sack of potatoes. I tilted my head and sighed loudly... My Gods, that's such an adorable-

"Sweet ass"

I sighed again, "Yeah..." Then I suddenly came aware of the jerk beside me "What the fuck??"

"No worries! I've been told what happened to the last man who put his hands on him, and believe me, I value every inch of my body and don't want any of my limbs pinned to your mast"

I fumed trying to keep my calm, and I went back to watch my angel, "You better keep that in mind, Zaire. I probably warn my people before punishing them, but in your case, I don't think I'll have that kind of patience"

He smiled uncomfortably, "I get it. You could kill me, but you spared my life. And I know that has nothing to do with the deal that slut made with you. I mean, if you wanted to kill me, you would've done so back in the cave, right?"

"Don't be so sure, little slave merchant" Then I turned to face him. I towered over him and wore a devious smirk, "I was very tempted to kill you. But I thought using a sword or a dagger would be very unsuitable for your title. I'd maybe burn you slowly with a *torch*, since you looked so fond of fire"

He swallowed and tried to compose himself, "I... I wasn't really going to scar him back there-"

"Well, we'll never really know that, will we?"

"Captain, I truly didn't know I was buying Martina pirates!"

I chuckled. People might refer to him as a *Lord,* but he's just a brat, "And now, *Lord Zaire,* you get to be one of them"

He kept looking in my eyes and I could see the hint of fear hiding in his, "Captain, I want to know if you really intend on taking me with you"

I smiled, but that didn't seem to ease his worries. I reached behind my back. He flinched and his eyes narrowed, but at least he didn't escape.

So I got me a brave prick.

I pulled out my dagger and enjoyed his breathing getting hastier. I leaned in and with one swift movement, I cut the ties behind his back.

He grabbed his wrists and started caressing the red marks, looking confused as he did so.

"Aren't you afraid I might escape?"

"I don't get *afraid* easily, Zaire. You sure witnessed that yesterday"

"But-"

"I won't force you to follow me. If you're on the ship, then you need to be under my command. I need to know that I can count on you as part of my crew. Otherwise, I might as well just keep you as a prisoner and roast you when we're out of meat"

"Holy Fuck! Do you people do that??"

I smirked, "With your attitude, I'm really tempted"

He gazed at me for a moment, then smirked back, gaining his confidence this time, "You really are something, Captain Agenor. Let me guess: You let me go knowing very well that if I escape you will hunt me down, and seeing how my dear bitch-sis made you cancel your last hunt, I guess you'd be eager to jump into another one"

I smiled smugly; I couldn't have said it better myself.

"**So**," he continued, "I actually don't have that much of a choice. My hands are tied either way"

"It's good to know I'm not getting an empty-headed"

"I still have a request, though"

I arched an amused eyebrow at that, "You didn't just use the word *request*, did you?"

"Just hear me out. I'll *gladly* join your charming crew, Captain, but I'll need to bring five slaves along with me"

"Five slaves?"

"Yeah. Two men slaves, I'll get strong ones. They'll be there to serve me, of course, but they'll also help with the raids and stuff"

"I see... *raids and stuff*" I crossed my arms waiting for the rest of his *wishes* to fall upon me, "And the other three?"

"Sex slaves, of course! We could keep them in one of the cells down the hull. Now I know your code doesn't allow women on-board because the ship might get *cursed* or something," he said that while rolling his eyes, "But these are not women, they're sex slaves. It's different! And it will give your crew the chance to fuck and have fun"

I breathed in and out slowly to control my temper, "Let me get this straight. Not only you want to bring slaves to serve you, but you also want to turn my hull into a whorehouse?"

"Yes! Think of the money we'll make! Sure, it will be nothing compared to business on land, but still, that's the best we could get in the middle of the fucking sea"

I hid a smile. This brat was doing his best to profit of his fucked up situation. I didn't care for him at all but I'm starting to find him amusing.

"Zaire, let me say this once and for all. You'll be PROFOUNDLY HAPPY to join my crew. You WILL become a pirate; you will wipe the floors when told, you will clean the shit house when told. You will pick up a sword and raid on other ships when told. And everything you get will be brought to me, and only *I* will decide if you're worthy to get a share. I'm not going to start a sex slavery business on my ship, that has no **fucking** sense!! And the reason I don't allow women on-board is not only the pirate code, but also to prevent my men from slaughtering each other because it will always come down to 'who will fuck first'"

I meant to go on when I heard my Nyx laugh and I went back to watching him. Baril was apparently swearing at Tren, who kept grinning and provoking the old man.

Zaire sighed beside me, "Fuck… Fiiiine! I just wanted to make the sail slightly interesting"

"I frankly don't fucking care, Zaire. You could choke of boredom and I still wouldn't care"

He sighed again, and after a moment, I guess he surrendered. He joined me in watching the scene around Nyx. A moment later he asked like he couldn't wait to know, "So that dagger on his waist is actually the one you used on that pirate Ken??"

"Aye"

"And today on Amos… Smart warning"

I grinned and saw that Nyx had finished carrying what the fucking old man wanted. So I headed to my tent.

∞ ∞ ∞

He walked inside and halted at the sight of the boxes, "Where did all of this come from?"

I stepped in front of him and scooped him up. He yelped cutely and put his arms on my shoulders to keep himself from falling

I looked up at his beautiful eyes as I carried him, "I missed you"

He smiled, his hands went around my neck as he tried to hide his shyness, "We were together a minute ago"

I nuzzled his chest and murmured, "I should chain you again. This time I'll tie you to me"

His right hand pushed my hair back gently, "I'm already bound to you", and with that, he leaned in and kissed me slowly. I immediately pushed my tongue in his mouth and kissed him eagerly. His honeyed saliva that tasted so sweet coated my tongue and my lips, sending waves of fire echoing through my body. I slipped a hand to grope his ass without putting him down.

Taken by surprise, he jerked a little and his hand flew to rescue his cute butt, "I think this is enough for now"

"*Enough*! Are you kidding me? We haven't even started yet!"

"We're in the middle of the camp, Agenor, we can't-"

Ughghgh... this privacy thing is a serious cock block! I walked a couple of steps and lifted the opening of the tent looking around outside

"Are you crazy?? Put me down! People will see us!"

Ignored him and yelled at the first pirate passing by, "You!!"

"Captain?"

"You will stand where you are and make sure no one comes in here. If I see a head pocking inside my tent, I'll cut it along with yours"

"A-Aye Captain! No heads inside! Got it!!"

I walked back in, "There. Fucking alone at last"

He hit my shoulder in protest, "Do you have to be such a jerk?"

I smirked, "You love my attitude, admit it"

He laughed and wiggled to free himself, "You said you had something to show me or was that just a ruse?"

I grinned and put him down, I turned him around to face the piles of boxes, "See these new boxes?" he nodded so I continued, "They're for you"

"For me?"

"Aye. I bought you some things yesterday with the money I got from the weapons," and I just couldn't refrain from kicking in some guilt, "I was thinking only of you while you were scheming to flee my camp"

But it didn't really work, it seemed like his mind was occupied elsewhere, "Agenor?"

"Aye, love?"

"Why are all the boxes wrapped with blue ribbons?"

"You like it? I told the merchant to get me the most expensive ones. He had a couple of boxes with real silver embroideries. I was about to get those but I thought if the boxes were too expensive, those wolves might try to steal them and that would put your life in danger. So I went for the second best"

"Ok, but... blue silk ribbons?? Are you certain these boxes were made for gentlemen? If Raya was here I'm sure she would've claimed them right away"

I hid a laugh and occupied myself in distributing small kisses on his neck. I should've known that he'd notice that. Actually, when I started ordering for silk and cotton bed sheets, a nice mirror, and hair clips... the merchant thought I was buying the stuff for a woman. So when I asked about the boxes, he happily produced these. And I just found them very suited to my sweet angel

"Of course, they're made for men... just a little fancy"

"A little?" he eyed one of the boxes suspiciously, "Agenor that one has flower embroideries on the side!!"

I laughed loudly, "Are we going to talk more about the boxes? Because the reason I brought you here is to try the things I got you"

"Things? Like, clothes?"

"Aye, including *undergarment*"

His eyes lit with hope at the word *'undergarment'* and I could barely hold in my laugh.

I opened a couple of boxes after I loosened their ribbons, then I looked at him, "I want you to try everything on for me. Let's see if the size fits"

He stared at the piles of clothes in the open boxes, but didn't dare to reach for them, "Agenor... I... can't accept these, you know I don't have any m-"

"Don't. You're mine Nyx", I said as I grabbed the first thing my hand landed on and pulled it out for him, "I know how uncomfortable you are with the clothes you have now. We'll be heading further north in the next sail,"

His eyes widened in surprise to my words. I smiled and continued, "Winter will hit us in less than a couple of months, so I want you to have all the warm clothes you need. I got what I thought necessary, but I'll get you anything else you need. I can even take you with me to town tomorrow and you can get what you need yourself"

He seemed to have lost words. He didn't look the slightest comfortable to accepting something for free, but I wanted to change that. With me, I wanted him to whine, hope, and wish to have things. It felt like he wouldn't do it right away, but something inside me was eager for him to ask for things... anything.

"... Thank you" was all he could manage. It sounded more like an apology than an appreciation. I smiled and tugged his shirt off to give him another.

As soon as the shirt was off, he looked quite uncomfortable. He moved his arms to try and hide his torso, but I pulled them away. My heart tugged at the purplish marks that covered his ribs from the beating he got yesterday

"Sorry... I look awful..."

He tried to turn away and hide. I held his waist to keep him still and leaned down to kiss his ribs slowly.

"Still hurts?"

"No, I'm ok"

Of course, you'll say that. I kissed him again on the stomach and he flinched, "That tickles"

A grin tugged my lips as I kneeled down and started working my mouth on his stomach and lower belly. His cheeks reddened. The small giggles that escaped him made me laugh, and they enticed me to dive even lower. I pulled the sweet flesh of the area right above his groin between my teeth, and he moaned deeply and held my head. I grinned while I continued to nibble on his sensitive skin. My hands that were holding his waist dipped under his pants to grab his ass.

With my teeth, I tugged on his ties and freed his pants. Pushing them to fall on the sand, I slid my lips on his half-erect member enticing a shiver to run through his body. I tilted my head and kissed his cute balls. I sucked on them making him buckle his as cheeks. I pulled his nuts in my mouth and enjoyed his voice that started enchanting my name

I lifted my eyes, making sure not to miss any of his aroused faces, and with one go I took all his member in my mouth

"Fuck... God, Agenor!!....."

The way he suddenly cussed was unbelievingly erotic. It made me groan deeply, and it seemed to weaken his knees because they buckled and almost surrendered. I wasn't in a mood to let him rest, though. I kept him in place as he leaned on me for support.

He looked down at me with desperate aroused eyes and I wanted nothing but to disappear in his sea-blues.

"A... Agenor.... Agenor-Ah!"

I slipped a finger and the surprise caused his sweet member to thicken in my mouth. I closed my eyes and tightened my mouth more, I made sure to breathe through my nose because I certainly didn't want to let him go yet.

My middle finger dipped deeper causing his back to arch, and I started moving it faster and bobbing my head up to tease his swollen head, and down to his hilt. His breath sounded accelerated and his slit started drooling on my tongue. I pulled out of him just enough for me to coat two fingers with his pre, before sliding them both into his sweet ass. Escaping the pain from the sudden invasion, Nyx moaned and stood on the tips of his toes. The sounds of his voice and those of my mouth around him made my cock throb in my now uncomfortably tight pants.

With my fingers pushing roughly up his ass, and my mouth working down on his shaft, his hands curled into my hair and his body started shivering and preparing for release, "Agenor... I... I can't... I'm going to come... Agenor..."

And as much as I loooooved to let him do that, the devil inside me decide it was time to punish my sweet angel for his deeds.

I pulled both my mouth and my fingers out of him. A helpless whimper escaped him and he looked at me with lost confused eyes.

I smirked and ran my thumb on my lower lip to gather his precum, then I sucked it provokingly. Another pleading whimper escaped him, and he leaned in to catch my lips hungrily.

Slowly, I guided him to lay on his back and leaned on him to continue kissing him.

"Agenor... don't tease me... please"

I chuckled between kisses, "Beg Nyx, beg for more"

"Please, I can't... please let me come"

I reached for one of the blue silk ribbons that lay around the open boxes and tugged them, "First I need to punish you for making me worry about you"

"Agenor... I love you! Please let me come!!"

Oh, my Fucking Gods! It took everything in me not to pump him free right now!

"Shshsh... Don't move Nyx"

His breathing hasn't evened yet. His eyes drowned in euphoria as he looked at me trying to figure what I meant. But by the time he did, I had already finished.

I sat back and opened his legs wide on either side of me. I groaned and my own blood pumped harder in my veins at the sight of his cock, standing in full attention, wrapped into the blue silk ribbon.

"Oh God! What the hell-"

He moved to release his sweet member, but I pushed his hands away and raised a satisfied eyebrow at him, "Hands above your head, naughty angel"

My voice was low and commanding. His hands were slightly shaking as he lifted them and stretched them beautifully above his head, giving me an even better view.

I tugged on one end of the ribbon and he jolted, "Damn! Stop doing that!"

I laughed and made a second loop with the ribbon around his balls. Then I pulled both ends, to tighten it before securing a knot.

Nyx's back arched and his waist convulsed trying to adapt to the pressure caused to his erect member.

I watched as he went back and forth between pleading and cussing. I pushed his left leg further and he winced and begged to come once more. Instead of answering his plea, I bit on his toes and sucked on his sole. Unable to bare his arousal, his hand sneaked in to touch himself. I watched in awe as his hand moved up and down on his own cock, caressing and squeezing further precum out, "Agenor... please...", he begged with a voice torn between excitement and embarrassment.

I smiled at my angel and removed his hand, keeping it with mine and holding it on the sand. I sucked my way down his leg until I reached his thigh. I licked his tender flesh, and without breaking contact with his bewitching eyes, I bit down into his milky flesh. Nyx screamed in pain before he bit his own lip to keep himself from screaming even more. His erect member throbbed and his balls twitched in the ribbon. I kissed the hurt thigh, and Nyx immediately started gaining his breathing back. His eyes blamed me for a pain I was proud to cause. But before he could calm down, I went and bit down again on the same spot while sucking to reveal the most beautiful mark.

His chest heaving and his body coating with a thin layer of sweat, he begged for me with his sweet, desperate voice, "I'm sorry... please, I'm sorry..."

"And...?"

"P-Please let me come! I can't take it anymore; I beg of you!!"

"Oh, my sweet little angel"

I leaned in and head tilted forward to meet mine in a starving kiss. I tugged my pants open and aligned my cock on his ring. I teased his entry and felt it twitch in eagerness to open for me, "I want you Nyx, I want you so Fucking badly... Tell me... Tell me what you want"

"I want you in me... please, I-I need you inside me!"

The voice that was pushing me to tease him more and more faded in the frenzy of my need to fuck him. And my cock dove inside him impatiently, pushing further and further and refusing to back out. A loud moan accompanied my invasion, as he threw his head back on the sand to take in the intoxicating ecstasy that we both felt.

I paused for a moment to allow his insides to adapt to my size, and I resumed ravishing his sweet swollen lips. His hips moved on their own causing a wave of pride to raid on my heart. I let him ease me inside him deeper before I started slamming my hilt on his ass. His leaking pecker wept between our groins, and I popped myself on my elbows to be able to look down and watch his swollen head, crushed between us, oozing pre on the soft ribbon.

"Mmhhhm Agenor!!"

"Nyx! Oh, **Nyx**!! Fuck you feel so fucking good!"

"AGENOR! I-I can't... I'm going to come! Please!!"

"**Fuck**!!"

My insides burned as I slammed harder and harder inside him. Our moans grew louder and none of us cared to hold them anymore. Unable to hold it in any longer, I pulled the blue ribbon free, causing my sweet Nyx to immediately arch his back and scream his orgasm that came pouring out of him in thick loads reaching his chest. His ass tightened around me and squeezed me inside, causing my own orgasm to tear out through me and fill his insides with my cum.

We both dropped on the sand, heaving and enjoying the ride down from our high euphoria. I leaned on my side and pulled him closer to me

"Oh, God... What have you done to me..."

I laughed, both still fighting for even breaths, "I made you mine, Nyx. And I'll continue to make you mine over and over for the rest of our lives"

He leaned his head my way and placed a kiss on my lips, "I love you Agenor... I'm so glad you saved me"

My heart was overwhelmed by his words. For some reason, I felt like I truly needed to hear that. But my attitude got the best of me, so I smirked, "Which time are you talking about?"

"Each and every time"

He kissed me again and I pulled him even closer. Our chests pressed on each other and my body felt hot once more when his warm cum spread on my skin.

I pulled on the cum-soaked ribbon, sliding it out from between us.

"So I guess blue is your favorite color?"

I smiled looking at his mesmerizing eyes:
"It is now"

∞ ∞ ∞

Chapter 15 ~ Closer... please?

∞ Ace's POV ∞

We walked back to the camp. Maren was talking happily while he walked backward or jumped around me like the monkey that he is. The large grin tugging his lips was so cheerful, it was getting seriously contagious.

"... so I decided to sneak inside and see what's going on, you know? But Britt said we should do as the Captain said and just wait for orders. So I went to look around instead, and I saw that new whore, Cherri, she was out but they were still fucking her. She looked like shit! I went back and told Britt, and you what he said? He wanted to go and watch! What a pervert, right? I mean, we're all pirates and all, but he's a perverted pirate, and he's big! So he's a big pervert pirate! ....."

I zoned out of his ranting. I used to just shut him up and tell him to go away and do something useful. I don't know why I didn't want to do that right now. His babbling wasn't bugging me as much. I actually rather liked his voice filling the silence in my head.

Suddenly I was stopped by a mate, "Captain ain't want anyone in his tent"

"What?"

"The Captain ordered no one to go near his tent"

Of course, Maren got intrigued, "Why? What happened? What's he doing? Who's with him?"

"All I can say is that the Captain wants some privacy"

Maren grinned mischievously, "*Privacy* my ass, that's not our Captain, that's more like Nyx talking!"

I sighed and turned to leave, but Maren decided he wanted to know more immediately, so he put his hands around his mouth and started calling for his friend, "Nyxyyyy!! Come out! Let's play something!"

And when he got no response, he just kept calling, "Nyxyyy! Let's drink!! Hey! Nyyyyxyyy-"

"**What**!!" an angry Agenor emerged from his tent. The pirate beside us went rigid like a plank. But Maren just grinned and joined his hands behind his head, "Captain! Have you seen Nyx? I'm looking all over for him"

The Captain rolled his eyes and cursed under his breath, then reluctantly motioned for us to follow him inside.

Maren threw his fist in the air and gave me a victorious smug smile.

As we entered the tent, Agenor's face lit up a little. He was sitting on a pile of boxes and leaning back some others. He watches as Nyx slipped a shirt on.

"Nyxy!! Where were you mate?"

"Hi Maren, what do you think?"

I walked to the side and settled myself on another box while I watched Maren roaming around Nyx and satisfying his curiosity by looking in the boxes.

"Whoa mate! All these are yours??"

Nyx looked both uncomfortable and embarrassed to answer. He just nodded and glanced at Agenor.

"Hands off monkey!"

Agenor warned, Maren pulled his hands away from the boxes and grabbed another shirt that lay on the side, "Waw, you really are lucky"

"Try that one, Maren"

"Really??"

Agenor glared at Nyx who only shrugged. It was too late to save the shirt though, in one second, Maren was wearing the new one. After complimenting him, Nyx pulled out a long jacket and started putting it on.

"Why's everything blue??"

"That's a good question, Maren!"

"Heh, so weird mate"

Nyx nodded in agreement. I smirked at my Captain's silliness. I mean, a blue shirt is one thing, but blue pants, bed sheets, pillows, handkerchief... He refused to buy anything that wasn't either blue, black, or red. And I'm starting to think my Captain is developing a blue-fetish. *Heh, I wonder if such thing even exists!*

"Maren, did something happen?"

"Why?"

"You seem... happy" Nyx accused while tilting his head to see more of Maren's face, "Please don't tell me you were with that slave merchant lady!!"

"You mean Enya? Nah, I wasn't allowed even near her tent. Can you believe that? I was literally jumping up and down and waving for her to notice me, but she didn't even look at me!"

Nyx sighed in relief, "It's better this way, Maren"

"How is this better?? Did you see how long and blond her hair was! She's a nice piece! But she has monster taste, I mean she chose Yeagar over me! I've seen him looming around her tent with his brother waiting for his turn. Something's wrong with her alright"

"She's definitely a bit scary", Nyx admitted, and Maren agreed, "Aye, she's not like the other whores."

He went silent for a few seconds, then eased into another subject as he checked his body in the new shirt, "I've been looking around the camp for you, Nyx, and I happened to see Cherri"

Nyx turned to him with a frown, "Cherri?"

"Uh huh"

"Is.... she ok?"

"She's conscious now, but damn she looks like hell. Just yesterday she looked so beautiful and young! Now she looked like her soul had left her. She doesn't talk, she's just staring and scared of what will happen to her"

Nyx looked very pained. His eyes lowered and his tone changed to sadness, "She went through a lot, Maren. Those thieves, they... hurt her badly"

"Aye, and she's not even used to being a whore and all. I heard her father sold her to Izel to pay his debt and Izel threatened to beat her if she couldn't get into the Captain's pants. So when Amos came to her with a plan, she just went with it"

Nyx went silent and it obviously didn't please Agenor, "She got what she deserved."

He said that with such finality that Maren flinched and looked away, pretending to occupy himself with something else. No matter how cocky he acted, Maren could never meet Agenor's eyes when he was angry.

Nyx, on the other hand, seemed to have gotten a bit better at it, "Her life wasn't fair, nor was her punishment."

"Did you forget what she did to you??". Agenor sighed, then continued, "She got herself into this mess"

"Yes, what she did was definitely wrong. I just...... I thought-"

"What?? You thought that you could save that whore??"

"No. I thought *you* could. I mean... you're our Captain, right? I just thought... you would find a way to make things right"

The tension that was rising in the air dispersed in a second. Agenor looked surprised to hear Nyx relying on him. In a way, he was both asking him to forgive Cherri and probably even keep her safe.

Maren, who was eying the situation cautiously, slipped in a comment, "Aye! If someone could, then it's definitely our brave Captain!" and he dropped his pants then immediately slipped his slender legs into a new pair, "Are you kidding? Not even her father could help her now! Actually, if she goes back to him, he might kill her for getting in trouble with Izel"

Agenor sighed and rolled his eyes at Maren's scheme to help the whore, the scheme that was working perfectly because Nyx's eyes widened in horror when he imagined the slut's father killing her

"Agenor?" he said pleadingly. My dear Captain looked cornered. He ran a hand through his hair and breathed a reluctant, "Fine. I'll send the bitch back to Izel with a word not to harm her"

"Really!" The appreciation in Nyx's eyes slapped a smile on the Captain's face.

Maren grinned as if he was the one being saved. He should be proud; the monkey played his hand well and even got to save the whore

"The Captain is **Awesoooome**!! Isn't he, Nyx?"

"Yes... Yes, he is"

Agenor's chest grew wider with ego. He tugged on the jacket that Nyx was trying on, "Feels comfortable? I can get you another one if you want"

"Thank you, I think it fits"

Maren pulled another shirt on and took a couple of steps closer to stand in front of me. He put his hands on his hips and started showing me *'his'* new outfit, "What do you think? Handsome, right?"

I chuckled and walked my eyes on his body. A light blue shirt and black pants that looked the nicest he probably ever wore or touched.

The collar was open wide showing his upper chest and his white skin. He had a very nice built; not too skinny, nor very muscular. I haven't noticed before how... perfect his body was.

I lifted my eyes slowly until I met his. A hint of fear and doubt drifted behind his cheerful smile. It was as strange as amusing to see Maren afraid of someone's rejection.

I looked past him to see Agenor failing to keep his hands to himself, despite Nyx's blushes and hushed protests. I grabbed Maren's arm and pulled him slightly to the right, blocking my Captain from seeing me. Then I slid my hand under Maren's shirt.

He flinched and I shushed him. He bit his lip and straightened his back in obedience.

Fuck, something was just so alluring when he's willingly submitting.

My hand ran on his chest until I reached his nipple.

"No. sound." I whispered my order, and he sucked his lip between his teeth and nodded.

I played with his bud a little causing small shivers to travel his body. I pinched him hard and he was barely able to muffle his moan.

Nyx and Agenor were laughing about something, totally oblivious to the scene behind them.

I moved to play with his second nipple, enjoying his control slowly breaking. I didn't stop though. My rule was clear and simple: this was to remain private.

I didn't get what made him offer himself to me, but I certainly was not going to reject him. It was a very odd; me wanting or accepting to be with someone other than a paid fuck. But it also felt curiously natural to have Maren as...... *mine*.

"...A....Ace...." he whimpered almost inaudibly, and his hand moved to grab between his legs.

I smirked, "Third rule, Maren," I said with a calm, amused, yet very low voice, "You are not allowed to touch yourself unless given permission"

"Wha-??"

"Want to be mine?"

He nodded quickly and without hesitation.

"Then you follow my rules. Only *I* get to decide when your cock can be pleased"

He opened his mouth and his lips were shivering, but he didn't find words.

He looked so damn adorable! Torn between his cock's needs and my orders. But his hesitation didn't last long, a couple of seconds later his hand reluctantly moved away, leaving the bulge in his pants unattended.

I smiled at his docility. He made the right choice, "Good boy, Maren," I said while my fingers resumed playing with his nipple, "From now on, you are *mine*"

The happiness that invaded his eyes was interrupted by my fingers twisting his nipple hard. Suddenly his whole body tensed, and he shuddered despite his efforts to remain still.

And when the shivers were gone, a wave of cuteness hit his cheeks as he raised his eyes to meet mine and murmured, "s..... sorry..."

It took me a couple of seconds to notice the stain on his pants. I laughed lightly causing his eyes to lit up with happiness again.

My Gods, this monkey is a fast comer! My hand landed on his head and I caressed him. Like a cat, he leaned in for me to pat him more, "You're adorable, Maren"

His eyes widened in surprise as if a compliment was the last thing he had expected. I didn't blame him, I wasn't much of a talker, and compliments were even rarer for me. His blush grew more furious, making me eager to ignore every warning in my head and pursue him for real... make him fully mine...

Fuck, I'm already looking forward to hearing his whimpers and pushing him beyond his limits...

∞ Maren's POV ∞

OHMYGODS! OHMYGODS!!

My heartbeat pulsed so fast, I was afraid the Captain might hear it and screw things up for me.

Did you hear that? His voice was low but he said it like.... like he actually meant it!

He said *I was his*! He said I was *adorable*!! I preferred being called strong and handsome, but I'll take adorable!! Adorable is so fucking awesome!!

No, I'm not awesome, **He Is**!! And he wants me! Can you fucking believe it? **MEEE**!!

I swear to the Gods my knees were ready to buckle and kneel before him.

He looked at me and smirked.

"You spoiled the new pants", he murmured in an amused but damn sexy voice

My eyes widened as I remembered that these clothes weren't mine! Shit!! If Agenor orders me to give the pants back, he could find out something was wrong and... Ace might not like that at all!!

The last thing I need is to disappoint him right now. I WILL NOT MAKE HIM HATE ME!!

I looked back and saw Nyx glaring at Agenor with his arms crossed. Agenor was pushing something his way and Nyx was scoffing

"Just try it"

"I'm not wearing a woman's dress, Agenor!!"

Oooookeeeey... that is a weird conversation.

I took advantage of them being busy arguing over a... dark blue dress?? That would look nice on Trixie...

FOCUS! I shook my head and decide to beat it. I glanced at Ace, it looked like he understood what I wanted to do. He nodded and I sprinted out of the tent before Agenor could even bat his eyelashes.

I walked into the camp. I didn't want to talk to anyone, I didn't want to drink, I didn't want to play with Trixie... I just wanted to....... think?

Ok, that's new for me.

I walked towards the forest. My feet led me to where I was earlier with... him.

My heart was strangely beating fast. There was no one around, yet I could hear his voice loud and clear ringing in my ears:

'You are mine'

Oh, Gods... I'm shaking! I don't think my heart can take this much!!

I mean, can you blame me??

I've been watching that man way before I joined Martina. From the first time he raided on my ship, I watched him slay his way through my crew like a sexy God of death. No one could stand in his way! Not even that disgusting pirate that used to treat me like a slave, force his foot in my mouth, and shove his fingers inside me thinking he could make a whore out of an eleven-year-old.

One slash. One slash with his amazing Tashi ended an episode of misery for me.

So imagine my surprise when I learned that he was only second!! I immediately thought something was wrong with that, he should be nothing less than a Captain.

My life was spared on that raid. Some suggested they'd take me to serve the winning crew as a slave, but the real Captain, Agenor, refused. I didn't want to be a slave, but I wanted to go with them. I actually asked him to take me, but he refused to have a child as a crewmember.

I was jumping from one crew to the other, some of them threw me away, others were raided on and killed... I've met and dealt with more people that a scholar could count. None of them had an aura as cool and strong as the owner of that Tashi.

With every sail, people started forgetting about my name. I became 'windy'; the brat that shifted loyalty on every other heartbeat. But to me, that name also reminded me that I had survived a hundred hells that I sailed through.

It took another long couple of years before we could meet again. I had joined Captain Kier's crew. He despised the legendary Captain Agenor like hell, and his hatred made me even more fascinated by the devil's crew. So imagine my happiness when we were raided on by Martina!! Fate had us meet again and I just had to join them!

When I saw the black flag approaching the ship, I 'failed' to inform my Captain at the time. I just took a place upon the mast and watched in awe as the Martina crew invaded my ship.

When the raid had ended, I actually managed to be on Martina's deck. I thought I had sneaked in when no one noticed, but they actually just ignored the little brat who managed to swing a rope. Captain Agenor was amused that I managed to 'break through their lines'. I told him that I wanted to be part of his team, but for the second time, he declined. He ordered his crewmembers to back off and threw me back on the other deck, after telling me I should be thankful that I was still alive. That's when I realized that by stepping on his deck without invitation, I had actually risked walking the plank.

I reluctantly continued to serve Captain Kier who had lost his leg that day. He became meaner than usual and his revenge against Agenor haunted every breath he took. He sent for his brother, who had recently started his own pirate crew back then, and decided to, I quote, 'Wipe the devil's smirk and piss on his deck'.

It seems like the heavens were listening that day because sooner than we thought, we were face to face with the Martina crew yet again. Captain Kier decided he wasn't going to wait for his brother and fired the cannons.

Once the two ships were close enough, I could see the devil standing proudly on his deck, and just beside him... *his second...*

Something inside me wanted to be on that deck with them no matter what. So I did the first thing that came to my mind: If I was thrown back the other time, it was because I had nothing to offer! This was my last chance, I thought. I needed to land on Martina's deck with something to offer NO MATTER WHAT!

I sneaked into Kier's cabin and tried to break the lock of his gold box. Gold is the most expensive thing and it's the best winning card a living soul could get.

Before I knew it, the Martina had already invaded the ship and Kier was fleeing into his cabin to hide.

That moment was both blessed and cursed. Kier found me grabbing a handful of his gold. He charged at me and pushed me away. He hugged the large box and started ranting like a lunatic that he was going to kill me and that no one was going to take his gold away from him.

That moment, I understood why Agenor hadn't wanted me among them. The Martina was one of the strongest wolves roaming the seas, and they got their fame because they were no weaklings. They were strong and merciless, and that's how I needed to be.

I grabbed Kier's sword and without much hesitation, I plunged it into his back. I guess I had missed the heart because he dropped his gold and turned to charge at me. He started choking me, but the bleeding finished him before he could finish the job.

I was scared. I was terrified! I was 13, I was old enough to have seen dead bodies that could cover the sea. But this was a Captain, and he was my first kill.

I wasn't about to lose my chance though, someone was already knocking on the door very calmly, and I could hear Agenor calling for Kier to stop acting like a coward.

So I took the best chance that I got in life so far; I grabbed a handful of gold with my bloodied hand, and I opened the door.

I walked straight to Agenor and offered him the gold, "Your gold, Captain Agenor"

He raised an amused eyebrow and smirked. Lou looked inside the cabin and told him about Kier's death. Everyone looked at my bloodied clothes, and when their Captain laughed loud they all echoed.

I sneaked a look at Martina's second and smiled at him in victory. He didn't smile. He didn't look the kind to smile much, **He Was So Damn Cooool!! And!** He was looking at me!

And that's how I joined the Martina. If not for that I would've been killed like all the rest of Kier's crew. But no, once again, I survived. And **for The First Fucking Time!** I was in a better place than the one I left.

"Deep in thought. That's new"

I was startled and looked up to see those intense eyes pinning me. I hadn't realized I was sitting down. I stood and smiled widely, my mind going crazy trying to say something that he might find cool.

But after a moment of just grinning like an idiot, my mind was exhausting itself to say something... anything!!

"It's strange..."

"What's that?"

The ghost of a smile appeared on his lips, "You, being silent. Looking so dazed and confused... I like that"

Of course, when I heard that last part, my mind decided to provide the most unexpected thing:

"I Love You"

His eyes widened a little in surprise. I was a bit surprised myself, but when it left my lips, it somehow felt like the most natural thing in the world

"Ace, I'm not confused. I love you"

He gazed at me intensely for a silent moment. A moment that felt like it would decide about my fate and whether I was worthy of feeling happiness or not.

That moment ended when he leaned in and took my lips.

I happily drowned in the feeling. I moaned and stretched my legs to meet his lips more. He pushed me back on the tree, his hand held my curls and tilted my head back roughly. Feeling his strength, a wave of shivers traveled down my spine. My mind was no longer in control as it willingly dropped all weapons.

I moaned and opened my mouth to invite him in. Instead, he pulled back. I whimpered and looked at him pleadingly.

"How many times did you come today already?"

I talk about fucking and cocks all the time with the mates without feeling the least ashamed of it. Why is it that when he's looking at me, I feel like an excited girl having an orgasm for the first time!

"Maren?"

Oh, Gods... the way he says my name...

"I'm waiting for an answer here"

"Three! I... I came three times today..."

"Mmmm... Is three enough for the day? What do you think, Maren?"

Fuck! Keep talking... just call my name and it will be four...

"Nnnn!!" His hand pushed against my groin, making me close my eyes in pleasure. It felt so fucking amazing! The tingling in my stomach was spreading fast and my head felt lighter.

He chuckled with his deep manly voice, "You're grinding against my hand. Are you even aware of that?"

"I... I'm sorry... I can't stop..."

"Don't stop. I came here for you, Maren. I thought I'd show you what I meant when I said I'd be making you mine"

His hands tugged on the pants and they were immediately yanked down with a confident move. His fingers wrapped around my erect cock and I hissed at the intensity of the feeling, "Oh Gods! I think I'm going to come again!!"

He laughed lightly while his hand started pulling on my member. He started moving up and down, squeezing on my length and teasing its head. I looked in his eyes. That hint of playfulness that swam around his cool aura made me surrender.

As if he read my mind, he smirked, and that was the final blow for me; my whole body shuddered as I came in his hand.

"You came already??"

I hesitate to answer. It... it just happened! I couldn't control it!! Damn it

He gazed at me for a moment, searching for something in my eyes.

Shit, coming so fast... AGAIN! He must think I'm ridiculous! I hope not, I don't want him seeing me like that! I want him to enjoy being here... I want him to be happy with me...

".... Ace...."

My hesitation seemed to have gotten him out of his thinking. He used his foot to step on the pants that were looped around my ankles, then he grabbed my left thigh and lifted my leg up, releasing my foot from the pants.

I put my hands on his shoulder to keep my balance. He didn't set my leg down though, he stepped even closer and out chests were against each other. My heart beat very fast, and I swear if it could, my heart would've flipped me off and went to keep his heart company in his chest.

So imagine its reaction when Ace's cock pushed between my legs! It seemed like my heart had stopped for a second, and my back arched when I felt him poking against my groin through the fabric of his pants.

"What's wrong, monkey? Lost your breath already?"

He started working his waist against me. His hand pushed my leg even higher, gaining more access for his excited cock to rub against me.

"Please... your pants... I want you to touch me... Ace, I want you..."

He smirked calmly and retreated a little bit, "Be my guest"

I didn't wait to be invited twice. My hands ran to untie his pants and release his cock.

I looked at his size and my mouth watered when I remembered the events from earlier in the day. I bit my own lip as my hands started working on his length.

Fucking Gods... I would never have thought I'd do this willingly to another man! But he's not any man... he's the Tashi fighter, the cool pirate... *he's Ace*

And as if my breath could be any hastier, Ace leaned in and whispered in my ear, "What do want to do now, Maren?"

Fuck, I knew what I wanted. I knew what I wanted so fucking badly!! But I was afraid... I didn't want to be rejected... if I ask for it and he denies me, I... I don't know what I would do!

"I... I..."

His hand pushed a few curls of my hair back, and he said with a very confident voice:

"I want to fuck you, Maren. I'm going Fuck your brains out and this is the last chance I'm giving you to save yourself"

My heart swelled with happiness and relief, "I want you to! I don't want to be saved!!" I stretched my leg as far as I could until I was able to lead his huge swollen head to lie between my butt cheeks, "Please make me yours, Ace! Please Fuck me!!"

Ace groaned deeply and attacked my lips. His kiss was very rough, and to my surprise, I liked it. **I LOVED IT**!! And I wanted more with every bit of my being. So I tried to do the same, I tried to tug on his lips and suck on his tongue. But he was too dominating for me to have a chance, so I ended up surrendering even more, barely keeping my sanity with my overwhelmed feelings.

When he broke our kiss, I was breathing in puffs. He tilted his head and brushed his lips on my ear, then he whispered an order sexily, "Put me inside you"

I was shaking all over. It was everything: his voice, his eyes, his thickness in my hand, his order!!

I obeyed immediately. His shaft was laying under my groin and between my butt cheeks. With my fingers, I started pushing the swollen head into my hole.

I pushed him more against me, but it didn't work. I whimpered, "It... It won't get in... I want you inside me but...."

It felt so unfair! I wanted him so badly! And he FINALLY wants me too!! And it was an order!

I looked at him apologetically while still trying to get him inside me. My body was craving him so badly that I felt tingling in the back of my eyes.

His hand moved down and he grabbed the back of my neck with the other. He kept me pinned on the tree when he took hold of his own cock and with one thrust, he was squeezed inside me.

"**Fuck**... Maren... You're too fucking tight..."

My back arched and I cussed and winced in pain. He was big... Shit, he felt huge!!

His hand went back to holding my left leg up, and his right one lifted my chin so I was looking into his eyes, "You're ok?"

I managed a nod and couldn't keep my eyes away from his face. He looked in pain... I felt so damn proud to make him look so erotic! I mean, Trixie never said he could make such a hot face!! She said he always looked emotionless. This wasn't emotionless! This was a heart-melting seductive look...

"Maren"

"Uh huh?" I managed between breaths

"Are you a virgin??"

Before I knew it, my face was struck by a rainbow of colors

"No-I-I slept with... many-so many!"

"Was there a man among those?"

I shifted uncomfortably, which was a very wrong move because his cock moved inside me and it hurt so fucking bad. I hissed and arched my back only causing for more pain to spread.

He winced a little. His free hand traveled around my shoulders and brought me closer to him.

"Shshsh... calm down Maren, I'm doing my best to wait until your ass adapts to my size, but if you keep moving might as well I be the one who fucks you"

HE'S HUGGING ME!!

My arms were thrown to hug him back tightly. I hid my face in his shoulder, "Yes... I'm a virgin. But I can take it! I'm big and strong and I can take it!! Please don't let me go"

I did my best to stop moving. And thank the Gods he was holding my leg because my knees were shivering.

"I'm not letting you go, Maren"

I looked up at him to see a playful smile. He leaned in to lick a tear on my cheek that I hadn't known was there, "It's too late for you to escape now. You're already MINE"

His waist moved and his cock opened a deeper way inside me. I moaned as he thrust in me slowly but not so gently.

The pleasure hurt.

It hurt so fucking bad, but I wasn't even close to admitting that loudly. I didn't want him to stop. Never!!

He was finally with me! He was **Fucking Me! And We Were Hugging!!**

And despite what I said about trying not to come fast, my dick was once more pushed to the edge, as it exploded between us.

And I felt thankful to all the fates because that didn't make him mad. On the contrary, Ace groaned deeply and used his hand to gather my cum and wipe it on my lips. Then he bit on them hard and increased his pounding inside me.

I was a mewling mess between his arms, as he thrust in me faster and his cock stretched my insides painfully. In a couple of minutes, I was already hard again, and my member wept between our bellies.

We both moaned in unison and shuddered when our orgasms tore through both of us. I watched his hooded eyes as he sent his last rough pushes inside me, and filled me with his thick milk.

∞ ∞ ∞

Oh almighty Gods and Goddesses
Oh, devious devils and powerful spirits
THANK YOU ALL
If one day I'm going to die, take my soul after my Master, owner, and lover Fucks me.
Take me then and I promise never to come back and haunt my killer.

I laid on my side between his arms, his legs on either side of me as I kissed every inch of his bare chest

"Maren"

"Nnnn?"

"If you don't stop I might Fuck you again"

"I don't mind……", and I kept distributing kisses on his skin

He chuckled. Shit, I could come just from his chest vibrating like that...

His hand caressed my lower back, "Are you feeling ok?"

I looked up to meet his gorgeous eyes, "No, you're so cool it's making me go insane"

He smiled and kissed me on the lips, "Why do I have a feeling you'll be taking control sooner than I could imagine?"

I laughed and snuggled closer, "Hug me more, pleaaase"

I can't remember the last time someone hugged me other than the whores I paid and asked them to. So when his muscles tightened around me, I sighed in relief. I was so grateful that he didn't let go, it felt like he understood my need, and if I dare say, he also wanted to hug me closer.

His strength barely allowed me to breathe. And the strange thing, I wanted more. I didn't need to breathe, I needed to be smothered by his arms,

I needed to be beside my lover.

∞ ∞ ∞

Chapter 16 ~ Oreo

∞ Nyx's POV ∞

"Hey! Focus, boy! You'll have to do it this time! I'll show it to you one more time, then you'll be on your own from now on. GOT IT??"

At moments like these, I feel like a thirteen-year-old kid with an unsatisfied parent. I sighed and faked attention as I watched Baril tear another lamb leg with a stick and set it above the fire to roast. He leaned down to adjust the burning pieces of wood, and I took advantage of the moment to look at Agenor.

He was laughing, listening to some story that Maren was telling everyone. But the tiger's eyes were on me.

He's so handsome! Look at him, sitting on the sand, surrounded by his crew who tore their minds to come up with stories and comments that would make his lips twitch. But to me, he would smile so easily. I was so proud of such a little thing, it made me feel... special. And I loved the feeling more than anything in this world.

I owed him a lot. And beside my life, my love, now I owed him my clothes and my new leather boots. He also promised to take me for a tour around town tomorrow. He insisted I chose something to buy other than the piles of clothes and weird jewelry that he got me. It felt like I had taken a lot already, but I ended up asking for something after all; books. We don't know if we would find any interesting ones on Esme, but he promised he'd get me several ones by the time we sailed. See how sweet and loving he is? He even remembered about my mother and promised to send her a letter from me in a couple of days.

I LOVE THIS MAN SO MUCH!!

I smiled at him, just a little in order not to be caught by the others around us. He never cared what they thought, which was understandable, he wasn't the one they teased or bullied if they caught anything against him.

So, like always, I tried to be cautious with the way I act with him in public, but I ended up not noticing when Baril's face was inches away beside me, wearing an ugly scowl, "Am I keepin ya from something, boy?"

I got startled and saw that he had finished with what he was doing, so now it was my turn to cut the poor lamb's other leg and roast it. I couldn't help the frown that formed, I like meat and enjoy eating a nice roasted piece, but I don't exactly enjoy handling large pieces of bloodied flesh

"I... I'll get you more wood!!"

"Oh no, now you're going to-HEY! **Come back here**!!"

I turned on my heels and sprinted away to the end of the camp where we kept a pile of chopped wood. I had to walk by the herd of slaves and the spears still made me very uncomfortable.

I started gathering some pieces when I saw Nash walking out of the camp and towards the forest. He was stomping, to say the least, obviously very annoyed. He was breathing heavily, glaring forward, and holding his sword; UNLEASHED sword.

His hair was messy, his skin looked sweaty and reddish, almost as if he was training hard. At the thought I remembered that he was with that slave merchant lady, Enya, I think. I felt embarrassed knowing about his activities.

I wasn't the only one, everyone heard their screams at one point or the other. But I didn't get why he was so angry if he was spending what pirates would consider as a very good time.

I hesitated to follow him. I didn't have exactly a good record with following people to the forest, so I stood my ground. He seemed to notice me though from the corner of his eye. He glanced my way, and when he did, I instantly froze.

He was crying.

The cocky bastard who always teased and bullied almost everyone around him...

The narcissistic pirate who thought the only existing being worthy of his respect was his Captain, Agenor, and deemed all the rest lower...

He was crying.

I wasn't estranged of the casual overwhelming emotions that led me, a man, to shed a few tears, but...... Nash wasn't like me

I always hated his smirks and his teasing. But I admit I preferred seeing him smile, even if it was for a smug joke that Lou threw my way and that he jumped in to have some fun at my expense.

The situation felt very weird. And it got even weirder when I saw Ajax and Yeagar head towards the fire on the other side of the camp; Ajax was laughing and smiling widely with a hand squeezing on his brother's shoulder, while Yeagar kept glancing very uncomfortably towards the silhouette disappearing into the forest.

If I stayed any longer, I'll be having a very angry Baril scolding me not so gently. I tore my eyes away from the trees aligning the forest and walked back towards the fire that was blooming beside the ring of rude pirates.

I looked at the brothers as they reached their mates. Some congratulated them for sleeping with the 'Queen of sluts', referring to Enya, and the others praised the way they stole Nash's fuck-time.

The brothers were both laughing and taking the compliments in stride. But again, Yeagar looked bothered and, unlike his younger brother, he remained silent.

I didn't really get what was going on anymore. I mean, I spent a lot of time during the last few months learning about my mates' personalities and the weights of power that reined the Martina. Everyone found the black brothers daring in the way they continuously teased the 'untouchable' Nash. But I always thought they were actually friends underneath that rudeness. Now I wasn't sure anymore.

And that wasn't all! I looked at Maren who was coming back from Agenor's tent with his wine. Ace had just said the word and Maren jumped to bring the Captain's drink.

I know, Maren admires his Captain a lot, but he never liked chores of any kind. And he never obeyed Ace without putting a fight!

Yes, look! I'm not the only one who finds it strange! Even Agenor is raising an eyebrow when Maren poured the wine to Ace BEFORE serving his Captain or even asking for permission to do so!

My eyes accidentally met Zaire's. He immediately winked at me succeeding in sending a chill of fear riding my skin.

I sighed. I don't know what was happening in this crew anymore.

∞ *Nash's POV (earlier during the day)* ∞

"OH! OH! OH! OH! OH! YES! MORE! FUCK ME MORE!"

"Yeah, oh fuck, you're so fucking horny... I'll give you more... I'll fucking tear you open... Yeah... Yeah, baby, your cunt is so-FUCKING BLACK ASSHOLES!! Get the Fuck out or I'll shove your dicks in your ears and-HEY! You fucking deaf cocks!! Are you the FUCK SLOW?? Can't you see I'm Fucking busy!! **I'm Literally Fucking!!**"

"Oh, don't stop! Move, damn it!!"

"Wha-??"

The slut whined and started humping her cunt on me. I wanted nothing more than to meet her moves and thrust harder inside her mossy cleft. But I couldn't help my boner that limped the instant those fucking-motherless-cursed-useless-assholes walked into the tent

"Sons of a whore! Get the Fuck out or-"

"Oh relax Nash" Ajax interrupted me, and of course, his fucking brother continued on his behalf, "We were invited in"

I frowned questioningly until Ajax leaned down and kissed Enya on the lips.

What the fuck!! I haven't done that with her yet, and she's kissing that piece of shit without any questions asked??

"What in the Fucking hell do you mean by '*invited*'?? Enya, what the hell? Hey! **Enyaaaaaaa!!**"

The fucking whore completely ignored me!! She was already busy kissing Ajax who kneeled on my right, and she was moaning with her tongue pushing its way down his throat while still straddling ME and grinding her clit around my cock!!

*My now **fucking limp cock**!!*

I started cussing and moving my waist around trying to disturb their kissing and almost succeeding in throwing her off me. The fucking son of bitch smiled in an amused way as he pulled away from the slut's demanding lips and smirked so fucking deviously:

"I'm actually stunned; I see you managed to tie him up." Then he added as if he was telling a not so embarrassing piece of information, "Did you know that no whore had ever managed to do that? The poor souls only got tied up and even left alone bound to some tree after he was done fucking them"

The fallen woman's face lit up with amusement. They both turned to look at me, then she ground her waist harder on me, "mmmm... I didn't know he was such a naughty, naughty pirate. He didn't put much of a fight to *my* demands"

I was about to curse them when Yeagar pulled my pants further down and under my knees, then he positioned himself between my legs. I immediately started swearing and kicking his ribs and sides the best I could with my knees, but the fucking load of muscles didn't seem to feel a thing.

He put his hands around the cunt that was now slipping her tongue down Ajax's pit once more. Then Yeagar grabbed her tits, "No one dares say no to you, princess"

"mmmhhh... I prefer Mistress"

"Hehe", the fucking younger black shit giggled, "I like that... *Mistress*" and she bit on his lips and dominated the kiss once again.

Yeagar's hands slipped from the whore's tits to her waist. Then his hands disappeared and I felt them grabbing my legs and pulling them over his, only to end up resting on my thighs. My Fucking Naked Thighs!!

"Don't you Fucking touch me, you motherless shithead!! I swear I'm going to gut you like a fish and feed your entrails to your asshole broth-"

I suddenly lost EVERY. FUCKING. WORD.

That dickhead Yeagar! Actually, it was his Fucking fingers! He was CARESSING my thighs with his fucking huge fingers!!

The younger prick was biting Enya's lips out of her face. And the older dick was sucking on her neck and placing kisses along her shoulder.

I couldn't see the pair of hands that I yearned to cut and feed to the sharks! Those fucking hands that were making me shiver by drawing teasing circles on my skin!!

But the worst news was the fucking tingles that were relentlessly sneaking to my groin.

A moment later, when Enya moaned in satisfaction and ground her waist on me again, I came aware of my own cock starting to get erect once more. The last Fucking thing I needed was to get hard in the presence of these two airheaded morons. And my cock being affected by.... some thigh tickling!?? What am I? A FUCKING HORNY TWINK??

I was boiling with anger already, so I took over bashing them with insults. I yelled my brains out for these sons of bitches and the slut to fucking stop making out while having my cock up her cunt. I cussed for them to leave and to untie me and to go fuck sheep and to die and to **Fucking Stop Ignoring Me!!**

"Ughghgh! Shut him up! His foul mouth is irritating me!"

"Aye Aye Mistress"

"Wha-What are you doing? Don't you fucking touch me! Ajax you fucking asshole son of a whore!!"

"Shshshsh... I'm just going to make you a little more enjoyable and much, much less annoying"

When Ajax said that, he was reaching in his pocket. When he pulled out a black handkerchief, I started shaking my head, "Don't you fucking dare! Yeagar! Call your fucking brother back! Yeagar, YEAGAR!"

I struggled but ended up having the piece of cloth tied around my mouth. Can you believe these fucking goat shits!

It didn't stop me from throwing their way every fucking insult a pirate knew, even if they ended up like colorful angry moans

"Nnn... Nnnnnn!"

"Better?" The asshole asked the slut, who slipped her hand in his pants and grabbed him, "mmm... Much better..."

Ajax untied his pants and lowered them to give the shrewd witch more access. She licked her own lips at the sight of his enormous black junk and put her white slender fingers around him.

I was now breathing in puffs already. And I watched those beautiful white hands slide up and down his cock making it harder by the second. The contrast of colors looked so beautiful, and it didn't help that he was moaning in pleasure with his head thrown back and his lips releasing a cuss after the other.

I was getting uncomfortable.

I was uncomfortable since these two bastards came inside the tent- No, scratch that. It was since they stepped on Martina!!

But right now it was another kind of uncomfortable. The kind that was making me heave and watch a fucking thick black cock that was getting my shaft harder

And the slut knows it because she can feel my erection harden inside her cunt and she's fucking smirking at me!!

Fuck, FUCK!! Kill me now!! And it didn't fucking help when the younger jerk put his left hand on my chest and started moving it around and touching my abs and shoulders while moaning.

I was so overwhelmed with confusion and anger that I almost forgot about Yeagar as I got used to his fingers drawing circles on my inner thighs. But now his hands moved to my ass. And he was pushing me upward to fuck Enya! The slut seemed to like it and asked for more, which he did by grabbing harder on my ass cheeks and moving my ass higher!

I glared, cursed, threatened! Nothing seemed to work! It only fueled their excitement and widened their smirks.

I felt the passion rise in me. I hated this humiliating pleasure in every way, but it still tore through me, eventually making me burst to relieve my cock inside the warm cold-bitch's cunt.

I fell limp, heaving and trying to catch my breath. But I haven't even settled from the euphoric feeling when I felt hot liquid coat my stomach and chest. I looked down only to see-

That fucking Ajax released his cock milk on me!!

I was fucking fuming like a bull! I thrashed and glared at the brothers that were immensely enjoying my misery. The young turd even dared to spread his cum further on my chest and started rubbing my nipples with his it!

I tried to avoid his hands, but every time I forced him to release my nipples, he came back to grab them harder.

Enya kept complementing the brothers and enticing them to play more with her slutty mouth. They glanced at each other and smirked as she leaned over me and started licking Ajax's cum off my chest.

I was mad. I was fucking furious, but at the same time, I watched her tongue as it flicked the white fluid off my chest, then she lifted her head to show me her tongue dripping with the thick white that came from a thick black cock. *Fuck that was fucking sexy*

I was pulled out of my daze with the feeling of my cock being painfully crushed when Enya's hole became suddenly unbelievingly tight. We both moaned as we were taken by surprise, and it took me a moment to realize that it was that fucking Yeagar's doing.

The bastard was pushing his rod inside Enya's cunt!! **While I Was Still There!!**

I groaned in pain and squirmed, trying to release myself from the whore, but the slut wouldn't take a hint, she pursed her lips and closed her eyes while she moaned like a cat in heat, feeling the thick cock that was sliding agonizingly slow, stretching her insides, and crushing my half limp prick in the process. And the even more frustrating fact was that I knew he was taking more space inside the bitch than I was! It felt like he was **fucking pushing me into a corner in there!!**

And just when I thought I've seen every possible shit today, I felt a couple of fingers forcing their way in my own back door.

My eyes opened wide, and I glared daggers at Ajax who was watching my face while biting on his lower lip. I shook my head, trying to make him understand that if he went any further I'd cut his balls and make him-

Uhghghgh...

His fingers were forced inside me so very painfully... the bastard used both his index and middle finger without even considering that his sausages could tear me up!

By now my body was shaking with every possible feeling. I writhed as Ajax's fingers moved inside me sending a very painful strike to my spine. I tried to breathe past the pain. But it wasn't easy to take a full breath with Yeagar that was **still pushing his huge fucking cock inside the shared cunt!!**

I stopped moving. I fucking surrendered. Aye. Let them fucking think that they won. I better give up now than let the small unfamiliar sparkles that started to weight on my heart develop further.

And it worked. The brothers looked at each other questioningly and then to me. Enya was squirming like a bitch and grinding her waist around us. She was asking for more and went to sit straight to take over, but Yeagar pushed her down with a dominating hand on her lower back, making her moan sexily in approval.

She grabbed Ajax's prick with her left hand and started yanking him again. Then she wiggled her ass asking for more, but the brothers didn't seem to notice her trials. They kept watching me, and for a split of a second, I almost allowed myself to think that they were worried about me.

After gazing at me for a moment, Ajax leaned over Enya's head aiming for mine. I sincerely feared what else he might fucking do? How else could he torture and humiliate me??

And my heart lurched when he placed a kiss on my forehead.

I blinked twice. I tried to gather my wit and find that rude devious brain of mine that would suggest schemes and ways to take revenge.

But... My stunned mind couldn't come up with anything. I dared to move my gaze to meet Yeagar's. He smiled gently at me.

He looked so... handsome... with his broad shoulders... those tattoos on his arms and around his belly button...

his hands holding my thighs... his black fingers digging into my white flesh...

He was beautiful...

My ass switched drawing my eyes away from Yeagar, following the heavily tattooed strong arm that was toying with my entry, only to meet a smug smirk and a pair of mischievous knowing eyes.

Ajax's smirk grew wider and I knew he was up to something. He pulled his fingers almost completely out of me, only to push them back inside quickly. My back arched causing both myself and Enya to moan loudly. His finger dove so roughly inside me that it made me involuntarily thrust into the slut's cunt. I winced and looked to see Yeagar still gazing at me, with the same pained expression as I had.

After a couple of minutes, he couldn't keep still any longer. It was already getting more painful as I was becoming harder because of the younger devil working my ass.

Yeagar grabbed Enya's hips firmly and started thrusting his cock with force.

I pulled on the restrains hard trying to escape the ripping feeling of ecstasy that was starting to drive me crazy. But with my cock inside the slut and Yeagar's tight grip on her hips, every time I was pushed backward, I was kept from actually moving or pulling my cock out.

I bit hard on the cloth in my mouth, channeling all the pain and crazy feelings into it. My skin was coated in sweats and I heaved loudly.

I couldn't keep the moans anymore. Neither could Yeagar nor did Ajax shut his mouth or stop releasing the enticing sex talk that was supposedly meant for Enya, while he was biting his tongue and raising his smug eyebrow at me.

The pleasure was beyond what I have ever experienced, and my mind was mounting waves of intoxicating euphoria as the handsome brothers alternated their ways into me. I felt and watched them create a rhythm making me penetrated, either way, every second;

when the manly one pulled out, the devious brother pushed and stretched my ass further...

and when the playful one pulled his fingers out, the dominating brother thrust hard and made the friction between our embracing cocks unbearable...

The crazy rhythm was sending my mind into a frenzy. We were all moaning and groaning in ascending pleasure. The voice of Enya's hand wanking Ajax's cock using his own leaking cum right beside me was making it hard for me not to watch and get excited like a pervert.

And every time I forced myself to look away, I was caught in the trap of Yeagar's deep gaze that felt like it knew every bit of my soul.

The black brothers were groaning and cussing. They looked painfully on edge...

They looked fucking beautiful...

My release was so very close. I wasn't fucking holding back anymore. I was moaning louder than the fucking whore lying helplessly on my chest. And if not for the cloth around my mouth, I would've been howling like a fucking wolf!

The first to give up was the slut. Her insides squeezed harder on both our cocks. She released her warm cum and Yeagar pounded even harder inside her, taking advantage of the slippery liquid coating our cocks.

I held my own orgasm, I desperately wanted to watch them more, and feeling every noisy thrust that Yeagar was sending against my cock with that enchanting mix of lust and pain swarming in his eyes.

Ajax's fingers vibrated and twisted inside me, I watched him orgasm while his eyes were glued to me, and he sent every bit of his cum on Enya's body, while some reached my own chin. I groaned deeply at the erotic sight, unable to keep the hungry look that took over my face. And that seemed to set Yeagar off. He groaned as his thick cock pulsed heavily against mine, and I felt a second load of cum coat both our cocks inside the warm cunt.

Ajax fell by my side. He put an arm over Enya and his hand landed on my shoulder and held on to me. We were all heaving and breathing in puffs.

The first to speak was Enya. She was still out of breath, but it didn't keep her from complimenting *the pirates' ability to draw loads of pleasure out of her cunt*, as she said.

Yeagar was sitting back, watching us... or what felt like he was watching me. I took a last glance at his heaving chest and naked body before I turned my head to look away. Ajax strangely put his forehead on my shoulder. And the feeling that sneaked inside me from such simple contact made me realize what just happened.

I panicked. I kept silent and calm, though. I didn't have the strength to do anything anyway. My body was tired but... the problem wasn't my body...

Enya climbed off me and went to stick her lips to Ajax once more. The whore.

I didn't know what to do. I was now totally exposed and for once in my life that bothered me. And the fact that it did bother me was even more annoying!!

Luckily, Yeagar didn't forget about me, he stood up and crouched beside me and fondled with my ties. His dick was still hanging so at least I wasn't the only one naked. It didn't seem to bother him the same way it was bothering me, though.

As soon as the ties were gone, I was putting on my pants and out of the cursed tent. I made my way through the set of slaves that didn't seem the least phased by all the noises that they witnessed. One of them handed me my sword. I didn't even register my own moves until it was fully unleashed in my firm grip.

I wanted to be alone. I had to fucking think about this thing that keeps tugging inside my chest even after I came.

So I stomped my way towards the forest looking for an answer to make this sickness go away... this thump that invaded my heart every time the thought of the color black came to mind.

∞ ∞ ∞

Chapter 17 ~ Hit the waves
∞ Nyx's POV ∞

"**Nyx! Nyx! Nyx! ...**"

My arm was shaking already. I need to end this stupid thing fast. God, why did I even agree to this?

" **Nyx! Nyx! Nyx! Nyx! Nyx! Nyx!**"...

Nope, I'm not that popular. It's just that they like to tease my opponent.

"You know, if you're not serious about this, at least pretend that you're trying", he said that while squeezing harder on my hand.

"I... I **am** trying actually" I smiled but ended up making an awkward pained grimace

"Heh, you call this trying? We've barely started and your arm is already- **why in the fuck's name are you all cheering for him!!??**"

"Becauuuse you're an asshole, Nash", "Aye", "An arrogant bastard!"...

Nash rolled his eyes as if he weren't fazed by all their remarks, but the pressure on my poor hand tells otherwise. I tried to hold my ground, though. It was all because of the real asshole, Lou. The jerk suggested this stupid arm wrestling challenge. I tried to pull away, but he declared me a coward in front of everyone.

I sighed. *Why in the name of God did I fall for that?*

"Haha!! I'll tell you why, Nash" *Uh-oh, not him, not now!* "Because it would be so fun if you were beaten by our pixie"

Nash's eyes narrowed, and before I could talk him back to reason, the back of my hand hit the large barrel with a loud thud.

Everyone laughed their hearts out. I pulled my arm to caress it and ease the pain, and I glared at Ajax, "Did you need to aggravate him like that?"

He raised a proud eyebrow and the smirk on his face contradicted his words, "I don't know what you're talking about"

I sighed and turned to leave. Assholes... I just thought maybe I'd test my strength a bit.

The tension between those two is so obvious! More correctly, the three of them, I mean, Yeagar is less asshole than his younger brother, but he also likes to set Nash off. If only Ajax kept his mouth shut, I'm certain I would've remained in the race longer!

I went to step down the stairs and away from the forecastle, but I was greeted by a wall. I raised my eyes to meet Lou's scheming eyes

"You want to play, do it with Nash. I'm done for the day"

"Ooooh? But the fun hasn't started yet! Come on, princess. One more round for the audience?"

I glared at him. He knows very well how much I hate to be called girly names! The others have stopped- ok, most of them have, but Lou is set on bullying me, "I'll pass on the honor, thank you"

"Hey!" Zaire called from the other side of the forecastle, leaning on the wheel and watching the show, "Need some help there? You just need to ask, cutie"

I rolled my eyes at his rudeness.

Why does everyone become a jerk when they're bored? And why am I the easy prey to tease around here!!

I went back to glaring at Lou to move away and let me go do something useful. He didn't budge, just kept staring with the hint of a smirk, waiting for me to get angry so he could earn a laugh. Sorry asshole, I'm used to your tricks by now.

"Nyx!"

"Yes?"

"Want to train? It's better than.... whatever you're doing over there"

I blushed when I realized I was too close to Lou and staring at each other for a moment now. So I pushed him away, and of course, that gave him a reason to laugh at me.

"I'll be ready in a few minutes, Ace!"

"Aye, and get my sword"

"Ok!"

I walked towards the cabin looking forward to it. I loved training with Ace. It has gotten much more interesting since Esme. He no longer just stands there bored.

Now he....... Well, he still holds his sword with just one hand, sometimes he doesn't even unleash it, he still wears that uninterested look as he'd rather do anything else than waste his time with me, he still drains me and slaps the back of my head to get me to concentrate more, I still spend most of the time getting back on my feet rather than actually fighting....... So, yeah... it is much better than before.

I felt my shoulders slump; who am I kidding? I'm as new as this as the day I stepped on this deck.

Syrvat

I opened the cabin's door and a comical sight welcomed me to wander further inside. Maren was busy, kneeling with a piece of coal in his hand while he sullied the wall facing the bed.

"Hey, Nyxy! Come here! Look!! Look what I wrote!"

His childish excitement made it impossible to resist smiling.

"Look! Tell me if it's correct!"

I moved closer to take a look at what he was drawing. A month ago I suggested teaching him how to read and write when I discovered that he never had the chance to learn. He laughed at me and dismissed me with a wave of his hand! But when I spoke of the matter again and Ace welcomed the idea, Maren became magically eager to learn. I wonder what happened to change his mind and the little fox refused to explain his change of heart.

I focused on the wall while I spoke, "You know Agenor doesn't like you writing on his walls inside his cabin"

"Nah it's ok. We'll clean it later"

We??

I tried to decipher his several attempts here and there. Then I focused on the one he was pointing to while grinning at me in anticipation.

I sighed, "I told you, Maren, I will not teach you how to write improper words!" I tried hard not to correct his mistake and hold it in, but in the end, I surrendered and blurted it out, "At least write it correctly, the word 'Ass' is written with double 's' "

"What? No! Open your eyes mate!!"

I frowned when I saw how angry he looked at me, "This is 'Ace' mate! Not ass! You're the ass!!"

My eyes widened at that, and I lifted my hands in the air to show him that I didn't mean it while holding myself from laughing, "Ok sorry! My bad Maren"

"Not cool, mate. Not cool"

"Don't be mad, why 'Ace' anyway?"

I knew I was prying, but I couldn't help it. Maren is being the same windy with everyone EXCEPT ACE!

I even thought Ace was holding something against him, which would make him do chores and be much more compliant to his orders. But whenever I asked, he would change the subject. Smartly, I might add.

"Why not your Captain's name?"

"Too long"

"My name?"

"Too complicated"

"Lou?"

He grinned, "Too asshole"

I laughed, " 'Ace' is written with a 'c' not 's'"

"Which one is that? The pregnant letter??"

"No, it's the half circle one"

"Ah! The bitten moon!"

"That's the one. Also, add an 'e' "

He grimaced when he failed to remember how to write it, so I gave a hint, "It's in 'Maren'"

"Oh! Yeah, I knew that!!"

I chuckled at his enthusiasm. It was hard making him remember the letters, especially when he kept whining about 'Why would we need so many', but then he started attaching hints to each letter to help him recognize them. I frankly wasn't comfortable with it at first, but then it actually looked like a clever way. Childish, but clever.

I let him try assembling the letters again and moved to one of my boxes to look for my black shirt, hoping it would give me more of a fighting aura with my training with Ace. Besides, I'm kind of fed up with the color blue. It's a nice color and all and I know Agenor prefers it, but almost everything I got is blue! He seriously needs to stop getting me blue stuff.

I removed my shirt when Maren called for me again, "Hey, is this correct? It's written like this, right? Right??"

"Yes, well done", I complimented him and he grinned widely in satisfaction, "Now, write a couple of times again so you wouldn't forget about it"

"AAAAAye!"

He went to focus on his writing again when he turned to ask me, "What're you doing?"

"I just changed my shirt. I'm going to train a little-"

"With Ace??"

"Yeah, I don't have the patience to face any of the others today. The last time I crossed sword with Yeagar I got beaten and laughed at! You're welcome to watch if you want"

"Yessss! Let's go!"

I grabbed my sword, or should I say Zaire's sword, "Wait, I need to go get his sword from the hull"

"I'll get it!"

"Maren, you don't have to-"

"Too late! I'm getting Tashi"

And he was out of the door in a split of a second. I laughed lightly, but when I turned and saw the mess on the wall my shoulders slumped, "Maren! You didn't clean the wall!"

Too late, I was stuck with the cleaning. He probably schemed this all along. I grabbed a cloth and drenched it with water. Then I kneeled, taking Maren's spot, and started rubbing the coal out.

When the door closed, I thought it was Maren getting back to help me clean his mess, "Maren, I'm only helping you a little-"

But a pair of strong arms went around me and a nose started fighting the collar for access to my neck, I couldn't help but shiver, "I didn't see you there, Agenor"

He sucked on my neck and grazed his teeth against the sensitive flesh, drawing a small moan out of me, "I missed you, my love"

"I missed you too"

"I'll tell that monkey to stay away and stop bothering you"

"Please don't, he's not a bother at all"

"He is when he makes you clean the ship's walls behind him because of his new hobby"

"I'm just glad he's into learning how to read and write. He thinks he's a pirate so he wouldn't need such things, but knowledge comes very handy once you acquire it"

He nipped on my ear while talking, "He should do that away from my cabin"

I turned in his arms, making sure not to soil him with the cloth in my hand, "Please bear with him. He doesn't like to say it, but when he's out there your dear subordinates keep teasing him and criticizing his handwriting or the fact that he still forgets some letters. Here he feels safer, so it's your crew's fault, and therefore your fault, *Mr. Captain*"

He chuckled with his gaze deeply into mine, "Fuck the crew, the only one I care about is here, in my arms, where he will always be"

I blushed as I felt the sincerity sneaking beyond his teasing eyes

"I... I need to go. I can't be thinking about you when I get my ass kicked in training. Besides, Ace is probably waiting already"

He leaned closer and our lips brushed lightly against each other, "Let him wait. Let the whole world wait"

He pulled his head back slightly, and I followed like a hooked fish. I claimed his lips and he smiled proudly to his triumph. I let my fingers go through his hair, but then I pouted and broke our kiss, "You're wet"

He chuckled, "I know, I'll get you wet too in no time"

My eyes widened and I felt my face blushing to my ears from his rude insinuation, "I meant your hair! And your lips taste salty!"

"Did you know how adorable you look when you pout?" his hands sneaked shamelessly under my clothes, one heading north to erupt tingles on my back, while the other dove down to cup my ass cheek.

But his attempts to distract me didn't work. I pouted more and accused him, "You went swimming without me. Again!"

"I'm not sure the waters are safe yet, Nyx. Once I am, I promise I'll throw you there myself"

"No throwing, thank you. I can manage on my own"

He smiled gently, "Now where were we?" he tilted his head and didn't wait for an answer. His lips already held mine and I found no will inside me to resist.

We enjoyed the gentle foreplay. Slowly kissing and allowing our tongues to dance and tease each other. I held his neck with one hand and threw the wet towel aside to free the other. I slipped my hand under his shirt and touched his warm back. He jolted from the sudden cold that held onto his lower back and arched it while he laughed, "You're a little devil, aren't you?"

I looked at him smugly, daring him to pull away. My amused look seemed to draw him into a gazing moment that I happily broke when my wet fingers traced upwards to awaken his spine.

When he didn't retreat, I decided to take things a step further and ran my tongue along his jaw, then I kissed his neck hungrily. I loved when he held himself back and let me enjoy him. It made me feel like an equal, at least when we were in private. He threatened my control when his hand clenched harder on my backside, but I didn't yield. I lifted his shirt to meet his wide, inviting chest. I slowly tasted him and smiled when the deep groans started rumbling under his skin.

He was getting restless by the second and his hands held and groped me more eagerly. I purposely ignored him, finding his impatience to be truly adorable.

But, after I started nipping at his flesh, his resolve was bound to break. He grabbed my arm and pulled me up to meet his lips again. And without breaking our kiss, he started leading me to a position where I laid on my back beside the wall, while he straddled me and leaned closer

"**Shiiiiiiiip**!!"

I immediately pushed him and propped myself on my elbows, "What? Did you hear that!"

"Aye, a ship. Nothing new" then he actually leaned in and resumed kissing me!

"**Shiiiip**!!", "Aye! Looks like a fucking trade ship!", "Wohooooh! Finally, something to do!"

"Nnn... wait... WAIT! Agenor! Your crew is going to raid on them?? It's not a pirate ship!"

"Why do you care, Nyx. I'll deal with them later; I have some unfinished business to take care of right now.... right *here*"

He ground his waist against mine and I gasped at the pleasure that exploded with the friction between our groins. And before I could even make sense of the situation or compose myself, the door flung open

"Captain, I think we found you a..... bigger prey"

Zaire said while he leaned against the doorframe. Our eyes met and he raised an *'I've caught you doing the naughty'* eyebrow. I flushed and looked away, leaving it for Agenor to deal with the insolent slave master.

"What do you want, slave shit?" he said without even looking back or letting me go

"Mmmm, I don't know... I thought I'd ask to be on the team that jumps for this raid, but... maybe it would be more interesting to stay here and watch you two" I didn't need to look to know that he was wearing a sly smirk

"Oh God" I mumbled, I can't believe he just said that!! I hid my face in the palms of my hands and actually preferred staying hidden under Agenor's body than facing the humiliation.

Agenor cussed under his breath and moved to sit beside me. I could feel his angry glare towards Zaire, "You fucking ruined it, you dumb fuck"

"Hehe, I still cheer for you two, you know"

"You know what you can do with your cheering? Put it up your fucking smug ass-"

"Okeeey! God! Please stop with the vulgarities already!" I stood up facing away from both of them and tidying my clothes.

Zaire laughed and didn't even budge when Ace had to sidestep to walk inside, "Captain, it's a medium trade ship. Would ten be enough?"

"Aye. Priority to those who didn't get a chance in the last two raids"

Ace nodded respectfully and headed out to execute his Captain's orders.

I sighed. Since Esme, we crossed two pirate ships. I remained inside this cabin the whole time and didn't even dare to party with them afterward. These pirates tend to get mean around raids, and, as pathetic as it sounds, my stomach doesn't do well around blood.

But this time it's not another crew. It's normal people! *Will they kill them all??*

I heard of ships sailing and never coming back. I heard stories of crews being burnt alive in the middle of the sea...

God, please spare the innocent from being killed or injured today

Agenor sat on the edge of the bed and was putting his leather boots on when he called his second just before he stepped out of the cabin, "Oh Ace! Count these two in"

My mouth opened in disbelief. I stared at Agenor waiting for an explanation that never came, and I could swear my heart stopped beating. Wait, what just happened?? Did he just-?

He couldn't possibly mean that I.....

"Thank you, Captain!" Zaire lashed his Captain an appreciating grin and a courteous exaggerated bow, then he turned to smirk and wink at me. When he noticed my confusion, he laughed loudly and left, "Great! Now I need a fucking good sword"

Once alone again, I gathered my focus and tried to talk... I need to talk him out of this insanity!

"Agenor..."

"Uh-huh?"

I thought of ways to put this without sounding rebellious or daring; the last time I challenged his order didn't really go well for me.

So I only managed to stand there, looking hesitant and anxious. Agenor walked closer. He looked at me and I saw no coldness or roughness in his gray eyes, if anything he looked sympathetic.

"Don't worry Nyx, this is bound to happen so just follow my lead. It's an opportunity for you. You will be fine."

He leaned down to place a kiss on my lips, then he grabbed his sword and strode confidently to the deck.

∞ ∞ ∞

Chapter 18 ~ Dilemmas
∞ Nyx's POV ∞

I kept clenching and unclenching my hands.

I took steady long breaths to keep the shiver in my body from showing.

My mind was going in every direction, trying to scheme a way out of this. Maybe fake sickness? Or get into an argument somehow and be 'punished' by staying in the cabin??

I sighed. I didn't want to ask Agenor for his mercy, he was clearly very insisting and even excited about this. And if I pushed him too far he'd probably think I was disobeying him and I frankly have no will inside me to make him disappointed in me... I just can't...

Someone held my arm, I lifted my eyes to meet Yeagar's. He smirked and put my sword in my hand.

I looked down and stared at the foreign sword. I never liked it. It was too cocky and obviously too experienced. A fighter needs to show humility or he might take innocent lives. This sword was the opposite, it used to serve a slave master and I was certain it caused too much misery in the past. I wasn't silly as to think that a sword had a power inside him as some did, but knowing its past was enough to make it unsuited for me.

"You'll be ok, just show us what you learned from that training"

Like what, falling on my ass?

I barely kept myself from answering. As if he read my mind, Yeagar laughed a little and took a step forward on the forecastle, staring beyond the waves at Martina's target. He, his brother, Lou, and Zaire are part of the group allowed to raid on this prey... this innocent prey...

"Nyyyyx! Stop slacking and come help with the galley!!", then the usual ranting started, "feeding a fucking thousand mouths in the fucking ocean without a bloody help form cursed pirates..."

Syrvat

This was the first time I considered Baril's voice as a way to salvation. I turned around aiming to be a good pirate and do as told, but before I could even answer or step down from the forecastle, Ace was blocking my way.

I looked at him pleadingly, but his gaze was nothing but cold and emotionless. He shook his head slowly wiping every shred of hope. I was about to ask why he's interfering when his eyes looked past me. I turned to see Agenor glaring daggers at Baril, who was in the middle of the deck.

Baril hurried to stomp closer, "Captain! I need Nyx today; he's going to help me prepare-"

Agenor glared down at him from where he stood on the forecastle, "Back to your galley, Baril. This doesn't concern you"

"Captain," Baril insisted, very courageously I might add, "The boy is not made for raids"

"I said, go back-"

"He will only get himself in trouble"

"That's not for you to say!"

"Well, I know he ain't going to like it and he could even get hurt while-"

"**Know your place, pirate**!" almost everyone flinched when the Captain yelled angrily.

Baril swallowed and looked a bit surprised like he didn't expect to get Agenor mad. It wasn't just because of today's event, lately, whenever Baril pulled me away from Agenor's side, he would get irritated.

This wasn't the kind of trouble I wanted to cause, especially not to Baril who obviously wanted to help me find a way out of this. And despite every instinct of self-preservation, I calmed myself and smiled at Baril the best I could right now, "Sorry Baril, I know you need help with the galley. I'll come to join you once I finish."

His frown grew deeper. I nodded to reassure him, and he just nodded back slowly, almost apologetically. He didn't dare to look at Agenor though, he just lowered his head a little in submission, and when I turned back to face the sea, Agenor walked back and took his place again beside the bowsprit.

I love him, but he's a total jerk sometimes.

I went to stand beside him. I told myself it was to prove that I wasn't going against his order, but in fact, I just felt safer standing close to him.

I tried desperately to find a proper reason for raising a sword against innocent people and stripping them of the fruits of their hard labor. I needed to understand, I had to make it logical somehow... It's no surprise that my mind came back at me empty-handed. Absolutely nothing...

I hated the feeling; the only word describing my state was *pathetic*. It seemed so unfair! I seriously wondered if the fates were pushing me to insanity by playing with my luck. I started to believe that I was cursed.

Once again, I was put on an impossible trial by my loved ones. I was to convince them that I was strong and worthy... In the past, I had to show that I was a good responsible gentleman and a worthy business manager. Today I had to prove the total opposite;

I needed to prove that I was a real pirate.

∞ ∞ ∞

We closed the distance between us and the escaping ship. The more we approached the more frantic the sailors of the other ship got. It looked like they had some strong fighters, which reminded me that it was a trading ship and not a fishing one; Merchants tend to hire strong men to protect the goods from... well, situations exactly like this one.

Their Captain kept giving orders to his crew. The merchant was pushed by that Captain into hiding and was nowhere to be seen once we were at a dangerous distance of them. Maren was monitoring everything with his monocular and told us that the 'rich dude', as he called, went inside the cabin.

The inevitable moment arrived when the other ship started aiming arrows to our heads. It wasn't damn easy to stay put while a rain of arrows fell upon us, tearing parts of our sail and menacing our lives. There were about seven men sending them our way, yet it didn't bother many of the pirates who stood their ground.

Agenor and Lou successfully broke every one that threatened to fall a few feet around them. Others, like Zaire and Ajax, ducked behind the edge of the ship to protect themselves. That was wise considering the danger of being hit. I watched with fearful eyes while I stood beside Agenor, almost behind him actually. As much as I expected myself to stand before him if danger hit, I took advantage of the swift swing of his sword and his confident, calm smirk that rubbed the difference between our strengths to my ego.

I jerked in startle when I heard a pained yell accompanied with colorful curses. I looked behind me to find J falling back with an arrow stuck to his left arm. I instinctively went to move him from the center of the deck and away from the next arrows that will hit. But I was pulled to halt when Agenor grabbed my arm and yanked me back, successfully saving my neck from an arrow that hit right where I was stepping a second ago.

I froze, looking at the arrow that oscillated viciously. Agenor's hand pulled me close behind him as he reprimanded me with a calm voice, "Don't move, Nyx. The arrows will stop in a minute"

He gave me a reassuring smile that I couldn't reflect. I just gulped and stood my ground.

Yeagar grabbed J's leg with one hand and dragged him across the deck nonchalantly. Then, between the teases and laughs of the audience, J was unceremoniously shoved below deck.

Unfortunately, the arrows only stopped when the ships collided. The pirates jumped off the deck, immediately engaging the swords that welcomed them. Agenor pulled me before him and gave me a push on my back; a silent order for me to follow their lead. I stepped over the edge and my feet met the foreign deck.

Somehow, Agenor was behind me but managed to jump before me and clear a safe landing for us. The second I lifted my eyes to take in my new surroundings, two men were charging our way. Agenor smirked wickedly and easily hit one in the face with his elbow and the other in the gut with his foot, successfully sending them both to fall a few feet away on their asses.

His stance, confident and his aura expanding, he was ready to conquer. I looked at him, noticing that hint of excitement that I only saw around raids taking completely over his charming looks. It's that look that usually made me avoid being around him.

My attention was pulled away by a sword aiming to cut through me. I moved mine to block the blow and sidestepped before hitting his shoulder with the pommel of my sword.

My moves were perfectly executed, but they were not enough to convince the fighter to surrender. If anything, I made him angrier. He started cursing a 'bloody pirate', and it actually took me a moment to realize that he was talking about me.

I was the pirate. I was the one invading his peaceful sail and threatening his life and the bread of his children.

I ignored my own consciousness the guilt that ate me up. I moved almost instinctively, feeling something clench hard on my heart. I attacked the big guy, avoiding his deadly swings and blocking his less lethal ones. He was adamant to kill me, but I couldn't give up so easily.

He was right. I was wrong. Yet that wasn't enough for me to surrender my life.

I ducked to avoid his blade and moved quickly to appear around him and I hit his right forearm with my blade.

His sword fell on the deck, its sound drowning in the screams and the swords clashing around us. He held his injury while glaring daggers at me and taking a step back. I held my sword up, defying him to lunge at me, while my eyes tried desperately to ignore the blood oozing out of his wound. I heard whistles coming from Martina and when I looked up, a damn crowd was watching while drinking and exchanging bets.

Suddenly, while I was looking the other way, my injured opponent jumped off the deck, favoring the coldness of the sea over my blade.

"Nooo!!" I called and ran towards the edge to grab him, but he was already out of my grasp. Immediately, I looked around to find a rope. I threw one end off the deck and attached the other with the ropes tugging the sail. When I looked back into the sea, I hoped to see a man holding tight, eager to save his own life. Instead, the man cursed me and turned to swim away.

I didn't understand. I didn't aim to kill him!

Yes, that's why you raided on his ship and raised your sword to take his life!

I couldn't respond to my own thoughts. And I watched as two pirates dove in the sea, pursuing the escaping man.

"**Nyx!!**"

When Agenor's distressed voice reached me, I thought he was in danger somehow. I turned around and immediately saw an ax towering over me and aiming directly at my head. I whirled around to avoid it and it cut through the edge of the deck with a loud thud.

"**Focus**, Damn it!!"

Agenor looked like he took a breath he was holding. I stepped back from the guy that was repeatedly aiming his ax my way. My heart was kicking fast and my breath heightening.

The sword in my hand. Use it!

Use the damn cursed blade!!

I panicked as I realized my arm no longer wanted to use the fucking sword.

"You think you can just drop in and take our money! You damn stupid little pirate!!" He roared at me and slashed his ax dangerously close to my stomach. My shirt got slightly torn and the sight of it made me freeze for a second. But the fear for my life forced me to regain my wits. I dodged the next hit, still unable to fight back. I just kept moving away and avoiding the heavy ax.

But by stepping back repeatedly, I was bound to be cornered. My hand held the sword harder but refused to raise it. Suddenly, an arrow drove its way to the huge man's arm, making him release an excruciating painful groan. He cursed and caught his bloodied arm. I looked towards the source of the arrow and saw Ace from our ship lowering a bow. His eyes as emotionless as always, unlike my frightened look and weakened stance.

The man growled; he was removing the arrow from his body. At the sight, an image flashed before my eyes; a slave lying on his back, his hand clutching at his crimson side, and his eyes staring accusingly at me... I shook my head to chase the image away, but it was as vivid as the day it happened a few months ago. I... *I didn't want to hurt anyone anymore!*

Syrvat

I killed and injured... this was challenging every damn principle carved in me since I was born!

This went against my own being!!

I found no other option than to avoid the opponent that was adamant on splitting my head.

I swiftly moved past him before he could deliver the next blow, and I avoided another couple fighting. I shamefully escaped from the ax that was stuck behind, meeting another pirate to target.

I looked around me heaving and trying to make sense of my surroundings; the deck certainly looked less busy. The number decreased significantly in a handful of minutes, and everything was happening almost at the same time. Agenor wasn't really fighting, just fending off those who attacked him, while his eyes remained on me most of the time. He wasn't helping me, just watching. I wondered if he was the one who gave the order for that arrow to hit the large man, and I hated the fact that I didn't know if I should be thankful or resentful.

There was only a handful that was still standing against us. My 'mates' already started vacating every useful thing from the hull: food, cotton rolls, silk rolls, weapons, some wooden boxes with fancy jars inside...

I witnessed a couple pushed down the deck with their hands tied, then it was their Captain's turn. Yeagar kicked his leg and forced him to kneel before he restrained his arms and shoved him to join his defeated fellows in the hull.

On the other side, Lou broke the cabin's door with his foot. Then he smirked and walked in.... he was going after the merchant. An innocent merchant who happened to somehow stray away from the guarded routes and who might pay for that mistake with his life as well as his crew's lives. And I didn't know what I could do about it... I'm so damn useless!

A weak pleading voice drew my attention. I looked to find a sailor almost crying, disarmed and falling back at the end of the deck, begging for his life to be spared from a deviously smirking pirate.

But Ajax didn't back off. He lifted his sword and actually went to stab the defenseless sailor. I yelled at him to stop and lunged forward, luckily blocking his sword just in time to save the innocent soul.

"Nyx?? Get the Fuck away! That's MY PREY!!"

I held his sword back using mine, refusing to move, "He surrendered!! He's unarmed and-"

"Who's side are you on!?? **Get Off My Fuckin Way!!**"

Ajax growled at me and pushed me back roughly with his sword. I almost fell, grabbing the edge of the deck to keep my balance. The sailor used a couple of seconds of Ajax's distraction to flee, but it wasn't long before Yeagar easily punched him straight in the face rendering him unconscious.

I was about to look for a way to reason with the predator pirate that was glaring like he wanted to bite my throat. And that's when I saw it in the corner of my eye.

Lou released a mocking laugh as he walked backward and out of the cabin. An angry young man chasing him with swift, elegant moves of his sword.

My body froze and my breath heightened at the sight. I gazed unbelievingly, ignoring Ajax's angry remarks.

"H........... Haven??" I mumbled.

"Hey! Look at me when I'm fucking talking to you!!"

Their swords kept clashing and separating, only to meet again. Under the crude cheering of his mates, Lou played skillfully with his prey.

I tried to move closer, still uncertain that my eyes weren't deceiving me. But as soon as I stepped away from Ajax, he grabbed my arm and pulled me back while stating that he wasn't done 'dealing with me'.

I pushed him away, but his grip only grew angrier. So I just moved enough to be able to see the face that I yearned for once again.

I wasn't imagining things... It... it was HIM! My cousin... my best friend was here!! And... Oh God, he was facing one of the most dangerous pirates!

"A..... Agenor!!", I called for Agenor and only then did I notice that he was already heading my way and glaring at Ajax. He thought I was calling about Ajax, I didn't care. The pirate released my arm as soon as he saw his Captain.

"Lou!!" I was so desperate that I didn't wait to talk to anyone, not even Agenor. I just had to stop that damn pirate from hurting Haven! But I was too late.

Lou had already disarmed him and was standing behind him, holding him still. Haven thrashed, trying to release Lou's arm from around his chest, but he came to halt when the sword approached slowly and settled on his neck. The pirate held him closer, then he leaned in and whispered words in his ear. Haven shook his head slowly, refusing whatever the asshole said that obviously scared him, and Lou only smirked wider.

I avoided the other pirates and ran their way, ignoring Agenor, who noticed my terror and was about to stop me, "No! Let him go, LOU!!"

Lou turned my way looking confused and bothered that I disturbed his damn bullying groove. "You hurt him and I swear I'll-"

"**Ughghgh!!**"

I gasped, feeling my heart stop when Haven succeeded in driving his small dagger into Lou's arm, despite the sword that was still pressed to his neck.

Lou groaned in pain. He didn't drive the sword further into my cousin's neck, instead, he skillfully moved it away to avoid injuring him. And almost breathed in, if not for the fact that Lou immediately grabbed Haven and hit him.

My friend fell on the deck with a loud thud.

I couldn't even move anymore. I lost every emotion as my eyes focused on the circle of blood that formed under his head.

∞ ∞ ∞

Chapter 19 ~ The unfilial heir
∞ Nyx's POV ∞

"**Haven**!!" I pushed every silhouette aside and ran to reach my cousin's motionless body. I kneeled down, my hands not even daring to touch him despite my heart that yearned to hold him safely.

With lips shaking and eyes staring in disbelief, I called his name over and over, begging him to open his eyes and answer me.

"Nyx"

When I lifted my eyes to look at Agenor, they settled on the pirate behind him. My blood boiled with fury as I stood and took a step forward. I punched his already bloodied arm as hard as I could, drawing a deep painful groan from him, "You fucking bastard... You damn monster, you killed him! He did nothing to you and you.... you...."

I couldn't even find the proper words. This all happened so damn fast and I was so confused; it felt so unreal! It can't be... It can't be fucking true!!

When Lou snarled and charged at me, Agenor pulled me back and turned me away from him while blocking his way to me, "Nyx, calm down-"

"Ca-calm down?? How could I when your damn crew killed my family!"

They all went suddenly silent as if my words actually made a difference for them. I could only hear my uneven breaths and I could only see the blood.

"What do you mean family??"

I looked at Agenor and saw deep worry in his eyes. I couldn't even try to stay composed anymore. My voice weakened and the words poured out without me thinking, "How could you, Agenor... You promised me... You promised as long as I stayed you wouldn't hurt my family..."

Agenor opened his mouth, but he didn't say anything. He was as confused as I am, but frankly that bring me any consolation. I was shaking badly already, unable to cry or even touch my dear friend. I just stared at him and around me in disbelief.

Even in my current state, I could feel Agenor's agitation. I didn't know if it was the anger or simple dislike of the situation, but it was emanating from him in heavy waves. He kneeled down beside the body and reached for it. That scared me. Agenor touching Haven scared me to no end. No matter what feelings I had for him, he was the devil pirate, and he was now close to my cousin... my bleeding cousin... my dea-

My heart pinched again at the thought. A long moment had passed without me even registering it, and I just realized that Agenor was holding my shoulders and saying something.

Something I couldn't believe

"Nyx! Hey, I said he's alive, you hear me??"

When his fingers ran through my hair, it sorts of brought my focus back to his words, "...alive??"

"Aye, he's just unconscious. You can see for yourself, Nyx. He's not dead"

I looked at Haven again and reached for him. I touched his wrist trying to feel his pulse, but I couldn't hear a thing over my shaking hands. So I put them on his chest and tried to focus the best I could. When the thump hit my palm, I breathed in and leaned my forehead on his shoulder, "Oh God thank you.... thank you..."

I pulled my cousin carefully and set his head on my kneeling thighs. My eyes were able to focus better now. I inspected him and found his head to be injured from the side, which was the cause of all the blood. I pressed on his head to slow the bleeding and pulled him closer to me while whispering in his ear, "I'm sorry... I'm sorry my friend..."

"Heh, that little wolf, he actually managed to stab me!"

The bastard Lou sounded proud as he spoke and went to crouch closer to Haven, but he immediately frowned when I glared and threatened him, "Don't you dare come any closer or I swear to God-"

"Nyx", I was interrupted by Ace who spoke with his usual calm attitude, "Your friend is regaining consciousness"

I looked down to see Haven's hand moving a little and his features showing signs of pain. I was so relieved to feel him move,

but......... I froze.

I actually didn't know what to do.

"I'll close your friend for you" Ace continued

"Close?"

"I'll stitch his injury; it doesn't look deep so don't worry. He'll be fine"

I nodded, then I felt Agenor's hands holding my shoulders from behind me, "Nyx, do you want him to see you?"

"What?"

He looked in my eyes as if searching for a serious answer, "If he wakes up and sees you, right now... Would you want that?"

Do I want that? Do I want Corail to know what I became? Do I want my dearest friend and family to know that I'm a pirate? That I was the one who invaded his ship and stole his business??

What would he think of me? What would he say?? Will he hate me, forgive me? Will he hide my secret or... report back to Corail and tell everyone that the Osborn's heir is now a pirate, killing and stealing from the weak...?

Will.... will they still love me? Will they disown me??

"Nyx..." Agenor urged for a response with a desperate hint in his voice. I kept looking at Haven's face as he released a moan, signaling that he'd be opening his eyes any second now.

I tried to think straight and take a very quick decision, but I failed, "I don't know..."

Agenor sighed. His arm traveled around my chest and he pulled me up with him. My hands reluctantly released my cousin under the soft reassuring words that Agenor kept saying to me. Then he pulled me back, leaving Ace to take my place and start working on the injury.

∞ ∞ ∞

Sympathetic stares... amused grins... bored looks...

I ignored all of them as I kept walking forward. I went into the cabin, barely able to stand. I dropped as soon as I reached the other side of the bed and under the small window. I joined my hands together, trying in vain to ease the trembling.

I was at a complete loss.

A moment later, Agenor walked into the cabin and slowly approached me. He stood in front of me, then I felt him pushing something my way. I raised my eyes to find his hand holding a sack, "Here. Your share of the raid."

My eyes widened at the sight of my 'prize'. And that this last straw that broke me, "I..... please don't make me take that" My eyes immediately blurred and I couldn't contain my sobs anymore.

∞ *Agenor's POV* ∞

Fuck... Fuck... FUCK!!

I dropped on my knees and held his sobbing body, "Ok, you don't have to! You don't have to, so just... Gods, please don't cry, Nyx"

He held onto me as his tears ran freely out of him. Damn it, this feels like a serious new low, even for me!! That fucking Pin, he suggested I'd give Nyx some of the gold we got and that it would cheer him up. Just because normal pirates stupidly grin at the sight of gold, he thinks Nyx would too! The stupid damn midget!!

How the fuck did I believe such thing!!

I raided on someone he knows and caused them harm, and now I'm paying him for helping me do that?? Why the fuck do I keep screwing up!! And who the hell is that Haven?? He said he was family... Shit... things got so fucked up very fucking fast

I swallowed the guilt that made me feel like a total asshole to the one and only person that I actually cared about. I hugged him closer burying his face in my chest, but his crying didn't stop.

Since I brought him on this ship, I saw his tears and heard his sobs a few times already. He never cried this strongly though. Now he's wailing and shaking severely! He's crying loudly, unable to compose himself anymore. He kept mentioning his family between sobs, but his weeping kept me from understanding the words.

"It's ok, your friend will be ok. I promise. This was.... just a fucked up coincidence, Nyx. I didn't... I never aimed to raid on your people! Please, don't cry, don't be sad, I..... I promise everything will be ok..."

I kept reassuring him and holding him close. He was shaking so badly and his breath was very dangerously erratic. I didn't know if he was in such panic because of that Haven guy being injured, or also the fact that he participated in a raid. Or maybe that hunter that tried to kill him with the ax over and over?

Gods, *I pushed him over his limit yet again.*

I promised not to go after his family, and here I am, breaking that promise. I didn't do it on purpose, but once blood is spilled, that doesn't really make a difference. .... Fuck......

He didn't push me away, though. I didn't understand why he wasn't trying to kill me right now! Instead, he let me hug him as he vented his pain and worry. And I bit my lip and took in his tears and his frustration.

He misses his family so much; I know that from the way he keeps talking about them happily despite not seeing them for months. And now he sees them get injured by the hands of pirates, and his MATES none the less!!

I kissed the top of his head repeatedly, tightening my grip around him as to tell him to not dare think about leaving me... I wouldn't let him. I will never allow him to leave! I'm aware of my own selfishness, but I don't give a damn! I shouldn't let him see or talk to that guy named Haven again. The way Nyx hugged him gently and protectively... Fuck...... Aye, fuck the fates! Fuck Haven! Fuck his damn family! How the hell did they find their way to him again?? We're in the middle of the fucking sea for Gods' sakes!!

I nuzzled his soft hair while my hand drew calming circles on his back. Time passed heavily, and it took him more than an hour to actually calm down, which left him feeling weak and sad.

Once I made sure he was better, I tore myself away from him. I needed to see what the hell became of that fucking Haven that came out of nowhere. And I hope he's damn fine because if not, I sincerely wouldn't be able to face my lover.

Nash gave me a quick rundown of the situation. Basically, everyone was tied up and kept down the hull of the other ship. They were almost finished carrying whatever they found to Martina. Ace climbed into the deck and walked straight to me, "Captain"

"Ace, you patched the kid?"

He sighed and nodded, "Aye. Turns out he's Nyx's cousin"

I cussed low and Ace nodded in understanding. A cousin, is that considered close family for landlubbers?? Fuck, now that I think about it, I think Nyx mentioned his name a few times. Gods, this keeps getting better!

Nash scoffed sarcastically, "Heh, what are the odds, right?"

Ace rolled his eyes at the comment. I wanted to glare at Nash, but I found myself agreeing, "This is so fucking messed up. Why the fuck would his cousin show up here from all the places? And why the fuck is he sailing in an unguarded area!"

"I don't know. I didn't get anything more out of him while sewing his head. He just kept fighting back, and even when he felt dizzy again, he calmed down a bit but kept swearing at Lou"

"Where is that fucker, by the way?" I asked as I remembered that most of this shitty situation is because that asshole hit the kid and rendered him unconscious and bleeding. **Right. In Front. Of Nyx**!! I mean, he could've fucking warned me or something, like: Captain, I'm about to fuck up so make sure Nyx is not a damn witness or something.

I groaned at my silly thought when Ace answered my question, "He stayed back", then he frowned a little and continued, "He actually likes watching that merchant cuss and challenge him. I was tired of watching him grin so I left as soon as I finished with the kid. He even forgot about his own injury"

I sighed and ran a hand through my hair, "Fuck, I don't even know how to answer that. But as soon as Lou gets back on this deck I'm going to kick his fucking ass!"

Nash laughed excitedly, "Aye!! He fucking deserves a beating! If you need a hand, I'm totally your man for the job, Captain. This is all his fault. That bastard is so fucking irritating; you should cut him a leg or something"

I glared at him, "Maybe I should start with your grinning face, Nash!"

He raised his hands in surrender and looked away, obviously still amused by all of this. Ace shook his head at him earning a glare back. I swear sometimes it feels like I'm surrounded by a bunch of kids.

"Captain, what are we going to do with the cousin?"

"I don't know Ace, I actually don't know."

"We could kill him and get this over with" Ajax poured some of his wisdom in, and I just noticed that he was standing close all along

"No one is touching him, you hear me?"

"A-Aye! Of course, Captain, whatever you decide. I just meant that if he can't go back to his island, he wouldn't tell them where Nyx is. And I guess that's what you want"

Nash scoffed and shook his head slowly, mouthing a silent 'idiot', and Ace took over the explaining because I obviously wasn't very eager to talk anyone out of their stupidity, "Haven didn't see Nyx yet. And unless the Captain allows, the merchant can't know his cousin is here. And if the worse happens, hurting Haven will only cause Nyx to be hurt too"

Ajax nodded and everyone fell silent.

Aye, unless I allow it... if Nyx talks to his cousin, who knows what he'll think?? He might want to stay on-board and sail back to Corail!!

Could I live with that??

Or, I could send the ship away and tell Nyx that they were simply gone. Then he wouldn't have any chance of meeting the merchant or talking to him. He wouldn't even have a choice or a say in the matter.

Fuck... what should I do?

∞ ∞ ∞

It was late at night already. I was still standing on the deck, arms crossed as I watched the other ship tied to ours with long ropes and chains. It reminded me of Regina. That ship was smaller but definitely better. It was the ship that brought Nyx to me. It was also the ship that threatened to take him away, so it bugged me as much as this one. And that makes me wonder if Nyx would have an urge to swim to this ship the same way he wanted to escape to his Regina.

Lou hadn't returned yet. My men told me he was keeping the situation under control on the other side. It was probably not a bad idea to keep him there for now. He would certainly prevent any further problems from happening. He's actually a pretty good pirate; he just lacks the will and the focus to become a Captain of his own.

I tensed when Nyx stepped beside me. I couldn't look at him. I didn't know if he still wanted to blame me more for the situation we were in. I'd understand if he did, and that's kind of new to me because I never liked to be blatantly accused, even of my own doings. But in this case, it was different. It involves Nyx...

The last few months went do fucking perfectly! Now I don't know what the hell he thinks of me.

If he wants to blame me again, I'd take it. I just don't know how to face him or how to respond. It feels like a weakness and it irks me so deeply! But that doesn't change the fact that once again, he's facing a fucked up situation.

We stood there for long silent moments before his left shoulder leaned on mine for support. I tried to ignore the tingles that erupted in my stomach, followed by a sense of relief that I was afraid to believe in and be disappointed.

"Help me", he mumbled

I looked beside me. He was tense from the way his fists clenched tight. I met his eyes and he was looking straight into mine, "Agenor, I... I don't know what to do. Please help me... tell me what to do"

My jaw tensed and my breath instantly rushed. And I couldn't believe the words that came out of me next:

"It's up to you, Nyx."

He frowned in confusion, "But..." His eyes looked up at me with a cute sad pout.

I can't fucking believe it, did I just give him a choice??

"I know your cousin is dear to you. He's ok now; Ace finished taking care of his injury hours ago and he's resting. I also gave orders for no one to hurt him so you don't need to worry about such a thing happening again. But what we do from here.......... I'll let you decide that. You decide, Nyx. And I'll give the orders that follow your decision-"

I was interrupted when his finger touched my nose. I looked down at him in confusion and he smiled at me, his blue babies still sad, but a playful little twinkle shined in them, "I'm not leaving you, Agenor"

My eyes widened in surprise. He smiled a bit wider as he caught the fear that I couldn't hide. He removed his playful accusing finger and pulled my arm, making me turn slightly to face him better. Then he said with confidence, "I know what you think of me. You still don't fully trust how important you are to me."

He waited for an answer to his suspicions, but I didn't dare confirm the truth.

"Nyx....... I love you so much"

I couldn't help the weakness in my voice and it amazed me how determined and confident he sounded as he responded, "And I love you, Agenor. I love you and don't want to live without you"

My heart beat so strongly in my chest and I felt like I wanted to kneel before him and do whatever he asked. He's so damn handsome... He's more beautiful than what my heart could take!

He says he doesn't *want* to live without me, he said. But Nyx, I....... I *can't* live without you

His sweet voice drew back to reality, with a tenderness I never deserved, "Agenor, I know this all went the wrong way and I know you didn't mean for any for this to happen. But I still need to make this right somehow. Haven is my uncle's heir and only son. He's a really good person, even better than I am. I can't let him get harmed again! I want to do something right, but I really have no idea what to do, and the only one in the whole world that I could ask help from, is you"

I swallowed and nodded slowly as I listened to every word he said. The way his mesmerizing eyes looked at me with hope, the cadence of his sweet voice, talking to me, venting his fears and pleading for help. I would be damned if I didn't wash his worried away.

"I will lead him to safety"

He tilted his head a little in confusion, "To Corail??"

"To the closest guarded island. I will sail with your cousin until he's free from danger on a guarded island with a threat to never leave safe waters again"

"Really? You would do that!!"

I nodded, "As long as he keeps to the guarded routes, he will safely sail back home"

A wave of relief settled on his face, and a smile started working its way to his lips. That until he remembered something else, "What about the others?? His crew and the guards that he hired?"

Two dead and seven with injuries or broken limbs

"Safe and sound. They're imprisoned in their hull and will remain there until I release the ship."

Now the satisfied smile completely landed, "Thank God! I actually feared for their lives. Especially that one who jumped off the ship"

Dead.

"Everyone's in the hull, except your cousin who's resting in his cabin"

"What about their business??"

"I'll leave your cousin enough money to buy food and rent more guards if he needs for his trip back home"

He nodded quickly, "Ok, that would be fine. Haven would probably lose a trade partnership or a client or two, but that's not important now, right?"

"Aye. Get him to safety. That's what you want, that's what we will do."

His arms suddenly sneaked around my chest and pulled me into a tight hug that I didn't expect, "Thank you! Oh God, I can't believe we could actually make this right!! I knew you could help!!"

I hugged him back and in his soft black hair. He kept thanking me and I focused on the feeling of having him in my arms, willingly hugging me and ignoring the pull to his home.

"..... My God, I just... I was so scared, but we will fix this! Haven will be safe now. I don't even know what the hell he was doing in this unsafe area! I'll need to ask him and tell him to never leave the guarded routes or he might get himself-"

"What??" That last part made my heart leap in my chest. I pushed him just enough to see his face, "You're going to talk to him??"

"I... I haven't decided yet. He could hate me for who I became...... But I have the chance to see him and tell him that I'm fine, and maybe ask him about mother and Raya-"

"NO"

He frowned in confusion and tried to pull back, but I held him closely. *I can't let him talk to his fucking cousin!! I don't care what Nyx thinks; his cousin could have other plans! He could even tell him some bullshit about his mother and it will be Amos and Esme all over again!!*

"If you talk to Haven, he will not leave you behind and go back. He will certainly try to take you away!!"

He shrugged innocently, "Not if I tell him that I'm ok and that I want to stay"

"Then what?? They KNOW you're doing well because you sent them letters saying so. But if they hear you're living with pirates, you think your mother will accept that??"

His eyes widened at the idea and he stuttered, "I-I will tell him not to say a word-"

Fuck... I continued trying to sound as calm and gentle as possible, "I can't have Haven knowing about you here and then lead him to an island infested with guards. The second he'll reach there, he'll tell them that we're keeping a nobleman and they'll send an army behind us. You need to choose Nyx, it's either talk to Haven and part ways here. Or keep the secret and escort him to safety."

I am cruel, I know that. After all the things that were forced upon him, I'm still cruel to him. I don't rejoice over his confusion and anxiety, but I'll be damned if I laid back and watched him get closer to his family and further from me!

He looked lost. He thought deeply for a moment, and each passing second proved how much he cared for this Haven person, and it weighed on my heart. Finally, his shoulders slumped in defeat and he broke the silence, "Safety. Please take him to safety"

I bit my tongue to keep a long sigh from ruining my plans. My hand landed on his hair to caress it and I smiled gently at him, "You made the right choice"

"I hope so... I just wish I had more luck..."

"Why would you say that?"

He chuckled sadly, "I wish this day wasn't such a disappointment. I wish the raid was easier. Maybe I'd be invisible or something, or at least I wouldn't drive innocent people to jump into the cold sea to save their life. I really wish I hadn't attacked Haven's ship. And most of all, I wish I could just talk to him like we used to and remind him that I'm here... I exit"

My chest tightened at how defeated he looked. And it evaded my logic that despite his own worries, he was still thinking about me, "But I don't regret being here, Agenor." His fingers reached elegantly to touch my hair as he continued, "I'll never regret meeting you. That was my blessing, and I wouldn't trade it for the world"

I met his loving smile with my lips crashing on his. We completely forgot that we were on the deck, with at least one witness looking down from the crow's-nest. I kissed him eagerly, unable to keep my hunger for him at bay, but a part of me also wanted to confirm his assertions. This doubt that I'm not proud of keeps me on edge whenever I feared for my lover. And it became a weakness that I both hate and welcome.

My hand kept his head from retreating and I tilted my head as I claimed his mouth. I sucked his lips and bit his tongue provoking a sexy moan from him. My kiss was strong and needy, and I reveled when I succeeded in coercing his tongue to a playful arousing dance that made my pants feel uncomfortably tight.

When I pulled back, he was deliciously blushing, with sexy half hooded eyes that stared at my lips in a cute heaving daze.

"I will never force you to anything again, Nyx. I won't force you to become a pirate if that would change who you are. I've watched you in that raid today; you fought bravely, but you were focused on the safety of others more than yours! That fear in your eyes when the guy jumped off the deck, I never want you to look like that ever again. You will be by my side. And you will decide on what adventures to live as long as you take me with you"

His beautiful eyes blinked to keep the tears back in a manner I was used to by now, and he asked cautiously, "I... I don't have to be in raids?"

I shook my head slowly, "Only if you wanted to."

His head lowered when a stray tear betrayed him, and he mouthed a very appreciating yet shaking 'thank you'.

I kissed his head tenderly, then I added, "You're my angel, Nyx. And I vow to stop tainting you."

"You think I'm an angel??"

"What? Can't you see the big white feather wings on your back??"

He chuckled adorably making me laugh. I rested my forehead on his, "Now, I'm sending for Lou to come to tell me himself what happened in the afternoon on your cousin's ship. You want to listen? Maybe ask him about Haven's health?"

"Yes! Yes, please", he nodded enthusiastically making me laugh and pull him in another hug.

Fuck, I actually never want to lose sight of this enchanting smile of his. And I'll be damned if I ever caused pain again. I will protect you, Nyx. I will keep my promise to never force you to do anything you didn't like. I'll be your mattress when you're tired, and your shield when you're in danger.

And since I, the devil, am protecting you,

no one will ever dare lay a finger on my angel.

Right?

∞ ∞ ∞

Chapter 20 ~ A pact with the devil's spawn
∞ Nyx's POV ∞

My jaw dropped as I tried to follow every single move on the other ship, "D-Did you see that!!" I yelled in frustration and got ignored. AGAIN!
"**Nyyyyyx**!! Galley, Now!" Baril asked for my help once more, and I lied, "BE RIGHT THERE!"

I pushed the hat back to see better and pressed my eye so hard in the monocular it felt like it was going to pop out the other end. Haven threw a punch and my heart leaped with it. The-the asshole punched back!!

"He's hitting him! He's trying to finish the damn job and kill him!!"

Agenor sighed and said calmly, too damn calmly, "He's not going to hurt him, Nyx. They're just...."

"**Just what??**"

"I don't know, playing, I guess?"

"You *guess*?? Haven's still injured... My poor friend, he's in pain- Look! He pushed him! He pushed him and... I can't be sure, but I bet the bastard is smirking like usual" I pushed his monocular back to him not too kindly. Agenor sighed again and ignored my glare, "I don't need the eye, Nyx. I can see from here that your cousin is the one attacking-"

"And Lou is hitting back! He's going to harm him"

His arms landed around my shoulder to calm me, "I'm confident Lou won't do such thing"

"You say that, but-"

"Trust me, if he wanted to, he would've done so days ago. It's like a routine, Lou lets Haven out of the cabin for some fresh air and the little one can't refrain from trying to defeat the pirate. If anything, maybe we should restrain Haven"

My teeth pressed hard on each other. I hated what Agenor was suggesting with every bit of my heart, "I bet my own life it's Lou's fault, Haven is too competitive and proud. I bet your pirate teased him somehow"

My body jerked when Haven got pushed back and almost fell. This is like the tenth time today! The damn pirates watching the scene beside us exploded laughing at my poor cousin once more.

"Stop being so rude!" I yelled and they only laughed harder.

"Oh come on. Admit it already. They go at it every day! It's like a very entertaining daily show"

I glared at Ajax and his older brother smirked at me from behind him. I rolled my eyes in exasperation, "Agenor, at least get Lou back. Send someone....... less asshole"

"That would be hard to find", Pin interjected.

I looked at him with confidence, "I'm sure we can find someone better". He looked back at me with a raised eyebrow and interest in his eyes, "Want to bet??"

I shook my head in disbelief, right before I glanced Ace passing behind us, "ACE!!" he stopped and I tugged Agenor's arm, "Ace, send Ace instead of Lou!"

Ace looked at me with the same unwavering boredom, "I don't really want to unless it's an order from the Captain"

Damn it, it sounded like I was the one ordering him

"Sorry, it was just... a suggestion..."

He nodded. EMOTIONLESS! I can never get used to that. But I'd actually prefer Ace sailing the other ship behind us. Lou has been doing a very good job keeping everyone safe and fed, also keeping the ship on the right track with a good distance from Martina; not too close so we'd sail without fear of colliding even at night, and not too far so we'd be able to keep an eye on their deck.

If only he could spare us his shitty attitude!! My God, it's almost two weeks now since he hit Haven on the head. And I swear I'm using cruder words by the day! That motherf-- no, that's too rude... **The bastard!**

"I'd take his place! I'm much more 'Captain' than Lou is, obviously"

I narrowed my eyes at Nash. Ok, he'd probably be less provocative than... Lou? .... that thought roamed a few seconds in my head before my shoulders slumped and I started massaging my temples, "This is hopeless"

"Wha-? Say that again, pixie!!"

Agenor chuckles, "He's right, Nash. You'll probably lose it with the first swing and actually go for the kill. At least Lou is having enough fun to ignore the boy insulting him-"

"He's not a boy!! He's a man! A very brave man! And a well-mannered one too! Haven doesn't insult people"

Agenor raised his hands in surrender. I turned my focus back to the other deck just when Haven lunged at a laughing Lou. He sent him a punch that Lou avoided easily, but instead of almost falling forward like he usually did up till now, Haven lifted his knee and successfully met Lou's groin. Haven retreated, leaving the pirate to fall on one knee while groaning painfully.

Everyone gasped, then the cheers and whistles filled the air. My dear Haven stood proudly and pushed the loose bandage on his head behind. His attention was brought our way, he strode to the edge of the deck that was closer to us and stood straight.

"Hide, hide, little kitten" Nash said and I just remembered that I was exposed! I immediately dropped to my knees and brought the hat further on my face to hide it. I first thought the idea of a hat silly, but I guess it's actually useful. I just wish it wasn't a pirate's hat, ahhh this is so embarrassing

I peeked under the hat and over the edge of the deck, and saw my dear cousin stretching his arms proudly in the air and............ *flipping us off??*

My jaw dropped and I focused with wide eyes to confirm... Yep, those are my cousin's both rude fingers.

Everyone cheered more and happily mirrored the gesture. I felt the glorious moment end quickly and hid my embarrassment by burying my face in the hat, as Agenor leaned down closer to my ear, *"Well-mannered,* you said? Hehe, I think I'm growing fond of Corail's 'manners' "

Oh God, Haven dear, please don't let these pirates contaminate you!

"Agenor, please tell me Lou didn't hit him back!"

I know my cousin is stronger than I am, but I've been living with pirates enough to know that someone like Lou could end him in a second.

"Nope, they're talking"

"Talking!! About what??" I snatched the monocular back from him.

"Well, I don't think the eye could help you with that"

The idiots laughed and started teasing me again. But I ignored them all and tried to figure if Haven was planning to attack again. I breathed in relief when I saw him leaning on the closer side of the deck while Lou stood up, not so straight, and leaned on the other one. And they were actually just talking. Good, I guess Haven is safe. For now, anyway!

"Wow! Your cousin is something, Nyxy!" Maren said as he landed from the mast a few feet behind me, making me smile, "Yeah, he's really something. He's cool, don't you think, Maren?"

"Aye! I'm interested. I'd love to meet him!"

Ace looked at beside him at Maren, "You would?"

"Aye! He looks brave! He's as weak as Nyxy but also amusing, don't you think"

"Hey! I'm not weak!!"

Ace nodded, "I guess he could be interesting to meet"

"I'm right here!!" They both ignored me on purpose, and Ace looked at Agenor, "I could take him there for a couple of hours, if you agree, Captain"

"Sounds good." Then he turned to me, "There, you wanted Ace to go and he's going, so please stop worrying"

Wha-! What changed his mind?? Did no one see what just happened!! My God these pirates are so idiot sometimes. And YES, my lover included!

Maren ran to bring Tashi and they prepared to leave immediately. As they climbed down the ship and into the small boat, Agenor gave them a few instructions, and I kept asking them to make sure Haven is doing ok and to tell Lou to back off, even if they were to threaten him!

"Don't worry Nyxy pixie! I'll protect your cousin". He sent me a wink as Armpit rowed the boat towards the other ship.

And I couldn't help the little part inside me that wished Maren would make a mistake and slip my name despite Agenor and Aces warnings. I know, I chose to keep him safe, but... He's Haven! My dear friend... and he's right HERE!

I sighed heavily. Agenor must've heard me because he patted my head and whispered calm words in my ear. Words that I was really in need for right now.

But I guess once Ace was on-board, he'd be able to tell if everything was going well. Yes, I trust Ace.

Sadly, I shouldn't have trusted my dear cousin that much. As soon as he felt a presence behind him, he looked back to see the boat getting dangerously close to him. He yelled something I couldn't hear, then ducked behind the edge of the deck.

I thought he went to hide, which wasn't cowardly because these are pirates! Damn dangerous teasing pirates!! But instead of hiding, he showed up with a piece of wood in his hand that only God knows **Why They Kept Such Thing On the Deck!!**

Haven aimed and threw the wood without hesitation to Ace's head. The tall pirate sidestepped, successfully avoiding the flying object. But poor Armpit, he was too focused on working the oars and the wood went straight to his knee, before bouncing up and being caught by Maren.

"Ouch, that must've hurt like shit", "Hehe, idiot fucker, I bet it's the smell that makes him that stupid", "hahaha!!"

I tried to ignore the mockeries, but they immediately stopped when Maren didn't spare time before throwing the object back and aiming for- *Oh God, I think I'm going to faint...*

"Fuck. You're ok??" Agenor asked worriedly while holding my waist and helping me stand

"They hit his head again... They killed him! Your crew killed him again!!"

Agenor went silent for a moment and a bet immediately started behind my back. A couple of seconds later, he patted my shoulder, "He's still alive, Nyx. Your cousin is tougher than you give him credit"

I opened my eyes to see Haven holding his forehead and yelling at an angry Maren over the deck. The pirate yelled back with his hands on his hips in his famous *'whatcha going to do about it'* pose. Lou threw a rope to Ace who immediately started climbing, making my cousin step back to keep his distance from the new pirates on his deck.

I tried to take the monocular back from Agenor, but he wouldn't let me, "Is he bleeding? I need to see"

"You've watched enough already, Nyx. Your cousin lives fine, and I hope he doesn't kill any of my men by the end of the day"

He said that jokingly, of course, Haven was the only one in danger above that deck.

"**Nyyyx!**"

"**One minute, damn it!!**"

I knew I shouldn't have said that the instant it came out. And it only took five seconds before an angry stomping limping Baril climbed to the deck with the ham knife in his hand. And that's one damn big knife

He glared at me and I looked past him to avoid his scary look as I sprinted towards the opening of the hull. When I started climbing down and didn't hear him stomping behind me, I looked back. Only to find him exchanging glares with Agenor. Shit, it's been this way since the raid; Baril would demand I'd be in the galley and Agenor would scold him for giving me orders. Now they're just glaring, but I know where that would lead to if Agenor snapped. I might be able to survive glaring to Agenor because he doesn't lash back at me, but it's not the same as his crew. And Agenor started threatening and getting angry at Baril a lot lately.

I walked back slowly and pulled Baril from his arm while smiling at Agenor. That didn't dispel the tension at all, but I guess it helped a bit since Agenor didn't look like he wanted to kill the old man anymore.

Once inside the hull, I removed my hat and did my best to help Baril with the galley and lead him back to telling old stories instead of bitching about things like my own life and future.

∞ *Agenor's POV* ∞

I walked inside my cabin and closed the door behind me. Nyx was changing into his bedclothes, which meant that he already finished cleaning himself and reading for the night.

I could feel his mind lost in thought when he pulled his shirt down, then went to put his neatly folded clothes in one of his boxes. He was bending over the box, my head tilted and I palmed myself at the sight of his cute tight ass.

I reached and fondled his right cheek that fit perfectly in my palm. Nyx yelped and turned around only to turn crimson from neck to ears as I smirk lightly and continue to harass his butt. I pulled him into a hug and I ran my left hand on his back, hoping he'd find some calmness instead of all the worrying he's been exhausting himself with lately.

My hand that was supposed to only make him relax sneaked under his shirt and started feeling the shivers on his skin. I smiled at him gently. He mirrored with that special noble kindness in his eyes. Then he stretched his legs to peck my cheek and put his arms around my neck, "Thank you for helping me with my cousin's situation. And especially for not listening to your airheaded pirates who suggested they'd keep Haven as a servant"

I chuckled, "I believe the one who came up with the idea was the slave merchant. My airhead mates only agreed to it"

"Yeah, innocent pirates" He rolled his eyes, making me laugh. He went to kiss me, but stopped remembering something, "Oh, please remember to go easier on Zaire"

"Why? Did the shithead say something??"

"No, he complains about everything, but you know he really fears you and so far he never went against your word. He gets bored sometimes and just wants to fool around, and you're ALWAYS angry with him. He has been enjoying himself and bonding with your crew much better than when we left Esme"

"It's because I don't need a 'Master' on my ship and he doesn't seem to understand that! He just pisses me off"

"He pisses you off because you didn't beat him up for what happened in that slave cell" he raised an accusing eyebrow and I didn't bother hiding a guilty smirk, "Well, 'beat him up'?... That would maybe make me feel better"

"He really respects you, Agenor. And he fears you. Besides, he didn't cause any trouble, not even when you allowed him to go on the raid"

He killed two of your cousin's crew. But sure, no trouble for me.

"I guess I could stop making the pirate life harder on him. Now, I have a feeling if you keep talking about him, that wouldn't help his case at all" I gave him a hungry look and he smiled dearly.

"See, you're too sweet and kind to be called Devil"

I laughed and pulled his waist closer. I leaned in and kissed him slowly, a real kiss this time; with demanding lips, saliva, and tongues tangling together. My body heated with the luscious sounds that our lips made while I enjoyed the feeling of him melting in my arms, "I want you to relax, Nyx. Stop worrying about the world and just be here. Be with me"

"Actually, I'm not worried anymore. I feel much better after Ace came back and confirmed that everything is ok. He even treated Haven and made sure the injury is healing nicely. I would really love to pay back his kindness, but I don't see how"

"You know, I'm the one who ordered him to check on the merchant's head"

He chuckled cutely at my childish claim, "I know, but still. Ace is always helpful. He's a good person and a very good second"

I closed my eyes while shaking my head and tsked playfully, "I knew it, I should've gone there myself. Then you'd be admiring ME right now"

"Mmmmm... Nah, I think I prefer Ace checking out on things on Haven's ship"

My jaw dropped at my little daredevil's revelation, "I'm the one you love! Your CAPTAIN!! And you have more faith in my second??"

"You're kidding, right? I've seen the way you 'check on things', *Captain*. All you do is just walk around and everyone fixes whatever pops into their mind, they're not even aware that you're not paying attention"

I laugh loudly at the snappy comeback, "My baby exposed me!"

He laughed lightly and stretched his slender legs to place a kiss on my lips, "You're not the only one watching me. I watch you too, my love"

"Fuck, I love it when you're horny"

"What? I'm not-" I stole his mouth and bit on his still swollen lower lip, hearing the first melody of a moan. I licked his flushed cheeks and sucked on his ear, while my hands resumed feeling his skin under his shirt. His dark blue shirt.

But as much as I loved that color on him, his naked skin was the best clothes he'd ever wear. I bit his earlobe, then I whispered seductively, "I think it's safe to say that the coldest days of winter are behind us, so we should put the 'no shirt in the cabin' rule back to the game"

"It's still a bit chilly at night"

I released him and took a couple of steps back. With one lamp lit and the moonlight sneaking from the small window behind me and falling in a circle around him, I eyed his confused beautiful orbs.

"Strip", I said. And his eyelashes batted in surprise. But I didn't miss the breath that he inhaled sharply.

"Agenor..."

I smirked, knowing that despite his hesitation, the thought is actually arousing him. I tilted my head and ordered again, slowly. No anger, no hurry; if anything I was enjoying the sweet remains of his noble denial, "Strip for me, Nyx. I want to feed my eyes on your beauty"

His head lowered slightly with a shy smile on his lips. He grabbed the hem of his shirt, and his eyes bravely met mine as he lifted his shirt slowly. After releasing his hair from it, my beloved angel threw the shirt at me.

My hand clenched on the shirt hard as he looked at me with daring flirtatious eyes. I bit my tongue to keep myself from ripping his pants out of my way and burying my manhood deep inside him. And I'm fucking glad I didn't, because when he slowly turned around and slipped his thumbs under his pants, I started heaving like a bull.

I watched with a daze and a watery mouth as my baby wolf started lowering his tight untied pants deliberately slowly, as he swayed his hips in small circular moves. Fuck, I could feel my cock twitching to claim him, and my eyes stared at the beautiful lines of his body as they followed the rhythm of his bewitching dance.

The cloth finally lowered to start revealing the delicious curve of his round ass, making me swallow loudly as I ate him with my eyes.

His dance stopped and his hands halted with it. I furrowed my eyes and I whined in protest, but when he didn't resume seducing me, I reluctantly lifted my eyes only to find that he was staring back at me with a provocative look filled with lust that contradicted his shy cheeks.

His pink lips tugged in a winning smirk before he bent his knees slightly and pushed the pants to drop on the floor with an elegant move.

I took in his entire naked backside. He was fucking beautiful, with nothing to protect him from the devil's eyes, but a nice black leather pirate collar. I released a heavy sigh while I stared at his ass hungrily, making my pants grow tented from the perverted thoughts that tormented me.

Feeling my intense look, the white flesh of his ass cheeks reddened. Oh Gods, his cute ass just got shy!!

He was turning to face me now, and as soon as I saw his erect member I was a goner; I approached him without breaking eye contact with his baby blues. I grabbed his collar gently and pushed him back, guiding him until he was lying on the bed for me. Then I hovered above him.

I removed his hand that attempted to hide his sensitive part from me, and I pleasured my eyes by watching every detail of his fair muscles and slender legs.

I was lowering my body on his when he propped himself on his elbows and met me halfway with a peck on my jawline, "Am I the only one to reveal myself? Seems unfair, don't you think?" he said with a seductive low voice, as his naughty right hand provokingly palmed my throbbing erection.

"Oh my," he added flirtatiously, "you're this big already"

"Fuck......"

I huffed, trying to ease the heat that exploded inside me. I closed my eyes and moaned with pleasure at the feel of the spreading waves of aphrodisiac caused by his small hand. He grabbed me harder and I was soon grinding against his hand in the search for more heavenly friction.

After making sure he had me moaning and groaning freely under his touch, he tugged on the ties of my pants, "Please?" he asked tenderly. And I cussed under my breath with excitement; His fucking cute politeness will be the end of me!!

But I didn't wait to be asked twice. I pushed my pants down and stepped reluctantly out of bed. I abandoned the pants before I climbed on top of my Nyx again.

He laughed slightly at my eagerness and his cheerful look made me smile. Then he reached for the hem of my shirt and helped me remove it. As soon as I did, his eyes were lost in a daze as they followed every muscle and bone on my chest. His fingers caressed my skin adventurously making me halt in my haste, and just watch him enjoy me.

But the rascal between my legs stubbornly demanded to be united with his baby wolf. And once I took a glimpse of his thickening member, mine went rogue on me. All I had to do was lower my waist and grind against him to make him cling to me desperately. I smirked at his beautiful reaction and started over... and over, and over. Just kissing and touching every part of each other's bodies while squeezing our cocks together.

I kissed his panting lips and denied him an easy breath. And his arms hugged me tighter and closer.

I couldn't wait any longer with my cock that was spilling already. I groped his creamy inner thigh with my hand before I pushed it aside to flirt with his entry. His butt cheeks clenched to protect him immediately and he looked beautifully embarrassed.

"Hey baby, relax... open for me, love"

I buried my head in the crook of his neck and laughed lightly at his adorable struggle. He moaned deliciously and I could feel his muscles clench and unclench in a fight between pleasure and decency. But I didn't wait for his decision; I pushed my middle finger past his tight ring making him moan deliciously. The devil inside me wanted to tease his angel, so after half a finger, I forced another to join his warmth insides.

"Ah! That... that hurts... God, slow down"

He whined, making me smirk and lie, "Aye, I am slowing down, Nyx. **There**"

"Ah!!"

I pushed both fingers all the way in and continued to coo and tease him, "Fuck, you're so warm inside, I can't wait to be buried in you..."

I started finger-fucking him as he whimpered, "ah... ah... your... fingers..."

"Aye, they're opening my baby slowly for me" I whispered as I scissored him nicely making him arch his back.

I continued moving my fingers inside him until I felt his walls relax more around them. Then I parted his knees further using mine and rubbed the swollen head of my shaft on his sweet throbbing entry.

I pushed my mushroomed head inside him making him awe and moan loudly. I stopped for a moment to smile at my heaving lover and allow his ass the time to adapt to my size. He smiled back at me with an enticing sign of pain nesting in his eyes.

He bit his lip in a weak attempt to control his own arousal, and I wanted to save that lip so badly... save it and bite on it harder with my own teeth. We both groaned in heat as I tugged his lip in mine, then I nicely licked the pain away. He responded to my teasing by meeting my tongue with his and coercing it to dive into his mouth.

My cock demanded attention again. I pushed it further and moved in and out of him until I was completely buried in his warmth. I circled my waist while inside him making him throw his head back and moan uncontrollably. I pulled out of him, then thrust my hips roughly. I fucked him harder by the second feeling my cock become thicker inside him, as his hands clung to me desperately and at one point, his nails started taking revenge on my back.

"Fuck, Fuck Nyx... you're so fucking good..."

"God... I can't... please... I'm going to... I'm going to come!"

I reached between us and grabbed his weeping cock hard. He tried to release my hand, but I smirked and pressed harder on his suffering member, "Not yet, Nyx. Hold it in, my love"

He whimpered and begged for release. I was at the edge myself, but I was enjoying this too much to end it just yet. I leaned in and started nipping on his upper heaving chest. With a hand grabbing his member, I used the other to pinch his nipple making him cry even louder. His body was shuddering in ecstasy while I tormented his innocent nipple and pushed my thumb harder on the swollen head of his cock.

My balls clenched and my release became imminent. I eased my grip on his arousal and started pumping it quickly, but Nyx immediately arched his back and shot his sweet milk on both our stomachs. My hips slammed harder against his ass riding his orgasm to the fullest, and before he could slump in relief, my own orgasm broke free inside him making him clench his ass around me as I kept slamming against him and shooting my loads with every thrust.

I laid on top of him as we both descended from the clouds we were riding. I could feel every hasty beat of his heart, and every heave of his chest. And his arms hugged me gently making me return the gesture with a tight embrace.

We sat at the side of the bed, doing our after-fuck ritual by teasing each other; something he called 'cleaning'.

I was grinning happily as I walked the wet cloth on his milky skin, and smiled as he used his wet cloth to wipe the sweat off my chest. I raised an eyebrow to his reddened face when his hand reached down to clean my junk. I let him take his time and finish wiping me to his satisfaction, before I took him by surprise and lifted his knee on my shoulder, leaned down, and licked his butthole clean to *my* satisfaction.

∞ ∞ ∞

Rumors have it that, just like the Gods, the devil never sleeps.

Lately, however, I've had this unfamiliar habit of sleeping, and I mean sleeping deeply to my heart's content. And it's all because of the 'innocent' noble who's adorably sleeping in my arms.

My eyes opened by themselves. I sighed when I noticed that we were still far from dawn. I peered down to see Nyx snug to my chest, breathing peacefully while I hugged him. I smiled slightly and watched him for a few seconds. His sight was like a lullaby that slowly brought the sleep back to me. So I surrendered to the *Nyx-effect* and I closed my eyes, thinking about the blessing of having my angel happily and safely trapped in my arms.

I almost drifted to dreamland when my ears picked up on a strange light movement and realized that it was the same sound that woke me up in the first place. I remained still as I focused on my hearing. After a long moment, the door of my cabin was fucking opening!

Despite being alarmed, I remained calm. I closed my eyes again and evened my breathing. Fuck, I would be much more confident to protect my lover if I had my dagger under the pillow like I used to. But Nyx barely likes moving around with it, let alone sleeping beside it! About a year earlier, I used to sleep with my sword beside me for Gods' sakes!!

The floor cracked slightly under the weight of the intruder. Whoever he is, he's one person, and he's not too heavy. Only ONE attacking ME?? He's either fucked up stupid or a too confident assassin!!

Protecting Nyx was my ultimate priority. No matter what, the first thing is to be between him and the stupidly daring bastard. My hand unintentionally hugged Nyx tighter as my mind worked a thousand ways to finish that plan and kill the fucker without even waking my lover.

I waited for the steps to get closer, but they were oddly taking their sweet time. After a couple of minutes that felt agonizingly long, I decided to take matters in my own hands and not wait to finish the motherfucker. But before I ended him, the intruder made his own move.

"Nyx??"

∞ *Haven's POV (earlier in the day)* ∞

"Fuck you"!!

"I'd love to see you try"

I lunged at him for the thousand's time and the result remained the same. He easily dodged my attack and I received the same smirk.

"If I had my sword in my hand, I would've wiped that smug smirk off your ugly face!"

"Oooh~, you think I'm ugly?" he whined pretending to be hurt. This ugly bastard is so damn amused by my misery; it's making me so fucking angry!!

"I'll kill you!"

"Come on, you've been trying for how long now... two weeks?"

"I asked you a damn question! Where the HELL are you taking my ship!"

He sighed and crossed his arms, "You know, I expected you'd be thankful by now. AND, I can't believe I'm saying this, not so rude! I've been allowing you to sleep in a nice bed with warm food and water for two weeks! I even allowed you to the deck-"

"On MY SHIP! And who THE FUCK you think you are to *'allow'* ME?? I'm not a fucking dog!"

He smirked again and raised his mocking eyebrow. I will tear his eyes away from his damn ugly face!

He thinks I should be thankful?? To what!! Attacking me? Hurting my crew? Stealing my goods? Taking my money?? AND GOD KNOWS WHERE I'M FUCKIN HEADING RIGHT NOW!!

My God, if father hears of this he could have a heart attack. Even if I make it alive, he'll be so disappointed and he'll ask why- wait... am I getting alive out of this?

I guess I am since they didn't kill me... but why? Shit, this situation is so fucked up... I can't die now! Not until...

When I realized I was staring at him, I turned around, released a loud frustrated groan, and headed back to my cabin. He laughed and I pulled every shred of patience left inside me to not turn around and kick his smugness out of him. I mean, who fuck he thinks is??

If allowing me on MY deck is a favor then I'll pass, and I'll shove his fake courtesy up his-

"Mmmmm... Nice ass!"

"Wha-" I looked back to find his perverted eyes glued to my backside

"I just noticed, did you know your ass gets angry too? It actually gets tenser and it clenches- Oh, did I get you mad, bunny?"

I ran and charged at him. My hand balled into a tight fist and went straight for his jaw. Of course, he sidestepped and dodged the attack just like I knew he would. His smirk grew wider and he grabbed me closer to him. And before he could give one of his wiseass comments, I lifted my knee and met a pair of unfortunate balls.

"FUCKCKCK...!!"

The hit was perfect. I probably couldn't win against him without my sword, but I wasn't a complete weakling either. And I put quite the strength in that knee strike. Enough to wear a proud smirk as I watched the crazy pirate crumble to the ground with a very satisfying painful groan.

I stepped back to enjoy the full picture and also avoid an instant revenge blow. I couldn't help the part of me that feared the damn pirate. This terror that I've been burying for days now, but it resurfaced to terrorize me from angering the big asshole.

I braved up thought. Never showing the slightest doubt in myself and always keeping my nose held high. With that thought, my chest tightened at the memory of someone dear to me; someone who would take a hundred criticisms with an elegant smile...

The asshole grabbed himself between the legs and sat on the floor of the deck. I guess this means we're taking a break. I sighed and leaned back on the edge of the deck across from him.

"Fuck... That was a low blow, my friend"

"I'm not your friend! And you deserve much more than a kick in the junk"

"Ugh... Shit, it really hurts"

I laughed when he winced and threw his head back. Yes, he totally deserved it.

We sent silent for a few minutes before I asked, again, "Please tell me the truth. Where did my cousin go after he left you?"

A knowing small grin tugged the side of his lips, and he answered without even looking at me, "Like I said, your cousin didn't tell his plans to the pirates who raided on him"

Damn it! He talks to me like I'm an idiot, but he knows nothing of the frenzy that my life has become!!

I realized the identity of my captors as soon as they raided on my ship. One look at their Captain made me recognize him from the 'wanted' papers I borrowed from the guards on Mila. And my suspicions got confirmed after I woke up and found myself unconscious and surrounded by them. The man who treated my bleeding head looked very familiar, I knew I've seen him before. And when his mates called his name, 'Ace', I remembered he was the second of the Martina crew.

As much I wanted to talk to them before, I never thought I'd actually meet them one day! I guess it wasn't that bad to get out of the guarded routes after all.

A few days after the raid, I confronted this fucked up pirate of what I knew. The way I figured it out amused him, but I admit that I kind of regretted it when he told me that their Captain Agenor, also very feared and known as the devil pirate, was going to execute me and make me walk the plank since I knew who he was.

I tried convincing this shithead that there was no reason for his Captain to kill me for just knowing who he was, but he said that Agenor would think I was here looking for revenge because of what they did to my family.

I kept my mouth shut around all the other pirates and tried to somehow get this bull to spill all he knew about the day they raided on Nyx. I'm aware of how illogical I sound, but I really hope he knows something... anything! I've been looking for him day and night for months now without the least trace of him! I even found his Regina, but I didn't find *him*...

Everyone thinks Nyx sailed for a vacation or something. I can't believe everyone fell for that!! He's Nyx!! He would never do such a thing and even if he did, he'd never leave without telling us face to face, and he'd never, **never!** leave his father's business unattended!

So many questions, so few clues!

But now I have to take this chance, even if it would kill me! I have to get this fucker to tell me anything that could be useful no matter how small because I've frankly already exhausted all kinds of means in my search.

Besides, that look the smug pirate gets every time I ask him, it's like he knows something, but for some reason, he's keeping his damn mouth sealed.

I was about to try and ask him again, maybe find some effective insults this time. And that's when I caught a movement in my peripheral vision. I turned around to find a boat coming from the other ship and approaching mine with three pirates onboard.

Maybe the assholes have decided of my fate and are now coming to lead me to my creator. Well, I won't be going down without a fight!! I looked around me and found a broken piece of wood, one of the remains of the cursed raid. I grabbed it and immediately aimed at the pirate standing proudly at the front of the small boat. I recognized him as Ace, but I didn't regret attacking him one bit. The pirate avoided my hit, though. He dodged it so easily, but at least it crashed on the stupid pirate behind him.

I smirked when I managed to hit the second pirate in this 'lucky' day. My smirk hadn't settled yet when the same piece of wood came flying my way and crashed on my head.

I awed and fell backward. Luckily I didn't faint or bleed. I lunged at the edge of the deck to get back at the young pirate with curls exploding around his head, "You fucking pirate!!"

"You started it first, *merchant*!"

"Tha-... That's not even an insult!"

"I don't care! Never aim at Ace again, you *merchant*"

"Fuck you!"

"Fuck **you**!"

He crossed his arms and pouted. I was planning to throw in more insults, but once the so-called Ace grabbed a rope and started climbing, I immediately retreated.

Oh God, this is it. Even if he wasn't going to kill me, he would definitely do that now that I attacked him! P-p-plank, he said? They will feed me to the sharks!!

I looked at the second of Martina nonchalantly exchanging words with the shithead called Lou. My eyes narrowed on his long sword making me gulp.

Shit, I can't die now! I haven't even found the tiniest lead to finding my dear cousin!!

When his attention was brought to me, I stood my ground and ignored the glares of the younger pirate who somehow managed to climb into the deck a blink of an eye. Ace approached me steadily making my heart threaten to stop in my chest.

"Your head"

Oh God, they want to cut my head!

"You ok? You're shaking"

"I-I'm fine"

"A headache?"

"Excuse me?"

"From the injury. Do you still feel drowsy sometimes?"

"N-No... I'm... better actually. Just the occasional headache caused by your pirate friend"

He grinned slightly and nodded, "Good. Now let me take a look so I can tell if it's been healing nicely"

I nodded. It was so weird, I was supposed to be scared or angry or something, but... it felt like I wanted to be polite to this man. ONLY this man though, because the other two are already getting on my nerves with their smirk/glare combo.

I learned that the young pirate is called 'Monkey', probably just a nickname though. And he looked like Ace's lackey or something.

Ace checked on me, then he went to make sure everything was going well with my crew below deck where they were keeping them as prisoners. They spoke alone, Lou and him for a while. Then he called upon the monkey and they all left my ship back to theirs.

I sat on my bed with a long sigh. I didn't know what I could do anymore; money, I spared. Time, I stole. Efforts and ideas, I'm sincerely out of those... Yet here I was, a prisoner in my own ship in a shadow area, and being led to God knows where...

"You're weary"

"You're smart" I said, sarcastically of course.

"What's wrong now?" he asked as if my worries could be any of his business.

When I didn't answer, he walked into my cabin and close to me, "Dinner should be here soon, if you're hungry"

I nodded. I can't believe it, but after two weeks of this shit and months of pure chaotic chase, I actually don't have in me to fight the asshole pirate anymore. I'm just... tired... desperate...

"Hey"

I lifted my eyes to meet his furrowed ones

"Are you feeling sick? Want me to get Ace back here??"

'Get Ace back here', like he fucking works for you, you bastard. He's the damn second of Martina. He's probably treating my wounds so he could put me in a whole where I'd fight a bear or something

"I'm tired..."

"...... Want to sleep a bit?"

"No. I just... I actually want nothing."

"Heh, well that's impossible. Everyone wants something, especially a merchant, right?"

He laughed at his own stupid joke, making me smile sadly, "All I wanted was to get my cousin back home safe... now not only have I failed to do that, even if by some miracle my men find a clue on his whereabouts, I won't be there to chase after it"

"You've been searching for Nyx?"

I hid my face in my palms when I felt like it could show too much emotion. I rested my elbows on my legs and sighed heavily, "Doesn't matter. Wherever he went I'm too far and too late anyway. I couldn't pick up any trail of him, and every day that goes by makes it harder to find him. Now I'm losing important clients, I'm imprisoned by pirates, my father will definitely know now that I've been doing more than just taking care of his trades, and the worst is that the last time I saw him I was mad at all my family and refused to even talk to him."

His voice sounded calm, but less smug than usual when he spoke a moment later, "If you do as the Captain ordered and stay put, I promise you won't be harmed. I actually know for sure that so far, he has no intent on killing you"

"I don't really care anymore, Lou. Even if he lets me go, I don't know what I would do after that... This is just too fucked up"

I bit on my lip, trying not to look more pathetic than what I felt. It was funny actually because, in much less complicated situations, I'd turn to the one person I trusted the most and ask for advice. So now I need his advice on what to do to find him...

"Haven", I lifted my eyes to see Lou standing in front of me and gazing at me deeply, "If you had to choose one thing, only one. What would it be?"

"What, like, anything?"

"Anything in the world"

I stared back at him looking in my mind for many things I could possibly ask for. It was weird how I found nothing other than the quest that kept me sleepless for the past months

"Nyx... I want to see him again"

The pirate's eyes furrowed and he looked and sounded strangely serious, "And what would you give up to see him?"

What would I give up? Money, time, power, business... you name it!!

"Everything"

"Even your life?"

I went silent for a short moment, before smiling and answering confidently, "My life"

He frowned, but more sympathetically this time. He looked into my eyes intensely and I looked up into his. A long moment later, I realized how long we were gazing at each other... a very awkward moment

I chuckled, forcing myself to sound humorous to avoid the embarrassment, "Now what, we make, like, a devil-pact where you tell me you know where he is and then kill me?"

I expected a snicker, the usual smirk, or even his eyes rolling. But what didn't expect was him, rubbing the back of his neck and mouthing a hesitant, "Well..."

∞ ∞ ∞

Chapter 21 ~ Cartes sur table
∞ Haven's POV ∞

I waited until it was very late at night, and I climbed the edge of the deck that was facing away from the pirate ship. I jumped and was embraced by the sea, no complain though, I didn't have the time. I swam around my ship and towards Martina, making sure not to awaken the stinky pirate sleeping in the small boat by my ship.

I swam, approaching my destination slowly. The long jacket was restraining my movements so I removed it and let float away as I moved further. I was following my heart, and my mind was screaming for me to turn around, but I refused to listen to logic. I usually calculated and planned everything I did. Right now I had no choice though! God knows if what Lou said was true, but if they know that he spoke I might never see my cousin ever again. This was my only chance, and since I already made a deal with a pirate, it was my last chance.

So there I was, swimming in the sea under a very dark sky; either heading for my salvation or complete hopelessness. In both cases, I was definitely heading for my death.

Damn the water was freezing! I was a good swimmer, but with my bones shaking from the cold, it took me a good fifteen minutes to reach the bigger ship.

I touched the ship while heaving, mostly from the cold and not the effort of swimming. I looked up, trying to find a way to climb the damn thing. I needed to get to the deck without alarming them. I definitely need to verify if Nyx was actually here before they noticed me!

I moved around the ship until I found the heavy chain linking the ship to its anchor. I looked back to see it that pirate Lou had changed his mind and came to claim my head earlier than promised. It was dark with enough moonlight to let me see my ship, now for from me, and the small boat still floating beside it. I breathed in and out; I was safe……… for now.

My hands grabbed loop after loop as I climbed the heavy chain. Soon, I reached the edge of the pirate's deck; it was at arm's length from me. My resolve decided to bail on me at such a critical moment. I tried to ignore my feelings and just do it, so I reached and grabbed the edge, but I pulled back when my hand started trembling. I clenched and unclenched it trying to ease the tension and my mind took the chance to do what I've been preventing it from: thinking.

I sighed and grabbed the chain again to keep myself from falling back into the sea. Yes, this was far from wise; if I'm found, I'll be most probably killed on the spot or worse, tortured! If I actually manage to find my cousin then I'll still need to hold my end of the bargain, which means...... handing my head to Lou. And even if I don't find him, I'm stepping on a pirate ship without permission. My head will most probably be severed by the Captain before Lou could collect it himself.

I held my neck, imagining the pain one would feel when they pass away. I was scared, hell I was terrified! I'm not the kind who gets frightened easily, but this... I was going to perish either way

My Goodness, am I ready to die??

Hell no! I still need to report back to father. I need to find a way to cover the losses of this raid or he'd be really disappointed. I need to go see if the people I sent came back with any news about Nyx. And mother, I need to buy her the silk she wanted again. I also have to take my crew safely back to Mila, I have people to pay and trades to finalize, I need to find a way to deal with the merchants waiting for the cotton and silk that I just lost... And most importantly, I need to find him... God, I desperately need to see him at least once before I die......

"Whatcha doing?"

The unexpected voice startled me as it tore through the heavy silence of the ship, making me yelp and almost fall in the water. I looked up to see that young pirate, monkey they called him, he was grabbing my soaked shirt tightly preventing me from meeting the sea.

He tilted his head waiting for my answer, which came humiliatingly stuttering, "I-I-I... I was..."

"Are you cold?"

"...... Excuse me?"

"Your hands are shivering, you're soaked and you can't talk straight"

"Y-yes. Yes, I'm cold"

"Well clinging to the chain won't help you. Come on"

He pulled me up and I followed until I was standing on the deck. I straightened my back and looked around me; this was it, there's no going back anymore. I was here. On the deck of the Martina pirate ship!

Fuck, I'm doomed.

"Now, I can give you dry clothes, if you want"

Clothes?? He's not going to tell on me to his crew??
If not, then I don't have time for this!!

I sighed and tried to get rid of him, "That would be quite generous of you, thank you"

He grinned, then put his hand on his hip and leaned on his right leg, "Ten coins"

I frowned, simply because I didn't understand what he meant

"For the clothes," he explained, "it will be ten coins"

"Really? Ten for a pirate's used shirt and pants?"

"If you want pants, that will be an extra seven coins"

"Are you serious??"

He shrugged, "Well, I don't think you should bargain much. You're stepping on a pirate's deck uninvited. The last time I checked people get killed for doing just that. Now, I'm being kind enough not to call my mates and wake them from their filthy dreams, but if you want clothes, you'll need to pay"

"I don't get it, why are you helping me? Why not just tell your friends and get all the credit? I mean, we just met earlier today and I'm certain you don't like me"

He nodded, "Aye, I don't like you. But I do like your-"

He stopped suddenly. I stared for a couple of seconds in his brown eyes before I realized! I stepped in front of him and held his arms, "Who? What were you going to say?? Please, please tell me I'm not mistaken and-"

His hand covered my mouth almost slapping me, "Don't raise your voice, landlubber. You're going to wake the others. Now, I know you deserve a lesson on how to be respectful to people like our great and amazing Tashi fighter, but if they catch you right now, you'll be getting more than just a lesson, if you know what I mean"

Part of that was gibberish to me, but I nodded frantically, making him release my mouth, "Sir, please. I... I need to see him!" I pleaded desperately and he looked at me closely, I thought he was giving up, but this young man is adamant on making me lose my mind before the end of this endless night, "What can you give me?"

I sighed, trying to control my temper. **I don't have fucking time!**

"I don't have anything right now" *Not even my own life, actually...*

"Too bad, can't help ya then!"

"Fine, I'll find him myself!"

I walked past him and towards the hull. When I was close to it, he snickered and said sarcastically, "Good luck finding anything down there! Too bad you were cheap to save your own life. It was nice knowing you, Haven. Wait, nah, not so nice after all"

Did... did he just help me??
If the hull is not the right way, then...

I turned and walked towards the cabin. Standing in front of the door, I looked back at the young pirate. His hand was clenched on a rope falling down from the mast. He looked at me with eyes filled with worry and I might even say fear. What was he afraid of? I'm the one walking towards death here.

When I reached for the cabin's door, the pirate grabbed the rope and hastily climbed up the mast like... ok now I get why they call him *monkey*.

I pushed the door, causing a small squeaking noise to erupt. It wasn't much, but since everything was silent, and considering this was the lion's den, the small noise was more than my frightened heart could handle.

The thought of turning around rushed back hard. *It's just an instinct,* I told myself, *just my instinct of survival.* I breathed to encourage myself, and the memory of my dearest friend and family wiped the hesitation away.

I stepped inside carefully. It was pretty dark, only a small window, casting a very dim light into the room. I opened the damn squeaky door more for more moonlight to flood in. And that's when I saw someone sleeping on the bed.

My feet immediately froze to the sight of the long gray hair of the so known Captain. I looked around the room and saw nothing else alive, so I was about to walk right from where I came and hope to close the door without waking the devil. But as my eyes adapted more the lighting of the room, I noticed the other person lying in front of him.

I stood there, blinking as my mind refused to process what my eyes saw. And before I know it, I called to him, "...... Nyx??"

In less than a second, a pair of eyes was angrily glaring at me. I couldn't even get my feet to move as he stood up and strode towards me, his feet light as a ghost and his eyes pinning mine coldly. I looked at him and I immediately knew he was going to kill me. I took a step back, reaching the area lighted by the moonlight that sneaked in from the door. As soon as I did, the menacing silhouette stopped and the gray eyes widened in disbelief. He recognized me, and for a second I wondered why he stopped.

"nnn... Agenor... what's wrong?" the black bed sheet moved as he sat up and rubbed his eyes sleepily. And when he opened them, he gasped sharply

He moved slowly out of the bed. After so many months of feeling empty inside, my heart resumed beating at the sight of him... and I felt alive again as I followed his every move, afraid that if I look away, his image might disappear like an illusion.

God, if this is a dream, please keep me forever asleep

"Haven?"

When his sweet voice called my name, I knew this was a reality. Without thinking, I rushed his way and threw my arms around him in a desperate hug, "Yes! It's me! I'm here, Nyx, I will save you my dearest"

"H..... How did you...?"

I smiled and pulled back, "I always knew not to believe those damn letters. I always knew and finally... here you are"

I gazed at his shiny eyes that never lost their beauty even under the dim light. Suddenly the room was brighter. My head snapped to the source of it and found the pirate, Ace, with his hand pulling away from a lamp, and slightly behind him was Monkey. I guess he did tell on me after all. He looked worried, almost hiding behind Ace. Why would he hide?? He didn't seem scared of me before. Unless... it wasn't *me* he was scared of

My eyes met the Captain's again. He was standing still in the middle of the room while glaring holes in my skull.

Shit, I can't be killed yet, I need to get Nyx out of here!!

I turned until I was facing them, my hand still holding Nyx's forearm to keep him behind me. My mind suddenly realized that he was half naked, and I pushed the thought away because I completely refused to think about why the FUCK he was lying half-naked on the same bed as the devil!

Even when I was looking away from him, my mind kept revisiting his picture over and over. A new memory... At last, I have a new memory of him after all the time I've been denied to look at him. A lump formed in my throat when I suddenly came aware that he was wearing a......... *collar*

How could they do that to someone like him!!

"Don't worry Nyx. I'll get you out of here. I'll get you home"

As soon as I said that, Agenor took a menacing step towards me, but I kept my ground. Agenor seemed to have stopped moving forward when his eyes glanced to Nyx, making me hold his forearm harder and push him further behind me. He called me and pulled my arm to make me look at him. And as much as I wanted to, I couldn't break eye contact with Agenor's intimidating aura

"Haven, look at me-My! You're freezing! You need to change"

When I didn't answer or look at him, he continued, "Please sit down, there's so much I want to talk to you about!" I know that tone of his all too well, that's the voice he uses when he's facing trouble and wants to calm things down.

I held his warm hands that were still pulling at my left arm, "We'll talk Nyx, we'll talk as much as we want right after I get you out of here"

God, I need to do something to protect him, I can't believe we're trapped with both the devil and his right hand facing us!! And from the looks of it, the Captain will not back down before he chops my head. Shit, I need to come up with something fast!!

"How did you get here??" Ace asked me with his eyes narrowing at me.

Despite the dire circumstances, I made sure to keep my stance straight and my eyes unwavering. This was fucked up enough as it was, I didn't need Nyx to know how much scared I was of these pirates who most probably tormented him for months... *Oh God, did they hurt him? Torture him??*

"You already took everything valuable we have, keeping not one, but TWO noblemen prisoners will only get you more enemies. And it would be even worse if you dare hurt us! Let us go and we shall not pursue you for what you stole"

Enraged for some reason, a tick formed at the Captain's jaw and he stepped closer, looking ready to rip my neck.

"Agenor-"

Nyx went to talk to him, but he was interrupted when other pirates outside called Lou and started asking him about what happened. *Fuck, I'm running out of time!*

As soon as Lou arrived at the cabin, with other heads that looked inside, but didn't dare interfere, he went to talk to his Captain, "Captain, I came as soon as-"

I didn't even register until the pirate was thrown back with a loud thud as hit large built hit the wall.

Lou, the cocky pirate, and the excellent fighter. I was told he was the one who defeated the Captain of my ship as well as many expensive guards. The pirate that I tried to defeat over and over and over... he was thrown against the wall with one punch!

"Oh, God!" Nyx gasped and went to interfere, but I grabbed his arm and pulled him while we both retreated back. *Damn it, even without our bargain he would definitely kill me now for getting him beaten by his Captain. He won't do it right away though, right?? He can't kill me in front of Nyx! That's part of the deal!*

The pirates outside were all watching with eyes open wide. Some of them cursed and disappeared as soon as they saw their Captain's stance. The young pirate was scared too, he stepped back and lowered his head with his hand still grabbing Ace's shirt. Ace was the only one who didn't flinch; he sighed and shook his head in irritation as if he knew of this outcome.

As soon as Lou tried to sit while grabbing his bloodied nose, Agenor kicked him in the guts and sent him falling again on the floor. But the Captain still had more coming. He grabbed Lou's shirt and pulled him up just to ball his fist and prepare for the next blow.

"**Stop!!**"

Nyx's yell surprised me, and I watched with eyes open wide as he strode towards the devil and pulled him back, separating him from the injured pirate. Then he stood between them and actually glared at him, "Are you out of your mind? What's gotten into you!"

"Stay out if this Nyx, this is none of your business!"

"It's **all** my business! And Lou didn't disrespect you in any way. He's not fighting back, not even protecting his face!! What did he do to deserve that!"

Agenor glared at Lou, who was now wiping the blood on his chin and leaning on the wall behind him, "He knows well what he did."

Lou's eyes strayed my way for a brief moment before he looked away in silence, practically confirming his Captain's thoughts.

Nyx sighed and his voice became lower, but not less assertive, "Well, please try talking first. Especially with those who are loyal to you. He didn't even say one word and you attacked him!"

"Why are you defending *him*? Weren't you the one who wanted me to kick his ass for tormenting *Haven*?"

I almost chuckled at the venomous way he said my name. Nyx pouted and shifted uncomfortably, looking very guilty. *Fuck, I missed this cute side of him*

"I... I just wanted you to keep him away from Haven..." he returned with a shrug. Then he gained his confidence back when he remembered something, "It was Nash who proposed to beat him up!!"

"Ooooh~! Look who learned to tell on people!" Another pirate came inside while smirking at Nyx who sighed, "Not now, Nash"

The pirate just laughed slightly and pushed his hair back. He stood beside the second with his sword resting on his shoulder. A few other pirates came in and a couple were actually teasing the very silent Lou.

Nyx walked past me to open a box, then he smiled at me and hurried back to hand Lou a blue handkerchief. Lou took it, but instead of walking out, he pushed Nyx slightly so he could face the devil, "Captain... I apologize for tonight, I didn't really plan it, it just..."

Agenor closed the distance between them and threatened with a low and enraged tone, "Get out of my face before I end you."

The pirate looked really hurt. It was so weird that he didn't seem scared of being beaten by his Captain, but rather ashamed of disappointing him.

Another one who was now leaning on the edge of the door with a sword attached to his waist smirked at me, "This is all *your* fault, you know?" then his smirk widened, "I say we punish him by keeping him for a while. I really need a servant after all"

I swallowed when all eyes turned to me. The so-called Nash smirked and pushed the scabbard slightly back with his thumb revealing a shiny blade.

"Leave him alone, Zaire. And please put your swords away, no need to tease him", Nyx said as he walked my way. When he stood before me, he smiled gently, "Don't mind them, they like to bully people. Are you ok?"

I blinked. I was the one who was supposed to ask him that! Somehow the situation had shifted... I don't know how or why, but Nyx doesn't seem in need to hide behind me. He actually looked more ready to shield *me*.

I opened my mouth to answer him, but as I looked at his eyes, the only thing my mind provided was a whimpering 'I missed you'. So I closed my mouth and chose to be silent.

Nyx leaned to his right and grabbed the black bed sheet, then he put it around my wet body, "You need to get warm Haven, or your chest might hurt you. Did you bring your medication with you?"

Now that he mentions it, I'm actually very cold. I pulled the cloth on me, "I did, but all my stuff was taken in the raid"

A wave of guilt washed over his eyes. He swallowed nervously, then looked away, "I-I'll find it for you"

The Captain moved and I stiffened. My eyes followed him as he grabbed a long black leather jacket that was on the table and put it on Nyx's naked shoulder. Nyx looked back at him and they exchanged gentle smiles before he pushed his arms in the sleeves.

Agenor's hands landed on my cousin's shoulders as if that was the most natural thing in the world. I glared at him and grabbed Nyx's arm and pulled him to me, but the bastard only squeezed his hands harder.

The sudden pulling in opposite directions had Nyx awe. I didn't want to hurt him, but I wasn't going to let him go either!!

"Don't. Touch. What's. MINE!"

My eyes widened at his insolence, "*Yours*?? He's not anyone's! He's not an object!"

We both moved closer to each other, but Nyx stood between us with his hands on each one of us, "Please don't do this! Agenor back off, and Haven please hear me out first!"

"I don't have time for this! I'm not listening to anything until I make sure you're safe, Nyx! I'm taking you back home-"

"He's safe here!! And you're not taking him anywhere!!"

"Oh my, this is really something", "Fuck, I should start a bet right away"... the pirates watched the scene with amusement.

I pulled Nyx and moved towards the door, "We're leaving!"

My feet halted when sharp swords left their scabbards welcoming us to try and walk through them. I cursed under my breath. And when I looked back, I found Nyx holding Agenor's arms to keep him from attacking me, "Agenor, please..." his voice weakened suddenly and he whispered, "you'll make him hate me!"

For the first time tonight, the coldness in the devil's eyes faded as he looked down, "I'm not letting him take you away!"

I was truly surprised at the hurt in his voice that suddenly lost all animosity. He didn't get any response though. They just kept a staring contest, and I guess Nyx somehow won because Agenor threw his hands in the air in surrender and walked back then reluctantly sat down on the bed.

"Good!" the so-called Zaire yelled from behind me, "Now who's in for some fancy wine?"

"Count me in! Why don't you serve us some, Nyx?" Nash added. Nyx turned to give him a half pout/half glare, but the pirate brushed it casually, "Oh come on, kitten, it's the least you can do for waking us I the middle of the night"

Nyx rolled his eyes, then smiled at me. He walked to the table and pulled a chair for me, "Please"

I glanced at Agenor, who was squeezing his hands together with eyes pinned to the floor. The pirates moved further inside the cabin and Zaire pulled a jar of wine and started drinking before passing it to the next. Nash stood beside him and they started laughing at something. Monkey joined in taking his 'share' of the wine as he called it. And Ace just sat quietly beside his Captain.

This... felt really, really weird. When I didn't move, Nyx smiled sadly and pulled a chair for himself. I looked behind me; even while knowing there were still pirates on the deck, the entrance looked much easier to escape from. But what is the point of leaving without Nyx??

I moved to sit where Nyx wanted me to. He grabbed a cup and politely asked for the wine back from the hands of the vultures. He poured some and pushed the cup to me, "Please have some, it will help you warm up"

I drank while Nyx went to open a box and bring something. When he came back, he grabbed the bed sheet from around my shoulders, "It's soaked already. Please change into this shirt, I don't want you getting sick"

I nodded and removed my shirt, then put the blue one that he handed me on. My pants were also cold, but he knows I wasn't going to change them now, not here anyway.

After that, he sat on his chair again quietly while watching the pirates, but not saying anything or even laughing with them. There was a weird sense of awkwardness in the air and it wasn't just because we were sipping wine with some of the worst pirates!

I gazed at him and smiled because he was avoiding looking at me. He was so nervous he probably didn't know what to say. Somehow it made me feel sad and oddly estranged

I leaned forward and grabbed his jacket gently. I closed it and started tying it. It was obviously not his since the shoulders sagged on the sides. He sighed soundly and his eyes lifted to hesitantly meet mine, "I... I'm sorry Haven... I have so much I wanted to talk to you about but I don't know where to start"

How about the reason why we're sitting comfortably instead of fighting these hooligans and taking cover in my ship!

"I'm here now, Nyx. And I'm not leaving without you. Until then, we can talk about whatever you want"

"What were you doing in a non-guarded area?? You know how dangerous it is!"

"Yet here you are" I mumbled. For some odd reason, it looked like he took that as an offense, which was the last thing I would do. "I was looking for you, Nyx. For months I've strayed away from my original routes to visit Shadow islands and look for you. But no one recognized you or could even give a hint! I've hired bounty hunters to trace you... Nothing! Not a damn thing for months! It was like you disappeared in the sea never landing anywhere!!"

He looked at me with a gasp and guilt filling his eyes, "Haven that's so dangerous!! What if something happened to you! You can't trust hunters, and you know that! They can lead you on with false information and-"

"I know, that's what happened actually. I was given false information and lost two months chasing it. Of course, I still paid the asshole, it's not like I want a hunter going after the family"

He shook his head slowly as if his mind was in denial of what I said. Then his voice stuttered slightly, "Why would you go so far?"

"I had no choice! What did you want me to do, go to parties and pretend as nothing happened?? **You Were Almost Killed!!** I told you a thousand times never to trust Terry! I told you to take a break, to leave everything behind and just come sail with ME! I go back from a stupid trade and find you GONE! Leaving nothing but a-a-a fucking letter!! How could you do that!!" I was standing and yelling. The composure I was supposed to keep and the strength I was supposed to have in order to lead him to safety completely broke. Now I was just really angry at him.

I can't believe he thought I wouldn't sail to bring him back!! That I would just let him go beyond reach? ALONE!

"............... I.......... I couldn't go back..."

"What about now? Let's leave! Or at least try to!! Why are we sitting here like this is the most fucking normal thing to do on a pirate ship!!"

The cabin went completely silent after that. Shit, Nyx looked ready to break if I pushed harder. *Either these scums are holding something against him or......... he really doesn't want to go back to Corail... with me...*

After a long few minutes of silence, he asked hesitantly, "How's mother?"

I scoffed, but when I raised my eyes, his were ready to spill, "Oh God! Is she sick?? Did something happen?"

Shit!

I grabbed his hand and looked straight at him, "She's fine. Your mother is not sick Nyx, believe me. The last time I saw her, she was in perfect health"

I felt a heavy aura crushing me, I looked beside me to see Agenor glaring at me again. *Damn it, if not for Nyx, he would definitely have killed me by now. Wait, why am I thinking that??*

"You looked troubled when I mentioned her!"

I shook my head while crossing my arms, "Your mother is not sick. She's doing fine. Too fine, actually. She was very worried after what happened, we all kept reading your letter over and over until it looked like it was written a hundred years ago. I tried to find any clue you might have left for me in the letter... something... anything!! We hired investigators to find you and I sailed to look for you myself. So imagine my shock when I come back and they tell me they received a second letter from you and that they already called the search off!! They actually believed you would sail away without even saying goodbye or talking to me. I tried to convince them that you weren't 'happily' sailing safely somewhere, that you would never do this! I kept telling them that you were in danger and that we needed to find you! I tried to make them see reason, but they said I would bring you bad luck is I keep saying that you're I danger and that they couldn't hear me talk about you anymore. And when I kept asking father to convince the guards to send a word out and keep looking for you, he said I should mind my own business!! So YES! I am troubled with them because they refused to listen to me! At least they were missing you a lot, but then it was all baby this baby that-"

"What?"

"...... Oh... yeah, Raya is a mommy now"

He looked at me in complete surprise, like he couldn't find the words to express his happiness. He just blinked as the pirates lunged towards him and started congratulating him, saying they needed to celebrate with some wine as if they hadn't finished the second jar already. Monkey was patting his shoulder, calling him 'old uncle' when Nyx looked my way again, "Is it a girl??"

"Áine and little Nyx"

"**Twins**!!"

I nodded and his eyes opened wide, then he turned to Agenor, who was already standing beside him ruffling his hair, with a tenderness I found myself not comfortable with at all

"Did you hear that? T-Twins! Raya had a boy and a girl!!"

Agenor smiled lightly, "Congratulations. Now you know your sister is safe"

Nyx nodded eagerly then he faced me and threw his arms around my chest, "Thank you! Thank you so much, Haven!! I know you've been through a lot because of me and I know I don't deserve kindness! You've always been there for me, even after what I became, here you are! I was going crazy thinking about Raya and if she gave birth or not... Oh God, a boy, and a girl! Just... Thank you!"

My chest tightened and I closed my eyes to finally feel him really close to my heart again. I hugged him back, ignoring the looks of the pirate who I knew was wishing me dead right now. Well, his wish will be granted soon, but not this moment; This moment was my last gift. I put my forehead on his shoulder and my hands clenched in the fabric of his jacket as I hugged him closer, forcing myself to only dive in this brief happiness and not think about my debts.

∞ ∞ ∞

Chapter 22 ~ Catching up
∞ Nyx's POV ∞

It was evening already and we were on the deck, still talking and laughing together. This day was magical; a part of me that was always feeling unsettled and worried, it now felt appeased.

My dear cousin is my best friend. He's the brother that I never had. I love him, and I took care of him, especially when we were kids. Since my father's passing and despite being younger than me, he was there for me; talking me out of my state of depression, forcing me to go horse riding with him, and even defending me when I got in trouble at work or with my stepfather, Terry. He was the only one telling me to take it easy, never once did he tell me to work harder or step up to carry my responsibilities.

And seeing all the difficulties I went through, especially when we almost lost my father's business because of my incompetence and passive attitude at the time, my uncle decided that Haven should take more responsibilities at leading his trading business, and he started sending him overseas on his own.

Back then, I had it rough with the abandoned ships and the scattered shipwrights and sailors, but it wasn't easy on Haven either.

My dear cousin never complained though. He usually opens up to me and pours all his hardships, but at that time he knew that I wasn't in shape to give advice or even listen. And whenever he came back, he would spend as much time as possible with me at the port, helping me sort payments and prepare schedules. HE IS SO SMART! I mean, I am not stupid, but I'm the kind who learns by practice and by applying what I read in books. Haven, on the other hand, he's born to manage business. He's so talented that he doesn't even take a break from his long sail before diving into my work and sort out my mess while giving me all kinds of advice. He is whiny, playful, and sometimes childish, but also brilliant, kind, and very trustworthy.

He sees me as a role model since we were kids. He has changed a lot since then. He used to get sick all the time and the most fun he'd have is when I visit and read for him. I proud to say that I taught him the passion of reading books. And when he grew up, his health got a lot better, so he made up for all the time he spent at home by making friends and going to parties. My cousin is so talented socially, much better than my humble self.

So here I was, sitting beside him on the deck, genuinely laughing at his stories and his jokes, while I ask him over and over about our family, and make him tell me how cute the tiny babies are.

My heart filled with happiness as he talks about Corail, and I'm so glad I'm able to hide the shame and fear swirling inside me.

"... whenever one cries the other follows. And they never, NEVER sleep away from each other! It seems they got used to snuggling together. Áine always sleeps and whines much more, but when she smiles you can't help but fall for her. She has your mother's blond hair and beautiful green eyes. While little Nyx has blue eyes and black hair, just like your late father. Your mother says he looks exactly like you when you were a baby! Explains why he's so beautiful...... And he's the perfect gentleman already! Unlike Áine, little Nyx doesn't mind being fed after his twin sister"

I laughed, "I imagine Raya has her hands full"

"You can say that, but her husband loves to hold them and I hear he even helps cleaning them while nagging about them taking only after their mother's side. He says that, but you can see how proud he is of both his wife and children. So I think they're not too much to handle for Raya"

"... Is she happy?"

Does she miss me?

Silly questions. And yet I felt so unqualified to ask them when I was the one who abandoned her. I didn't even know if it was my own fault or not anymore. That didn't really matter much since someone needs to take responsibility either way. I just... I need to hear that my dear sister is living happily... despite being *my* sister

Haven stared at me for a minute, then he answered with eyes that couldn't hide his sadness, "She's happy, Nyx. Raya has her husband and mother beside her. My mother also visits a lot, as you know, so she has many people to rely on if she ever needed anything. But her happiness will be complete if she gets to see *you*! And I..."

I embraced myself for what was coming. This is the conversation I've been avoiding since Haven saw me.

I went to talk, but the lack of words made me close my mouth silently. When I didn't say a thing, Haven continued, "Nyx, you know all about me, my cousin. You know I would never want to harm you or wish you to be hurt in any way. Please talk to me, tell me why the hell do we befriend these pirates? Why are we not at least trying to get away from them! We have to go home Nyx. Together, you and I, we'll go back to Corail, I promise this time you'll find more support than before. I know how hard the last years were for you, I promise I will help you much more just... come with me. You need to! I... I really need you with me, Nyx"

As his green eyes implored me, I felt deeply guilty and utterly lost. As I failed to justify my passive attitude yet again, he grabbed my hand, "Nyx, I-"

Suddenly haven froze and looked alarmed as he stared the other way. I followed where he was staring only to see Britt walking closer to us with his face emotionless like always and his steps heavily pounding on the deck. Haven tensed and stood up defensively from where he was sitting on the edge of the deck. I chuckled; he wasn't used to being around Britt, but the big guy is actually very nice. No one seems to share my opinion about him on this ship though, not even Agenor! But that doesn't keep me from being right.

Britt halted when he reached us then he just stood there, staring at Haven. The giant man wasn't threatening or anything, he just liked to intimidate others using his large form, and it worked with everyone; I could see my poor cousin swallowing.

"Hey Britt"

He nodded at me and pushed something in my hand. Then he looked at Haven again, before turning around and disappearing into the hull.

"God, that's a fucking huge pirate!!"

"Don't be rude, Haven" I opened the pouch of leather that he handed me and smiled, "He actually found your medication! See? He's a very nice person"

"...... I could never use 'nice' to describe that"

"How long since you had your medication?"

"...... two weeks"

I knew my cousin too well to detect when he was lying to me, so I asked again with a tone that demanded the truth. He looked away and mouthed a weak, "A month, maybe more"

"Haven... you know how important this is for your health. Why would you risk-?"

"Why? I'm fed up with being so weak! And that shit is useless: If I take too much, it hurts my stomach, too little and it practically has no effect whatsoever! Besides, when I take it for a long period, it affects my concentration. And I needed to be awake and able to think in order to find you"

With the little courage I had, I faked strength and confidence, hoping as a lousy cousin and older friend I still had a say in his life, "I will prepare your medication for you-"

And the old Haven was back in a blink of an eye when he whined in protest, "Nyyyx~ I really hate the taste!"

"I'm sorry, we don't have honey here, but you still need to take it. I can' believe your servants let you do as you please"

"They're *my* servants! They obey me"

"Look, I'll make half the usual dose for today; with everything happening, I don't want to overwhelm you. And starting tomorrow you go back to the daily dose. Please, Haven, all I want is your well-being"

"Fine." His hopeful eyes looked at me and he added with a hesitation that made me feel so guilty, "I'll take it every day if you're there to hand it to me"

"I......... I'll go prepare this"

With that, I cowardly turned away and paced towards the hull, fleeing from the confrontation and the hurt took that I caused to my brother.

∞ ∞ ∞

The galley was empty since everyone had dinner already and started drinking or slacking somewhere in the ship. I lit a couple of lamps hanging on the walls, then I pulled the cleanest round kettle and used it to heat some water. Once it started boiling, I poured some of the herbs from the leather pouch into the water. I had to keep the fire low but going, so I blew lightly on the burning pieces of wood every minute or so.

It was strange that I was enjoying the silence around me. God knows how much I missed my cousin, but it seems my fear of facing him was even bigger.

So far the day went really well; we talked about many things and I got to know the details about Corail and Haven's work, I went to thank Lou for his help. I wasn't as stupid as to believe that my cousin discovered my whereabouts on his own. And despite not knowing the reason behind his sudden generosity, I still owed him the happiness of meeting my cousin and hearing the news about my family.

Lou was sitting against the edge of the quarterdeck when I found him, and he looked in pain. I guess Agenor's hits were really effective if only a couple could make someone as strong and experienced as Lou move with difficulty. Thank God Agenor didn't go further than delivering a couple of punches or he might've actually killed his crew member. Yes, Lou can be a huge jerk sometimes, but he wasn't a bad person, at least when he wasn't teasing me with Nash. In the end, I expected him to be resentful towards me for what happened to him, to my surprise he just smiled and nodded.

When Agenor joined us, it felt awkward at first. It didn't seem like Agenor was angry with him anymore, so I left them alone and went back to my dear cousin. A while later, the pirate was already making his Captain smile and laugh.

Yes, it was a perfect day.

And the only way this perfection would continue was if Haven refrained from asking me questions that I really didn't know how to respond to.

He will demand to know what happened to me, why I changed, and I want to do with my life. He will expect me to go back to Corail and face the pirates to gain my freedom.

I do want to go back to Corail; it might sound childish, but I miss my mother. I also miss Raya and I deeply want to see the cute twins... but that is not an option for me. I don't know if Agenor would actually let me go if I asked him to. Even if he did, I'm too attached to him to leave.

I blew again on the small fire and sighed.

I love him; it's as simple as that. Despite everything we have gone through since the day he saved me from drowning, I came to rely on him in so many ways. As much as I invested in my business, I'm so glad that my uncle was taking care of it now. God, it's like a huge load was removed off my shoulders and I can only be relieved. Now I can't imagine myself being able to carry that load again.

That's not all, I don't know if I even deserve to! I'm not a gentleman anymore. Or am I? God, I don't know who I am. All I know is that now I'm a pirate, I eat from stolen goods, I raid, I fight, **I KILL**!

I'm no longer the promising son and heir, I no longer make my family proud

"You ok?"

Agenor's calming voice reached me, but I didn't dare look back. I didn't want him to see my eyes right now because I was trying to blink the tears away.

I hummed in response and occupied myself by blowing lightly on the fire. He walked closer and hugged me from behind. I closed my eyes to feel the blessing of being beside him. Whenever my thoughts tugged me in a thousand ways, being close to Agenor made them quiet down and gave me a warm sense of security.

"Thank you"

He leaned down and kissed my temple, "For what?"

"For not lashing out at Haven, and for letting me talk to him all day"

It was actually a miracle that he didn't attack Haven already. I wouldn't forgive him if he did, but still, he didn't even yell or insult him despite his hot temper. For that, I was truly grateful.

"I would do anything for you, Nyx... Anything to keep you mine"

I blushed at his response; I didn't know if that sounded rather possessive or childish. Either way, it was very heartwarming

I couldn't help but confess my thoughts as I held his arms that were hugging me tight, "I love you, Agenor"

My lover froze for a second, then I felt his smile widen as he kissed my cheek, "I adore you, my love. And I hope all your worries be dispelled soon"

"I... I don't have any worries"

"I can almost hear your thoughts-"

"I'm just going to finish preparing Haven's medication. I'll make sure he drinks it all, or at least most of it. I think my cousin is growing to become stubborner than before"

"Nyx, you're escaping again"

My silence confirmed his accusation. I was a weakling and a coward; that thought had a truly bitter aftertaste.

After a moment of heavy silence, Agenor rested his head on my shoulder, "What's this medication good for?"

He was asking about Haven's illness. My cousin didn't like talking about it with others, but as a close friend and family, I was aware of it since we were kids.

"Haven used to suffer from troubles with his lungs, especially when he was young. He used to spend all his time in his room, the slightest change in the air or temperature would affect his breathing. As he grew older, he became stronger and much healthier, but he still needs to take this medication"

"He didn't take it for the last two weeks... Is he sick now??"

"He hasn't taken this for a while now, but thankfully he's alright. But seeing the bags under his eyes, I believe he's not sleeping well. He gets like that when he's stressed and it aggravates his illness. These herbs help him relax and sleep too, so it's important that he takes them. From what he said, he had been overworking himself a lot lately, yet he still unable to get a good night's sleep. And all of this is..."

My voice trailed at the end and Agenor caught on it, "What is it?"

I sighed, "It's... It's my fault Agenor... It's my fault that he's trying so hard-"

When his arms suddenly left me, I felt abandoned for a second. But then he turned me slightly to look in my eyes:

"I hate this, Nyx"

I didn't know what to say to that, he was seeing my weakness and I hated that too! So all I could respond was a useless but sincere apology, "I know... I'm sorry"

"No, I didn't mean it like that! I hate that you belittle yourself, like this cousin of yours is somehow better than you"

"You don't know him, Agenor. He is better, he's so kind and helpful! Unlike me, he never hurt anyone... The mere idea of him finding out who I became and being disgusted with me-"

"You don't need his approval! Why can't you see how perfect you are? You are strong and brave... you are unique, Nyx. And the only one you're allowed to seek approval from is ME! You challenged pirates countless times, for Gods' sakes, both drunk and sober. Why can't you face this cousin of yours?"

"You think I didn't try? I tried all day, but I kept failing!!"

"Maybe you need a drink" he raised an eyebrow, and despite the difficult situation, I found myself chuckling at his absurd suggestion

His face lit up and he pushed a strand of my hair back, "This is how I always want to see you, smiling"

His eyes gazed at my lips making a blush creep up my neck and settle on my face. He leaned in and pecked my lips, and I welcomed him by cupping his face and kissing him back. His arms pulled my waist closer to him while his teeth teased my lower lip.

My mind was drowning in the pleasure of the heated kiss when both Agenor and I heard something that made us turn to face the door.

My eyes widened when I saw Haven, staring at us in complete confusion as he breathed heavily

"H... Haven"

I went to walk towards him but he shook his head and took a step back, "You-... you-..." he was trying to talk but his breathing kept interrupting him. I tried to calm him down, and so did Agenor

"Haven, please, listen to me"

"Hey, calm down or you could faint"

Agenor was trying to help, but as soon as he approached him, Haven panicked even more and walked backward to escape from him. Before any of us could reach him, he was already falling on his back.

I gasped and reached forward to keep him from injuring himself. Luckily, Lou was right behind him and he caught him before he touched the hard floor then helped him sit.

Lou winced in pain, but he didn't let go of Haven who was still scrambling to get away from Agenor .... and *me*

Agenor lifted his hands in surrender and retreated to show Haven that he wasn't a threat to him. With that, my brother stopped trying to move away and just sat there, leaning on Lou, as he fought for a decent breath

"What the fuck happened??" Lou was confused as he witnessed one of Haven's attacks.

"N... Nyx... you... you..."

"Haven, I-"

"No!....... It-it can't be!" his breaths were getting shorter and more painful, which meant his confusion was only growing further

"Please stop talking, you're panicking and it's very bad for your health, if you calm down you'll feel better very soon, please Haven" I stepped forward, but when he flinched I immediately halted.

This is my fault! This is entirely my fucking fault!! He saw me kissing a pirate... a **man**! God, what will he think of me now! I didn't mean for any of this to happen, I never meant to hurt him!

I felt hands holding my shoulders, and that's when I realized that I was crying. I was shaking under the weight of Haven's disbelieving eyes and the sound of his wheezing breaths. He was still panicking and he really needed to calm down or it could get more serious!

I fought against my own cowardice and went to sit right in front of him, "Haven, I'm so sorry! I swear to God, I will explain anything you want, but you need to calm down for now, please..."

I held his hand in mine and he responded by shaking his head again while his eyes darted back and forth between Agenor and me, "You're... you're with him?... H-How?... Why *him*??"

When he didn't push me away, I dared to put a hand on his chest. I drew circles in a slow and a gentle motion, just the way I used to do when we were kids. I forced a smile and tried to calm him, "shshsh I'm here, Haven... you'll feel better, I promise"

We stayed like that for a few minutes; his eyes staring at me, still confused and in denial, but they seemed more focused now. The wheezing faded painfully slowly, leaving him exhausted.

Once he was able to draw a decent breath, he leaned forward slightly to part from Lou's hold. I didn't know what to do, so I dropped my gaze to the floor and waited for his rejection to hit me

∞ ∞ ∞

Chapter 23 ~ Parting ways
∞ Agenor's POV ∞

'my cousin is kind'...
'my cousin is smart'...
'my cousin is so helpful'...
'my cousin is famous with the ladies'...

All the times that Nyx had spoken about his legendary cousin came rushing back like an angry wave. I never gave it much thought before or at least asked about his damn name. Hell, I didn't even know he was talking about ONE COUSIN!! He praised him so much that I assumed he had many!!

my cousin this, my cousin that... **A cousin out of this freakin world!**

From all the oceans and seas, the legendary fuck decided to sail in ours! The lucky bastard...

Damn it, I shouldn't have pushed Nyx to raid. It started so well, though; I felt so proud of him actually fighting and defending himself on his own. He was a little too hesitant to strike, but that was expected of someone as principled and innocent as my cute angel. And I was ready to wait, push him step by step and watch him get used to being the attacker, and becoming a real pirate.

Gods, the way he moved his sword against those fighters, so elegantly and beautifully... Ace's training certainly gave him the strength to strike and to raid. And when the skilled guard surrendered and actually preferred jumping out of the deck than facing his blade, the whole sea couldn't drown my pride of his memorable performance.

Then *he* happened, making everything go south. I never want to see the agony in Nyx's eyes again, even if it meant that he wouldn't raid with me. That incident with his cousin not only messed with his head, but he was feeling so remorseful that he's basically begging this damn man for forgiveness

And here I stood, barely able to hold my frustration and discomfort at the sight of my lover caressing another man, a man he deemed as his best friend and only brother.

Brother my ass! He thinks I don't notice the way he looks at my lover!! The way he follows him with his eyes all day and recounts the measures he took to try and find him!

I mean, what *cousin* hurries to sail to a shadow island and into an unguarded sea after receiving the whiff of a rumor, without even confirming it first!! I might be a pirate, but I know pretty well what brotherly love is, and every instinct in my being is screaming at me to pull my Nyx away and hide him from this unwelcome visitor.

But no, I had no right to hide what was mine right now. If I pulled Nyx away, he might actually hate me for it. So I had to watch and remain silent as he held his cousin's hand with teary eyes that were pinned to the floor in shame.

Lou was standing on another wall, with a deep frown and questioning eyes; he tried to understand what had just happened, he wasn't aware of Haven's illness after all. He was staring between me and the cousins, with a hand on his side; he was clearly still suffering from my beating yesterday. I might have fractured a rib or two... he totally deserved it though; going behind my back and telling on Nyx! Damn, when I remember what he did I feel like I want to kick his fucking ass again!

A few heads peaked through the door of the galley, but I glared at them and they retreated. Not completely, of course, just enough for me not to see them.

My gaze fell again on a couple of birds sitting on the floor. After pushing Lou away, Haven moved to lean against the wall. He looked suddenly extremely exhausted; his skin was very pale and his eyes so tired and unfocused. I took him for a fighter, the way he put up with Lou and tried to hit him, but now he looks... frail.

Nyx stayed silently in front of him. He stopped touching his chest and calming him, but he didn't let go of his hand.

He was waiting...

Aye, he was waiting for the rejection to come. And as much as I hated the fact that this Haven's thoughts mattered to him that much, I couldn't do anything about it... Only try to make this easier on my Nyx.

∞ ∞ ∞

After a while, a long one I might add, Haven's face started gaining color. People who could get this sick usually avoid sailing, which meant this incident didn't occur often for him.

Nyx didn't calm down though, no matter what time passed, he kept biting his lip and sneaking looks at his cousin's way. Common sense probably suggested these two should be left alone, but I was in no way going to leave my Nyx with him.

Eventually, Haven spoke, his voice weak and extremely hoarse:

"Cold...... I'm cold..."

He didn't even look at Nyx when he said that. But that didn't matter to Nyx, who nodded and patted his cousin's hand, "I'll get you a jacket! I'll be right back, Haven"

With that, he shot me a sad look before pacing out of the galley and towards the deck. Haven threw his head back and just stared at the ceiling, looking quite sad and deep in thought.

Lou moved closer to him, but he didn't move at all. In a minute, Nyx was already back, holding his long jacket in his hand. He carefully put the folded clothes it in Haven's lap, and then he pulled out his blue handkerchief and wiped his forehead gently, "Haven... I want you to know that I-"

"I'm tired."

"Oh... Ok, here, let me help you up. I'll take you to my bed, you need to rest and we can talk-"

"I'm going to my ship" Haven pulled himself up and tried to straighten his stance.

"You can stay with me so I could help you if you needed-"

"My ship."

The decisiveness of his tone made Nyx flinch slightly and stop trying to help his cousin walk. Haven left the galley with nothing but a simple, "Let's go" to Lou.

I didn't need to see my lover's face to know that his cheeks were definitely wet right now. And despite his cousin's cold attitude, he hurried to grab the kettle and take it to them before they left Martina.

Haven was already climbing down to the boat when we reached the deck, and Nyx looked lost on what to do. I feared he might ask to go with him, so I acted first; I called on Lou, who turned around and nodded at me in obedience, "Captain"

"Take his medicine with you" I motioned for the kettle in Nyx's hands. Lou frowned, but he nodded and grabbed the kettle anyway. When he did, Nyx couldn't hold back from insisting, "Lou, please make sure he drinks this, if he's too stressed he might get sick again during the night. I'm so sorry Lou, but... just for tonight, please make sure he doesn't get sick again! If he coughs too much, send for me. And tomorrow I'll watch him myself and take care of his medicine"

Lou looked taken back by Nyx asking him for something. He patted his head and reassured him, without his usual sarcasm or toying attitude, "I'll make sure he takes his medicine and sleeps. Just... stop crying, it doesn't suit you, Nyx"

With that, and after making sure I had no other instructions for him, Lou climbed down a rope and joined the boat that started roaming away immediately.

With shaking shoulders and sniffles, Nyx stood there on the deck, watching the distant ship for a while, long after his cousin had disappeared in the darkness of the night. I thought I should let him vent his sadness instead of dragging him inside, so I put an arm around his shoulders and wiped the escaping tears.

"No... this won't do... I have to go with him", Nyx turned to me and continued, "Make them come back! I have to be there for him!"

"You can't do anything more for him now. Just let him rest and tomorrow you can talk to him again"

"But Lou won't know what to do if Haven's health worsens! I need to be by his side, please-"

"I don't think he would want that right now"

The hurt that invaded his eyes was so contagious that I sighed and ran my fingers through my hair. He moved closer and started whispering, "H-How about we send Ace there?"

"Ace??"

He looked around us, making sure no one would hear him, and then he continued whispering, "I know I can't ask anything from Ace, but you're the Captain, and if Ace is close to Haven, he could interfere faster in case he gets sick again. Please, Agenor... I don't know what else I could do..."

My Gods, begging... whispering... and hands clutching at my shirt! He's so fucking cute!! His adorable teary eyes will be the end of me

"AAACE!"

"AAAAAye!", an immediate thump on the deck announced a presence behind us, "Aye Aye Captain! What can I do for you?"

I frowned as I looked at the monkey that dropped beside us, "I was calling for Ace"

"Aye! And I will relay your message! You can tell me, Captain, and I will go tell Ace!"

I raised an eyebrow at that. Ace was already walking out of the hull and he pushed Maren's head down to shut him up as soon as he reached us, "You called, Captain?"

"Aye, you will spend the night on the other ship, just in case his cousin gets sick again"

He looked a bit confused before he said, "But I don't really know how to deal with his sickness"

"Doesn't matter, Ace. From all of us, you're the best at this anyway"

"Understood"

"Aye aye, Captain! **We** will leave immediately!!"

I turned to Maren, "*we??*" and he gave me a wide grin. I looked at Ace who shrugged, so I let it go in an attempt to shorten this endless night, "Fine, just don't bother Ace or Lou". He grinned widely and ran into the hull after announcing that he'll get Ace's sword.

Sending Ace was actually an excellent idea if it would make Nyx less worried about Haven, and most importantly, less eager to chase after him.

∞ ∞ ∞

Unlike the expected, Haven didn't show up the next day. Nyx kept monitoring the deck since dawn. And when his cousin finally came out of his cabin around noon, the bastard stood on the deck facing the other way and didn't look back.

By the end of the day, Nyx was tearing up inside. He felt so down and rejected, and I hated to see him like that. He asked several times for me to let him go to him, but I couldn't let him. So he went to the water room and decided to keep himself busy by filling different small drinking barrels with water.

I couldn't watch him sigh anymore, so I nudged Armpit and ordered him to accompany me to the other ship.

When I stepped on the deck, I was met with Lou, Ace, and Maren who were drinking. Lou was worried about me coming there without Nyx, but I wasn't about to clarify my actions to anyone so I just walked into the cabin.

I found Haven sitting on a chair; still a bit pale with darker bags under his eyes. He was staring at the kettle that was on the table beside him and holding Nyx's black leather jacket in his hand. As soon as he saw me, he tensed and stood up to face me. I caught on the fear in his eyes and in his stance before he could hide it with a layer of coldness in his stare.

I paced towards him making him retreat, "You're coming with me"

"Excuse me?"

"You. Are coming with me."

"No. I am not! And how dare you give me orders?"

That was supposed to make me enraged, but surprisingly enough, I was actually amused! I had missed the occasional '*How dare you*' that Nyx used to throw my way every now and then. And at the same time, it hurt to notice the resemblance between them.

When I smirked, he frowned in confusion and stuttered a little, "I-If you're here to kill me, do it here. I won't die in front of Nyx, that was the deal!"

The deal??

I turned to Lou, and when he scratched his head and looked away, I knew my fellow pirate had cooked something. I rolled my eyes and went to face the green-eyed mouse again

"Even pirates keep their deals. I know that's written in your code somewhere"

"And the deal is...?"

"Not to hurt me in front of Nyx! Do that, and I promise not to fight you"

"So, you care for Nyx?", I said sarcastically

"What do you mean? Of course, I do! He's my cousin!! I care about him more than you do and obviously much longer!!"

"Yet here you are, spending what's probably the last chance of you talking to him in your cabin, while he cries his eyes out thinking that you hate him!"

His eyes widened and his voice toned down, "He's... crying?"

"What do you think? If you knew him so well, you should've known how much he misses his fucking family! He keeps talking about you people like you're the Gods themselves! His family is so dear to him and they always were his first priority! I thought someone like you would at least be aware of that"

"............ he... he doesn't want to go back with me... I don't get it"

"It's not that he doesn't want to, he can't"

He stared at me for a few seconds before he realized, "YOU! You're the one who told him to act like he didn't want to come home!!"

"No, I didn't order him to act like anything. But aye, I am the pirate who saved your cousin's life and the one who's keeping that life as mine"

"My God... how... how could you!! Just because you saved his life, doesn't mean you can take it!! He's a person! A nobleman!! His life is more precious than all of yours combined! What is it that you want, money? Ships?? I can give you all that, just give him back to me!"

"He's not yours in the first place to take back!"

When I yelled at him, he flinched in fear and hurt of what I just said, then he didn't think much before lunging at me and trying to punch me.

I easily sidestepped and grabbed his hair, then in a blink of an eye, I had my dagger threatening to cut his neck. Maren, who was watching from the door, took a couple of steps back and instinctively hid behind Ace. The latter stood his ground and only frowned, while Lou ran inside the cabin, "Captain, he... Nyx wants him safe..."

His pathetic attempt to save the smaller man made me glare at him, "I don't care about the deal between you two as long as it stays the fuck out of my way. And you," I pulled Haven's hair a bit harder, "next time, think twice before attacking a pirate Captain"

With that, I pushed him away, sending him towards Lou. I made sure to push him hard enough to make Lou wince from the impact, "Now that you know that I CAN hurt you but am NOT going to, I think you'll understand me better."

The merchant rubbed his neck and glared at me while standing on his own.

I sighed and made my voice calmer before continuing, "Recently, I gave your cousin a choice: go back to Corail or sail with me, and he chose with his free will"

He shook his head, "I... It can't be... why would he?"

"Because he has a new life now. He's still the principled landlubber that doesn't take shit from anyone, but he managed to earn his own place on my ship. It wasn't easy for him, but I guess you know how brave and patient your cousin is once he sets his mind on something. If you talk to him and ask him, I'm sure he will tell you the exact same thing."

He looked very confused and his hand clutched at his own chest. His breath sounded shorter and hastier when he answered, "But... what about... me..."

I sighed.

I wanted to curse him and accuse him of being manipulative and a liar, but the way his breathing became dangerously erratic last night and the way he panicked, he was obviously not faking it. A part of me hated him for being honest, for being a 'good cousin', as Nyx called him many times before, while the other part couldn't blame him for it. I mean, from what my lover said, Haven stood by him in many ways at times that I wasn't even there to help him. He also went as far as to look for him in unguarded areas; even I couldn't get myself to truly hate him.

"Haven, look at me", I said, as gently as I could manage right now. He raised his gaze to meet mine and I couldn't help but hate the loss in his eyes that resembled my lover's.

"You are welcome to stay on my ship and you can leave whenever you want. You have my word as the Captain that as long as you don't stir trouble, you will not be harmed."

Everyone looked pretty surprised at the offer, especially Haven himself, who stared at me with wide eyes, "You're inviting me to stay on your ship??", when I nodded he continued, "For what in return exactly?"

I chuckled, a merchant can never stop being one

"Nothing in return, Haven. Only your obedience as someone who sails under my command, nothing further"

"I don't believe you. People always want something back, especially a *pirate*"

I swallowed the spark of anger that spread at the disgusted way he said that, "The Captain of Martina never goes back on his word. Someone like you, I'm sure you did your research about my crew. I'm also certain the rumors confirm that I always stand by my word. And if you really need a reason, let's say that I know how important you are to Nyx and that I'm doing this for his sake, not yours."

He stared at me for a moment, looking for a lie in my words. Finally, his eyes narrowed and he said as if he couldn't believe his own thought, "You love him..."

I answered without hesitation, "I do. I love Nyx, and I promised to make his dreams of sailing and becoming a navigator come true"

"...... he told you about that?"

"He tells me many things. Everything, really. And he wants to stay because he loves me back"

He shook his head in disbelief, "You... a pirate? Why??"

I smirked proudly at the thought of Nyx choosing me, "Even the devil has his charms"

Haven obviously didn't like my answer, but I didn't expect him to, nor did it matter to me. All I needed was to make him go talk to Nyx and convince him that he doesn't hate him or reject him in any way

"Is..... Nyx angry with me?"

"No, just very sad. He thinks you hate him for falling in love with me and preferring my ship than your home"

"How could he expect me to accept him being with a *pirate*!"

I shrugged, "I think what bothers him the most is the thought of you not accepting him getting fucked by a man"

His eyes widened to my crudeness. Then he cursed under his breath and looked away.

I was missing my angel already and needed to wrap this up fast, so I walked closer to Haven, "Now, I'm going back to wipe my lover's tears, you know, the ones that you caused. You're welcome to join me"

His shoulders slumped in defeat, "Please take me to see my cousin."

∞ ∞ ∞

I lead him directly to the water room where, just as I thought, Nyx was still working. We could hear the voices from the hall.

Nash, Ajax, Zaire, and Britt were beside him. Britt just smirked while the others teased him.

Nash hovered around him while he ignored them and kept working, "Oh~, come on pixie. I know you want to try arm wrestling again, I miss beating you at it"

"I'll pass, thank you"

Zaire, who was sitting on a barrel beside Britt, lifted a jar, "Come on, cutie. It's too late to be that gloomy. If we're not asleep, we should AT LEAST drink, right?"

Nash snatched the jar and poured the liquor into his mouth. Once finished, the jar was immediately taken by a drunken Ajax who drank some more before pushing the jar to Nyx, "Little ladybuuug, you know you want to join in the fun"

"Stand back, pirate!"

Everyone turned to find the owner of the unfamiliar voice, including Ajax, who took a step back and tried to focus his eyes to figure out who was talking.

Haven didn't even flinch as he walked inside to shield his cousin and glare at all of them, "Mind your manners and be respectful when you speak to a nobleman!"

Nash's jaw dropped while Britt and Zaire shared an amused look. Ajax just tilted his head in confusion.

"Haven!"

Haven turned to face a very surprised Nyx, "Why do you allow them to address you like that?"

Nyx smiled and put away the cup that he was holding in his hand, "You're... ok?"

Haven nodded with a small smile. They stared at each other a few seconds before a tear betrayed Nyx's control, "I'm so sorry..."

Haven reached and hugged him, and fuck it took everything in me to hold back from throwing him onto his deck, "You have nothing to be sorry about"

"I... I didn't mean to... I didn't know I was going to become *me* and-and I didn't want to make you sick, I'm truly sorry Haven"

Haven pushed him back to look into his eyes with a smile, "You're still the perfect gentleman that I know. I shouldn't have left you yesterday; I should've listened to you. No matter what you chose and..... who you chose to be with, you will always be dear to me, you will always be my best friend"

Nyx broke into more tears, and when he hugged Haven again, his eyes looked up to me and he gave an adorable appreciative smile after mouthing a silent *'Thank you'*.

And fuck, did those words mean the world to me.

Of course, the moment of 'feelings' came short when Zaire and Ajax hugged each other and fake-cried. Nash was cracking up at the scene, while Lou wore a freakin wide grin.

Gods, to think that these idiots were MY idiots...

One look towards Nyx, I knew that his worries were being swept away. And I felt so fucking relieved, until Haven pulled him by the hand and out of the water-room with nothing more than a simple, "Excuse me, I need some private time with my cousin"

I expected Nyx to say something, I don't know, maybe *'I want Agenor to be with me and hug me while we talk because I love him so much and he's more important than family'*, or something like that. But nope, Nyx followed him without even sparing me one look, leaving me to drown in the sarcastic comments of my loving crew.

∞ ∞ ∞

(about a week later)

Haven refused the offer to sail with us. When I asked him again earlier in the day, he looked at Lou then back to Nyx and me, "Sorry, I would love nothing more than to stay with you, Nyx, I just... I have some debts to pay before I could take such decisions"

"I truly apologize for all the trouble that my disappearance has caused you and my uncle..."

"Don't worry, it's no trouble at all, I just... really worry about leaving you here, Nyx"

Nyx shook his head and smiled, "Please don't, I actually am happy, Haven. I haven't been so in a while"

So here we are: we reached the guarded island Sejour. I released Haven's ship and his men as soon as we spotted the island so we wouldn't be seen by the guards.

Nyx insisted on getting on the island and making sure that Haven reached safety. He also wanted to meet the Captain of Haven's crew, they seemed to know each other from before and Nyx wanted both Haven and this Captain to tell his family that he's doing fine and living well on his own.

I was very hesitant to let him go, despite believing him when he assures that he'll be back in no time, I didn't – and will never – completely trust his family not to attempt to take him away from me. But the idea of others seeing that he was doing well would definitely be good for his family, and by consequence will make him less worried while staying with me.

I chose to drop sail near a tiny island neighboring Sejour. Most of my men had bounties on their heads, dead or alive. So I had to make do with Lou and Zaire to escort Nyx to the port of Sejour where he planned to meet his cousin, then Zaire will bring him back to me, while a couple of other mates will buy some food and booze.

I let them go, but my heart refused to settle down. A couple of hours later, I was walking the streets of Sejour with a hood on my head to avoid being recognized by the guards. It didn't take long to spot Haven's ship in the sea, and also find his men that were carrying what they needed for the trip back to Mila. Like promised, I had given Haven enough money to hire a few more men for the sail. I also noticed the few guards protecting their goods; which only meant they already told about being raided on by pirates. I never expected them not to notify the guards, but seeing them only urges me to get my Nyx out of here as soon as possible.

When I found him, he was talking to Haven and his overly grinning Captain, with Lou and Zaire on either side of him. Nyx handed them the letter he wrote to his family and the Captain happily took it before he shook Nyx's hand vigorously; *I swear to the Gods if he touches him again, I'm going to raid on his ass again!*

I sighed to control my temper and approached them a bit more. I noticed Zaire was looking elsewhere; he was frowning and staring at a man who was walking by. Lou asked him about it, he just sent him a dismissive wave and walked away to follow the man.

I was about to go after him and check the reason for his odd behavior, but I couldn't let Nyx get out of my sight right now. So I watched until they finished talking and Haven hugged Nyx tightly. When he pulled back, he squeezed Nyx's arms a little, refusing to let go. He was asking him something with a serious look and got a reassuring nod as a response from Nyx. But he still didn't let go.

I was fucking right, Haven couldn't just sail and leave Nyx behind. He probably thought he could take him with him, now that they're practically alone and guarded against pirates!

I took a couple of steps further, making myself visible to Haven, who looked pretty startled to see me there. Lou noticed my presence immediately and shot me an amused look.

As revenge, Haven kissed Nyx's forehead and cupped his cheek gently, making my heart burn with jealousy.

My Gods! Just Fuckin leave already!!

I walked even closer and finally, he got the message and let go of him.

"Will I ever see you again, my friend?"

"We will certainly meet, Haven, many times! I will send you a letter, tell where we're heading and you could meet with us!"

"What about now, where are you heading now?"

"... I... I still don't know, but I will find out and we will definitely work it out"

"It's ok, I know where the Martina crew is headed. Zaire and I spoke about it with the Captain. I will make sure we meet again" Lou said, then he moved to stand beside Haven

"What's going on here?", It took Nyx a minute to figure it out, "Wait, are you going with him!?"

Lou smirked and Haven nodded while trying to manage a smile, "He's sailing with my crew for now"

"When was that decided! And why?? Hey, is he blackmailing you??"

I almost chuckled; my first guess was *'Aye, he's totally blackmailing him'*

"My, my, our ladybug is working its head like a real pirate now, I'm so proud of you, pixie"

"Don't be rude!" Haven scolded Lou, then turned to Nyx, "I just thought I'd hire someone strong and he agreed"

The merchant's Captain called for him, saying the guards wanted to talk to him. Lou sent me a nod as a respectful farewell, while Haven looked very apologetic as he hugged Nyx, ***again!!***, then walked away with Lou on his tail.

Nyx was obviously very surprised to know that Lou decided to leave with his cousin. Lou told me about this a few days ago. I was surprised to hear it too, but I can't deny being happy about it; with Lou beside Haven, the latter will not dare say anything about the true whereabouts of his cousin.

Nyx after parting with them, Nyx looked around him searching for Zaire. A minute later, he was already worried and panicking. He started pacing around and even bumped into someone. I couldn't let him be lost like that any longer, so I sneaked behind him and put my arms around him.

He got startled, and when he turned around and saw me, he gave me a cute happy yelp before hugging me back. I pulled him away from the busy crowd, and we headed back to Martina.

∞ ∞ ∞

knock knock knock

"Captain! Dinner is ready!!"

"... Agenor... dinner..."

"We – will eat – later – " I answered my sweet angel while distributing small openmouthed kissed on his shoulders

"mmmm... okay"

He moaned and threw his head back, giving me more access to his sweet flesh.

knock knock "Captain! I got you your plates!!"

"Just put them – down"

"But it's ham!! If you leave it out here"

"If anyone touches our dinner, I will cook them alive! Now leave us. The fuck. Alone!!"

"Hear that, monkey? He will cook you alive"

I sighed and shook my head as I tried to ignore Baril's ranting with Maren. My attention was drawn by a sweet laugh from Nyx who seemed quite amused by all of this.

He faced me and stretched his legs to meet my lips with a burning kiss. Fuck, I missed touching him and kissing him like this. With that fucking cock-blocking cousin, we were barely alone whether it was during the day or at night! Now the disturbance was finally gone, and I got my lover all to myself again.

I kissed him hungrily drawing erotic surrendering moans past his exquisite lips. When he pulled back, his eyes were already drowning with desire. And before I could dive into another adventurous kiss, he cupped my face with both hands, and said in a low, seductive voice, "Have I told you how handsome you are?"

I laughed, feeling my ego swell with his words, I put my forehead against his and answered playfully, "I don't think you did. I would love to hear you say that and more"

"Well...", he smiled and blushed beautifully, then he gathered his courage before lifting his blue beauties to meet my gaze, "You are by far the most handsome person I know. You are so strong, Agenor, and you are so kind to me... I am truly thankful for all the patience and generosity you showed my cousin since the raid. I never dreamt of seeing him again, let alone spend days with him talking and catching up. I even got to hear about Raya's twins! My God, I love them without even seeing them. I'm sorry you had to risk walking into a guarded island, and I'm sorry you had to give up someone as important as Lou. I know how highly you think of him; I just hope he doesn't drive Haven crazy with his teasing"

"Haha, Lou **is** capable of that, but that's your cousin's responsibility now. I'm certain he will be safe from here on, so I never want you worrying about him again.

And Nyx, know that whatever I did, it was all for you, *my love*"

∞ ∞ ∞

Chapter 24 ~ Pyry
∞ Ace's POV ∞

Gods, the things this monkey makes me do...

"mmmm"

"Can't you wait until we reach land?"

"Please... I miss youuuu~" he whined cutely and a playful smile tugged his lips as soon as he saw the amusement in my eyes

"You have a mast waiting for you, remember?"

"J is covering for me"

"J? And what did you give up for that exactly??"

"Nothing, I did him a favor! He was complaining about you telling him to help you move some stuff to the deck, I told him I would do that if he took my place up the mast"

I raised an eyebrow at him, "Then aren't you supposed to be working right now?"

"I am, I will, right after I finish kissing you..."

He went back to kissing my chest, occasionally he would stretch his legs and suck on my neck a little. I ordered him not to leave marks on me whenever he did that, and I try not to mark him either. I don't care if we're found out, but I don't want him being treated as the crew's bitch. He's smaller and he's weaker than most in a real bout. I could protect him, but I don't have enough authority to keep pirates away even when I'm not beside him, unlike Agenor, who fends off the hungry wolves just by using a collar that reminds everyone who Nyx really belongs to.

Maren started grinding on me. My, his honest eagerness is what makes me give in to his desires... our desires

I felt my temperature rising and my lust started to take over my senses. Fucking cute monkey... We established that I owned him and that he was to obey me, yet here we are; whenever he started something I could never find it in me to push him away.

I grabbed his cute firm ass, "Are you so impatient that you'd to make us hide and grind?"

He looked up at me with a small pout, "I really miss you! I think about you all the time, and it gets me so horny, but I'm not allowed to touch myself. I want you to touch me so much... and I want to lick you everywhere" and then with a mischievous smile, he added the magic word, "please, Master"

I stared at his eyes a little, taking my time to enjoy his begging and make him worry a little. About a minute later, he was already scared of actually being rejected.

I smirked and saw his playfulness regain its usual spark in his brown eyes. I leaned in to kiss him, just before our lips touched, I pulled back a little. He whimpered and his hands grabbed my shoulders to lead himself closer to my face. I smirked and watched him fidget in my arms a little before I met his sweet lips with mine.

The horny teen moaned and opened his mouth for my tongue to invade. I leaned slightly forward, kissing him vigorously and making him soon lose breath. His grinding followed a quicker rhythm before he shuddered in my arms and broke the kiss.

I laughed lightly at his defeat. I couldn't help but be smug every time I made him come.

His cheeks turned crimson; a beautiful color that only lit his face whenever I had him squirming in my arms.

"I think this was the fastest I've seen you come", I teased. And the little monkey didn't even bat an eye as he answered, "I don't know, but I have come from just watching you before"

"Watching??"

"Aye! I watch only you when I'm at the top of the mast and you're on deck!"

"Aren't you supposed to watch the sea?"

"But I feel much happier looking at you!! I never get tired of it. You're amazingly handsome, so tall and so brave! And when you're not around, I think of the lines of your strong body... the movement of your muscles when you swing your Tashi... the cool look in your eyes when you're uninterested... and the way you stand near Agenor as an equal when you're clearly much more awesome!! My Gods, every time I think of you I get so fucking hard!"

He resumed grinding his body against mine halfway through his declaration. And Gods know how every word increased my arousal. His unlimited honesty made my heart feel unfamiliarly open and fragile to only him.

"And all I want is for you to notice me, to know I'm there, thinking of only you! But sometimes.......... I wait for you to remember me and just look up for a second... and when you don't, I feel so lonely... so void"

I frowned at the sadness that flooded on his usually cheerful face. Fuck, his mood changes and his big loving puppy eyes are going to make me go insane.

I squeezed his ass harder in my hands and leaned down to kiss his fear away. I kept sucking on his tongue and biting his lower lip until his eyes had nothing but lust once again, "You little cute troublemaker, you make my body crave your eager daring touch, you make me sneak away from a whole damn crew just to fuck you and now you protest that I'm not giving you enough attention?"

"I... I always miss you, Ace!! And... do you really think I'm cute?"

"Aye, I find you very sexy. It actually makes me want to give you more chores"

"I-I can totally do anything! Anything, Ace, as long as it means you're thinking of me!"

"Ok, now you're being cute on purpose"

He gave me a beautiful, shy smile. Fuck, he makes me want to talk and... express myself. That's so not me!

But I guess being shy is definitely not his usual self either. I couldn't stay still any longer, so I pushed his pants down to reveal his firm butt. Instead of retreating like anyone taken by surprise would, he held onto my shoulders and wiggled his ass to help the process.

"Maren, I miss you too sometimes, even if I'm not looking up"

"Really? -Ah!!"

He yelped delightfully when I moved my hands on his ass and pushed both my middle fingers against his hole, "Shshshsh, don't be loud"

He sucked his lips between his teeth and nodded eagerly, and his breath immediately hitched when I pushed my groin against his. I enjoyed the tingling friction, feeling both our groins grow.

I knew how tight he was, but Gods, it aroused me so much to push his limits. I watched the pain and lust mix in his eyes when I pushed both my fingers past the ring of his ass. His mouth opened in a silent cry of pain, and he stood on the tips of his toes, trying but failing to evade my invading fingers.

Once both my middle fingers were halfway inside him, I halted to give him the opportunity to breathe. He looked up at me and I gazed at his luscious lips that trembled while looking so... weak and lonely. I leaned in, giving his lower lip a small lick before sucking on it and kissing him roughly.

Maren held onto me, a hand on my shoulder and the other grabbing my arm, he didn't resist one bit. He never did, and the thought of him never ever doing so filled my ego. I pulled both my fingers sideways a little, and the stretching made him moan deliciously in my mouth. Like tasting a fine wine, I took my time with him; pulling his erection closer against my groin, rubbing my tongue against his, squeezing his milky ass and moving my fingers to torment his butthole. And he kept moaning and saying incoherent words that I never let him finish. Fuck, I was leaking already. And from the feeling of his member that poked against mine, I knew my little pet was about to come again.

My Gods, I could milk him or hours and wouldn't feel bored... Damn, it would be great if I had the chance to enjoy him to my heart's content

My thoughts surprised me a little, but... what surprised me more was the realization of the feeling that was filling my heart right now. And I also realized that the same sense of warmth, pride, and happiness were present every time I had him this close to me. It was like he filled a void in my life that I never even cared to address.

I was stretching his entry harder while thinking, and a sensual moan accompanied with him starting to shudder in my arms made a word pop in my mind......

love

Shit, am I in love?

Unfortunately, my thought was interrupted before I could get to the bottom of it when I heard mates talking and getting closer.

I parted from Maren who looked at me with lost and confused eyes. I put a hand on his mouth before he could protest or beg and immediately pushed his head down while I ducked a slightly behind the pile of boxes and rubbish that we threw in this storage room.

"Thank you, Britt! I'll find them myself" I heard Nyx say

"Aye, call me if you need anything"

Wha-? Since when was Britt a 'call me if you need anything' pirate??? Fuck, that whale is a weird pile of puzzles

I stayed still as Nyx pocked his head past the door frame and gave the room a quick scan. Then he carefully wandered inside towards a specific pile of stuff.

It was unfamiliar to see Nyx here. He was allowed to go wherever he wanted on the ship, but Agenor told him to avoid the lower levels and he abided. He wasn't scared of being hurt by any of us anymore, but we're pirates; a few drinks can lead a drunken pirate to forget his Captain's orders and cause troubles. Usually, we handle any accidents occurring between us without a big fuss, but Nyx, no matter what Agenor said, was not a pirate.

So there he was, going through the things we got from his cousin's raid. I was surprised to see that he was touching those, he had made it pretty clear that he didn't like hearing about the treasures, nor have his share of the things we got from that raid.

I felt tugging on my pants. I looked down to see questioning eyes. I mouthed a silent '*Nyx*' and Maren rolled his eyes. He pulled my hand away and mouthed a '*what's he doing?*'. I looked up to see Nyx smiling affectionately at a..... bunch of books??

He pulled the first one and stared at the cover before opening it and kneeling beside the books. I looked down to Maren with an amused look and said very quietly: '*reading*'

His eyes opened wide: '**Now!!**'

I chuckled and looked up to see Nyx pulling another book, organizing the pile and starting to skim them one after the other.

A few minutes passed with Nyx obliviously enjoying his cousin's books, and Maren pouting with his arms crossed. Well, can't blame him, he was interrupted right before he came. The gods, his lips look so inviting when he tries to look angry... I reached my hand and played with his beautiful rebellious brown curls. He leaned into my touch like a satisfied cat looking for more. Then he tilted his head back and started licking my fingers. And Fuck, the tingles erupted in my groin when he kissed and bit sexily on the flesh of the palm of my hand. I was about to release an uncontrolled moan, so I pulled my hand and went back to caressing his hair.

When my attention went back to Nyx, I guess that didn't sit well with the mischievous monkey kneeling in front of me. The young wolf tugged my shirt, and when I looked at him, he was using an invisible piece of coal to write on the boxes beside us: 'I LUV YU'

I smirked at his cute big eyes that stared at me with pride and longing. I nodded and wrote an invisible 'LOVE'. He grinned and licked the side of his hand, then he wiped the already invisible writing, and rewritten an 'I LOVE YU'

Well, that was close enough for me. But just before I could flatter my monkey, someone else came into the room.

"I was looking all over for you"

Fuck, now I'm hiding from Nyx AND MY CAPTAIN!

"Sorry, Britt and I were chatting and he told me about Haven's books"

Chatting??

"Chatting?? With Britt!?!?"

"I told you he's a nice person. When I told him I already read all the books you got me several times, he suggested I take a look on Haven's. I can't believe you people threw books in such a place"

"You were clear about not wanting anything from the raids, especially that one, so I didn't want to bring it up"

"Well, that rule doesn't apply on books"

Agenor laughed and Nyx continued, "Besides, two of these are mine"

"How so?"

"See that" Nyx opened the cover of a book and showed the first page to the Captain, who crouched before him and read:

'From a reading enthusiast to another, I share the humble thoughts of a scholar on his journey to find the truth in the ocean of knowledge that is this world, Sir Elec Bence, from Lyrma'

Agenor checked the cover, then raised his eyebrows, "The author himself dedicated this book?"

"Yes, to me!"

"You? How could you tell?"

"Haven always made sure to dedicate the books he bought for me, either it was a librarian, a scholar, or the author himself. This time he sailed to Lyrma before he went off route and into an unguarded area. And he got this for me! Can you believe it? I was away, but he still remembered our little tradition"

Well, of course, he remembered Nyx. In fact, his cousin got raided on because he was looking for him.

Agenor smiled, in a fake way, I might add. I almost chuckled at his obvious annoyance; my dear Captain never liked the way Nyx spoke of his cousin.

"I remember he used to get you two books. I guess he got cheap this time"

"Oh no, look!" Nyx pulled another book and handed it to Agenor, who tried his best to behave and keep his discontent to himself, "Like always, he teases me by bringing a book in a foreign language, even the dedication"

"Maybe in our sails, we could find someone to read the book for you"

"Really?"

"Aye, we can try and I'm sure we'll find someone"

"That would be so amazing! And I'll send a letter to Haven with a thank you and a translation. My, I can imagine his reaction"

Agenor closed his eyes and shook his head slowly making Nyx pout a little, "What?"

"Nothing. I just can't believe how happy you get every time you touch a new book"

With that, he leaned in very close making Nyx blush immediately

"Agenor, people might see us"

"Let them. Those hooligans have seen much more, trust me"

"What about Maren! He's still an innocent kid-"

Innocent??

"Innocent?? Huh, that's a good one. I really don't give a damn who sees us"

"But..."

"Believe me, no one will dare interrupt us, Nyx. The only one who did is not part of this crew anymore"

Nyx looked down regretfully, "Maybe... maybe we should've waited more for Zaire"

Agenor sighed, "I did wait. Three fucking days! And that ungrateful bastard disappeared without a word. I spared his life once. And by not chasing after him that day, I spared his life again"

Aye, five months ago after we separated with Haven, Zaire was nowhere to be found. The Captain sent mates to look around the guarded island, but he was already gone. Some of us, including Nyx, thought maybe he just got in trouble or was delayed. So Agenor waited a couple of days more before we sailed. We couldn't stay any longer in a guarded area, and Agenor never actually trusted the slave merchant. Even when the merchant insisted on helping to protect Nyx while he said his goodbyes to his cousin, Agenor followed them and refused to let Nyx alone with Zaire, especially with Lou sailing with Haven.

"Hey," Agenor said to Nyx while touching his hair gently, "don't be sad over someone like him"

"...... Many people miss him, you know. He was a tease, but he was also fun to be around. He respected you so much! I actually thought he liked you as a Captain and enjoyed being with us. I still wonder if I was wrong..."

"To be honest, I was a bit surprised too. But back then, all I cared about was getting you away from -euh..."

Haven

"From who?"

"From...... that island! Aye, that island had many guards and if anyone recognized you, they would try to take you away from me"

Nyx swallowed my Captain's not-very-smooth-lie and smiled, "Well, they will know that I will never allow them to keep me away from the love of my life"

Agenor's breath halted, and it was very understandable. I was surprised to see Nyx bravely open and eloquent about his feelings, and it made me happy for my Captain who was now grinning like a fool.

Nyx pulled Agenor into a heated kiss. I sighed and looked down to find Maren hugging my leg with his head resting on my inner thigh. He looked sad and left out, but so beautiful with his ass out in the open. I ruffled his hair and his face lit up with happiness to that simple gesture. I kept playing with his curves until the daredevil decided to start sniffing my crotch and grazing his teeth teasingly against my groin.

He walked his lips on my covered member and started kissing and biting on the cloth of my pants slightly. Fuck, he was getting me so hard and I couldn't do anything about it right now, only wait for us to be alone again. But I wasn't close from pushing him away. A moment later, his fingers fondled with the ties and he released my junk then immediately put it in his mouth.

I bit my lower lip to control my groans and took a handful of his curls. He remained still to adapt my size to his throat, but his lips kept moving slightly further every few seconds until I was almost fully buried past his luscious lips. My breath was accelerating and I felt my body get hotter the more I watched him.

As to provoke me even more, he sucked me hard and started moving around me. I tried to swallow the excitement, but a small groan already escaped. And as soon as it did, we both froze like rocks, waiting to know if we were heard.

"W-w-what was that?? Oh my God, please tell me that wasn't a rat! D-Do you have rats here??"

Agenor sighed and pulled away from the kiss, "Looks like we do". Shit, he said that so calmly and with an amused tone of voice. He didn't even sound surprised! And now I was certain he knew that they weren't alone in here.

Nyx moved around, and from the sound of it I guessed he was gathering his books, "God have mercy on us...... w-what should we do!??"

"Do? Well, the mates could catch them and roast them. These *rats* sound quite big, I'm sure they'd make a satisfying snack"

"Ewww! Please tell me you're joking!"

"Haha! The next time they catch a rat, I'll make them give you a piece. You might like it"

"I'll pass. God, I think I'm going to throw up"

"Hahaha!"

Their voices faded slowly as they climbed to the upper level of the hull. As soon as the voices died, I grabbed a very silent Maren. I made him stand up, then I pushed him against the wall

"I-I-I-I'm sorry! Ace I'm sorry, please..."

He sounded too scared for my liking. *Did he actually think I might hurt him or something??*

The mere thought of that disgusted me. So the first thing I did was sneaking a hand around him and grabbing his penis.

"Nnnngh... I-I-I didn't mean to; I just couldn't wait! Please don't end our relationship"

I tugged on his member and started rubbing him roughly, "You've been a naughty boy, Maren. What happens to naughty boys?"

"They... They ask for forgiveness? Please, Master... I really love you"

I pulled his head to look him straight in the eye and smirked at him. He immediately relaxed in my arms, "I'm not mad at you, my pet. But you still need to be punished"

I grabbed my own cock and pushed my swollen head into his tight ass without any warning. He was about to scream but then he shut his lips, making sure not to make the same mistake twice.

Actually, I was the one who groaned, but still; the thought of him making me unable to control even a fucking moan was embarrassing! He needed a punishment either way, and I was glad to deliver that.

I didn't wait long before I shoved inside him again, going deeper and making his back arch beautifully. Before I knew it, he was leaning forward as much as he could with the wall right in front of him. I instantly tightened my hold on his member, making him throw his head on my shoulder:

"Tsk, tsk, tsk. You were about to come, weren't you, pet?"

"P-please... I have you inside me AND holding my cock! This is too much, please let me-"

"Oh no, not so soon. I need to punish you, remember?"

"**Gods!!**"

He tried to move his waist and get some friction, but I kept my hold firm on his shaft. Not painfully though, just enough to keep him from coming. And I smiled when I remembered that he was denied to come earlier too. My my, this was probably the worst punishment for this quick-milker

My own cock called for attention and started throbbing eagerly inside him. I started moving in and out of him, and as soon as his ass was stretched enough, I started pounding him hard. He covered his own mouth to keep himself from breaking the rules again, while I made sure to torment his ass and drive him crazy by sucking on his neck and biting his sweet flesh repeatedly.

I felt myself grow even more inside him, our breaths followed the same hasty rhythm and our hearts beat together. And FUCK THE GODS for their bloody teasing, because just when I was about to come, I heard voices approaching.

Maren's mind was above the clouds. He didn't even hear the loud approaching quarrel. I leaned forward and shushed him quietly, while my free hand hugged him to calm him down. I was actually very pleased when he didn't resist me slowing the pace so suddenly, and just leaned back to feel my hug.

My cock was throbbing; I could neither remove it and lose the sweet contact with Maren's cute ass, nor fuck him and make our presence known. So I just caressed Maren's chest a little and remained still.

I tilted my head slightly and looked back towards the door; two idiots emerged. The blond one, with the usual anger problems, grabbed the other one's throat and pushed him against the wall:

"I told you a Fucking thousand times. **Do Not. Touch Me There!! In Fact, Do Not Touch Me At All!** I don't care if you tell other people about what happened! I will fucking kill you before you could finish! I will cut your balls and fed them to the sharks! And then I'll gut you and-"

Ajax smirked and I was very surprised when he grabbed Nash's ass with both his hands, "I told you, it's not my fault. Your ass calls for me"

"**I will kill you!**" Nash went to unleash his sword, but Ajax laughed and skillfully pushed the sword back into the scabbard. Nash groaned and gathered his fist to punch the cocky pirate, but his hand halted when the third asshole caught it

"Ajax, I told you to leave him alone"

"Oh~, but he's so angry! It's adorable"

"I'll show you, you motherfucker!!"

Yeagar manager to pull Nash back enough to spare his younger asshole's life, "I apologize for my brother. He's a bastard"

Ajax frowned, "You're a bastard too!"

"Aye, but I don't act like it"

"I don't fucking care!! I want you black shits to leave me the fuck alone!"

"Hey, we just wanted to recall some memories," Ajax winked suggestively and continued, "veeery awesome memories, remember? The kind of memories you want to keep secret, but also want to live it over and over and over..." he took a few steps towards Nash, who took a step back before groaning angrily and pulling out his sword

"Fuck!" With that, Ajax was running out with a furious Nash on his tail. Yeagar only smiled before following them up.

As soon as they left, I FUCKING breathed. Fucking Gods are certainly making bets on this fuck!

I turned to my cutie and found him silently licking my forearm. Ok, that was strange and ticklish. I chuckled, and when he turned his big brown eyes to look at me, I smashed my mouth on his. Fuck the world, Fuck the Gods. I let him moan as much as he wanted, and I resumed fucking him hard, not taking the time to start slow anymore. I just pulled out almost all of my shaft and thrust it all back in. My hand eased the grip on his cock and he immediately moved his hips for more friction with his tongue chanting my name. I fucked him harder and rougher until he shuddered in my arms. I felt his sweet milk soil my hand while his ass crushed my thick cock painfully inside of him. With a groan, I rode his orgasm then mine tore through me seconds after, filling him with my own milk until it oozed out of him.

When I pulled out, his knees gave up and we both sat down. He moved so he was between my arms, the way he liked to snuggle every time we had sex. I swear, sometimes it felt like he did all of it just for this moment of cuddling. At first, I found it weird, now I like it and it felt so natural.

He looked up to meet my eyes and smiled at me. We didn't say anything, just took our time to gaze at each other.

"**Laaaaand**!!"

We both laughed

Well, Fuck you Gods, this time we already finished fucking.

∞ ∞ ∞

I was giving orders to the mates to prepare to get to the shores. Pin showed up proudly with the straws in his hand and everyone started praying. The Captain and I stood back and watched. Nyx also stood back, but he was only trying to avoid the mates who were pushing each other to get the first pick.

For the first time, Maren got a short straw. He looked like an abandoned child. His eyes were pleading mine to do something. He wanted me to use my position as the second and get him out of his duty, that was out of the question. I leaned in a little when others were occupied by the straws and whispered, "In three days, I'll be fucking your brains out"

He moaned and pouted even more, looking so damn adorable. I just laughed and followed my Captain to the boat.

We hit the shores of Pyry leaving a few men on Martina. Everyone got busy making the tents and organizing the empty barrels and the boxes; they all knew they could only go look for whores once they finished setting up the camp.

Nyx was looking around, unsatisfied with our surroundings. It's understandable with this island; Pyry is known for its harsh winter blizzards and ghostly forests. Legends walk the seas about the people who stepped on it and never came back or those butchered by the ghosts as sacrifices or just for fun. Even without the stories, Pyry does creep the weak hearts. The beach is poor with sand, and it mostly has deep cliffs and tiny mossy rivers. It's covered either with rocks or leafless trees. And despite that, the forests are still very thick and challenging.

We don't expect to find the need stocks and whores on Pyry, but this island is surrounded by a set of tiny ones that we will target later for food.

"**Nyyyyx**!! Move your ass and come to start a fire!"

"Coming!"

Nyx was about to do as told when Agenor grabbed his arm and pulled him back. Then he glared at Baril, "His ass is staying with me"

"I need his ass to help me set for lunch! I can't feed these fuckers alone!"

Agenor took a threatening step towards the old man, "I'm talking his ass with ME"

Nyx put his hands on his temples and shook his head, "Could you stop mentioning my ass!! And please don't fight"

Baril just ignored him and continued, "Where?"

"I'll show him around the island. It's his first time on Pyry"

Nyx looked behind him and to the silent trees, "I... don't think we should go there. That forest looks...... I don't believe in ghosts, but maybe w-we should stay here, the beach looks fine"

"Don't worry, I'll show you beautiful places behind this forest. Let's go" Baril started limping towards them and the Captain snarled his way, "ALONE."

Baril rolled his eyes and focused on preparing lunch with the usual love in his heart and a smile on his face, while Agenor nodded at me and lead a reluctant Nyx to a walk among the ghosts.

After lunch, those who weren't on guard duty left the camp to look for women to fuck and people to rob. I made sure I had enough sober mates to avoid any problem happening, especially in the absence of Agenor.

I expected him to come back by the end of the day like every time they leave for one of their private trips. At least then I could get drunk. But to my surprise, they didn't show up. They must've decided to have more 'private time' or forgot to come back all together.

But by the afternoon of the following day, I decided to send a group to look for them just in case. Nash volunteered, and so did Ajax and Yeagar. A hell of curses broke between those three on who was to accompany who. I let them argue and started weighing the idea of going with them myself to make sure things were done well and fast. Don't get me wrong, I fully trust my Captain's strength and decisions, but there were times when he sent us all to hell and just did what he wanted, and in this case, he might decide to spend our whole stay on Pyry alone with Nyx. And, like always when he takes decisions like that, I show up and coerce him back to his loving crew.

I came out of my thoughts with Ajax laughing at an angry Nash. Fuck, that Nash sure is snappy lately. I'm certain Ajax and Yeagar deserve what they're getting, though. Damn, they're so noisy I might as well go get our Captain back ALONE.

I looked at our ship. *What would Maren be doing now? If I knew him well, he's probably watching me with his monocular.* I smiled at the thought and grabbed my sword, deciding to accompany those jerks for the search.

We hadn't even set foot in the forest when hell broke free.

Dozens of pirates suddenly attacked us while screaming *'revenge'*. Some of us were lucky enough to have a weapon in arm's reach, but many others were injured during the first few minutes of the attack.

I immediately unleashed my sword and threw the scabbard away. I swayed my sword and took the limbs and lives of every bastard who crossed my way.

We managed to kill all the bastards. But as soon as we were the only ones standing, another dozen emerged from the fucking forest of ghosts.

It went on like that until nightfall. And Fuck did we fight; we haven't had a straight attack like that in years! My first thought was them being rogues, but it turned out that they were pirates. I guess they didn't know who they were raiding on; rare are those who stand against our crew.

We had no more attacks that night, but damn we had to keep most of those resent awake for surveillance.

I hesitated on what to do; send everyone around the island chasing after our Captain, or stay and guard the camp. After much thought, I decided on the latter; I had to keep the crew together and wait for those who went to the neighboring islands to get back. If they were still alive, that is.

The next day, the crew was gathered again. I frankly did not expect more raids, but that's exactly what happened when the sun took its place in the middle of the sky. This time, more came. Many more. Usually, an attack never contained so many people. And it seemed like they were looking for something.

We tried to know who they were or who they fought for, but the only thing they kept saying was '*revenge*' or '*revenge the dead*'. It was only when one of them yelled at his mate '*Where the fuck is the boy?*' that we realized they were here for *someone*, not something. Our minds instantly went to the only one we found worth such measures: The nobleman

Someone was trying to take or kill Nyx.

Hours and hours passed while we continuously slaughtered all our opponents, and it seemed like the strongest among them were kept for the end. Nash, J, Yeagar, Britt, Ajax, and many others fought nicely. I didn't have time to make them spill out clearly the reason behind these attacks, so I knocked out a couple of them and kept them alive for later interrogation.

When I looked around, every one of us was busy with one or two of them. I was about to go help Nash, who was surrounded, but the situation got way shittier when Armpit yelled:

"The **ship**!! Me gold!! Me four coins of gold! The motherfuckers are raiding on the ship!"

One of the mates pulled a monocular. I instantly snatched it and looked in the eye. Several boats surrounded the ship and our mates were fighting them successfully. Then by heart almost stopped at the sight of five men climbing the shrouds, all closing in around Maren who was already engaged in a fight.

Fuck, Fuck, FUCK!!

I didn't get it; Why the HELL?? He's on the mast and all those are targeting just him??

Why the FUCK was there so many going for Maren when the others were fighting about one fucker each!!

Maren saw the approaching pirates, he immediately grabbed a rope and skillfully swung towards the quarterdeck while avoiding all those at arms' reach of him. And I almost breathed in if not for a bastard who threw a knife at him midair, sending him to falling the sea

"**Nooo!!**"

I yelled loudly and threw the eye away. I ran into the sea and towards the ship. Before I knew it, another commotion had started behind me. I looked back quickly to find more fucking pirates; they looked even more skilled and strong.

I knew I had to choose between heading to Martina or helping the mates on the beach who were clearly tired and outnumbered. But for once, I didn't really think. My body, mind, and soul called for me to save Maren and kill those who wanted to kill him.

And only one thought screamed painfully in my head:

Don't you fucking die on me, my love!!

∞ ∞ ∞

Chapter 25 ~ Ghost from the past
∞ Maren's POV ∞

Fucking hell! Things got bad real fast!!

I was up on the mast, ogling over Ace with my monocular. He looked dazzling as he gave orders to everyone, *so Fucking sexy!*

I sighed... why am I here alone and he's there alone? Why can't we go on adventures together like when Agenor takes Nyx? Nyx is so damn lucky... We should be together, Ace and I, hugging and kissing

Aye, he fucks me, I suck him, then we kiss... and we cuddle!! I love cuddling with Ace, he has strong arms, and he squeezes me so damn close to him... It's definitely the best place to be! In his arms... for always and always!!

Fuck, suck, kiss, cuuuuddle~

Fuck, suck, kiss, cuuuuddle~

I sang with eyes closed while trying to bring back the memory of the warmness of his hug.

I opened my eyes again and lowered the eye a tiny bit. The sight made me suck my lower lip between my teeth. *Gods, he's so damn handsome! And I get hard every time I watch his tall stride and his amazing ass... shit, I think I'm drooling*

I wiped my mouth and went to watch my God again, only to see a bunch of men emerging from the haunted woods and attacking our crew.

Shit! I started panicking and my breath hiked immediately. I used the eye again to find Ace and only breathed when I saw him fighting with his Tashi that slay a hundred men every hit!

Ok maybe one or two, but his fighting was still so awesome and absorbing to watch!

I warned my mates on the ship, a couple were drunk and the others went to try and wake them up. Meanwhile, I kept guard, on Ace of course. I accompanied him in his glorious and beautiful battle and wished I was there beside him. Gods, he's so Fucking hot!

This wasn't the first time it happened, we get attacked in the sea as well as when we land. Sometimes, thieves or rogues would take us for a weak crew that just came back tired from a long hunt, and they try to steal our treasures. If they knew who they were facing, they would run with their tails between their legs. It goes without saying that since I joined the Martina crew, we NEVER lost! We always managed to protect our money and gold. Sure, a few were killed over the years, but that was nothing compared to other crews that faced total annihilation.

This time was a bit tough though; the mates were fighting the attackers nicely, but the fucking assholes kept coming out of the forest like cockroaches! And the fight would barely slow down or halt for half an hour or so before another started. The more time it took, the more I got worried. I didn't worry about Ace's safety, I knew my sexy man was the hottest and strongest EVER! But I was certain he was getting too annoyed because of the continuous fighting and I wanted so badly to be there beside him.

I asked permission from J, but the fucker refused to call the small boat back saying no matter what, we had to abide by the rules. I wished I could just ignore him and leave the ship, but rules are rules. And our Captain, as well as Ace, took this kind of shit seriously; hell, Agenor would kill me himself if I defied his rules! So I ended up flipping J off and going back to watching my owner with heavy sighs.

My stomach protested and I groaned. I was so tired from spending all this time in the crow's nest without moving. And I was so damn hungry; the mates on the beach didn't get to buy food or send us anything. We had to stay to guard the ship, and yesterday the mates didn't bother sharing whatever crappy food was left. But for the first time, the food wasn't my priority. I was getting really anxious with this shit that was taking too fucking long!! It was the afternoon of the second day and the fuckers were still coming at us! We never had these many raid on us, and I swore they weren't from the same crew from their clothes and the way they fought!

I was pulled out of my daze when I heard screaming. I looked down to see one of my mates, wobbling on the quarterdeck with a knife stuck in his guts. As soon as he fell on the deck, dozens of men jumped onto the deck from different angles.

Bloody Fuck! They swam here and I didn't even see them coming!

It was too late to warn everyone; they were already fending the intruders. I was about to go down and help, but I preferred to keep monitoring the beach. I took another look in the eye to see that Ace was still doing well, fighting beautifully, then I looked around our ship. The damn rats were still climbing into our deck so this might take a while. In the meantime, I really couldn't ignore what was happening on the beach, so I went back to watch the glorious Tashi.

A few minutes later, all I heard was a loud, "I GOT HIM!!" that erupted right behind me. I turned and barely evaded the sword that cut into the crow's nest right where I was. I shifted my weight on my hands and used my legs to push the fucker away from me, sending him flying with a loud thud as he landed on the deck. I looked down to see him unable to stand, he thrashed and spat blood. I pulled his sword that was stuck in the wooden nest beside me and grinned at the pirate.

With difficulty, he pointed at me, "The mast!......... I found the fucker...... **Get him!**"

What??

He was making too much noise for an almost dead dude, so I send his own sword to finish him up. I grinned proudly at the perfect throw. And then I sighed; if only Ace was here to see that...

The unlucky pirate stopped moving when the weapon cut through his chest, but other eyes were already snarling at me. *All of them at once?*

And before I knew it, five of them were climbing the shrouds and laughing loudly:

"Catch him!", "Aye! Let's end this fucking hunt!!", "**He's Mine!!**", "Heheeeh! No wonder the others couldn't get him on the beach! The bitch was hiding here!!", "Waiting for **me**! Hehehe"

The Fuck are they talking about?? Shit, are they after ME??

"Hey, whatever the fuck this is, we should talk it over a nice beer, right?"

"Dead or alive!" a voice emerged from right behind me. All I saw was a tense rope in my peripheral vision and I knew someone climbed faster than the others! "I prefer **dead**!! Hey bastard, you're *windy*, ey?"

They know me??

"**Maren**! What the Fuck?" J yelled, but immediately got his hands busy with two other pirates. Fuck me, I was to face these crazy sons of bitches alone. And instead of pulling my dagger and fighting, I did what I do best when the situation gets tricky: Save my fuckin ass!

I jumped back and off the nest to escape the pirate behind me, but my shoulder already grazed the edge of the ax that he was aiming at my head. I grabbed the closest rope and hissed when the wound in my shoulder protested. My hand involuntarily released the rope making me almost fall, but I managed to catch it again with my other hand. I looked at the wound and was relieved to see that it wasn't serious.

"Captain *Kier* says hi from beyond the GRAVE!"

My whole body shuddered at the mention of his name. My eyes widened in disbelief; *H-h-h-how?? He's dead! He's fuckin dead!! So was all his crew!!*

The pirates were climbing closer while laughing evilly at the mention of that dreadful name. I felt my foot being grabbed and pulled, I almost lost balance and fell, but before they could pull me down further or surround me, I grabbed another rope.

I had to fuckin stay away from these lunatics!

I bounced on the mast, pushing my legs hard and barely escaping a couple of swords. I swung the rope nicely and aimed for the quarterdeck. A few pirates were fighting with a mate, but I could land and avoid them easily.

One of those I left behind yelled, "**You Ain't Getting Away Windy**!"

I didn't even get to look back before the rope in my hands went completely loose. They must've fuckin cut it!! And all I registered, was the few pirates who ran towards me before I was swallowed by the sea.

I opened my eyes under the water and the first thought that came to my mind terrorized me; I saw Captain Kirk, his face was so close to mine, looking straight at my soul with horror, his eyes leaking with blood, open wide and staring furiously at me. The image was so vivid that my heart jumped in my chest and I gasped in terror, swallowing the salted water. I tried to push the floating figure away from my face, but his ghost refused to leave me in peace.

I was pulled by my hair. I coughed and breathed the clean air. A strong arm immediately strangled me. I tried to break free from whoever was holding me tight; I pulled my dagger from behind me and took a swing in an attempt to stab the man behind me in his side, but the damn bull caught my hand and squeezed so hard that I cried in pain, my dagger fell off my hand and sank into the sea. I thrashed in his grip; all it took was one punch to my cheekbone to make my head buzz furiously. I couldn't fight anymore, but the pirate still continued with a few other punches, making me sag in defeat, with only one thought holding my consciousness...

Ace...

"I got him!", the man who held me yelled with his thick, rough voice, "The prize is mine! Now back off, motherfuckers"

"He's *ours*, we all helped catch the boy, so why don't you hand him over, and we shall all split the prize"

"**Fuck you**!" his arm squeezed harder on my neck making it even harder for me to breathe, then he added with a lower voice, "I'm taking this little one to meet our Captain myself, he has been waiting for you for years now"

Th-th-their Captain?? years!! Where will they take me?? Oh, Gods, the dead pirate is back for revenge! W-what the Fuck is happening!

I was breathing even hastier now, shaking from the mere thought of my former Captain's ghost coming back from the valley of the dead to haunt me and get its revenge. I lifted my eyes and saw several others jumping into the sea and swimming our way, and ALL my mates were busy fending for themselves!

Several men surrounded us quickly and tried to talk to my capturer again, "I say we kill him. We cut him and take one piece each to the boss, he said to get him dead or alive, right?"

The man went silent for a moment, then his sword pressed to my neck dangerously making me gulp and lose all hope, "The head is MINE!!"

I flinched and closed my eyes to receive my end.

The ending was less painful than I thought, it actually didn't feel anything at all. I peeked to take a look at the valley of the dead, only to find myself still surrounded by the bunch of pirates that wanted to take my life. And instead of their snarls and scary faces, they were all gasping in surprise and terror and staring at the man that was holding me. I looked above my shoulder and my eyes widened at the sight;

the shiny end of a long sword was emerging from his mouth and pointing towards the sky, his eyes staring at the void as he choked on his blood. I was still consumed by the sight behind me, unable to explain any of the events of this cursed day. Then the strangest thing happened, the tip of the sword plunged back into the dying body and disappeared! And before I could even regain the ability to move again, my feet were pulled down making me sink into the water.

My heart was beating so damn fast, and the only explanation my mind could provide was that the ghost of the dead Captain was drowning me in the darkness of the sea. I panicked even more and I tried to counter the strength that was leading me to the bottom. Suddenly, I was no longer being pulled deeper, and I was pulled into a very familiar warmness.

I stared in desperate happiness at the beautiful face that presented itself in front of me.

Ace!

With his sword in one hand and his other one around my waist, he pulled me to him in a firm grip, then swam away from the herd of pirates that were above us.

I lost every urge to breathe or break free as I looked at his godly face. All I needed was right here, in my arms. My heart was warm again; I wasn't alone anymore! I couldn't stop shivering, only hold on to him as strongly as I could manage in this situation.

We emerged a couple of minutes later and gasped for air. The pirates yelled loudly as soon as we did and immediately headed our way. Ace cursed and resumed swimming right away while dragging me with him

"Fucking heavens! Why in hell are they chasing *you!*??"

"It's th-th-the ghost! The Captain's ghost! He's back for me, he wants to kill me!"

"What in the **fuck** are you talking about!"

"C-Captain Kirk!! I killed him! I killed him and he's back to kill me!!"

"Maren-"

"No, I swear! Those bastards told me themselves! They said they were taking me to him! They want to cut me to pieces, Ace, they want to a cut me and take me to the dead guy's ghost!"

"Calm down! There's no fuckin ghost!!"

"I-I-I don't want him to take me! He'll bind my soul for eternity! I don't want to be a slave ghost"

And before I knew it, I was wailing and begging in despair. Ace tried to get me to calm down but I couldn't ease the panic that embraced my heart.

I don't want to meet the ghost of the Captain I killed in cold blood! I don't want to be tortured by him for eternity! I don't want to leave Ace behind!

I cried and held onto Ace who cursed every time he looked back.

We reached the beach and he pulled me out of it with a firm command, "DON'T SAY A THING!"

I nodded and shut my lips tight to prevent myself from talking. Ace was heaving but he didn't wait, he pulled me behind him and immediately attacked a scary looking pirate. I wanted to fight. Aye, I will fight, right after I make sure Kier's ghost hadn't found me yet! I stuck behind Ace, my head thrashing right and left, looking for any signs of a cursed spirit.

Nash looked our way and yelled, "ACE! Where the fuck did you go!!" he barely finished those words, then got back fighting with a heavy man who seemed difficult to finish even for Nash. Nash looked tired and very annoyed. The others weren't in their best shapes either.

Nash seemed to have an advantage as his opponent kept retreating and he kept charging at him mercilessly. But at one point, Nash yelled with all his might, "**You fucking cockless cunt!** This is my best shirt!! I will Fuckin **cut your balls**!"

Before we knew it, the heavy dude was running into the cursed forest with Nash chasing after him.

"**Do not follow them! Stay on camp! Naaash!!** Fuck!" Ace tried calling him back, but the bull-headed Nash didn't spare him a look as he disappeared.

"I'll get him back!!" Yeagar threw at Ace before he finished a couple of pirates around him and ran towards the damn forest. And of course, Ajax followed him leaving a trail of curses behind him.

Soon after that, one of our mates approached us, "It's HIM they're after!"

"Go back to protecting your crew, Tren"

"Why the Fuck should we protect HIM??"

"I said **Go Back**-"

"Ney! I ain't giving my life for that mouse!"

A couple of other mates approached us, glaring daggers at me with eyes that spoke of their intention to attack me. Ace breathed in, failing to calm himself as his calm voice sounded so threatening that it gave me shivers, "You're part of the Martina crew and your Captain's orders oblige you not to turn your back to your mates! Now go back to protecting the camp or-"

Tren ignored him and tilted his head towards the others who joined him with his small piercing eyes still on me, "I say we give him to these bastards and get this shit over with!"

I trembled and held tighter on Ace's shirt.

"You say you want to rebel against your Captain's orders, you piece of shit?" Baril yelled from a dozen feet away

"Oh yeah? Where is the mighty God, by the way?"

Ace tensed at Ken's words. *Shit, shit, shit! They were starting to doubt the Captain's authority and that could only end really bad, and the first one who will get hurt in this fucked up situation will be me!!*

Before Ace could answer, another bastard attacked us. Ace turned to cut his head, the move was successful, but something happened in the blink of an eye.

Ace suddenly groaned and froze. Then he turned slowly to face our mates again, and when he did, I saw a dagger stuck to his back.

His hand reached to his shoulder and he managed to pull the dagger out. Without any wait, he sent the dagger back to its owner; right between Tren's eyes.

The pirate fell backward motionless, the other mates watched him, their eyes looking weary to Ace as they took a few steps back.

"Anyone who even thinks of betraying any of the Captain's rules will face the same fate!"

The mates gulped and retreated. A couple ran away immediately, while the others went to receive those who were swimming towards us and arrived at the beach.

Baril complimented the shot and whined about wanting to kill Tren himself. As for me, I felt like my soul had left me already. I stared in complete shock at the crimson smudge that widened before my eyes.

This... is... blood......... Ace's blood......

Because of............ me?

I did that to him......

I.......... Ace's blood...

I stepped back slowly, the word 'blood' ringing fiercely in my ears. I gathered enough consciousness to hasten my steps. So I turned back and started running.

Unfortunately, I was only a few steps away before Ace caught my arm again, "Where the FUCK you think you're going??"

I shook my head, "I... I'm sorry! I'm so, so sorry!"

My tears escaped freely as I watched Ace's so handsomely confused face. I opened my mouth to explain, but no words came out. Only more tears

I looked down and tried to step back again, but his hand squeezed tighter on my arm, "Are you Fucking kidding me? You walk away and you'll be killed on the spot!"

"**I Can't Risk You Getting Hurt Because of Me!!** I... I can't... Better I get killed than you, Ace! Please let me go!"

"Are you insane!"

"Not really, " Britt added. Ace glared at him, but the big fellow continued talking, "As long as he's here, they will keep coming for him. Just take him and hide somewhere"

Ace stared at him for a couple of seconds, then he turned towards the camp again, "BARIL!"

Baril answered without even looking back, "Just go! We'll hold them back!!"

"You're coming with us" Ace told Britt, who nodded and followed us.

Ace dragged me while we ran into the haunted forest. I couldn't help turn around in panic every time it felt like the ghost was about to reveal himself and grab my soul.

We could hear the voices of the pirates get closer and louder in the forest, which only meant that they knew that I was no longer on the ship on in the camp; they were after us even here in the forest!

We met a few ones, they didn't outnumber us by much so it was easy to finish them. But every time we did, the commotion of the fight made the others get even closer.

When it sounded like none of them was close enough to attack us, Ace pulled me close to a large tree with big roots while Britt stood guard behind him.

Ace held my face that was still trembling and spoke in a calming voice, "Stay here. You need to hide until we figure this shit out"

My heart burned and my eyes stung again, "Ace! Don't leave me!"

He frowned and a tick formed in his jaw; he wasn't sure of this; he was still debating whether to leave me or not. But then his eyes looked so saddened. *Damn it, I know I was causing him so much harm and trouble, I know being with him is putting him at risk! But now that he wants to leave me... no... please don't...*

Please!

He closed his eyes for a few seconds to gather his determination, then he pushed me further, making me duck, then crouch and get under the heavy curvy roots. I was involuntarily resisting every move, but I ended up under the tree, sitting with my legs pulled to my chest in the very cramped space.

"Ace..."

Britt cut a few branches from another tree, then handed them to Ace who started covering the hole under the tree. I didn't know what to say... I had no right to ask to be with him, yet I wanted nothing more than to have my eyes on him at all times

He put so many branches that the roots were almost covered completely. When I could see nothing but a small opening, I felt so desperate that I whimpered, "Ace, please don't abandon me..."

"I promise to never abandon you, Maren. Just stay still and don't move no matter what you hear. I will come back to get you as soon as I can"

Then it got darker. All I could see was the branches close to my face and the tiny light that sneaked in. I kept whimpering and calling for him, I know what he ordered, I just couldn't...

When I heard no more noise at all, I hugged my legs tighter as I shivered and cried silently.

I was alone...
In the haunted forest, with a ghost and a thousand pirates on my trail...
And he wasn't here with me...
Ace was gone...

∞ ∞ ∞

Chapter 26 ~ Whips and hopes
∞ Zaire's POV (two days earlier) ∞

whoosh

The cracking whip whooshed in the old hut. It was like waves... like the rhythm of a heartbeat. Once it's gone, you know it's coming back again, and if it doesn't, it's usually bad news. You are no longer pained by the sting of it, you only wait for the next... and the next... and the next... And the fact that I could still hear it, the fact that the whip was still slicing the air and my flesh with it, was the only proof that I was drawing a breath.

I was a Master. A powerful young man who owned over a hundred slaves, and traded a dozen every day; from sex and servant slaves to fighters and guards. Hell, I even sold a couple of slaves to a crazy wife who was conned into fake rituals that sacrificed humans for beauty or to get a soul in her womb.

I lived through life managing to escape the plots of a crazy older sister who tried to kill me a thousand times during her teen years. Yes, my family was crazy. As crazy as men could be...... except for my sweet mother.

She was the light to our dark lives. She was the only one who didn't blame me for coming to this life, despite the cruelty that I caused her as a baby.

whoosh

My father and sister called me an abomination, and that's exactly what I am. The day I was born, my mother bled so hard that the healers were barely able to bring her back from the valley of the dead. And once she recovered enough, they broke the news; mother wasn't able to give birth to other children anymore.

I never fed from her because I had rendered her so weak that she was unable to gather enough milk in her breasts. My father, sister, uncles, and cousins, they all cursed me. Strangely enough, I never batted an eye to their behavior towards me. It was like a lifestyle that I managed to adapt to quickly. It actually made it easier to be respected in the slave market. I trained my heart not to hate them to the point of plotting their deaths, only keep whatever hatred, self-pity or sadness inside me and away from the prying eyes. And certainly, having my mother on my side was the only, but sufficient, proof that I deserved to walk this earth.

I was thirteen when that changed.

Father was used to enjoying his own slaves, but it all went south the day he decided to bring a mistress back home. My mother hated her. Despite her weak health, she fought with him over and over. She even turned a few slaves against the mistress with the help of my loving sister. While drunk, my father confined to me, the young boy, for the first time in my life. He told me how strong and capable he was, how he wanted to have a young, beautiful and strong woman ruling over his business by his side instead of the weak old one.

I understood him. I never accepted the mistress, but I surely understood my father's ambitions and lust. He was a man, and nothing teaches you about human lust more than working in the slave business. It was clear to me that my parents would never go back to their usual relationship, especially with my mother who couldn't even spare a smile to her husband anymore, and not to mention Enya who fueled mother's jealousy and slapped the mistress several times causing my father to strike her back.

whoosh

I acted as my mind dictated was the most logical thing to do. I walked down to the dungeon of our second mansion, where we kept most of the slaves. I chose a couple of fighters and sent them to guard the mistress's bedrooms. Then I selected a gentle looking man to serve my mother. I took him to our servants who cleaned him and dressed him properly, then I presented him to mother after threatening to cut his throat if he did as much as forget to bring her a cup of water. I instructed him on what meals, tea, and wine she preferred, and I ordered him to keep her company and hug her if she felt angry, lonely, or sick.

Things got much smoother after that. But that was only for a few months until mother's health gave up and she passed away.

I witnessed the death of my mother, sprawled on her large bed, my sister kneeling beside her and crying. I didn't cry. I was deeply sad and feeling quite lost, but I hid it like I was used to with any of my feelings. At the time, I was still young, and I wondered why was it that I couldn't scream or wail like my older sister was.

It also struck me when I walked out of the room and found my father there. His usual upright large shoulders were slumped in defeat, his hands gathered in tight fists, and his forehead was resting on the wall while he shook slightly and the tears fell freely from his eyes.

I didn't understand. I thought father hated her, yet there he was, crying like a child... While the actual child was unable to do so. *What a fucked up family*, I thought. Little did I know that I haven't seen the half of it.

A familiar crushing heaviness fell upon my senses again, and I mistakenly thought I could surrender to it.
WHOOSH, "Don't you FUCKIN dare sleep!"
I winced at the pain. Something in me smiled at the agonizing feeling that reminded me that I was still alive, and my mind traveled away from this hut again.

My sister couldn't absorb what happened. She kept trying to take one of our lives: I, for being born, my father, for betraying our mother, and the mistress for replacing her. We weren't a set of gullible sheep either; we watched our backs, each for his own.

We managed to outlive her schemes. And every time Enya failed to put a snake in my bed, or send a sex slave with a dagger to the mistress, she would grab a poor soul from the dungeon, and she would torture the unlucky him or her until her rage was sated. And most of the times, she only stopped after ordering her slaves to dispose of the body.

Our blessed lives went on like that for a few years. One day, Enya killed a nice piece of a sex slave that father intended to sell to a rich Lord. Father slapped her hard across the face and threatened to kill her.

That was the last night anyone had spoken to father or his mistress. My dear sister poisoned them, then she walked up to me with the widest smile and radiant face I had ever seen her wear, "Two for three, little brother. Two for three"

I smiled back at her and simply walked away. I had to make sure most of the slaves were in their cells to avoid any form of riot, and that no one profited from these events to escape.

But, unfortunately... *one slave did*.
whoosh
I took my father's place, finding no difficulty to do so. I was raised surrounded by slaves and I knew every single method to train, force, or threaten them. I also knew a few slave markets on some shadow islands inside out, so the business never even slowed down on my hands.

Back then, my sister never showed interest in taking any responsibilities in our business. She only cared for the slaves she fucked, and the servants that she tormented. So I kept providing her with trained rough male slaves that would fuck her brains out and make her wake up late after I had left to our second mansion or the market.

I knew of the abundant love that Enya bore for me. So it didn't surprise me in the least when she practically sold me to a pirate.

If anything, I was a little surprised that she didn't take the chance to kill me. Maybe she actually loved me even a little, after all?............ Nah, she most probably wanted me to suffer knowing I couldn't survive in the pirate world.

Pirates are way better than slaves. They live for themselves, and most of the time they can choose who they take orders from. But they both share the fact that their lives are frivolous; they die easily at any moment and no one would give a shit.

I didn't have a choice in the matter though, I went from being a slave merchant and owner of more than a hundred lives, and became a pirate who can't even raid without the consent of his Captain. And what a Captain he was.

whoosh

Captain Agenor had one of the scariest reputations in the shadow seas. I was, unlike my usual luck, unfortunate enough to imprison him. Fuck, the mere thought still gives me shivers. Oh, and I didn't stop there, I almost fucked his personal pet /slave /pirate /lover /highborn. Can you blame me? The guy had the most beautiful eyes I had ever seen! And I could feel the daring and the nobility deliciously ooze from his glare! And Fuck was I right, he was actually a nobleman. An innocent one! How rare is that! But once I got to know him, I saw that he had his own kind of strength. He was a good person. And teasing him never stopped amusing me.

But his Captain was a totally another story. It took me a couple of weeks to accept my fate, but even after I did, Agenor never gave me a chance. I observed the Captain and the way he interacted with his crew. I couldn't understand how he could inspire their loyalty and respect without training them? It takes whips and threats to do such a thing! It eluded me. And the more I watched him and wanted to understand him, the more I felt like many of the others; I wanted to follow the man.

Yet every time I tried to talk to him, he would threaten me. My goodness, I who was immune to other people's loathing and death threats, I who survived living with the creature from hell called Enya reaching to grab my soul every day, I got caught in the web of a pirate Captain, and I felt like I wanted to make things right. I apologized, I befriended the pirates, who actually were quite amusing and not as dumb as I thought, I got into a couple of friendly bouts just to show him my strength. I wanted to prove that I was worth something even without my slave guards. I even made Nyx laugh a lot whenever I wasn't teasing him!

Nothing.

Agenor never trusted me. And whenever I was too close to his pet or almost alone with him, he was there, silently threatening me.

whoosh

All I actually wanted was a chance. And after several months, I finally got my chance. Twice, actually. And with my fucked up luck, I managed to fuck things up both times.

The first chance was when I was allowed to raid with the pirates. I was bored beyond belief, but I mostly wanted to impress the Captain. But we ended up raiding on the nobleman's cousin. Apparently, some people sincerely love and care for their family. And Agenor was busy watching Nyx during the raid and then fixing the cousin fuck up later. I never got the chance to tell him how many fighters I finished in the first minute only of the raid. I didn't get to tell him that I was the one who cleared the path to the fancy whine and silk rolls that were in the hull. I'm aware that it wasn't a big thing, but that was all I could think of in the middle of the fuckin sea.

And then I asked to escort Nyx on Sejour since many of the pirates had bounties on their ugly heads. I was surprised to see that Agenor accepted. Everything was going according to plan until I saw a familiar face in the crowd.

"You're daydreaming again?"

I raised my eyes at the source of my torment and smirked, "My sis says hi"

Before I could even blink, his fist crashed on my jaw. I was pushed back with the strength of the strike and my body wanted to retreat, but the shackles wouldn't allow it. I spat my blood on the muddy ground, then looked at him again, only to find him glaring at me.

Uh-oh, that's not good. Judging by his glare, I won't be eating, drinking or sleeping for at least three days. Fuck, this is like five months ago all over again. It was idiotic of me to think that he got bored of torturing me. But it's not like I have a say in this, is it?

It was interesting to know one's limit. And this sucker certainly tested mine; Now I know that I can live for at least five days without food and water, but the worst was the lack of sleep. His men would take turns to keep me awake for several days without rest. I blink an eye, I get whipped. I curse, I get whipped. I ask for food or water, I get whipped. Hell, even if I do nothing at all, I freakin get whipped.

During my whole life, I never faced hunger and thirst as I had for the past five months. On Sejour, when I followed the familiar face in the crowd and got caught, I actually had the audacity to think that I was part of a crew... that someone would come looking for me... How the FUCK could I believe such thing!! My **Fuckin** family would set me on fire if they could, and I trusted a herd of wolves to care about me?? No wonder Agenor left without sparing a look behind. Why would he!

The first couple of weeks that I waited to be rescued were actually more painful than the torture I had endured since then.

I was brought out of my thoughts with another painful punch in the guts. I groaned and heaved helplessly.

Gods, damn you all for playing with me. And fuck you all if you think I'd give up my life that easily.

"Remember *this*?" The tall infant pulled his shirt to reveal the snake brand on his chest, "Remember the day you gave me THIS??"

Yeah, yeah. I Fuckin branded you. Big deal. I kept telling this guy that it's what merchant slaves do with slaves. It's my fuckin job! He just keeps asking over and over like he's someone special or something.

"I can't take off my clothes in front of my crew because of this humiliating scar!!"

"......... Why in hell would you undress for your crew? Is it a kink of yours-?"

Ok, I should've seen the next punch coming.

"How do you like the taste of your own medicine, *Master*?"

Damn, punching a hungry stomach over and over is really fuckin painful. I grunted in agony, then gathered my strength to open my dried mouth, "Now that I tried my torturing methods, I'm actually more proud of them"

WHOOSH *WHOOSH* *WHOOSH*

"Ughghgh!!"

My back arched at the violent whip, then it slumped in fatigue.

This motherfucker's name is Theron. He's a piece of shit of a pirate and he used to be one of my slaves. That happened a few years ago, I was sailing back to Esme when this asshole raided on me thinking he could defeat my well-trained fighters. I spend day and night preparing them to protect me or to fight in battle pits, and he thinks a bunch of drunk dogs would scare them? I crushed his crew like a bug before I imprisoned him along with most of his mates.

"You know... when you dragged me into your dungeon, I still had hoped that you'd make me a fighter, but no. You handed me to that monster you call sister!"

What do you want me to say to that? Sorry?? I'm not fuckin sorry! You were a fuckin slave and I had every right to skin you alive!

"...... Try living with her for twenty years"

He looked disgusted for a moment. Then he stepped closer, keeping his face inches away from mine, "She tortured me... She humiliated me!!"

It was years ago, yet he looks as if he came out of her room an hour ago. I remember the day his luck had brutally abandoned him when my dear vipera set her eyes on him. Enya demanded to have him and I indulged her wishes. I actually took pity on him and branded him myself before handing him over. I am not a merciful Master, but it's loss of time and money to damage the goods. And if I left it to my sister, with the pirate's misplaced arrogance, she would leave him with at least five bleeding scars. Now he blames *me* for it? He witnessed himself my sister's deeds. For more than a year, my sister showed him hell, even after having her way with him.

"I remember the smile on your face when Enya cupped your junk and declared you hers"

"She's a devil in disguise!! How the hell was I to know that such beauty would be so fuckin cruel!!"

Fuck, I almost laughed at that. Sometimes I get my hand on a sweet slave girl or a twink, when they're confused they look adorable. But a tall hunk of a pirate, confusion looks so stupid on him.

"I thought you had your revenge, already"

"What, for your father? Are you fucking me!! Aye, I killed your father and his mistress. But I only did that with the help of your fucking sister!"

"And you were able to escape slavery that night and get back to piracy. Congratulations"

"You ruined my Fucking life!! My reputation as a pirate Captain, my gold, my men, my ship, **my brother**!"

I shook my head slowly, "Oh come on, you know he brought it upon himself!"

His face distorted into an angry snarl, "**I would've saved him!**"

I sighed, trying against my own usual self to calm him, "No Theron, you couldn't. You said so yourself, your brother kept running after the devil and challenging him. He was bound to fall. I lived with Agenor's crew long enough to know their strength. And I know you couldn't 've saved him"

His eyes widened and he froze in thought. Fuck, it's like every time he hears the news for the first time! I hate it when he froze like that. He's so fuckin disturbing to watch.

Yes, it appears that this Theron fuck had a brother, Captain Kier or something. Agenor annihilated his crew, and now Theron is after him for revenge. He says that he could've reached and saved his brother if I hadn't enslaved him.

He was to thank me for saving his life if you ask me. Slavery is no fun, but it's damn certainly better than crossing the valley of the dead.

So, Agenor was right after me and my dear Enya on his list of death. Oh, and he claims that Maren killed his brother, something about treason?? I couldn't believe his words, even if I saw it happen. Seriously? If the pirate could be killed by Maren, how could he be a pirate Captain?? This happened years ago, and Maren is still a boy, no more than sixteen, I think! Must be a reaaaally lousy Captain. No wonder Agenor got fed up with him and ended him.

I sighed when I remembered my own list of fuck-ups with Agenor. I betrayed him. After a month of torture and sleep deprivation, I broke. I told this fucker that

Agenor was heading this way, to Pyry. I don't really regret it. The man was so happy he gave a fuckin whole day to sleep!! But it doesn't change my deeds...

Which brings us back to right now, because Agenor was supposed to reach this island a few weeks ago. So now Theron thinks I lied, and the kicking, whips, and sleep deprivation resumed action.

I get it. Not IF, but WHEN Agenor knows, I'll be dead. Actually, I might be killed long before that because of this fucking slave. I just............

For once in my life, I'm really hoping for one thing...

I hope I die without Agenor knowing of my betrayal.

The unfamiliar feeling weighted on my heart again. I think this is what people call sadness??

I wasn't certain but doesn't feel good, nor light. My eyes drifted slowly leading me towards a depraved sleep.

But before I could reach heaven, his fingers ran in my hair. I felt shivers of disgust break across my skin, waking me more roughly than the cracking whip, "You know, I saw you before. Aye, before the cursed raid. You were younger, walking proudly behind your father. I followed you and tried to talk to you, but you unleashed your dogs on me!" his fingers curled in a painful grip and he started pulling on my hair, "Your men beat me to death thinking I intended to harm you when the only thing I wanted was to talk to you!"

Ok, this is the first time I'm hearing this. And after much consideration, I admit I was in the wrong.

I should've ordered my men to kill this disgusting unrealistic bitch. I swear to the Fuckin Gods that he's a lunatic with his crazy mood swings.

His grip eased on me little as he continued with a smile that looked like he was recalling the past in his fucked up head, "Then I saw you. The day of the raid, I never thought we would meet again, but we did! And I told my men to kill everyone......... Except *you*"

"Yeah well, you should've told them to do something they could handle"

"**Don't you fuckin get it!**", his hand pulled on my hair again and his other one squeezed on my neck to strangle me, "**I wanted you for myself!** If you didn't betray me that day, I would've kept you safe, with **me**!! Now look at you, look where you've gotten without me!"

Actually, I've gotten here because of you and my dear sis

"I... I would've taken care of you... I would've loved you..."

Shit, is he fuckin serious??

I, the slave merchant! He wants ME to be his bitch?? A PIRATE'S BITCH??

I couldn't help my eyes that looked him up and down, as much as I could handle with him choking me. Then when my disgusted eyes met his hopeful ones again, my eyebrows elevated and I answered with words dripping of sarcasm:

"I'll pass the dazzling offer"

All I saw was his head back up a little, with a fierce snarl tugging his lips. And then he brought his forehead crashing on mine, leading me to a forced long awaited sleep.

∞ ∞ ∞

Chapter 27 ~ His weakness
∞ Nyx's POV ∞

"I can't believe I followed you here"

"Hehe, I can't believe you're actually scared, Nyx"

"I'm not scared!!" Damn it, that was too loud. I shrunk a little as I looked around us to check the trees again for any monsters.

"I keep telling you, I have a bad feeling about this"

I was looking behind me when I voiced my concerns for the hundredth time. And when I bumped into something rigid, I actually yelped!

Then I pouted when I saw the wide grin that tugged Agenor's lips. He leaned down to place a chaste kiss on my mouth, and then he pulled back and smirked, "Do you have any idea how adorably cute you are when you're scared?" Then his arms pulled me closer to him and he his face dipped in my neck, "I think you're doing it on purpose to lure me"

"Lure you? **Here**?? God, how could you be in the mood in such a... creepy forest?"

He pulled back to watch my worried face, then he spoke slowly and too gently, like talking to a child or a stupid person, "It's this way because many storms hit this island all year long. The trees can't hold their leaves and sometimes the branches get torn and thrown away. That's why you never find an actual path in here. The eerie feeling along with the ghost stories make people actually believe that the forest is cursed. But I promise, there are nooo monsters, ok?"

I sighed and mumbled, "You say that, but... "

He caught my lips again and spoke while kissing me over and over, "I'll take you to see a beautiful cliff. We can even jump it if you're up to it"

"Jump? Off a cliff?? Sounds like a suicide plan"

"Not if you're with me, " he winked and gave me his seductive killer smirk, "Besides, there's a nice river underneath it"

"I don't know... I think crossing this forest is adventurous enough for me"

He laughed loudly and I really wanted to shush him.

We walked more in the forsaken forest while Agenor kept telling me entertaining stories about things that supposedly happened in here. I listened carefully, absorbed by every event he counted. A particular story was about a woman who was wrongly accused of cheating on her husband, and to prove her loyalty and honesty, she had to spend one night here alone in the middle of a blizzard!

Of course, like most of his stories today, the woman never came out of the forest and her limbs were found, cut neatly and scattered in different parts of the forest.

"It is said," he continued as he pinned me slowly to a pale tree, "that her head remained alive, able to see, hear, and talk. And every being who came across it and looked in her lifeless eyes had to swear of her innocence, or..." his voice trailed and his hands sneaked under my shirt and around my waist, "they would perish, and his soul will roam in this forest forever, thirsty for both the living and the dead"

I gulped and tried to hide my fear, "Tha...... that's an interesting story"

He smirked and leaned in closer, while his fingers skimmed lightly on my lean abs, teasing my skin, "This forest is quite interesting, don't you think?"

I nodded absentmindedly

"Would you like to go look for it, together?"

I seemed to forget what he was talking about as I stared at his smirky inviting lips, "together?"

He smirked wider and nodded, then his voice became thicker and more seductive, "Aye, together"

"Ok"

"Aren't you scared to meet the woman's head?"

I shook my head slowly and leaned in, joining his lips with mine

Even surrounded by creepy trees, he manages to look so outstandingly sexy... He makes me talk about death and ghosts and yet still feel hot for him

Shit, am I a sex freak??

"You're blushing... Now I know you're being cute on purpose"

With that, he licked my lower lip and I immediately welcomed his tongue. God, I think if a monster showed up, I'll lift a finger at him asking him to wait until I finish making out with my sexy devil.

And make out we did. I put my arms around his neck, while he kissed me vigorously, moving his head to explore every angle of my mouth. He was cupping my ass already, and I don't know where I had the audacity to do the same for him, only I went a bit further when I sneaked my hand under his pants and held onto his backside.

He laughed at my daring action and immediately lifted my left leg. He wrapped it around his waist and settled between my thighs

"I see my angel is being naughty already, " he rolled his waist, successfully drawing a moan from me, "Gods, I miss being completely alone with you"

I smiled at his sweet words, "Me too, I miss being only with you"

I pulled my necklace that was resting peacefully on his chest. Then I leaned in and buried my head in his neck and kissing him gently. With Agenor, I could get uncharacteristically daring. Even when I push him or initiate something, he never makes me feel overbearing or shameful. On the contrary, I feel his happiness with my actions; he usually holds back and curiously waits to feel my every move. And that compels me to try and be even more playful while taking advantage of his unusual patience.

His hand covered my head and pulled me even closer to him. I was taking my sweet time, distributing slow open mouth kisses on his neck and upper chest. And I reveled every time I made him flinch. But a few minutes later I noticed that he wasn't chuckling or kissing me back anymore, just looking around us.

I tried to pull back but his hand denied me that. I moved his hand from my head gently and wiped my mouth with the back of my hand, "What's wrong?"

His eyes met mine and he put on the fakest smile, "Nothing, love"

His unconvincing reassurance made me worried, "Agenor?"

"I thought I felt a movement in the trees"

"Haha, nice try. You should know by now that I do not scare easily"

"Are you sure?" he answered smugly, still looking around us. Then he stepped back, "I guess I was wrong, or maybe it was just a bird or a rabbit"

I thought he'd at least say 'rabbit ghost' to scare me. Whatever.

We kept moving while enjoying more and more disturbing stories until the weird trees cleared a little and we came to the cliff.

There wasn't a wide sight as I thought there would be, but it was beautiful nonetheless; it was a valley between the cliff we were standing on and another that we even higher. An angry river ran at the bottom with huge green trees that added a nice touch to the pale scenery.

I approached the edge as much as I could, which is a good couple of steps away from it. I listened to the echoes of the running water and breathed.

"This place is really nice"

"I knew you'll love it", he pulled the jar of wine that he brought with him and wiggled it, "A walk and a drink!"

"Shouldn't we discover the surroundings first? This seems like an interesting place"

He sat down right at the edge with his feet dangling in the air and I felt a shiver cross my spine with how close he was from falling, God forbid

"Believe me, this is as far as this island gets interesting. Besides, we won't stay much before getting back to those dumb asses so might as well start drinking"

I looked at him warily as he raised the jar in an inviting gesture

"What's wrong, brave one? Scared of some height?"

"N-no! Height doesn't *scare* me, especially not *this* height, it's not high enough to scare me-"

He interrupted me with a smug chuckle, "Just stop babbling and come sit"

I was too close already, so I couldn't help but kneel and slowly crawl the few feet left.

He laughed and I rolled my eyes. When I reached him, I was already lying on my stomach, carefully taking a peek of the river.

"Yes, this position feels much safer" I said.

He ran his free hand in my hair and kissed my head gently, then murmured, "You should crawl towards me more often.", his hand settled on my neck and his fingers reached to caress the skin under the collar, "Next time I want you to look me straight in the eyes, bite that delicious lip and undress"

I blushed at the image, "Shameless", and I tried to hide my embarrassment by snatching the jar from him, making him laugh loud at me.

Yes, my gutsy unabashed pirate is a huge pervert.

A pervert that I love.

Besides, one can't crawl AND undress.

.... Can they??

I drank some wine and passed the jar back to him. Propping my head on my hands, I watched the nice scenery and we went back to talking and enjoying ourselves.

∞ ∞ ∞

"We should get going if we want to get out of the forest before sunset" Agenor said as he looked behind us, then I felt him tense suddenly

"You're ok?"

He didn't answer me. Instead, he stood up slowly with his eyes never leaving the forest.

"Are you trying to scare me again? Because I'm telling you, it's not going to work"

When he didn't answer me, I started to get worried myself. I crawled back from the edge of the cliff and stood up. Agenor walked closer and stopped right in front of me. His stance was very protective and it made me anxious. I looked around but saw nothing. Yet with the way he reached back to hold my hand, I was certain we were in danger.

We were being followed.

I had no clue other than Agenor's behavior itself. It was odd though, Agenor usually faces his opponents straight ahead and doesn't prefer waiting. But something in the way he kept his focus on our surroundings told me he didn't want to confront them right away for some reason so I kept silent.

The second Agenor put his hand on the handle of his sword, I panicked. I tapped on his hand that was holding mine. He looked back at me and immediately wiped the frown on his face, but not before I caught on it.

I smiled and said with a low voice, "Agenor, it's ok. We can beat them"

His eyebrows arched in surprise then he sighed and nodded.

"How... many do you think they are?"

"Too many. But you don't need to worry Nyx. You won't be harmed; I promise"

I breathed and did my best to believe neither of us will get hurt.

"Do you know who they are? What they want?"

"No, but they're too fucking skillful"

Indeed. We've been trying to spot them and I am yet to see or even hear any of them!

Then he mumbled, "If I were alone I would've fuckin ended them already, but-"

He stopped himself before finishing that sentence. The meaning was quite obvious, though: *He was weaker because of me*

"We're surrounded"

Shit

"M-maybe we should try to get back to the camp again?"

"Aye, " he said that absent-mindedly. My suggestion wasn't really brilliant, but my brain could offer nothing else. Seeing the way Agenor was worried really shook me to my core.

My hand shook a little and caught Agenor's attention. He turned to look me in the eye and said a confident, "We will be ok"

I nodded, trying not to reveal how fearful I was. He pushed my hair back from my face and mumbled, "I need you to run, Nyx"

I gave him a quizzical look and he continued, with the same calm, low voice, "I will create an opening for you. On my signal, I need you to run to the camp and not look back. With your sense of direction, I'm certain you won't get lost. Can you do that for me?"

"I will not leave you-"

"I'll be right behind you. They will be on our tail the second we run and I need to know you're in front of me when they attack"

I gulped and couldn't answer him. It seemed logical for us to run, but why would he be the one to stay behind!! I'm as worried about him as myself or even more!

"Don't overthink it. Just trust me ok?"

I don't know what came over me as I stared at his eyes. An ominous feeling that I should not look away from him invaded me and I refused to turn my gaze away from him. As if he felt my distress, Agenor smiled in an attempt to ease my worries, but strangely, that just made me want to throw myself in his arms, hug him tight and not let go.

His deep sarcastic voice cut through the silence, "Wow, I guess you don't trust me after all"

"No! I trust you. I do"

"Good. Because I think they're going to wait for nightfall to attack, and I intend to cut their plan short"

Cut short?

He let go of my hand and walked closer to the trees and I got startled as something was shot right to Agenor's head. Agenor immediately unleashed his sword and cut through the flying object, and I watched as the small arrow with large head fell in two pieces.

As soon as the broken arrow hit the ground, a few men jumped out of the forest and lunged at Agenor. They looked hideous, their faces painted black and white, their clothes filthy and torn, and they had weird looking necklaces that resembled sets of teeth or small rocks. They ran towards Agenor with their backs hunched forward like a herd of animals.

I panicked and pulled out my sword. My hands were shaking and I got even scarier when more came out and ran straight to Agenor while screaming and making weird noises.

I attacked without a second thought and managed to push a few, keeping the from aiming at Agenor. But in a few minutes, we were already surrounded by the filthy animals from one end and the cliff from the other.

I managed to injure about four of them while Agenor killed more than a dozen. A while later, I was panting heavily as we stood side by side and glared at the men that were continuously snarling at us.

"Well, well. Finally, we meet"

A man walked out of the forest. He was tall with his hair falling on his shoulders. He was wearing nothing but leather pants and a sword tied to them on the side

Agenor glared at him with a hell freezing look, "Who the Fuck are you?"

"Now, that is very rude of you", the man said calmly, "I've been dreaming of the day we'd meet for years, and this is how you welcome me?"

When Agenor didn't answer, the man raised his head and declared proudly, "I'm your nemesis. And I'm here to collect your head"

Agenor snorted, "*Nemesis*, huh. I didn't know I had one"

"And that's your mistake! How could you not know about the Captain who has been coming after you for years!!"

"Years? Mate, seems like you lost your way in the seas. You should've hired a navigator"

The man's hands gathered in fists and he frowned angrily, "I didn't get lost! I-"

"How old are you anyway, boy?"

"**Fuck you!** I'm not a fucking boy! I'm a fucking Captain! I'm the nightmare that will kill you!!"

"Well, you don't look like a Captain to me. And I certainly never heard of a pirate crew from the Akaiton clan"

The man smirked, "Nicely observed. I wouldn't expect less from the devil. Aye, these are Akaiton hunters, but they're not part of my crew. They're only here for the gold"

"Mercenaries? That gives me an idea of how strong your crew is"

" **Fuck you!** My crew is fucking strong and we have a fucking reputation that puts yours to shame!"

Agenor raised an eyebrow and the other one continued proudly, "I am Captain Theron!"

I tilted my head to look at Agenor when he didn't answer. He looked like he was still waiting for an explanation, which clearly aggravated our opponent, "Theron! I'm Captain Kier's brother!"

"And?"

"AND. I'm here to FUCKING take revenge for the massacre of my older brother and his crew!"

"Are you fucking kidding me? You've been following me for years for that dead goat?"

"You would be wise not to insult my brother or I'll-"

"What? Kill me? You already said that like a thousand times"

I whispered to Agenor, "You're making him angrier!"

He smirked, his eyes still staring at the so-called Theron, "Prepare to do as I told you, Nyx. And careful not get hit or even touch those arrows. The Akaiton hunter clan is famous for using poison"

"Poison?? God! Agenor that thing almost hit you!!"

"As far as I know, it causes sleepiness"

"Oh, that's... not too bad, is it?"

"It is if you're being chased by fuckers. But too much of it can get one killed"

"Hey!! Are you fucking kidding me?? You dare ignore **me**!!"

Theron yelled and I flinched, "Shit, you got him angry again!"

Somehow, I still hoped they'd talk again and sort this amicably, but before they could say anything, one of the hunters threw an arrow at us. As soon as Agenor voided it, the other hunters moved to attack us too.

It went on for a while, Agenor didn't break a sweat and still managed to fend for both of us. But with the flying poisoned arrows, it wasn't an easy task at all. Theron kept ordering the I did my best to help but the fight was seriously wearing me out; both physically and mentally with all the blood and the animosity in the fight.

Agenor noticed that. He doubled his speed and whirled while moving from my right to my left. On his way, he sliced through three men then deflected some small arrows. It was so fast I didn't even see the arrows before they were broken.

"Nyx, **run**!"

No

Agenor kicked another hunter and pushed one away

"**Now**!"

His order was so firm that body moved without even thinking.

I ran.

"Get the small one!! Don't let him fuckin escape!" I heard Theron yell behind me, but when no one lunged at me immediately, I knew Agenor kept them busy.

I ran alongside the cliff and felt my heart tighten in my chest.

I'm running. I'm running and leaving him behind by himself!!

It seemed like no choice was the correct one. I run and I could call for help, but I'd be leaving him alone. And if I stay, I'd be in the way because he's obviously exhausting his efforts in protecting both of us!! Damn it, why am I so damn weak!!

My whole being screamed for me to go back. To stand with him no matter what! And I couldn't continue running anymore. I halted and turned around. A few were after me, but Agenor got most of them already. I was about to start running back at him, when Theron pointed somewhere behind around me, "Varg!! Get that one!!"

I looked behind my left shoulder and saw a bulky, sunburnt skin man approaching me slowly. He wore clothes similar to my crew. He had a big dagger on his waist and a huge bat in his hand. He smirked evilly and walked towards me, "Here here, cute kitten. I'm going to take good care of you"

"**Nyx! Runnn!**"

"Don't you Fuckin let that one escape, Varg!!"

I couldn't even look at Agenor. Everything happened so fast! The big guy called Varg swung his bat at me and I ducked to avoid it. I was able to evade his next swings, but I was retreating and getting dangerously close to the edge.

Varg kept calling me kitten and grinning like a crazy person as he chased after me slowly. At one point he reached at me with his hand and I had to quickly roll on the ground to escape.

I involuntarily let my eyes search for Agenor between the ugly beasts surrounding him. He was successfully pushing them back but they kept coming at him. I saw Theron raise his hand and yell at the hunters, "Arrows!! I want a fucking arrow in his head!! I want the fucking devil **on his knees**!!"

And to my horror, several ones pulled out their arrows and threw them with their hands towards my dear Captain. I panicked even more, my knees trembled and I couldn't keep myself from yelling his name.

Luckily, he deflected the poisonous weapons, but such luck didn't last at all. I heard a wild groan and I turned to find Varg very close to me with his bat elevated and ready to strike. It was too late.

I raised my sword to lessen the hit. The bat clashed with the blade and my sword flew away. The blow was so strong or me, I was pushed back and lost my balance. Before I knew it, my leg stepped into the void and I found my whole body going after it, falling in the valley.

"**Nyyyyyyx!**"

I clenched my fingers stronger on the edge of the cliff to which I was barely hanging. I tried to pull myself up, but my right hand and feet slipped and I almost fell again.

My heart pounded like war drums. I tried to even my breaths, but I was too distressed to calm down. I looked down and saw the rushing river. But before I'd meet with that if I fell, I'll certainly fall on the rocks and trees first. God, the view got me even more terrified with my hands that were continuously slipping slowly.

I looked towards Agenor and my ears caught on him yelling and calling my name over and over. I couldn't see him well, but I saw a couple of hunters being thrown into the valley. Their screams as they fell and the way those screams suddenly disappeared made me whimper.

"**Nyyyx**!! I'll get to you! Don't let go! Don't fuckin let go!!"

I swallowed and did as told. I clutched my hands more on the edge of the cliff and tried to ignore all my fears and just focus on Agenor's voice.

Not a minute later, a distressed 'No' that Agenor yelled alarmed me. I groaned in pain when something stepped on my left hand. I raised my eyes to find Varg, standing on the edge of the cliff and evilly grinning down at me.

"Surrender," I heard Theron say, "Drop your weapon or I get your little pet killed"

No, no no no...

"**Get the fuck away from him!!**"

"Drop. Your. Weapon!!"

Don't, Agenor please don't!

Vrag pushed his foot slowly, making me slip further down the cliff, and my heart sank at what I heard next

"Ok, just stop. It's me you want, just let him go"

"Agenor don't!!" my words were useless by now. And I saw with deep pain as Agenor's knees fell right on the edge of the cliff so he could look at me. I shook my head slowly.

Don't surrender... not for me... not ever!

He was breathing in puffs angrily, glaring dagger at Varg. When our eyes met, he nodded at me reassuringly. I couldn't help the whimper that escaped me seeing him on his knees with his hands lifted in surrender. Suddenly, an arrow hit his shoulder and he groaned in anger more than pain, then removed it instantly and threw it in the valley.

Oh God, the poison!! Those damn arrows are poisonous!!

Theron cursed and yelled, "**Hit him again**!"

I yelled his name as two other arrows hit his arm and thigh. Agenor cursed and removed the one in his arm, but before he barely removed the other when his body tilted to the side.

He took one last look my way before falling unconscious.

∞ ∞ ∞

Chapter 28 ~ Please wake up
∞ Nyx's POV ∞

"Noooo!! No, no, stop! **STOOOP**!"

I yelled with all my might, as I watched the horrible scene in front of me.

"See that, Varg. The devil isn't that scary once he's asleep, is he?"

Varg responded with a hideous laugh. I tried to move, but he pulled me back roughly by my arm. His grip felt like it was breaking my bones and no matter how much I tried to hit him or punch him, he just laughed at my weakness.

"I've been waiting for this moment for years" Theron said as he moved his dagger threateningly over Agenor's body, "I came out alive only to find my dear brother dead. Murderer! I had to find my brother's hidden gold, and then I got a ship and a crew. I had to sniff your trail in the fucking wide seas. Now I finally got you under my mercy" he moved the point of the dagger slowly until it rested dangerously on his chest.

As soon as the dagger touched Agenor's skin, my heart sank in my chest and my knees wobbled. Instead of giving into the fear that was consuming me, I lunged forward and managed to free my hurting arm from Vrag, "Don't you dare touch him, you bastard!!"

I lunged towards Agenor, who had his hands in shackles and tied to a branch of a large tree. His feet were barely touching the ground and his shirt was torn open.

And his eyes...... closed...

His helplessness felt so unreal. Every second I expected him to open his eyes and smirk at his coward opponent. But he didn't move a muscle. He didn't retaliate as he should've. His head hung low and he remained vulnerable to the threatening pirate.

And I wanted nothing more than to hold him and protect him with my own body. But before I could touch him, Theron pushed me back and I stumbled into Varg's hold yet again. I yelled and cursed them both only managing to draw mocking hideous laughs from Varg, who grabbed my hair and kept pulling me back and forth for his own entertainment.

"Stay out of this, little one. I don't intend to kill you, you're my gift to someone important." Then he turned to Agenor again, "You, on the other hand, I will torture you for every bit of misery I went through. I already trapped your stupid crew and soon their heads will be brought to me. I will take over your ship and your wealth, and I'll compensate all the gold I spent on the fuckers who are tracking you. I will let the world know that *I, Captain Theron,* got the devil on his knees begging for my forgiveness"

He walked the dagger on Agenor's abs and pushed slightly further. A couple lines of blood started sliding out of his body.

"Hehe, the kitten is crying. Look how he's shaking! He's fuckin scared shitless" Varg laughed lightly and I just noticed, indeed, I was trembling and crying. I thrashed to move away, but I couldn't approach him. Everything felt so unreal. *God, I was so fucking weak. With no dagger or sword, I was completely useless!! What can I do to save the most important person in the world for me? What can I fucking do!!*

When Theron drew another cut across Agenor's chest, I felt a bile rise from my stomach. Before I knew it, I was leaning forward and I threw up.

"Fuck! The fucking shit puked on my leg!!"

I was heaving and trying to control my breathing. But Varg was already roughing me up and hitting me on my sides.

Theron laughed at the scene. But when Varg didn't stop, he ordered him to, "Don't ruin his pretty body, Varg"

Varg didn't listen. He continued to pull my hair to draw me closer, and then kick me with his hands or knees. He wasn't giving me deadly blows, but he was rough enough to keep me from protecting myself or even looking up.

I was on the ground trying to protect my stomach when Theron pulled his arm, "Hey! I ordered you to stop!!"

Varg released his arm in a displeased manner and glared back at his Captain, "Why the fuck would you care?? You got your fucking revenge! Now I get to have my own fun until I get the gold I was promised!"

"I told you, you will all get your gold once those rogues and the rest of our crew comes back from raiding on Martina! As for this one, he is not yours to have fun with"

"And why the FUCK not??"

"Because I am your Captain and I said so!"

Varg didn't move, only kept glaring and waiting for a more convincing answer.

"Because I Fucking have plans for him already. I didn't think I'd have him, but now that I do, I will use him"

I sat up with difficulty and watched Varg step closer to his Captain, "You want him for yourself, don't you? We can share him. I am part of this shit as much as you! Besides, you already have your own toy"

Theron met the threatening stance with the same and smirked, "Aye, I have my own. And the little one is now part of my victory as well. I GOT HIM, I will do whatever I want with him!"

"Which is??"

"I'm going to make him my slave's slave"

What the hell was he talking about??

"Are you serious??"

"Aye, he loves to play Master and he seemed to talk about him with interest. So maybe if I give him this present, he'd agree to be my slave without resisting anymore"

Theron was grinning widely at his own absurd words. I didn't try to understand though. I pulled myself away slowly while Varg told his Captain how crazy he was and that his plan, whatever it was, would never work. I pulled myself up and approached him...

I was finally able to touch him. My poor Captain was hit and beaten all night. I touched his injuries that were still slowly bleeding. I tried to stop the bleeding with my own hands. I couldn't hold back the whimper that escaped me when my hands coated with his blood. I raised my eyes to meet his sleeping face, "Agenor, please wake up! I beg of you, you have to escape... please..." I released one of his injuries to touch his face. I lifted his head, shook his shoulder... nothing.

I stood on my toes trying to reach the knots of the ties that were holding him hanging. I was too fucking short to even touch the ropes.

A weapon... I need a weapon! I have to save him no matter what!

"What are you doing?" I whipped my head around to see Theron standing close, staring at me, while his subordinate glared at all of us from behind him.

I immediately stood between him and Agenor, putting my arms behind me to hug him, "Don't hurt him. Please don't hurt him! I can get you money! Just let him go and he'll give you anything you want! Please-"

"Are you fucking joking right now?"

My shoulders shook as another tear escaped, "I'll do anything... please just... don't hurt him. I beg of you"

He narrowed his eyes and kept staring at me in silence, then he crossed his arms and said like he was in deep thought, "I don't see it... I mean I get it, you're very handsome and you have all that 'I'm a highborn' thing going on, but..." he walked closer and I pressed myself more against Agenor, "I don't get why he likes you. I've seen him own much better-looking slaves, both men and women!"

"I..... I don't know what you're talking about"

He suddenly pushed my leather collar with the point of his dagger and pressed it against my neck. I went completely still, barely controlling my trembling, my only consolation was that his dagger was pointed at me and not at Agenor

"He blabbed about all of you when he was half conscious, even that fucking murdered called windy, but you! Your fucking name kept popping out over and over. Why the Fuck is that??"

I opened my mouth to answer, but words failed me when I saw the anger in his eyes. His mood changes so fast, I feared if I voiced the wrong words he might kill me on the spot.

My God, if I'm dead, who will help Agenor!!

I sucked my lower lip to keep my tears at bay. No matter what I faced since I sailed with my stepfather, it didn't seem like I became any less of a weakling.

"Please, sir... just spare Agenor..." was all I could whisper without crying.

I felt a sting on my neck from the dagger, then Theron's deep angry frown dispelled in a second and he was smiling apologetically, "Shit, sorry!" then he used his thumb to wipe the blood off my neck, "I said I'd keep you clean for him. Well," he put his hands on his knees and leaned down a bit so we were face to face. Then he added without dropping his smile, "If he likes, then it's for the best, right? What's the point of asking if you already fucked, huh? I'm fine with sharing as long as he's mine at the end of the day"

I didn't understand any of what he was saying, nor why he was smiling all of a sudden. But when he tilted his head and asked, "What do you think? Can you make him happy for me?"

I don't know why I nodded at that moment. I had no idea what I was agreeing to, but anything seemed better than making him angry and letting his attention go back to Agenor.

"Excellent! I can't wait to break the news for him. Do you think he's awake yet?... Nah, I think he's still asleep. Probably dreaming about me whipping him, right? Hahaha"

He was laughing so hard to his own words and somehow his craziness felt as threatening as his dagger. I peered behind him to find Varg still glaring at me with such hatred that it made me look away to avoid him. My hands held tighter on Agenor's legs behind me, while my eyes trailed back to the dagger in Theron's hands.

If I reached for it and failed, will he kill me? Or would he let it go because he apparently had plans for me? Wait... what did he want with me?

I paled when I remembered him saying 'slave's slave' earlier. I've never heard of such a thing but it had the word slave in it, twice!!

Damn it... Agenor, please wake up!

"Theron! Therooon!!"

"**What**?? I told you to fucking call me *Captain*!!"

The skinny pirate came to halt a few feet away looking alarmed and breathless, "O-o-o-ur men! Our men were killed!!"

"What? How the fuck!"

"The Martina crew! They killed them!"

"Did they get any gold, at least?"

"Euuuh..." the pirate took a couple of steps back before he answered, "They were beaten at shores"

Theron approached the pirate threateningly, "Are you telling me, the team I sent did not even get to raid on the ship??"

"Actually... Captain, I'm talking about the mercenary pirates and some of ours..."

"**What**!! When the fuck did I send all those??"

"I did", Varg answered confidently, "You were busy with your revenge against Agenor. The shitheads you sent were wiped out in five minutes, so I sent others too"

"Who the **Fuck** you think you are to order **my men**?"

Varg didn't even care to answer, nor did he stop glaring back. Theron ordered him while pointing his dagger at his face, "I say who attacks and who stays back! Now go gather the rest of the men, remind them of the gold that awaits them and **Wait. For. My Fucking Orders**!"

Varg glared at me again, then back at his Captain. I, on the other hand, had my attention on a rusty sword in the skinny pirate's hand. I didn't allow myself to think much, I took advantage of them all focusing on each other instead of Agenor or myself. And I lunged at the pirate.

Just like I predicted, as soon as I moved, Theron tried to catch me. I ducked, though, managing to escape his hand. In a second, I was holding the pirate's sword and threatening to cut his throat:

"Come any closer and I'll kill him!!"

The skinny pirate shrieked and started calling for his Captain's help. The latter, however, sneered and unleashed his sword, "I thought. **We. Had. a deal**!" he said very slowly while walking closer

I knew that the one I held was a losing card facing people like Theron or Varg, who strangely did not move to help his own crew.

"We do have a deal, let Agenor go and I will... do whatever I'm supposed to in this deal of yours"

He eyed me silently for a few seconds, unfazed by his subordinate's whimpers. Then he grinned, "I guess pretty people are idiots. You, little one, are not in a position to negotiate. But as a gesture of good will, let me help you with the problem at hand"

He went to strike the pirate, his own crew!! I pushed the unlucky man away and move to the other side to escape the sword. But Theron didn't stop, he struck again quickly and I managed to block him. His swings were very strong, but thanks to my training I was able to keep up to him. His laughs resonated as he kept attacking me, while I did my best to keep us as far from Agenor as possible.

I even thought I could take him down, all until the sword in my hands gave up and broke in half.

I fell on my back and his sword was immediately threatening to puncture my heart. I panted and raised my eyes to meet his, expecting the crazy happy look he had a few seconds ago when we were fighting. Instead, he was smiling calmly, "Good. You move well, not bad for a little one. Now, up you go!"

He pulled me by the arm and started walking, "I want to show you to someone. Don't be scared, he prefers bravery. Just be quiet in your corner and loud in bed, for now, keep him nice and good until I get back. I have to see about those motherfucking sea wolves. Shit, I can't believe they killed half my men already in one day! Those useless assholes. But don't you worry, I will win. I have to win! I will show the world my revenge for my brother to rest in peace, I'll show the slave Master how capable I am! -"

One second he sounded proud and the next angry. His attitude was unpredictable! I interrupted his ranting when I managed to hit him right across his jaw. *Fuck him if he thought I'd follow obediently!*

He didn't react much though, he just spat and smiled at me with raised eyebrows. Before he could dive into his craziness again, I punched him again between the eyes. This time he grabbed my hand and cussed, "Will you stop doing that! Fuck"

For a second I felt guilty, why wasn't he riposting?? He didn't even look angry! He's so damn confusing

He grabbed my arm tighter and walked again while babbling some insanities about me being 'the worst pet'. I looked behind me to see Agenor left alone, *unmoving*. I had no idea where Theron was taking me, but I certainly didn't want to leave without Agenor! I didn't try to punch him again, instead, I kicked him in his right leg as strongly as I could. Theron hissed and released me to hold his aching leg and awe like a child. I didn't let his weirdness distract me and went straight for his dagger.

My fingers barely grazed the weapon when I was yanked back. My eyes caught on Varg's snarl before I was thrown in the air. I landed on a tree, all the air whooshed out of my lungs before I fell dead to the world.

∞ ∞ ∞

Chapter 29 ~ Illusory smile
∞ Nyx's POV ∞

I opened my eyes with difficulty to find myself in an old hut, lying on the hard floor in a corner. I gazed at the ceiling and failed to recognize it. My senses started coming back when I heard a voice that felt quite familiar, **"Is there a limit to your fucking madness!!"**

"Whaaaat~?? I thought you'd appreciate the present. You know I'm your Master, right? I'm not supposed to suck up to you, you fucking shit!"

"And you had to kidnap **him**?? He's **his**!"

"Yep! And now he's yours"

"Couldn't you grab any of the fuckers who could actually handle your crap?? Why don't you use your fucking head!! Didn't you see the damn collar around his neck?? He's the Captain's!!"

"*I* am the Captain!"

"I'm talking about the **real** Captain! MY Captain!! And you hurt his most precious treasure!"

I turned my head and my neck protested. It must be from the impact on the tree earlier. I saw Theron, with a hand rubbing the back of his neck in front of someone who was standing and bound with shackles in the middle of the hut. I tried to focus my eyes to see the person, but he was facing the other way.

Theron pouted, looking hurt, "But... *I* am your Captain"

"Fuck, this is fucking useless. I am in deep, deep fucking shit already" when the man's voice started rising, I was shocked to recognize the slave Master that we parted with about five months ago, Zaire. But now the overly confident Master sounded more distressed and exasperated than I ever witnessed, "I'm fucking sick of looking forward to death at every fucking corner!! I lost everything. **Every Fucking Thing**!! And now all I hope for is an hour of shitty sleep without being kicked or whipped!! Agenor never trusted me to begin with, now if he knows I was here when his beloved pet got taken, he will think I betrayed him! He will come after **me**!!"

"No, no, no. Shshsh," Theron reached to hold Zaire, "I will protect you. *I* am your Master now, *I* am your Captain, and I'll prove to you I won't let that fucker touch you. I already got him begging for my mercy and I'll-"

"Wait, what?? Agenor is..."

"Aye", Theron said proudly, "I got the devil trapped. I had him bound in shackles since yesterday! I admit I was happy with it so I decided to let you get a good night's sleep. Besides, I thought you lied about them coming here, looks like I misjudged you"

I felt my throat tighten and my eyes became blurry at the image of Agenor, poisoned and hurt...

Theron patted on Zaire's head and the latter sneered at him, "Get your fucking paws off me! I spoke of that when I was in severe need of sleep!!"

"Still counts as help though, right?"

"Un-fucking-believable... Reasoning with you is like talking to a chicken!"

Theron immediately gathered his fingers and hit Zaire in his stomach. I winced when Zaire groaned in pain, but I held my breath to keep myself from uttering any sound.

"Just because I'm being good to you doesn't mean you have the right to talk back at your Master!"

Zaire coughed and groaned again. He was never one to admit weakness and finding him like this felt so unfair.

What the hell is happening... why is everything so fucked up!!

"Look. You can pursue your fucking vendetta against me or Agenor or even go after your dead parents for all I care. Just, keep *him* the fuck out of this. He's not like us, he can't handle your shit. And he never asked for any of this. So just let him go-"

"Let him go?? I thought you'd be happy to have him? I almost fought Varg for him!"

"You let that bear touch him??"

"He just roughed him up a little. And why the fuck would I care? I have the devil in my hands, and I got you as my pet. Fuck, I'm so happy that I could actually pass on getting that little fuck windy. Now all I need is get my hands on Martina's gold. I don't intend on paying those asshole mercenaries, so we'll go far from them and live well! Fuck, I can't wait to brand you"

"I... I'll leave with you. I don't have much choice, but I......... shit. I promise not to go against you anymore. I'll even let you brand me if-"

"**Really**!!"

"**If.** you send Nyx back safely to Martina"

"Nyx??"

"Him, the highborn"

"Oh, I told you, I'm already ceasing that ship. It's just a matter of time"

"Just hand him to the second of Martina and do whatever the fuck you want after that"

I couldn't believe what I was hearing. I call myself a pirate, I consider myself part of the crew, and I do my best to be seen as equal. But I never, truly never, thought any of them would risk their life for me. And it's the newest member who does that? I was certain it was due to his loyalty to Agenor, who refused to accept him very stubbornly. And seeing the way he suffered for months, alone... I felt guilty for not looking for him myself back in Sejour. I just kept asking Agenor to send someone. Why didn't I insist more? Why didn't I go by myself??

Theron inspected Zaire closely, then he sighed, "I don't understand, if you're willing to make a deal for his sake, why not keep him? Or maybe...... you love me?" he asked very hopefully

Zaire snickered, "I'd rather bathe in horse crap"

Theron glared at him, "Don't tell me you love the highborn? Or... is it their second??"

"My Gods!! That's it! I can't even try to follow your fucked up logic. Damn it, you're giving me a headache again"

"I will kill all that crew! I'll fuckin dance on their graves!!"

"Be my guest if you can, you bastard"

"Aye, I can. I fuckin can. And I'll start with Agenor's head, how about that? You'll see how strong I am once I become the new devil of the shadow seas! Then you'll BEG to be my slave! What do you think, want to witness his death?"

My breath stopped at the mere thought of it, and I closed my eyes to keep myself from whimpering. After a moment of silence, Zaire spoke very threateningly, "Now you listen to me, you piece of pig shit-"

"I don't take orders from you!!"

And Zaire suddenly yelled, "**Yes you do**! And the second you doubt that, rub your filthy fingers on your fucking nipple and see whose seal is engraved on your heart! **I branded you**! And no matter what that messed up head of yours tells you, you are **My. Slave**! So you listen. And you Fuckin obey!"

Theron kept silent in complete astonishment, while Zaire continued with a very commanding tone, "You will not touch Agenor. He's a fucking pirate, they all die in this fucked up business, but HE will not die on the hands of a slave! He will die **old** in a **fucking raid** with a **fuckin sword in his hand**! And I swear on my mother's life, you do him harm and I'll whip you so hard, you'll throw up your mother's milk!"

It took a moment for the threat to settle in Theron's mind. Then he said very hesitantly, "You... you still want me to be yours?"

"What?? Is that all you got from what I said!"

"Well, you did say I was your slav-"

"**Captaaaaain!**"

Suddenly the skinny pirate came in screaming, "The hunters! The hunters were-were-were killed!!"

"**What**?? Who the fuck sent them!!"

"It looks like Varg sent them hours ago, and now they're only a couple left and they want to beat it! We don't have men left to get the gold! How will we get the fucking gold??"

"Go gather the men left! I'll fuckin get my gold myself", he lifted the cloth covering the door of the hut. And just before he left, he halted to look back at Zaire. His frown turned into a warm smile with a head-tilt, "You think about what we discussed, ok?"

Theron immediately left the hut and started cursing and yelling, obviously arguing with Varg among others.

∞ ∞ ∞

"Fucking psycho ape, my head will explode just from listening to his demented thoughts"

Zaire cussed and insulted Theron repeatedly. Then he sighed and tried to look behind him, "Nyx... Hey, wake up, cutie. You need to get the fuck out of here immediately"

"......... Sorry..."

"You're awake?"

"I'm sorry Zaire. You were being tortured and we..."

"Can you move? Did they hurt you??"

"He... he's poisoned... They poisoned him and I couldn't stop them! Then they... they hurt him and injured him! He's bleeding right this second!" My voice stuck in my throat and I couldn't stop the tears that escaped my control.

Zaire cussed then asked me again, slower this time, "Nyx, there's hope as long as he's alive. Just tell me if you can move, you have to! my shackles are tight so you'll have to get out of here on your own"

"I can't... my hand is bound too"

I pulled my right hand that had a small shackle on it. I tugged on it more, but it was made from iron and linked to an iron pole stuck into the ground

"Fuck"

"I'm sorry... I can't help any of you"

"We'll figure this out. At least they didn't get Maren, right? I mean the kid is tough but he wouldn't even stand a week of their torture. Besides, it looks like those pirates are giving them a headache, so they'll keep them busy for a bit longer. Try to rest a little for now. It might seem unnecessary in these conditions, but they could keep you without food and water for days. So just try to gather your energy until I figure out something with that crazy head"

∞ ∞ ∞

I closed my eyes and thought of the one thing that would calm me.

I saw him wink at me sexily as he steered the wheel. In my imagination, he blocked the wheel then strode my way. As soon as he reached me, he put his arms around my waist and pulled me closer. I smiled and stretched my neck to kiss him. He met me in the middle and I could feel his smirk grow wider as I kissed him more; the pervert loved me initiating romantic gestures. His teeth tugged at my lips hungrily and I put my arms around his neck. We were on the deck yet completely alone.

He pulled back, leaving my heart beating only for him. He smiled down at me gently, his silver hair falling on his right shoulder like a silk cloth. I gazed at his gray eyes and he stared back at me.

He was breathtakingly beautiful. He smiled genuinely, looking so happy

So......... *safe*...

"Nyx... it will be ok"

Zaire's voice made Agenor's picture waver and disappear. Then I realized that I was sobbing silently. I answered him with a muffled hum and tried to think of any way to help us out, to save Agenor.

∞ ∞ ∞

Before I knew it, someone charged inside the hut angrily. I tensed and pulled myself back against the wall at the sight of Varg.

He was fuming in anger and kept walking back and forth in front of Zaire. Suddenly, he grabbed a whip from the floor and started whipping my mate irritably. I gasped in horror at the scene. And I... I couldn't even speak while facing such cruelty, so I shamefully failed to defend someone in need.

Zaire met the torture with great endurance. Around the seventh whip, he commented sarcastically, "What, did your Captain spank you in front of your friends?"

Varg looked like he could kill him. He threw the whip aside and started punching Zaire and cursing Theron over and over, "He wants to command everyone! He wants to fuckin get everything! I'll show him, I'll show him who the real fuckin Captain is!! I'll take the fucking gold! I'll take the fuckin pets!! **I'll Be the Devil**! I'll show that motherfucking slave bastard!!"... he went on and on until suddenly, his eyes set on me.

His movements halted immediately and his eyes widened as if he didn't know I was here with them. Zaire spat and said with a very tired voice, "Hey, is that all you got? Come on, I expected more"

Varg didn't respond though. He pulled back and started walking slowly towards me. Zaire kept calling for him to go back, but only got ignored. I pulled myself up and wiped my lingering tears with my forearm.

I was more scared than ever. Every pirate I met had motives; they acted either based on money, power, or just for some entertainment. This one, on the other hand, looked like the only thing stirring his actions, was anger.

As soon as he was at arm's reach, he threw punches directly to my face. I successfully ducked twice, but that seemed to anger him even more. He groaned loudly and reached to grab me. I sidestepped, but I couldn't get far when my wrist pulled me back. It was a lost fight with the first hit that landed on my forehead.

Everything went eerily silent. His fist felt like iron that was about to crush my skull, and it sent a violent wave of dizziness to my head. I crashed on the wall, but he instantly pulled me by the collar and threw me on the floor.

"The fucker doesn't even have Kier's gold anymore! He fucking spent it all on this stupid revenge! **He's been lying to us all**! He can't fuckin pay us, the mercenaries will tear us to limbs!! I will fucking kill the bastard!! He wants to fuck everyone! Let's see how he's going to stop me now!"...

I lost focus on his words when he started kicking me everywhere, and my body felt number with every blow. Then he took into punching me in the face again. I tried to protect it with my arms the best I could. I kicked his leg, making him groan in pain, and I took that chance to punch him in the stomach with my right hand.

That made him stop to glare down at me, "You're fuckin strong for a kitten. Unfortunately, you ain't strong enough!"

He leaned down and I closed my eyes, expecting another punch. I felt a sudden weight instead, and when I opened my eyes, he was straddling my waist. I thrashed my legs to throw him away and even hit him on his sides. I yelled and screamed for him to let me go, while Zaire kept calling him and insulting him to leave me alone.

He grabbed my right forearm and squeezed it, "You're too damn loud for a sex slave!"

His hand clutched harder on my forearm and I screamed in excruciating pain. I tried to release it, but he laughed at me and pressed even more.

"Aaaah! Please... please stop!!" I whimpered and begged for him to release me. And he only let go after my arm gave up in his hold.

I felt a heavy wave of faintness when he unclenched his paw. My arm fell beside me, unable to move anymore. I groaned and tried to get a hold of my consciousness as the hut started swirling.

Agenor......
Agenor.........!!
'Nyx...'

I heard his answer in my mind, but he wasn't there beside me. Varg didn't leave me any time to even understand my own thoughts and I was too confused to comprehend what just transpired. He grabbed my other hand and held it to my chest. Then I felt the painful sting on my cheek.

My ears buzzed from the impact and I gasped. More from the realization of what happened, rather than the pain itself; he had backhanded me so hard, my vision got distorted. Varg was laughing hysterically and calling me demeaning names, ranging from 'mewling kitten' to 'slave bitch'. All while continuously slapping me, with the occasional punch and hair pulling.

It was completely futile to try to move or protect myself, with his weight on me and my wavering consciousness. I closed my eyes and just willed myself to wait for the pain and humiliation to end.

Suddenly, the realization hit me that he wasn't slapping me anymore. I tried to focus my eyes to see if I was finally spared, when I felt his hand between my legs and then I was hurting a lot, "A bitch has no need for a prick!"

"G-get your filthy hands off me-!!", I barely managed to say

"Hehe, you still have the strength to talk! I'll fuckin tear your tongue away from your fuckin face! I'll also cut your manhood and fuck your asshole, let's see how Theron will still claim a cock-less whore!"

"No.... no...."

"Yeees, fuck yes!" he kept grinning evilly and painfully squeezing me in his palm, "What, can't get hard? I bet you look fuckin good with a leaking hard cock... **Come on**! Show me your prick is useful or I'll fuckin cut it off!"

Kill me...

I didn't know I had voiced my thoughts until he answered, "Oh, I will gladly kill you! But first, I'll take whatever pleasure I could get. I'll fuck you open, maybe Theron will know he's no longer in command once he sees what I had done with you!"

Please kill me!

The torturous pain ascended to my stomach, making me spasm uncontrollably. I tried to release my hand from his grip, but he was pushing it so hard against me that it felt like my chest was also about to break. My humiliated desperation didn't seem enough to get him off my case, as he kept groping me mercilessly and demanding that I get hard.

∞ ∞ ∞

"Help!"

Zaire was yelling with all his might, and Varg threatened to break his limbs if he didn't shut it. Then he went back to focus on getting me aroused after giving me a few more slaps.

Seeing how unresponsive I was, Varg cussed and started tugging on the ties of my pants. I moaned and tried to move my free hand to cover myself. All I got was a killing shot of pain from my forearm to my spine.

"**Theron**! Get your ass in here! **Therooon**!!"

Vrag stood up and went to Zaire. I feared for his life, but Varg didn't hit him. Instead, he pulled out an iron key and released Zaire's shackles. Zaire fell on the floor with a loud thud and he groaned painfully.

"I hurt you and he'll fuckin act like a caring mother. But if he doesn't find you, he will fuckin flip. Come on, it's time for you to get the fuck out of here"

"Wait, what about Nyx? Give me the kid too! I'll only leav-"

Varg kicked him, then dragged him out of the hut. Zaire didn't look able to fight or even walk.

I moved my left hand with difficulty. I pulled my pants, but my fingers hurt too much for me to use. So I lowered the hem of my shirt instead and covered myself.

I was now left alone. Drowning under the unstable roof that moved like waves. I heard some voices outside. It sounded like a strong wind and people running and calling for each other in panic. Yet my unstable hearing filtered all the sounds but those of the whistling wind.

All other voices seemed to morph into Agenor's... My throat constricted and I closed my eyes, unable to stop the tears.

∞ ∞ ∞

"Everything is going fucking shit crazy!" Varg came barging inside. He tugged my collar and glared down at me, "He's gone to get the gold himself and even took most of the pirates!!"

"please..."

"Fuck! I'm going to challenge him when he gets back! I'll fuckin become Captain, take all the gold and the ship!!"

"... Agenor... please let me see him... I want to see him..."

Finally, when he heard me, he halted and looked me in the eyes. He didn't say anything, just kept staring at me with his angry look. I pleaded again, my voice barely audible. He held my chin and pulled my face closer, "You are actually pretty when you cry, aren't you? Did you cry like this to make the devil want you? Did you lure him with those eyes..."?

I tried to look away or closed my eyes, but he slapped me and demanded that I looked at him. I begged him once more and when he didn't slap me, I actually thought he was going to let me see Agenor. Instead, his hand dipped between my legs and he said in a low disgusting voice, "How about I fuck you right in front of your former Master? Maybe that will make those beautiful eyes cry more, or are you a bitch that only gets hard when a big dick is thrusting up your ass?"

No words could describe the disgust and dizziness that I was feeling. The repugnant and dishonorable feeling of his hand made me wish for a thousand deaths.

Suddenly, the hut started shaking strongly and the voice of the wind grew louder.

"Fuck, he's back! I wonder if they got the gold... Shit, I can't believe those hunters were right, we're getting a fucking windstorm! You, I'm taking you with me"

"No! Leave me alone! Please, let me see Agenor!!"

"Your fucking Captain is probably dead by now! Theron is back and he's having trouble controlling the remaining pirates! I convinced most of them to flee anyway! And even if he got Martina's gold, I'm going to take his fucking place! As the new leader of the shadow world, I will have you as my bitch. And if you're still alive when I'm bored with you, I'll sell your ass to a horny wealthy Lord. But for now," he pulled the iron key and released my shackles before he yanked my face closer to his and grinned evilly, "let me feel what it tastes to fuck the devil's whore"

Only God knows where I got the strength at that moment to crush his nose with my fist. We both groaned in pain. He grabbed his bloodied nose and I cradled my hurting hand.

Varg's curses were drowned in the noises of the rising storm. I pulled myself away from him in a desperate attempt to flee this lowly pirate. But I couldn't move fast enough with my suffering right arm.

"You fucking little wolf! I see you still have the strength to fight! I didn't want to use this so soon, but" he reached for his pocket and pulled a small bamboo container, "this Akaiton poison will make you into an obedient doll"

He inserted his thick thumb in my mouth, forcing it to stay open and making my head tilt back. And with his other hand, he crushed the container making the strange liquid leak into my mouth. At the first taste, my tongue and lips went completely numb. My throat started gagging and burning immediately, feeling like I swallowed a flaming torch. Then my whole body felt unbearably tired all of a sudden, with a heavy unseen weight crushing over me. My senses dulled rapidly. Everything went completely silent and the hut started to look reddish; the redder it got, the darker my vision became.

The last thing I saw was a beautiful shade of silver before everything disappeared.

∞ *Agenor's POV* ∞

'help...'

'help me!'

'How could you sleep? How could you let them take me?'

'I'm scared Agenor, you know I can't handle bad, rude people!'

'I'm in danger... SAVE ME!'

My body jerked when the image of him falling into the valley and screaming for me to save him. My senses suddenly started working again with great difficulty. My eyes opened and my head immediately felt dizzy. It took me long moments to keep my eyes open enough to figure where I was.

The first thing I came aware of, was the immense pain in my whole body. I tried to move but hissed as the pain got stronger on my chest and stomach where I could feel the burning ache of the injuries. I gazed around me, everything looked a bit red or purple, and everything was swaying a little despite my efforts to focus. My arms felt unbelievingly sore and it took me another moment to know that I was tied to a branch in the middle of the forest and what looked like a small camp.

Pirates were running here and there, sometimes stopping to poke me or talk about me, completely oblivious to the fact that I was awake. They were preparing to move because of the rising heavy winds. I pulled on my shackles hoping to break the branch, but I wasn't strong enough. My body was still low and not very responsive.

Nyx... where is my Nyx...

"Those bastards! They killed my army!! I'll show them! I'll fucking show them!"

"Captain... **Captaiiin**!"

"**What**!"

"Most of the living mates ran to our ship! They want to set sail before the tempest!"

"Fuck, I even lost the hunters and the few remain ones escaped during the raid. Shit, shit, shit... this is all getting out of control!"

"Aye," the pirate said in a crying voice, "we didn't get the goooold...!!"

I opened my eyes a little to see Theron waking back and forth in front of me.

"... think... I need to fucking think... I got my slave, I got his slave, and I got the devil. Now I need to go command my ship or those bastards might sail with it without their Captain! Aye, my prisoners and the ship. Forget about windy, I don't need him anymore. That should do it, for now, prisoners... ship... Aye"

"C-Captain..."

"Go get my prisoners; we're heading for my ship!"

"I-I-I'll get the rest of your gold, Captain!"

"No, there is no fuckin gold anymore"

"No!! The gold! Kier's gold!!"

"How do you think I paid for those mercenaries and the fuckin hunters??! Some of them actually came with the hope of getting their hands on Martina's gold! Hehe, at least those fuckers are dead, right? Or they might come after me for their payment"

"But... you promised that-"

"I don't need your pathetic whining right now! **Go. Get. The. Prisoners**!"

"Euuuh... I was about to tell you, Captain... the slave got away"

"**What**!! When? **How**!!" Theron grabbed the pirate's shirt and the pirate squirmed to release himself, "I was told the last he was seen was when Varg threw him outside the camp!"

"**Fuuuuck**! No, no, no! This can't be happening... I finally got him!"

The wind blew stronger, almost throwing the pirates away. Theron grabbed his hair tight and went into a frenzy, "I-I-I'll kill Varg! I'll fucking kill him right now!! No, I'll go find my slave first... I can't lose him! Wait, I'll take Agenor with me, after all the fucking trouble I've been through to get my revenge-"

"Captain, we need to leave for the ship!"

"The ship!! I need to get to my ship and take control over it once more! I can let a herd of idiots have it... but I need to find the slave Master first..." he touched over his heart and looked quite lost, "Aye, I need to find my Master... I'll FUCKIN GET MY SLAVE BACK!! And I'll give him his gift-Wait, what about the little one?"

"Still in the hut......... with Varg"

"**Fuck Fuck Fuck**! If that ape touches him, my slave will go shit crazy on me! I need to save the little one. But I still need to find my slave first! He must be lonely in this cursed forest! W-wait, my ship..."

I watched him pace crazily around, unable to decide. I didn't get half of his crazy shit, but if the tug in my heart is true, the 'little one' would be Nyx! Gods, he has to be ok. Don't let him get harmed!

During his ranting, his mate already fled and disappeared into the forest. With my right hand, I grabbed the shackles to lift my body a little and worked my left hand outside of the iron ring. I grunted in pain when I felt the bone in my thumb break, only then was I able to free my hand.

And as soon as I did, I reached and pulled Theron by the hair. My hand hurt like hell, but I managed to swallow the pain and use it the best I could. Taken by surprise, Theron went to unleash his sword, but as I pulled him to me, I wrapped my legs around his arms, prohibiting him from moving them.

I snarled at him and his features immediately looked like a scared and a very fucking surprised child

"**Nyx! What the fuck did you do to him!**"

"Shit! When did you wake up? Those fucking hunters, they said three daggers would keep you paralyzed for at least four days!! Those fucking cheating-"

"**NYX**! Where the **fuck is he**!!"

"Th-the little one? Aye, I didn't touch him! I swear I didn't! I was about to go help him! I was just about to-"

I dug my fingers in his hair and neck and I was sure I draw blood, "You take off these shackles and you lead me to him, or I swear to make you taste the wrath of a thousand hells!"

"A-A-Aye... Euuuh, you see, I really need to go-"

I dug my fingers more making him wince. I used the pain from my hand to fuel my anger and my snarl, "TAKE ME TO HIM!"

"Look, I-I-I'll make a deal with you. A-Aye, a deal! Just look down"

I peered to my side where he jerked his head and saw his hand holding a dagger to my thigh. He probably thought I'd be scared, but nothing would fucking scare me right now, because I was already terrified about what happened to my Nyx

"**SPEAK OR I'LL FUCKING KILL YOU!**"

"Th-that's really scary, b-but if you kill me, you won't get to save the little one, aye?"

A strong wind blew almost knocking him off

"Fuck, I really need to find my slave. Look, I'll free you and tell you where to find the little one, and you let me go find what's mine"

I stared at him looking for a hint of a lie.

Fuck, I let him go and he might kill me. Then I wouldn't be able to see my Nyx! But what choice did I have right now? It sounded like my lover was in imminent danger...

My heart fell at the thought that Nyx might be needing me right this second. And I couldn't waste a moment more.

"You hand me the Fucking key for these shackles first!"

"Aye, aye, I swear I will! I actually can't let the little one get hurt. He could get mad at me if I did. Besides, this way I'll tell him that I handed the prisoner back to you and he'll let me brand him! Fuck, this could actually work!"

He was suddenly very cheerful and I swear if not for my worry about my Nyx, I would've snapped his neck.

I eased my legs from around his arms and pulled them away. We eyed each other for a moment as he moved back and I sincerely feared he might leave without fulfilling his end of the bargain.

"There," he pointed towards the end of the camp, "I left your little one in the hut over there. Now, I'm going to give you the key and leave... very... quickly..."

He said while reaching for his pants and taking out an iron key. He pushed the key towards me very slowly, careful not to let me grab him again. I reached towards the key, and then I suddenly caught his hand. He tried to pull back but slipped with a yelp. He panicked and I could just pull him and fucking kill him since I already had the key in my hand.

But I was running out of time.

I let go of him making sure to release the key from his hand and into mine. He fell back on his ass and cursed, before running towards the forest like he was hunted by the hounds of hell.

I used the key to open my bounds, careful not to drop it. It took me a moment to do so with my broken thumb. As soon as I was free, I fell on the ground. I did my best to walk almost properly, especially with my lingering daze and the wind that kept getting stronger. With uneven steps, I headed towards where Theron pointed, hoping to find my lover.

∞ ∞ ∞

As soon as I reached the hut, all the pain in my body was forgotten and replaced with a burning rage at the scene before me.

The son of a bitch pirate called Varg was kneeling inside the hut.

And there *he* was... unmoving, eyes closed, in a most horrible state. The pirate threw broken small pieces of wood aside and laughed, "There, fucking docile. Like the good highborn bitch that you are"

He took his thumb out of Nyx's mouth and pulled his thigh, parting his legs apart.

I will hardly remember what I did at that moment. Between the daze that my mind was still fighting, the pain and guilt in my heart, and the burning red rage, my body was moving on its own. I first twisted Varg's head enough to hear a slightly satisfying crack of his breaking neck. I pulled him back and threw him on the ground. I made sure to keep him alive though. I didn't wait to register his pain or startle or fear or whatever the fuck he could've felt during those brief moments. I just took one look at my angel and started breaking Varg's limbs one after the other, over and over at different angles. I found an iron key on the ground and used it to tear his flesh. I only let the key go after I stabbed him with it in the groin.

I stood above him, heaving with intense fury while I watched him spasm. My eyes were tainting everything fucking red, so I only recognized his blood from the liquid that started making a pool around him. He was still alive, dying slowly. His body distorted in a weird position. The only thing he could still move was his eyes that were darting everywhere in disbelief. Everything else was either broken or pieced.

His eyes fluttered slowly, signaling his imminent death. I pushed him on his back with my foot, and stepped on the iron key harder, making it tear deeper in his groin. He gasped in a silent scream, while his rotten soul left his body.

∞ ∞ ∞

I dropped to my knees before *him* and stared in disbelief. Even with my weird colored sight, I could sense how pale he looked. He was alarmingly unmoving, making my heart tighten dangerously in my chest. I moaned when I saw his severely bruised forearm, and I knew from the way it laid beside him that it was severely damaged. I couldn't feel my own aches anymore, only the torturous pain in my heart.

I pulled his pants up and took off my torn shirt to cover him with it. Then, very slowly, I gathered his hands to his chest and pulled him carefully between my arms.

"Nyx... wake up, my innocent love...... What have they done to my little angel?"
Droplets of water fell on his cheeks.
It was raining, inside the hut.

∞ ∞ ∞

Chapter 30 ~ The devil's woe
∞ Agenor's POV ∞

His dazzling smile decorated his face as we sat on the front edge of the ship. I was on the jibboom facing the deck, and him very close to me, facing the sea. I loved that setting; I was the first to advance through the sea while keeping an eye on the whole ship, and he... he was the nearest... the most precious.

I was counting some events from my past, making him awe and laugh every few seconds. Of course, the forecastle soon got crowded, but somehow in my eyes, the crowd always dissolved in only him. The melody of his laughter was an everlasting charm. I could drink his smile and stray in those eyes for eternity.

Aye

Look at me

Allow my soul to be willingly lured to your enchanting gaze

And I shall need no seas to sail to, other than the blue of your eyes

Let all my heart's wishes be joined in one; for I, the devil, only wish to see that beautiful light

So look at me, my love

Look at me, my angel

Look at me...

Please look at me...

By the Gods' names Nyx, open your eyes and look at me!!

I panted heavily as I cradled him in my arms. Silent, unresponsive, completely still. The memory of his laughter drowned in the noises of the stormy winds. I ran my useful hand carefully on his body inspecting him. I couldn't rely on my tainted vision, but it seemed like he had no bleeding injuries.

I called his name, spoke to him, begged him even!

But he didn't respond.

What were the Fucking Gods doing again?

Were they Gods screwing with me? Punishing me??

I didn't know

Was Nyx punishing me??

I didn't know either, but I definitely deserved it.

"I'm at fault, Nyx... I should never have left with you alone! I get it, I Fuckin get it! It's my entire damn fault, I understand so open your eyes for me, ok? Please... just talk to me..."

I leaned down and kissed his forehead. I wiped some drool off his cheek, not knowing that the liquid was actually the same substance that paralyzed me and colored my sight even until now.

Suddenly, the hut started shaking violently. And not a few seconds later, the roof completely flew off. The shackles started clicking obnoxiously and the poorly built hut was obviously about to be blown away.

The boxes and objects of the camp started moving around. I had to take Nyx somewhere more secure.

I very carefully gathered him in my arms. My broken hand protested very painfully, but I made sure not to drop Nyx and to hold him as close to me as possible.

I walked away from the camp. My distorted vision didn't allow me to figure out our destination, but I couldn't remain there. I walked further as fast as I could with the strong winds and my unsteady steps.

I fell on my knees a few times, either pushed by the winds or tripped by roots and fallen branches. I made sure not to drop Nyx though. And the last time I tripped, my shoulder landed on a big rock. I groaned in pain and checked on Nyx. He hasn't moved or even winced once, which terrified me to the core.

The wind suddenly got very strong and dangerous. I couldn't venture with Nyx and risk facing the core of the storm, so I took refuge under the rock that was slightly bent to the side. I laid Nyx and covered him with my own body, making sure not to put my weight on him.

The weather got angrier by the minute. I ignored the branches that kept scratching my back over and over. I tried to focus on Nyx; I rubbed his cheek and his jaw, I kissed his temples repeatedly, and I tried in vain to feel his heartbeat through his chest, but all my senses were jammed because of the poison and the storm.

So we lay there for Gods know how long while the storm tried trying to rip us apart and throw us away. All I could think about was my innocent lover. I kept talking to him, calming him and encouraging him to open his beauties for me.

∞ ∞ ∞

By the time the storm calmed down, hours had passed already. My body felt very numb and my broken hand was even more difficult to use. I carried Nyx again and walked, hoping to head towards our camp. The winds were still rising, but manageable, and the forest was once again disfigured with all the branches that eliminated any paths that existed the day before.

An hour later, I heard some voices. My senses were still imperfect and I couldn't risk facing more pirates with Nyx in my arms. So I hid behind a tree and waited for the voices to pass. To my utter relief, it was none other than Ace accompanied by a couple of our mates.

"Ace"

"Captain!! We finally found you!"

"You know the way back?"

"A-aye... Captain, you look..."

"Not now, Ace" I said as I walked out from behind the tree and the mates gasped at the sight of Nyx and me. I ignored them and started walking with Ace right by my side

"I assumed you might sail Martina away from the island"

"We did, just slightly east. Now the ship is back right where you left it, Captain"

"How did you know where to look for me?"

"I was searching for you with Britt when we ran into Zaire"

"I figured that fucker was the slave Master Theron was blabbering about"

"Aye... I admit, I almost killed him when I saw him. I was so fucking enraged and I knew he had something to do with this. But Britt came between us. He was right, Zaire is yours to judge, Captain"

"Where the hell is that shit?"

"I sent him with Britt to be locked below deck. But before he left, he told me about your whereabouts and........."

"What?"

"He... he told us Nyx was in danger and unable to protect himself. I apologize, Captain, I tried to get to you both in time, but we ran into more of their men and-"

"Stop talking Ace."

Fuck, it wasn't his responsibility to apologize for. Nyx is mine to protect. And I failed to do so miserably.

Gods... why punish me using him? Haven't you played him enough?? Haven't you abandoned him already! Why come to seek him so soon!!

A lump formed in my throat. I couldn't speak or even think anymore. I just walked as fast as my body could; my priority was to get Nyx safely on the ship in order to examine him and try to get him to open his eyes. Ace kept trying to tell me about this important thing that he needed to do on the island before we set sail. I repeatedly told him to shut up and leave it for later. I needed to get Nyx to safety first, then I'll be able to deal with whatever other matter.

Once we got to the ship, I froze on the small boat; I was unable to climb my Fucking ship with Nyx securely in my arms. Ace offered to help, but I snarled at him and ordered everyone to back off.

Baril climbed down to join us and stood in front of me, "Give him, I'll get the boy to the deck. I don't think he should stay here with his current state and his... torn clothes"

I cursed and glared at him. The old man just sighed and waited. I couldn't believe I was releasing my lover to someone else's care, especially when he was completely helpless.

Gods, what have they done to him!

My heart protested so hard. But after long moments of waiting, I reluctantly put Nyx in Baril's hands very carefully. Baril climbed while talking to Nyx and telling him that he will be fine and safe while snarling at his mates and threatening them to back off and go watch something else.

∞ ∞ ∞

I barely pulled myself up the rope once when Armpit started yelling, "There! Those motherfucking pirates!! They're leaving the island too! Let's raid on their fucking asses!!"

"Aye!!", "We'll empty their Fucking guts!", "They killed and injured our mates", "No one touches Martina and lives to tell the story!", "Feed them to the sharks!!" "Allow us to raid, Captain, and I'll wear their balls for a necklace!"...

I let go of the rope and jumped back on the small boat. I looked towards the island to see another ship circulating it and probably intending to come towards us. My crew became more and more agitated, you could hear their snarls and the echoes of their foul insults cover the still agitated sea.

They wanted revenge.

I looked up to see Baril disappearing to the deck with my sweetheart in his arms, and something clicked in my head. I ordered everyone on the boat to get on the ship. Hearing my decisive and commanding tone, none of them hesitated to obey silently.

Except for Ace who approached me and said as calmly as he could manage, because something in his voice was alarmed and that only added to my fury

"Agenor, I'll stay with you. I won't leave your side-"

"Climb to the deck, Ace. And wait there"

"I'm not leaving your side again, Captain! I'm your second. We will go to hell together."

I sighed. I didn't have the time or the patience to think. So I did exactly that; not think.

I calmed my breathing and let the beast of revenge take over my senses.

"Roam", I ordered Ace. And he obeyed immediately.

My men called for me and begged to join us or for me to at least allow them to rain cannonballs on the enemy's ship. I didn't answer them, only stood silently at the front of the advancing boat, my gaze colder than ever and my heart dead to all feelings.

When we got close, we could see the commotion on the ship before us. The panicking rats ran everywhere while preparing their bows and swords. I ordered Ace to halt when we were still far enough from their arrows.

I removed my sword and set it in the middle of the boat. Ace immediately stood and did the same. I stared at him for a second. It was unnecessary to try and keep him from coming along so I let him do as he wanted.

I dove into the water with my second right on my trail. We dove deep enough so the enemy wouldn't spot us. We swam under the ship and rose behind it. The idiots weren't even monitoring this side of their ship. We climbed silently, and as soon as our feet hit the deck, we were attacked. My body moved on its own as I slit, ripped and broke every throat and heart on the cursed ship.

It didn't matter much that my left hand was useless. By the time the fight ended, I was walking between scattered corpses. I was certain a couple must've managed to hide somewhere in the hull and I was about to enjoy ripping their bodies out of their hiding. But the memory of a certain someone waiting for me made me want to jump off this ship immediately.

So Ace and I did just that, right after I set the whole damned thing on fire.

∞ ∞ ∞

Once on the boat again, I put my sword back in its scabbard. We roamed our way back to Martina and away from the burning ship. I just took revenge for my angel's misery, yet my heart doesn't feel a bit of relief.

Only guilt. Only fear.

"Captain, I..."

"Speak Ace. You wanted to say something since we were on the island. Either spit it or shut it because I'm definitely not in the mood for hesitation"

"I... I need to go back to Pyry"

"Why?"

"I hadn't reported to you what happened in your absence. I tried my best to keep the crew together, but things still got too fucked up"

"Did we lose mates?"

"Aye, five were killed and..."

"And?"

"Some escaped. I'm not certain, but I think they're at least nine. And... I killed one of ours..."

I sighed. I was the most aware of how difficult it was to keep my crew at bay. I harbored very strong pirates and they can get competitive or too ambitious for their own good. I never had trouble controlling them though, and in such circumstances, it's already recommendable that Ace could manage things so far. I am yet to hear details about what happened behind my back, but his self-blaming tone shows that he went through some tough decisions.

"Our crew is far from perfect, Ace. We are sea-wolves, and those who died knew what they signed up for. The ones who escaped will regret it as soon as they hear about our victories us again and they'll remember that they cowardly forfeited their share of the gold of years' worth of raids. As for the bastard you killed, I won't even ask who he was. Since it's you, I'm certain he deserved it."

"He did! It was Tren, he wanted to start a riot in the middle of the fight. I tried to reason with him, but he attacked me so I killed him"

"Is he the one who stabbed you in the back?"

"Aye. And... Captain... Nash, Yeagar, and Ajax went missing"

"Fuck" those three troublemakers again. I highly doubted that they escaped, especially Nash and Yeagar. But where the Fuck were they?? Shit, when I find them I'm going to skin them alive!

"I apologize, Captain..."

"You did your best, Ace. You should get your wound treated when we get back to the ship"

He didn't answer me. He went silent for a moment and I knew he wasn't finished. This damn trip back to the ship feels too fucking long.

"I swear to God Ace, just speak your fucking mind!"

"Captain... I need to find Maren-"

"Maren?? I thought they didn't get him!"

"Aye, he was in danger when we were attacked so I hid him in the forest-"

"Fuck, Ace. That damn storm made the forest almost unrecognizable again"

"I-I had no choice! It was all I could do to protect him! But it's been almost two days already. I was busy fighting and trying to find their camp, then the Fucking storm happened and I..."

I cursed under my breath and ran a hand in my hair. I knew I lost a few mates, but I never thought they got that close to Maren and the ship. I can't fucking let Ace go on land again! I need him to take care of Nyx

Nyx... I wonder if he opened his eyes... My Gods, what am I to do if he remains unconscious??

My mind was too fucking jammed to realize that Ace had stopped roaming and was looking at me, waiting for my orders.

For once in my life, I didn't want to command. I didn't want to be a Captain. I just wanted one thing... one person, and that person was attacked, hurt and out cold. I felt both eager to go back by his side, and afraid of the state I'd find him in.

".........-genor... my slave...... Agenor!!"

We heard yelling in the distance. The voice was barely audible with the sound of the winds and the burning flames. I looked to Pyry to see someone calling my name. It was none other than that Fucking crazy head Theron. He was waving and yelling. It seemed like he was carrying something. When he noticed us looking at him, he lowered his burden and sat it in front of him.

Ace reacted first. He instantly gasped and grabbed his Tashi. I looked closer and recognized Maren.

Shit, how did he put his hands on him??

"**Maren**!"

Ace yelled, but Maren didn't react. He was just sitting there, looking weak and unresponsive.

"Captain..." he pleaded for me and I nodded, "Let's get the monkey back"

Ace lead the boat towards the island. As soon as the boat was close enough, we both jumped off it and paced towards the bastard.

Theron looked terrified. With his eyes going back and forth between Ace and me, he was grabbing Maren's arm to keep him from falling on the sand. When we came quite close, he pulled out a knife and pointed it at us.

"W-w-w-wait! Don't get any closer or I'll slit your throats!"

"Maren!! Maren talk to me!" Ace called for Maren but the boy didn't answer. He looked pretty roughed up from the storm, with traces of scratches on his clothes and his body. Ace called again and Maren moved just enough to shake his head while mumbling, "No... he can't... he promised..."

I was glaring at Theron, who was now retreating a little. He obviously regretted making his presence known. I took a step towards him while glaring and he jerked. It looked like he was about to flee any second now.

"What the Fuck did you do to my mate?"

My voice was oozing threats and Theron shook his head quickly, "Nothing! I swear this is how I found him! He was moaning and mumbling something about a promise, he wasn't even protecting himself from the winds and the flying branches! I didn't recognize the boy so I knew he must've been part of your crew. I'm here to do you a favor!!"

"You want to tell me that you didn't do any of your crazy shit and just wanted to deliver him back? And risk losing your FUCKING NECK??"

"Maren..." Ace stepped closer to them and Theron retreated while pulling Maren back with him. Ace lost his patience and yelled at Theron, "**Let him go!** Or I swear you will be wishing for your own death!"

"**Wait**!! I-I'm here to make a deal!"

Of course you are

"I will let him go, I-I won't harm him if you agree to my deal!"

Ace turned to me, "He's Fucking playing us!"

"NO!! I always keep my word! ... or try to... the point is, I'm not playing games here!", then he turned to me, "Your Captain knows that I keep my end of the bargain"

He was referring to the deal we made when I was still locked in chains and looking to find Nyx.

Nyx...

I pulled my sword out slowly, "You have five Fucking seconds to confess your motives before I die the sand with your blood"

He froze for a second, then hurried to explain himself, "My slave!! I want him! I searched for him, but I can't find him, and I'm sure he went back to you! I can't lose him too, he's all I got and he's Fucking **MINE**!! M-maybe your men got him since they were already invading the forest by the time the storm started-"

His time was up. I strode towards him making him fall back on his ass. He was looking at my sword with mortification and he pulled Maren to his chest to protect himself. He was still carrying the dagger, which made Ace and I halted from getting any closer and risk getting Maren hurt.

"I-I-I'm not lying!!"

Ace snarled at him, "We don't have slaves on our ship!"

I snorted, "Zaire"

Ace looked at me questionably while Theron nodded vigorously, "Aye! Zaire, he's my slave! He branded me and now he promised he'll let me brand him if I gave the little one back, and I did! ..."

He went on ranting like that for a few minutes. Enraged one second and eyes full of promise the next. He kept insisting on his ownership over the slave merchant and counting some inexplicable pieces of events from his past.

I just gazed at his crazy talk. When I didn't answer, he halted suddenly and looked about to cry, "You... won't give him back to me, will you..."

His shoulders slumped in defeat and his arms retreated from holding Maren. He pushed Maren towards Ace and released his dagger that fell on the sand. Ace immediately grabbed Maren and moved back.

I watched Theron curiously, wondering what the hell was happening in his insane mind. He folded his feet and hugged them, then he mumbled while staring at his feet, "I gave up everything... All I wanted was to keep him... he put himself on my heart, how come we're not together??", he lifted his gaze to look at me, "Why wouldn't you give me what's mine? I gave you back the little one, haven't I?" Then his eyes widened in anger, "**Don't Tell Me He Was On My Ship**!! Did... **Did He**

Burn!??" his angry features completely wiped away in a split of a second and he looked behind him, then to me again, "No, that couldn't happen, ever! Wait, is he still in the forest? Is he waiting for me!!? **Tell me!!**"

I didn't know the reason behind his obsession with Zaire nor the relationship between them, and right now I didn't give a shit. I could easily end his misery with a swing of my sword. But something in his sincerity even in his threats told me to judge him at a later time.

I can't stay long. I had somewhere to be. Someone precious needed me

I lifted my hand and pointed at Martina the way he did when he told me about where Nyx was, "There, the one you're looking for is on my ship. Be my guest"

His eyes opened wide as he stared at the ship. Then, without looking at any of us, he stood up and walked slowly to the boat.

I looked to find Ace holding Maren's face in his hands, "You hear me? You are Fucking fine! You're just tired from the storm and you need water. So stop Fucking scaring me!"

I was surprised when he slapped Maren slightly, then he grabbed his curls and shook him, "ANSWER ME!"

Maren's eyes seemed to refocus and the first thing he whispered was, "Ace?... you came back to me..."

Ace cursed and hugged him close. Maren was whining and whimpering in coarse voice and Ace kept patting on his back. And I couldn't believe that I actually felt jealous that moment... So I ordered them to get to the boat with a lump in my throat.

∞ ∞ ∞

When I reached the deck, Baril was already in my cabin. The crew was cheering and praising the work of art that bestowed on the enemy's ship that was still in flames. Some others pulled away from me and gave me gazes of fear. I ignored them all and just hurried to be by Nyx's side.

I ordered Ace to examine him and tell me why he hadn't awakened yet. He took Maren to the hull and ordered someone to give him plenty of water then came back. He ordered everyone outside, only Baril remained with us. Then Ace sat on the side of the bed and grabbed Nyx's wrist.

I stared at Nyx and felt my limbs slightly tremble. I couldn't believe how terrible he looked. My sight was losing the sickening tint and I could clearly see how hurt his poor right arm was. His once cheerful face looked extremely pale with scratches on his cheeks. His clothes were torn and dirty. The rags of my shirt covered his waist and it reminded me of his torn pants.

He wasn't smiling at me... he wasn't looking at me...

"He's too weak. His right arm is hurt badly, but we can deal with that later. His pulse though... Was he poisoned?"

"N-not that I know of!"

He opened Nyx's eyes one after the other. I gasped in disbelief and tugged on my own hair when I saw the redness in his eyes.

Baril cursed, "Bloody hell!!"

"He's... he's possessed by the devil!!" a mate peering inside uttered, and I almost snapped his neck if he hadn't escaped.

"He was definitely poisoned" Ace said then looked at me while investigating my face, "Zaire said that you were poisoned and rendered unconscious. Maybe Nyx will wake up in an hour or so, but..."

"What??"

"Captain, your eyes look normal"

"I still have trouble with my senses including my sight. I still see a bit of purple on every fucking thing"

"I guess Nyx was given the same poison, then maybe he's weaker or he was given too much of it"

Ace checked Nyx's pulse again. I was pacing back and forth now, unable to calm down.

"Agenor... I..... frankly don't know this kind of poison"

"What the FUCK is that supposed to mean??"

"It means I don't know how to treat him or when he would wake up"

"No, no, no, Fuck no... this can't be happening!"

Ace swallowed and went back to check on Nyx's body. He looked at his arm again. Then he declared that Nyx might have a broken rib from the bruises that covered his chest. My heart lurched painfully at the news and I felt like I wanted to kill someone...

Ace investigated his body more. And when he removed the cover to reveal his waist. I went to order him to cover him but I went completely mute.

On his lower abdomen, as well as his thighs and close to his member, Nyx had scratches, small cuts, and bruises.

Ace immediately pulled the bed sheets and covered him. Then he went to check on his legs. Baril suddenly whispered me in complete surprise as he looked at me wide-eyed, "Captain, it's ok, the boy will be ok"

I didn't care what they saw. My knees buckled and I fell on the floor crying.

This was my fault! My sweet angel was living in peace and all I did was ruin his life!

I should've been in his place right now! He never deserved any of this!

This was my damn fault...

"I have to save him... I can't watch him like this and just wait! His state could be deteriorating as we speak!! I have to do something..."

"Captain, we should look for a healer"

I nodded and grabbed Nyx's hand in mine, "Aye, we'll set sail immediately. To the closest island to Pyry, Ganae"

∞ ∞ ∞

Chapter 31 ~ To Ganae
∞ Ace's POV ∞

I closed the cabin's door behind me and sighed heavily.

Captain, hang in there... Nyx will not die, we will definitely save him so please... don't look so defeated...

I've never seen you like that!

I felt so annoyed as I realized I was unable to help my Captain and friend in his most difficult times. I couldn't heal Nyx. In fact, I knew nothing about that poison and I was no expert on poisons!

I sighed again and pushed my hair away from my face in frustration. All eyes on deck were on me, waiting to hear from their Captain.

"Avast ye! Captain's orders are to sail to Ganae immediately. It should take a couple of hours for us to be there, so get to work. If I see anyone slacking or hear about a fight, I will personally deliver you to the Captain, I'm sure he'd welcome the chance to tear more limbs"

"Aye Aye!" everyone yelled, before scramming to do something useful.

My eyes caught someone moving beside me. I looked above my shoulder to find Maren, barely standing.

"What the hell are you doing on the deck? I told you to stay inside the hull, you need to rest!"

He looked at me hesitantly and said with a hoarse voice, "I... I want to stay beside you..."

His words took me by surprise as his big brown tired eyes stared at me hopefully. Gods, I wanted nothing but to hug him and take care of him right now.

I refrained from doing so in front of this big audience. So I threw him on my shoulder and carried him to the hull. I scolded him for disobeying me, which answered the surprised looks that headed our way. At the same time, I kept throwing commands at the pirates in order to sail as fast as possible to Ganae, the closest inhabited island.

Once we were in a room alone I set him down. Before I could do anything, Maren grabbed my hand and pulled it to his chest, "I'm sorry! I'm so sorry! Don't be mad! Please don't leave me!"

I stared at him for a few seconds, *was he still scared? Still afraid I would leave him??*

I couldn't help but feel sad for his doubts. I pulled him and hugged him tight the way that always sated him. My fingers traveled among his curls to hold his head closer to me:

"I would never leave you, Maren. I came to get you, but it was later than I should, and you went through that fierce storm alone! I'm so thankful to you for coming out of that cursed forest safely, and I'm so glad you're back in my arms...

I probably did nothing to prove it, but... I love you, Maren, I will never let you go. I will never leave you"

He pulled back enough to look me in the eyes and I couldn't help but smile at the rare blush that took over his cheeks, "You... you love me...?"

"Aye. I have no doubt about it, I am in love with you"

He sniffled twice cutely then buried his face in my neck while holding me with all his might, "I..... I wov you"

I chuckled at his distorted confession and he continued sniffling, "Ace, I love you so much more"

I sincerely doubt that

Aye, the scare I felt when he was attacked and thrown off the deck, the anger and desperation that invaded me when he was surrounded by the enemy in the sea... and the deep guilt that ate my heart when I left him alone in the forest...

This young man has devoted himself to me completely. And with that, he sneaked beyond the roughness of my soul and settled himself so comfortably in my heart. I sincerely doubt his feelings for me could measure to the love that I hold for him.

"I'm sorry... for being scared and for acting the way I did on Pyry... I'm not a crazy person!! I just... got really, really scared... I'm sorry for doubting you, Master"

I smiled at his sincere apology and kissed the top of his head, "You remained alive, Maren. That is all I wanted from you and you obeyed, so I'm very proud of you. And I promise to protect you better so you'll never face such danger again"

His shoulders trembled to signal more tears. I caressed his head and teased him slightly, "Hey, hey now, I never took you for a crybaby"

"mmmm..."

A moment later, when the sniffles slowed down, I decided I had to go back on the deck and see if Agenor needed anything. The mates were afraid to even walk close to the cabin, and I doubt the Captain would leave Nyx alone.

Before I went back to dealing with our shitty situation, Maren pulled on my arm and asked very hesitantly, "Will Nyx be ok?"

"I don't know, Maren. I sincerely don't know" his blood flow was dangerously weak and he was unresponsive to everything I tried, "we will do our best to save him. In the meantime, I want you to rest well and drink as much water as you can. You can go eat anything you want from the storage room. Try to eat slowly or you might upset your stomach. I will make sure Baril won't bother you. Just eat and sleep to regain your strength."

"Ace... Do you think the Captain will......"

"What is it?"

"A-Agenor... will he blame me for what happened? Will he punish me with the slave master??"

I sighed and caressed his back, "It wasn't your fault, Maren"

He nodded in my arms. *We both knew that wasn't enough to convince the devil.*

Fuck, it all depended on how things go from this point. I hope Nyx got better

For Nyx's sake

For my friend's sake

And for all of us

∞ *Yeagar (a few days back)* ∞

I ran behind the idiot as fast as I could into this eerie forest, following the sound of clashing swords and agonized screams. I was slowed down twice by new attackers. And when the third bunch of fuckers surged from behind the trees, I knew I would lose track of him if I stayed to fight back. So I left them in my younger brother's care, and ran further into the forest, ignoring his curses and insults for leaving him behind.

Fuck, I can't believe that idiot ran after the enemy alone! He's probably the only pirate in all the vast seas that couldn't control himself when challenged or insulted. Gods, I always enjoyed his lack of patience and his foul retaliations, but today... he could seriously get himself killed!

I jumped on the huge tree roots and quickened my pace. I needed to get to him fast! Ace was right, in that situation we should've stayed with the crew, we should protect our gold and wait for our Captain's return, not wander alone in the fucking ghostly forest!!

Damn it, I need to find the bastard alive and get him back to the camp before Agenor returns. We ran so much we've probably crossed third of the island already! It will be fucking difficult to find the fucking way back.

Shit, if we're late the Captain might think we deserted them! Fuck, it would be hard to convince him of otherwise if he already set is mind. Maybe I should go speak to him alone first?...... Nah, I should send Ajax to test the waters, hehe

I smiled slightly hearing my brother's insults in my head. I halted for a second to walk my sword through a couple of fuckers that emerged from the trees. Then I listened to the forest carefully. I could hear the commotion from behind me ensuring my brother's safety, but the sounds from the other direction had completely died.

I resumed running and finally reached him. He was surrounded by corpses, facing the other way with his sword in his right hand. At first, I was relieved that he defeated all his enemies. Good, I wouldn't expect less from the auto-proclaimed Third of Martina.

But when I walked closer, a sturdy pirate was holding his injured leg while limping towards him with his tick short sword in his hand.

He didn't look back. He remained completely unmoving despite the obvious threat behind him.

I lunged at the pirate and finished him quickly. I looked around to make sure we were not in danger anymore, then I approached him.

"Nash?"

My mind refused to expect anything bad. All I could think of, are the possible narcissistic comebacks and the heroic bragging he will now throw my way.

I walked closer and around him, only to gasp at the atrocious sight that met me.

Nash was standing with a profuse stream of blood falling from his face and soaking his shirt. His right eye was looking aimlessly ahead, while the left one...

His head turned slightly my way, but before he could see me, his body surrendered and fell.

"**Naaash**!!" I caught him before he could hit the ground. I looked closer to the wound and cursed.

My brother joined us and immediately started blabbering, "You Fucking turd, you left me to fight those rats alone while you played the hero? You better not've been pretending to be the only one who ran after- .... him......... W-w-what the fuck happened? Why is he covered in blood?? Nash? **NASH**??"

"He got stabbed in his left eye" I said as I tore my shirt and started covering the wound and tying it

"N-no... how could-? We were right behind him!! H-how-"

"We don't have the time for that, Ajax! Help me stop his bleeding"

My brother nodded frantically. He acted cocky all the time, but right now he was obviously too shocked to think properly. I wouldn't blame him; I didn't know what I should do either

"Yeagar, he... he's not talking..."

"He was standing when I got here. I think it has been at least ten minutes since he got stabbed"

"Is that good?? He'll be ok, right? **Right**??"

"Calm the Fuck down! I don't know if it's fucking good or not, I'm not a Fucking healer!"

We finished tying the cloth around his head, it was already getting soaked

"Fuck, this is no good. He definitely needs help-"

We were interrupted by a couple of pirates that were surprised by their dead fellows. Ajax didn't lose a second to attack them, his current anxiousness definitely helping with the way he quickly finished them.

"Yeagar, we can't stay here!"

"Aye", I gathered Nash in my arms and stood, "we need to get him help as soon as possible"

"We... we can't go back to the camp!! It would take hours and the way there is infested with fucking pirates!"

"Aye, I'm not sure Ace could help much either..."

"W-we can't let him bleed to death!"

I gritted on my teeth trying to come up with a solution fast. I turned to Ajax and asked him to climb the highest tree around us and see if he could spot anything in the distance.

He did as told fast. A couple of minutes later he was jumping back down, telling me that we were very close to the southern beach of Pyry. I didn't have time to reflect much, and I went with the first possible way out:

"Ganae"

"Wha-?? Another island??"

"Aye, it's the closest inhabited island to Pyry and that beach you saw is the closest place to sail to it from Pyry"

"Wait, maybe we can find a village here, we should at least try-"

"There are no fucking villages on Pyry!! Ganae, on the other hand, has a couple, so there has to be some sort of healer there"

"But we're not even sure!"

"Do you have a better choice because I can think of none that could save Nash's life!"

I started walking towards the beach, Ajax right on my heels while still bitching and checking on Nash all the time. Once there, Nash looked around and shook his head, "Fuck, fuck, fuck!! There are no Fucking boats! We can't fucking wait for one, we can't even look for one or we might get attacked again! We won't be able to protect Nash properly if we're outnumbered again-"

"Calm the fuck down and let me think!"

Ajax kept muttering and looking around us. I set Nash on the sand to check on him again. Fortunately, he was still breathing and his heart was beating.

"How far is this fucking Ganae??"

"Maybe an hour or two with a good ship. It will take longer using a small boat"

"We will swim"

"Are you serious??"

"Aye! That's the only way to get *him* on that island fast!"

"We can't risk it with him in this state! How will we even carry him??"

"I'll carry him on my back, just help me tie him to me so I could use both my hands" he crouched before us and tugged on Nash's arm

"Wait-"

"We have no fucking time to wait!! He's fuckin dying!!"

I stared at him, completely confounded. He was right, we had no fucking choice. But that didn't mean it was less dangerous for both Nash and the person who'd carry him!

"Wait here" I stood up and went to the line of trees at the end of the beach

"Hey! Where are you going??"

"Just wait until-"

"We don't have the time to wait!! I'm taking him to the water"

He went to pull Nash when I used my sword to strike a tree with a few hits. I started working on the trunk of the tree while I spoke to my impatient brother, "I know you're a good swimmer, Ajax," *the best between the two of us, actually*, "But no matter how good you are, you won't make it with him on your back. Even if we carried him in turns, we still risk getting too tired to reach the other island."

"So what? Are you going to make us a boat with your imaginary shipwright skills??"

"No, you idiot, I'll just tie enough wood together to carry him on it. That way he will stay above water at all times"

"Oh...... I'll help you then"

"Aye, let's just hope we don't get hit by a storm before reaching Ganae. Pyry is not exactly known for its welcoming weather"

Nash, hold on to fucking life,
it's going to be a difficult journey, but we'll definitely get you there!

∞ ∞ ∞

The swim was far from easy. It actually took longer than we expected and we had to stop a couple of times to rest and breathe, we were beyond exhausted. We didn't follow a straight line to Ganae as we were swimming blindly towards it, but luckily we didn't miss it by much and we finally walked on its sand.

The first thing we did was pull Nash out of the water, then we both dropped on the soft sand for a minute. I checked on Nash beside me, his bleeding wasn't fatal, but it didn't stop. And now the few wooden tree trunks beneath him were partly soaked with blood. Fuck, we were lucky we weren't attacked by fucking sharks on the way here!

I released Nash and carried him on my back before I stood up.

"One... Just one Fucking minute more..."

"We don't have time, Ajax, we need to get him treated fast" I started walking, and when my brother didn't follow, I added, "or we might lose him"

That was enough to get him off his ass, cursing and racing before me, "I'll go before you to look for the town! Once there I'll fire some woods or something for you to follow. In the meantime, I'll be looking for the healer there, so you better not slack, older brother!"

"Aye!"

I watched my brother disappear into the trees with surprise

"Did you see that, Nash? Ajax is working his head, probably for the first time in his life. You better not give up, my friend"

It wasn't long before I saw a line of smoke heading to the sky. And as soon as I got there, Ajax met us to lead the way, "The healer is preparing the medicine, I already told him what to expect"

"He wasn't scared of dealing with pirates? What if he escaped, Ajax??"

"Believe me, he wouldn't even reach his own door before we catch him. He's like a fucking snail"

The huts that we walked by were all closing, everyone afraid of us, pirates. When we got to the healer's home, I first placed Nash on what looked like the man's bed. Then I turned to meet the healer. As soon as I did, I saw why Ajax called him a snail. He was old, very fucking old. The old man grabbed some items and walked towards Nash. He started looking at him here and there, and then he looked back at us and spoke, VERY FUCKING SLOWLY, "Not good. Your friend is dying. Let's not bother him on his way to the Gods-"

I stiffened and glared at the old man, Ajax already had his hands fisting the old goat's clothes and lifting him in the air, "He's Fucking breathing and his heart is Fucking beating! Now you fix him, you Fucking old shit, or I'll send you to meet your Gods with my bare hands"

The threat looked effective as the old man raised his hands in surrender, "Fine, fine. I'll try, but you need to pay first-"

"How about I hand you your head for payment? Is that enough to get you to Fucking MOVE??"

"Aye aye aye, I get it, I get it so let go" As soon as his feet touched the ground, the old man started mumbling, probably thinking we weren't hearing him, "Every time a fucker sets foot on this fucking island, it has to be a fucking pirate. They come and go as they fucking please, fucking the women and stealing the fucking meat. Then in the winter, where is the meat? Oh, it was swallowed by the fucking damned pirates who don't even pay..."

One thing was sure, the old shit hated pirates. I wanted to shut him the hell up, but the slow fuck was already working on Nash, so I ignored his ranting. I watched as he removed the soaked cloth from around Nash's head. The wound was very ugly and it now bled even more. I've seen blood countless times in my life, this was the first time that my heart clenched at the sight.

Ajax was tapping the floor with his foot nervously. We tried to help the old man the best we could, but the shit had his own agonizing pace. Among the blabbering, he announced that Nash had lost a lot of blood and that he could still die. Of course, we renewed our threats and pushed him to work fucking harder.

Once he finished cleaning, closing and putting smashed herbs on the wound, he wiped his hands on his clothes and dismissed us with a simple, "Now leave. I'd like to take a fucking nap"

I sat beside Nash, looking at his pale face, "We're not leaving until he wakes up", then Ajax continued, "And you better hope he does because if not, you better say your prayers, you fucking shit"

The old man sneered, then threw the things he used in a corner and left while grumbling something about cursed pirates. I wanted to ask about the damage, but the least of it was clear to us. Nash lost his left eye.

"Fuck, this is my fault. I should've tackled him as soon as he started after those motherfuckers!"

I sighed to my brother's guilt, "No you couldn't, he's fast enough to outrun us, so don't blame yourself for what happened-"

"You! He's fast enough to outrun you, not me! I could've gotten to him in time if I wasn't slowed down by those bastards in the forest!!...... I mean, look at him... I've never seen him like this before"

"Let's just hope he wakes up and gets well. Everything else is manageable"

"But, what will he say when he knows that the Martina sailed without us??"

Aye, good question. Being part of Martina is probably the most important thing for Nash. He's proud of his position and brags about it day and night. I chuckled and said while touching his cheek, "He will certainly throw a nice fit"

∞ Nash ∞

My consciousness returned to me very heavily. I was dizzy without even opening my eyes that felt even heavier. I moaned, feeling a killing thirst in my throat. I must've voiced my need because someone immediately brought some cool delicious water to my lips and ordered me to drink.

I drank to my heart's content and it helped clear a big part of my dizziness.

"Wh... where am I?"

"You're still on land. You're safe, Nash"

I recognized Yeagar's voice and it brought be a great relief for some reason.

"What land?"

"...... Don't talk yet. Gods, I'm so fucking glad you woke up! Just rest more, mate"

"What the fuck happened? Why can't I open my eyes?? And this fucking headache..."

"You... you've been hit in the head. We brought you to a healer and wrapped the wound tightly for it to heal"

I reached for my head and felt the cloth around it.

"I don't feel pain... why can't I feel the injury??"

"The healer said he gave you some herb to calm the pain so you could heal better. How do you feel?"

I sighed and cursed under my breath, "Shit, so much for the future second of Martina... getting fucking stabbed in a stupid fight?? Fuck, Ace must be laughing his ass at me right now"

"Hehe, I'm so relieved to hear you bitch about Ace"

I moved my hand in the air the best I could to hit the bastard, "I'm not *bitching*, you smug fuck! Don't think just because I'm hit that you can beat me! And you better not be fucking smirking right now! Give me my fucking sword and I'll fucking show you!! Wait until I remove this shit around my head and I'll-"

I felt his breath closer and his hand holding my left arm and upper chest, "You have no idea how worried I was when you got injured, and how happy I am now to hear your voice"

His voice was getting closer and its tone getting thicker and more seductive

"Wh-what are you doing??"

He whispered while his lips grazed mine, "I need a proof that this happy moment is real"

Before I could even answer, his lips were locked on mine. I was surprised. Aye, I was taken by surprise and I was injured and confused, right? So I guess it was fine to give in to the sweet feeling without a fight... just this once...

His chest rumbled above me as a moan left him, leading me to release one too. Yeagar was never loud in his kisses, and he rarely moaned, unlike his noisy brother. Hearing Yeagar and feeling his excitement made me grow down there. I don't know what the fuck the healer used on me, but the herb's effect didn't reach my pants at all!

Yeagar pulled back to let me breathe, then took my lips again. It was weird that I didn't even complain or insult him by now. Aye, I'll blame it on the herbs

I heard a gasp and Yeagar leaving me instantly, "What? Who's there??"

Yeagar went silent for a couple of seconds, then he answered me calmly, "Nothing, it's no one. More importantly, do you still feel ok?"

"Aye. I just feel a bit dizzy"

"Good, healing will take some time, so you need to be patient and rest well"

"I-I know that! I guess I have no choice. At least until this fucking cloth is removed"

Yeagar held my hand and asked, "Hey, can I kiss you again?"

I opened my lips to find an insult, but all I got was more excitement

"Since when do you ask, you bastard"

"Hehe, I'll take that as a yes"

My mouth was covered again, this time it felt much less gentle. It was delicious and arousing, with a hint of impatience. I moaned as his lips moved faster. He bit on my lip roughly and when I opened my mouth to curse him, his tongue dipped to fill me.

He bit my tongue and sucked on it, only when I felt a hand groping my junk did I realize, "AJAX YOU FUCKING BASTARD!"

"Feew! You noticed? Good, now we can get serious"

I pushed him and kicked with my legs. Aye, I was dizzy and feeling numb, but when it came to kicking Ajax's ass, my body didn't fail to find the will for it.

"Get off me, you Fucking perverted cunt!"

"Hahaaah, already so energetic! Gods, I'm dying to celebrate you being alive! I bet it will help your healing if I fuck you"

"Wha-!!"

"Ajax, he's still sick. I only allowed you a kiss"

"Who the fuck are you to allow or deny such thing!!"

"Oh, don't be a grumpy old man, Yeagar, you'll get your turn. You can suck him for now"

"You pirates finish fucking and then you leave!"

"Wha-? Who's that?? Who else is in this fucking room?"

Yeagar laughed lightly and caressed my hand in his, while his brother's voice came closer, "Damn, I'm stiff already..."

I felt more hands on me and my pants disappeared. Fuck, I was too weak to push the bastards away!

Gods, kill me now

Or not, better kill them and save me, so I can watch them die with my own eyes

∞ ∞ ∞

Chapter 32 ~ Prayer
∞ *Agenor's POV* ∞

I used a cloth to wipe the sweat off his forehead.

"We're almost there, my love. Just hang in there a bit longer..."

I wasn't certain, but his breathing seemed shallower. He also looked paler. He was getting weaker without proper treatment. It made me doubt he could open his eyes without the help of a good healer.

Ace proposed to fix my right hand and the injuries on my arm, thigh, and chest. I just let him cover the deepest injuries that were caused by the poisoned daggers. Then I told him to leave me alone and go make sure we were heading as fast as possible to Ganae. The island had a couple of towns, as I remember. But a healer... and a good one for the matter!

.... *Gods, for once spare us your fucking games*

I went to hold his hand in mine. In my distraction, I forgot about my fucked up hand and moved it only to wince at the sharp pain that spread to my arm and spine.

I looked at his forearm that was a bit swollen. Fuck, if my hand hurt this much, how would his poor arm feel...

I sat beside him and held his hand in my useful one while talking to him and begging him to open his beautiful eyes. Then I remembered the way his eyes were invaded with the strange purple color... I gritted my teeth to keep a deep groan inside. It felt like the heavens were cursing me.

But why use *him*?... how could they tarnish those beautiful sea-blue eyes?

"Captain"

Ace's voice came from behind me. He was definitely standing close, but with my disturbed senses and confused thoughts, it felt like I was far from him, far from reality. I only gained some focus when I heard what he said next, "We're at Ganae"

I pulled Nyx's hand to my chest, "You hear that? We're already there! Just a bit more, Nyx... only a bit more..."

I decided against taking Nyx to the island. I might've killed and burned my enemies back on Pyry, but I still held a great fear for him from the land. Instead, I sent Ace along with Britt and a few others to find me a healer.

I didn't expect them to return fast. In less than an hour, my door opened and Ace walked in with Yeagar. Yeagar greeted me while looking very cautious. I immediately understood his silent fear. He was afraid I'd hold him responsible for leaving the camp along with his asshole brother and idiot mate, Nash. Aye, I probably wouldn't have let the matter go easily before. Not today, though. Today I don't give a fucking shit

"Where's the healer? You found one so quickly??"

Ace nodded, "Aye. Yeagar, Ajax and Nash were already boarding on a small boat to try and find us. The healer was already with them"

I turned to Yeagar who was frowning at the sight Nyx, "How did you know we were needed one?"

"I-I didn't, Captain. Nash is injured and I forced the Healer to sail with us to keep treating him until he fully recovers"

I nodded, "Fine, just bring him in already"

Not more than a second later, Britt walked in with an old man in his grip. The old man looked about to lose his soul as his eyes traveled frantically on the pirates around him. He started ranting very slowly, "I-I-I haven't done anything! I-I-I didn't want to sail with those fucking fuck-heads!!..."

Britt pushed him towards the bed and the old man lost his balance. If Britt wasn't keeping a strong grip on his arm, he would've fallen.

"I need your skills, old man. Can you heal him?" I said as I stared at Nyx's silent form. I was unable to keep the desperation from showing in my voice.

Aye, I was desperate... so fucking desperate!!

The old man gazed at Nyx and cursed under his breath.

"I'll reward you generously, old man. Just heal him!"

He wasn't listening to me, just shaking his head and sneering. He was examining Nyx's body with his eyes while ranting with a low voice, "Fucking pirates... Bringing me busted eyes and busted asses... Fucking me and fucking themselves... Now, *this*?? A fuckin highborn!! They fucking raid on him and want me involved?? The guards will be on *my* ass! This shit will totally ruin my future, after all the fucking fucks, I end up spending the rest of my days on the Island of the Forgotten? With the criminals and the fucking thieves!! Fuck... a highborn!! they beat him up, fucked his arm and poisoned him, probably took all his fucking gold. Maybe he had some fine wine-"

Before I spoke, the old man was in the air, dangling with Britt's grip holding his shirt from behind his neck. Britt sneered in anger and glared, "What fucking future are you talking about?? Now you listen, you old shit. I heard that you only get to do what's fucking asked from you after a nice threat, we don't have time for a fucking miserable old man! You will either do as the Captain ordered with your mouth shut or-"

When I suddenly remembered what the healer said I raised my hand to stop Britt. Britt immediately halted and lowered the old man, "poison, you said? You can see that he was poisoned??"

"A-a-aye!" the old man was shivering after Britt's threats, "H-h-h-his fingertips! The highborn boy's fingertips are black, a-and his lips"

I grabbed Nyx's hand, then looked at his face. I wasn't certain, but now it was confirmed. The old man was right. At the end of Nyx's fingers, the skin under his fingertips was dark. Also, his usually pink lips were now tainted purple.

Lords... the poison had invaded all his body!

Nyx, please... don't.........

My heart was too heavy to allow me to speak. Instead, noticing my silence, Britt pushed the old man to sit on the bed, "GET TO FUCKING WORK! Your life is the price of failure, old shit"

Ajax came in to bring what looked like the healer's duffle. Ace dismissed everyone after he told them to sail away from Ganae, just in case. He closed the door and remained alert to any command.

Britt towered over the old man, urging him in his work with threats when needed. And I stood there, watching the foreign hands, examining and touching my dearest.

After checking all Nyx's body, including his eyes, ears, mouth, his injured arm, fingers, and toes, the old man went back to his ranting and started working.

He chose some places in Nyx's body and started applying pressure on them. Ace stepped in to help after silently looking at me to ask for permission. I didn't like it, but it was better that Ace's steady hands helped him.

The old man declared that Nyx's right forearm was broken. He said it needed some kind of herb and careful treatment or it might get infected. He also announced that Nyx had at least a fractured rib and that he shouldn't be moved much. My heart sank deeper with every revelation.

And the last one wasn't less painful.

Nyx wouldn't regain consciousness unless he defeated the poison, which will take at least a few days. And if it takes longer, Nyx's body could give up due to the poison and the starvation.

I felt like nothing of all of this was true. My heart was in so much pain that my mind fell into denial. This couldn't happen, this just couldn't happen!!

I didn't even register that I was retreating until my back hit the wall. The old man was working on Nyx's good arm and his upper body, while Ace did the same on his legs. After a while, the old man told Ace to cut Nyx's fingers slightly. Britt provided a dagger that Ace used.

Small drops of blood started oozing from the tiny injuries in his fingers.

Blood... black blood! I gasped at the dark color and the old man defended himself, as if afraid to be stricken, "I-I-It's the poisoned blood! If we get most of the poison out, the boy would have a better chance of surviving"

The old man waited for an approval from me that never came. So he went back to pressuring some places, massaging, and then squeezing for more black blood to come out.

The black poisoned blood mingled with the black sheets of the bed. I stared in disbelief at Nyx's poor state... and the more I looked, the more I ached myself. I wish I was the one lying on the bed instead of him... I wish I was strong enough to keep him safe! It felt like all I did was throw him to the enemy with my own hands. My eyes walked the angry bruises on his body and the image of that motherfucker Varg hovering over him and laying his fucking filthy hands on him!!

Fucking son of a bitch! He roughed him and hit him, and then he poisoned him!
he almost...... almost...!
If that bastard Theron hadn't released me......

The guilt burned my heart with insatiable anger as I sank to the floor. *My beloved never deserved such cruelty! Why would the fates be so vicious to an innocent angel?? My sweet lover never held a chance to those ghouls!*

I closed my eyes and did what never done before...

I prayed.

To whoever God was listening. Even Nyx's God who discarded him... I prayed.

I would give my soul to whoever saves him. Just, please... bring him back. *If I'm unworthy of your mercy, please be kind to him...*

.

Hours passed and the old man approached me, "I guess you're the Captain here, young man. I did my best to save the highborn. I'm nothing but an old man, so it's on the boy now to live or give up"

I nodded and the old man breathed. Britt pushed him towards me and the healer cussed under his breath before muttering, "I-I-I will take a look on y-y-your hand now". It was more a question than a statement. I shook my head slightly to refuse his help. I didn't deserve it. I didn't deserve anything anymore.

"Captain," Ace stopped the old man from leaving, "if your hand gets you sick, you won't be able to look after Nyx. Please reconsider and let the healer treat your hand. I will help him and we'll be fast"

Britt didn't wait for an answer. He lifted the old man and sat him in front of me. I just looked ahead towards the bed and let them do whatever they wanted. Under the healer's recommendations, Ace pushed my bones back to place to align them.

Then he put some prepared herbs on it, the same they used on Nyx's poor arm. And also like Nyx, they attached my hand to pieces of wood to keep it from moving.

The process hurt. With every bit of pain, I felt momentarily better. As if it was my punishment for not protecting the fallen angel... my angel...

∞ ∞ ∞

"How is he doing?"

"Same."

Ace nodded and looked back when a commotion broke on the deck. He went to open the door and see the reason behind it.

"What's going on out there??" I asked him in annoyance and he sighed, then shook his head, "Nothing important, Captain. It's just Nash going after his mates. It seems like he had just figured that he lost an eye"

"Fucking idiot"

"Aye, indeed. I'll make sure to put him back to bed"

I nodded and he left. It was the third day already since we found the healer. Nyx's state didn't get better, but it didn't get worse either. His eyes... still unmoving.

I sighed and caressed his hair again. Feeling another fever, I grabbed a clean cloth and put it on his forehead. He's been going in and out of fevers since yesterday. Even the healer said we could do nothing about it. This morning, the old man and Ace removed some poison from Nyx's body again, until there was only red blood coming from the small wounds. And the healer announced he'd no longer bleed him. Only wait for him to wake up.

I kissed his pale lips again, careful not to hurt him or lean on his hurt chest, his ribs needed to heal too. The small injuries on his body looked better with the treatment of the old man, even the scratches on his thighs and private area. Even with one hand, I made sure to clean him and put his pants back on, my gentleman would hate to wake up and find himself dirty or naked.

I chuckled painfully at the thought while my finger caressed his cheek:

"Wake up, Nyx. It's time to open your eyes, my love" I said for the hundredth time.

"nnn"

A small moan left him and I almost died in happiness!

"Nyx! Nyx, talk to me. Please say something, Nyx!"

He moaned again confirming that it wasn't an illusion. I smiled widely, but then Nyx's moans turned to pained ones. He immediately started thrashing and trembling, his useful hand moving in the air as if he was fighting someone back

"Nyx! It's me, Agenor! You're back on Martina... you're fine!"

I said as I fought to keep him still without hurting him. Soon, the cabin was full of pirates, talking to Nyx and helping me keep him still.

When he finally stopped struggling, he slipped back into unconsciousness while taking away my hopes.

But then he slightly opened his eyes only to close them a second later.

The beautiful color that appeared was soon gone. But I was happy, I was Fucking happy as I noticed that his eyes were no longer purple.

I breathed deeply and just stared at him. Somehow his face now looked better, like he was more alive. The mates were laughing and calling Nyx a daredevil. I dismissed them to be alone with my Nyx after the old man checked on him.

I was more than exhausted, but I couldn't close my eyes. I had to keep watch over him and make sure his health doesn't go south again.

It was night once more. I lied beside him and watched him sleep under the dim light of the lamps. My eyes opened wide when he slowly opened his.

He was fighting to keep his eyes open as he tried to focus on the ceiling. I couldn't believe he was back to me!!

"Hey..." I murmured gently. He turned slowly and looked at me. His eyes took their time to focus, and I knew when he recognized me.

I knew because a tear dropped from his beautiful blues.

"No, no, no, please don't cry, Nyx... please..."

His voice was very hoarse and low as he said with difficulty, "Y..... you're crying too"

I kissed him and hugged him carefully, "You're back, Nyx. You're back to me, my love"

"I'm sorry... ", his shivering hand traveled slowly until it touched the scars on my chest and more tears flooded his eyes, "I couldn't protect you... I'm so sor-" his crying took the best of him. I couldn't believe he was the one voicing the apology

I was the devil, I was evil

He was the angel; he was pure

A thousand years of sorrow wouldn't pay for what happened to him. But if he figured that out, he might blame me. He might hate me...

So I kept my excuses and pleas to myself and just kissed his forehead and carefully hugged him again, enjoying him awake and back to my arms.

You are alive, Nyx. That's all that matters for now. It will be ok, even if you're crying; it will be ok as long as you're alive.

I'll wipe those tears and fears away, and draw that radiant smile back on your lips.

A sudden sadness raided on my heart when I realized,

there was only one remedy for my angel to be truly safe again.

Chapter 33 ~ While you can...
∞ Agenor's POV ∞

I sat on the jibboom, silently smoking a cigarette and ignoring the few still awaken mates who tried to get me to join their drinking.

It's been about two weeks already since Nyx woke up. His health recovered nicely. He's still a bit weak and he barely eats a thing, but at least the days of him throwing up all the time and getting menacing fevers were gone. Knowing that he's better made me feel alive again.

But no matter how good his health became, his low mood refused to give him some slack. He has been able to stand up and move around for a couple of days now. He still got dizzy easily, but the healer said that it was to be expected. His forearm has healed well and he no longer had pain in his chest, which meant that if he had a fracture in one of his ribs, it healed as well. But he hadn't stepped outside the cabin once.

Actually, he hadn't looked me straight in the eye either...

Aye, he has always been too proud and sensitive, unlike us or any of the people I met in my life. I don't blame him; his sensitivity is a part of him that I adore. But in this case, and just like I predicted, it won't pass without causing a heavy strain on his pure heart.

For the past days, I shadowed all his movements. Yet with his silence, I couldn't help but feel like I was smothering him.

"Come on, I told you, the eye-patch suits you marvelously, me lady"

"You call me that again and I'll make you wear one on each eye!!"

Ajax laughed and Yeagar didn't lose the chance to jump in, "Seriously, it makes you look more like a pirate"

"I already AM a pirate!!"

"Aye, but... you wear clean clothes"

"Just because I don't wear rags and have a stinky ass doesn't mean I'm less of a pirate, you fucking assholes!"

"Still, if you're going after the title of Second of Martina, maybe you should get a wooden leg too? Look, even the Captain agrees, don't you Captain?"

Ajax said as he offered me a drink again. I just nodded to get them to leave me alone. They went back to their commotion and I sighed. I threw my cigarette in the sea. Then I stepped back onto the deck and headed towards the cabin.

I nodded at Britt, who was sitting by my door drinking. Whenever I left my cabin, he'd be there, silently watching over Nyx. I knew that a couple of low lives on my ship despised Nyx, thinking he was the reason for me not being there with them when they got attacked. But none of them had the guts to voice their thoughts, let alone act upon them.

That didn't mean that I ignored the matter. As a pirate, you'd always have someone against you. And when others could live with that just fine, Nyx was a whole other matter.

I pushed the door open and was greeted with the sight of him under the dim light of a lamp, sitting on the bed facing the window.

I grabbed a big cup from the table and handed it to him, "Want some water?"

He eyed the cup and nodded without hesitation. I sat beside him as he emptied the whole thing in his stomach. Water was the only thing that Nyx never refused. Since he woke up, he was parched all the time. So I made sure that he drank as much as possible. I believe that actually helped with his recovery.

Once he finished, I placed the empty cup on the floor beside the bed.

"Want to read something?"

He shook his head slowly, "I don't think I'm up to it. I feel tired"

From the looks of it, he was also a bit dizzy

"How about we lay down for the night? It's pretty late now"

He sighed and nodded, then moved slowly to put his head on his pillow. I walked around the bed and lay behind him.

I held in a heavy sigh; here we go for another long night.

With everything going on, his tiredness was very expected. But his sleepless nights are only adding to his fatigue.

Like every night, we lay down. I waited for him to sleep, but he spent hours just staring at the moonlight. Whenever I moved to look at his face to check on him, he closed his eyes faking sleep. Yet the rhythm of his breath, the occasional sighs and the uneasiness on his positions, they all proved that he was wide awake. The first nights, he cried himself to sleep silently. I've seen enough in my life to know that he was tormented not by sadness, but by fear. Now that he no longer did that, he just waited until lassitude took over his senses and forced him to sleep, which usually happened around dawn.

Sleep eluded me as well, as the fear of him slipping away from me took over every night. I remembered the chain and almost moaned nostalgically. Gods, if I had him in the chain, I'd certainly be at more ease knowing that he'd remain by my side even if I drifted to sleep.

I looked at him and smiled at the familiar attraction that I had for him. Whenever I was this close- no, actually whenever I laid eyes on him, I couldn't be satisfied unless I touched him. With either a gesture as simple as ruffling his hair, or a much more satisfying invasion of his body... I just needed to touch him...

With that thought in mind, I scooted closer to him. My arm drapes around his waist and I pulled him closer to my chest. I pushed his pillow away and replaced it with my arm.

Only then I smiled. Aye, this was much fucking better.

I noticed him looking back at me, but when our eyes met, he soon looked away, "You're smiling..."

"Aye. That's what happy people do, don't they?"

He didn't answer. Instead, he tried to smile but ended up making an awkward grimace. I sighed inwardly. He never knew how to lie, not even now.

I leaned in a little and kissed his cheek, "How can I not be happy with such a gorgeous man in my arms?"

I knew that poor compliment wasn't enough to raise his spirit. I just hoped the sincerity would bring him to smile, even a little.

"You... you really think I'm..."

I frowned slightly and my heart tugged knowing exactly what he was thinking. I leaned in and nuzzled his cheek, "I never had the slightest doubt"

I heard a small sniffle before his hand cupped my face. I lifted my head to watch him. His eyes were staring at my lips and once more, I was hopelessly lost in their beauty.

He pressed harder against my chest as he moved slightly to lie on his back, then he pulled my neck with his hand and met my lips with his. I froze; my eyes open wide for a few seconds as I didn't believe he'd actually do that!

Oh, Gods, who knew a bit of fucking sincerity could achieve so much!

His lips innocently moved against mine. I didn't lose any time to pull him closer and take control over the kiss. I knew that being gentle and cautious was the wise thing to do, but... I was fucking hungry for him!

My lips were more demanding as they sucked on his. I peered to check for any discomfort and was met by his closed eyes and blushed cheeks. And Fuck that did it for me. I was already aaaall up in attention.

I bit on his lower lip, drawing a sweet moan that I missed so much. Then I pushed my tongue inside to meet his. My excitement was rising steadily and so was *his*.

When I felt him pocking my thigh, I couldn't help the victorious smirk that tugged on my busy lips.

I sneaked a hand under his shirt to caress his lower belly. Then my hand dipped south to hold him through the fabric of his pants.

The way he gasped when I fondled him fueled my greed. So I kept squeezing him and caressing him roughly, making him moan and breathe faster, until he was full and stiff.

I moved to straddle him, my body still leaning so I could get a close look on his dazzling face. I tugged on the ties of his pants and said with a seductive voice, "Show me how hard you are, love"

I barely finished those words and the color had totally left his face.

He was looking at my hand on his pants. Suddenly his breathing hiked and he pushed me away. I was stronger than to be moved by his weak arms, but the horror that suddenly raided on him made me retreat and move away. As soon as I did, he hurried to get off the bed, holding the hem of his pants tight, making sure they're in place

"L-l-l-let me go... don't you dare touch me!!"

His voice was so weak and low, yet the terror so loud and clear. Nyx soon realized what he was doing. The regretful eyes that stared at me obviously didn't know what to do anymore.

"S... sorry... I'm not ready, Agenor... I'm so sorry..."

I hurried towards him and pulled him into a tight hug, "It's ok," I said, "everything will be fine, Nyx"

That's what I kept repeating to him.

But I knew nothing was close to fine.

Indeed, that night he didn't get any sleep. So I took him out to the deck for some fresh air. We remained mostly silent but made sure to keep him close.

'Touch him' my stupid mind kept urging me, 'Touch him now while you have the chance'

I couldn't ignore the stupid thoughts compelling me to touch him. So I kept an arm around him as we stood on the deck.

A while later, he asked if he was allowed to go see Zaire. I was surprised that he asked specifically for the slave merchant. It goes without saying that I didn't deny his request. In fact, I held a lamp and lead the way. Before we got inside the cell, Nyx took the lamp from me and went inside. As soon as he did, the slave merchant greeted him and asked for his health.

But the two weren't alone, were they

"Little one! You're actually alive! I'm so glad I saved your pretty ass! It's me, you remember me, right? I'm the nice-evil pirate! Hey, could you ask your Captain to release us? Or at least tie us closer to each other. This close-far distance is killing my balls!"

"Shut the fuck up, you lunatic bastard! For fuck's sakes, I think I'm getting crazy from listening day and night to this fucking bastard! Don't mind him Nyx"

I watched from outside as Nyx grabbed a jar of water and let Zaire drink to his heart's content. Then, after a brief moment of hesitation, he did the same for Theron.

"I'm sorry, Zaire. I'm truly sorry for everything you've been through. If only we didn't leave you behind..."

"Heh, don't worry pixie. I'm tougher than you think. Actually, the worst of it all is being stuck with this prick in the same cell. He NEVER fucking shuts up!"

"How could you say that!! We're sharing such an important experience together!"

"PLEASE! Someone, just stab him with something already!"

"Isn't he adorable? He's training to be a slave, so he's using the word 'please' more often now" Theron said.

"Call me *adorable* or Fuckin *slave* again, your shit-head, and I'll get my mates to roast your prick! Been a Fucking thorn in my ass ever since we met"

"Aaah~, I'd like to be much more than just a thorn in your ass, sweetie. Oh shit, now I'm fuckin hard again"

"You-!"

Oddly enough, I heard Nyx chuckle. He kept listening to the crazy shitheads and hiding a laugh. Then Zaire suggested Nyx got back before the beast, and I guess he meant myself, came to look for him.

Nyx wished them a good night and walked out of the cell. He immediately handed me the lamp, then his hands wrapped around me and he hugged me tightly.

Needless to say that, the next day, I released the slave merchant. As for the crazy head, I let him roast more and sent my minions to torment him for a while. But in the end, seeing the way Nyx insisted on visiting him every day, the lucky bastard got released too.

I can't say everyone liked my decisions, but I never thought twice about those fuckers' wished. They just had to abide by my orders or fuckin jump in the sea.

∞ ∞ ∞

With the days, such happy moments were rare. Nyx went back to work in the galley, becoming more reserved. And at night, intimacy was a risk I didn't have the heart to take again.

But even though his sadness disappeared, sometimes his worries resurfaced in the form of anger. So, unlike before, now it wasn't unheard of to find Nyx arguing with a mate.

"**I told you**! Books are more precious than life!"

"That is just fucking stupid. What good is a book going to do you if you're dead, huh? You're going to bring them along to the valley of the dead to keep you company, ladybug?"

"No, but you can't sit your ugly ass on them either!"

"My ass is not ugly, princess. Ask Nash"

"Keep me out of this, Ajax! Nyx should kill you, for all I care"

"Besides, Nyx, you're the one who put it there and forgot to put your stupid book back to your fancy box!"

I've been told Nyx was steering trouble again, and now I'm heading towards the lower hull. Each time, it was about something really stupid. But it was actually Nyx who wouldn't let go despite the others' attempts to turn it into a joke and just laugh about it. And this time, it was between him and Ajax, apparently about some stupid book.

"**Books are not stupid**, you idiot!"

I was there just in time to see Nyx yelling at Ajax and actually lunging at him. I pulled my lover back and behind me as I glared to Ajax to retreat. It immediately worked for Ajax, but my lover was tougher than that

"If you touch any of my books again, I will teach you their respect!"

"Oh yeah, you think just because we fear the collar in your neck that we can't teach *you* how to talk to those who can crush you like a fuckin bug??"

"Why wait, Mr. pirate, let's try and see who's going to stir the other's regrets!"

"AJAX, heal!!"

Nyx went to attack the pirate and I easily held him back with one arm, while I glared at Ajax. The light dimmed suddenly. I looked behind me to see a very pissed Britt glaring at Ajax. I gritted my teeth. The last thing I needed was a real fight between my men. If this went further, you'll find Britt against Ajax and his older brother Yeagar. Nash will jump against all just to have some fun.

I raised my hand to stop Britt. He growled and stepped back slightly, but didn't entirely back down as he still sent glares of death to Ajax, who was giving him a *'Bring it on'* look.

Yeagar grabbed his brother's neck and pushed him down to a forceful bow, "Stop making trouble and apologize to your Captain, you bastard"

"Hey! You're a bastard too! Besides, I wasn't the one who started the challenge-"

Yeagar pushed him to bow again, with a clear order this time, "Just Fucking apologize, you turd"

Ajax scoffed. And when his eyes met mine, he seemed less reluctant to follow his brother's orders, "S-sorry, Captain. It wasn't a real bout. We were just having a nice talk about a stupid book"

"**I told you! Books are not-**"

"Nyxy!! What'cha doin?" Maren appeared from one of the cells at the end of the dark hall, with Ace right behind him. Ace's hair was oddly disorganized, while Maren was having trouble tying the laces of his pants.

Ace nodded at me and pushed Maren towards Nyx. Maren walked around Ajax and Yeagar and grabbed Nyx's arm to pull him away, "Come, mate. Let's see if we can get Baril to spare some apples"

It was hard for them to walk past Britt. And I only sighed when the three of them climbed the stairs and headed to the upper level of the hull.

I raked a hand through my hair and released a heavy sigh.

"Captain," Yeagar started while his brother eyed me cautiously, "This was nothing important. Let's go get a drink, shall we?"

"Ajax. What in hell were you thinking? You know Nyx is the Captain's property and not to be messed with?" Ace reprimanded Ajax who lifted his hands in defense, "It was just talk! I wasn't going to touch the kid, I promise!!"

This was fucking silly. I was about to walk away but decided against it. I faced Ajax and glared at the slightly shorter pirate, "I know Nyx is reaching beyond his means by challenging any of you but don't Fucking care! If I ever hear someone took a swing at him, I'll personally cut their arms and make the motherfucker walk the plank!"

"C-c-captain, I swear I was never intending to hit him! I just... just nothing! It was nothing I swear!!" Ajax defended himself, and his fear made me calm down.

"You know that despite his anger, he actually cares about each one of you, hooligans. I don't see why, but he's always defending you or asking me to get you fuckers more food and better clothing, somehow he believes feeding your guts is my duty." I sighed then added, "I don't ask you to indulge if he's in the wrong. If that ever happens come to ME and only ME! Got it?"

"Aye, aye!"

"Loud and clear, Captain. Now, about that drink"

I patted Yeagar on the shoulder, "Start the rounds, I'll join you soon"

I climbed to the upper level of the hull, leaving behind a better mood among the mates as they started talking about the party they're about to start.

I first headed to the galley. I didn't find Nyx, so I went to check in my cabin next. Before I went inside, I saw Britt sitting with his back against the mainmast. The huge fellow was already drinking directly from a small barrel.

As soon as he saw me, he pointed to the sky. I looked up wondering what he meant until I realized it.

I climbed the shrouds swiftly. When my head poked in the crow's nest, I couldn't help but smile.

My kitten was sitting there sulking while hugging his stup-...... not stupid book.

"Hey"

Nyx turned to glare at me, "If you're here to yell at me, go ahead. But I'm not apologizing to that insolent pirate! How dare he treat a book so lowly?? Should've taught him respect!"

"Aye, I totally agree" I said as I climbed into the nest.

"You do?"

"Aye, that's why I've chained the insolent bastard in the cold cell."

"You did what??"

I took my time to answer. I moved to sit behind him. With both my legs around his, I enjoyed the way his ass fit perfectly between my legs.

"Wh... where's Ajax now??"

I smiled inwardly at his worried thoughts over that bastard.

"As I said, he's a prisoner for now. Don't worry, tomorrow he's walking the plank and he won't bother you anymore"

"**What**! Are you serious!?"

I remained silent and he did the same. Not for long though, because he couldn't swallow that someone he knew was in danger.

"...... It wasn't just his fault... Agenor, please don't punish your men, not because of me anyway..."

"He should know better than stir trouble. I hate quarrels between my men, and he should've known better"

I hugged him to my chest and he held my forearms, "Actually, I think it was my fault, not his. He was irritably insolent and I... I don't know why I was pushing him to fight with me... I'm sorry, I don't know what's gotten into me. Please don't hurt your own men for something so silly!"

"You certain? I could at least kick his ass if you want?"

He shook his head, "No! We won't fight again, I promise. In fact, I'll go talk to him later and clear this silly misunderstanding. So... no need for the plank and the scary things"

I chuckled and kissed his temple, "As you wish, my love"

He smiled in appreciation, "I think lately I've been more bothering than helping to your crew... even to you... For that, I sincerely apologize, Agenor"

I kissed him again, "It wasn't your fault. My men are a bunch of wolves. They can be very irritating even to the most patient people"

He shook his head, "No, it's me. I get this angry feeling sometimes and I can't stop but look for trouble! I can't believe I became like this..."

We both remained silent as I enjoyed nuzzling and kissing his silky black hair. I tried to find a subject to talk about that would cheer him up.

"Did you know that Ace and Maren are together?"

"mmm... together? together in what??"

"Like, doing it together"

"Ok, but doing what?"

My sweet innocent oblivious angel

I tilted my head to look at his confused eyes, "They're fucking, Nyx"

"What! You mean, like... They're together??"

"That's what I said"

He halted to think and the silent gasp with his mouth left open as he thought about it was beyond cute

"Oh, my God! H-How... WHEN?? I mean, I knew Maren fancied Ace, but... are you sure?"

"Aye. They were fucking just before they came to us when we were down the hull."

"**What**!!" then he whispered adorably, "How did you know that? Did you *see*??"

"No, but I know my men."

"My, my... that is some interesting news!"

He was smiling and talking to me, and he was actually looking me in the eye without the usual fear or sadness. Gods, I would ask them to perform in front of him, if that would keep him smiling

"Nyxy! Got you an apple! Oh, Captain, welcome to my humble home"

"I thought this was *my* ship"

"Hehe, well my name is right after yours on the crow's nest! Nyxy, you look funny"

Nyx was staring at him with a grin on his face. I guess he was still digesting the information

"M-maren, h-hi"

"h-h-hi" Maren answered while mocking, "here, got you an apple. And one for me"

"What about me? You didn't forget your Captain, did you?"

"Nope! I actually got three, but I gave one to Ace! I don't think Baril will let set foot there again for the day, so... you share with Nyx"

Maren was sitting beside the crow's nest as he bit into his apple. Nyx grinned wider, "You gave the apple to Ace?"

"Aye, why?"

"Nothing, just didn't know you to be so generous"

"Oh, true. But Ace is different."

Nyx turned to give me a '*did you hear that!*' look

Maren tilted his head, "You two are scheming something"

Nyx fidgeted, I guess he could keep a secret, "Maren, are you and Ace, like... a couple?"

Maren's eyes widened and he almost choked on his apple. Once he stopped coughing, he put his finger in front of his mouth to shush Nyx, "Don't tell anyone, ok? Ace wants to keep out relationship secret"

Nyx immediately gasped, "So it IS a relationship!"

Maren swung his feet under him playfully and looked proud, "Aye, it's LOVE, and we FUCK, like... a lot! It's the whole love fuck from all angles. A. MA. ZING!"

Nyx blushed hard and put a hand over his mouth, "My God, Maren. What has Ace taught you??"

"Huh, more like what I taught *him*!"

"Taught what to whom?" Zaire poked his head from the other side of the nest. I rolled my eyes, "Another one..."

"Hey Captain!" he said enthusiastically, "Nice sunset, don't you think?"

"Not anymore"

Nyx nudged me to be *nicer* to the slave merchant and tsked and looked away.

Maren snickered and decided to be on his Captain's side, "We're talking about how Theron keeps trying to slip it to you"

"**Maren**!!"

I laughed while Nyx tried to help the weak, as usual, "Please don't be rude, Maren"

"What? I spoke nothing but the truth"

Maren said innocently, yet the one I took for weak was far from it. Zaire smirked and commented casually, "Well, at least I'm ruthless enough to actually protect my own ass. Someone else, on the other hand..."

Maren's eyes instantly filled with fear of being discovered. Gods, Ace got him nicely trained

"Wh-who do you mean??"

Zaire smirked and his eyes twinkled with mischief, "Did you know that Nash was fucked by Ajax?"

"**Whaaat**!!" Both Nyx and Maren yelled at the same time

Zaire nodded while I remained silent. Actually, the poor one-eyed bastard is fending off both brothers. But I kept that knowledge to myself.

Fucking Lords, the Captain goes for one sweet prey, and the whole damn crew follows.

Zaire and Maren started discussing it excitingly while Nyx tried to understand their indecent insinuations.

That, until someone called from the deck, "**Zaire**! My little slave bird! **Come fly into my arms**!"

"I'll throw myself just to break your neck, you crazy fucking bastard!"

"Hahaha! See? My slave is so romantic!"

"Who the FUCK are you calling a slave!! You piece of stinky goat shit..." Zaire kept insulting his ex-prison companion as he climbed down to the deck.

"Captaain!! Your drink is ready!", yelled Ajax from the front deck. He was most probably trying to make up for what happened earlier.

Maren grinned evilly, "Well, I'm going to tease more information out of Ajax" With that, he grabbed a rope and immediately dropped in front of Ajax with an idiotic grin.

"My, my... so many things I didn't know about..."

I won't even mention why my dutiful subordinate Lou left the exciting life of piracy. If Nyx knew, he could faint. But that cousin of his definitely deserves it!

I laughed at the idea, and Nyx leaned back on my chest, "Agenor..."

"Aye?" his voice was hesitant, yet still sweeter than any voice I ever heard. Especially those that were now singing to the rising bloodied moon in the horizon.

"Agenor, I......... know we haven't been... I mean... lately..."

I leaned down to kiss his shoulder, "I'm happy as long as you're smiling, Nyx"

"I will try my best, I promise. I don't know how long it would take me, but..."

My breath heightened slightly at the annoying thoughts that roamed in my head again. Thinking of only what's good for him and damning myself to hell, I gathered my courage and spat it out, "Nyx, I... I've been meaning to ask you something"

"What is it?"

I swallowed and clenched my hands in his shirt, holding him closer.

Once again, my mind urged me,

touch him

either chain him again no matter the consequences, or...

touch him while you can.

"My sweet angel... Would you like to visit Corail?"

∞∞ *TO BE CONTINUED* ∞∞

Epilogue

Hey pirate fans,

The storyline is still going further. More pirate romance with all these characters and more in the second book "*Pirate chains ~ Corail*".

Will Nyx choose home over his pirate-career? Or will he choose to leave everything behind and sail with his Captain?
Also...... will the Captain let him come along?

Answers and more will be found in the next book ;)

Grand merci to all pirate fans for reading and enjoying my first story ever!
And for those who follow to the next journey with Agenor and Nyx, I promise action and plenty of sexy scenes ;)
See you all in the next and final book!

Author note

Dear reader,

I hope you enjoyed this book.

Once again, the journey of Nyx and Agenor continues in the third and last book, "***Pirate Chains ~ Corail***"

Please take the time to write a review on Amazon. For any comments, corrections, ideas, etc. you can reach me on my Wattpad page https://www.wattpad.com/user/Syrvat **or email me at** syrvat.novelist@gmail.com

Also read
∞ Pirate chains ~ Corail ∞

∞ *Aella* ∞

∞ Miroir ~ The pirate whore ∞

Made in the USA
Middletown, DE
11 January 2019